Louisa Heaton lives on Hay[...] with her husband, four child[...] has worked in various roles in the health industry—most recently four years as a Community First Responder, answering 999 calls. When not writing Louisa enjoys other creative pursuits, including reading, quilting and patchwork—usually instead of the things she *ought* to be doing!

Traci Douglass is a *USA TODAY* bestselling romance author with Mills & Boon, Entangled Publishing and Tule Publishing, and has an MFA in Writing Popular Fiction from Seton Hill University. She writes sometimes funny, usually awkward, always emotional stories about strong, quirky, wounded characters overcoming past adversity to find their for ever person and heartfelt, healing happily-ever-afters. Connect with her through her website: tracidouglassbooks.com.

Also by Louisa Heaton

Resisting the Single Dad Surgeon

Christmas North and South miniseries

A Mistletoe Marriage Reunion

Cotswold Docs miniseries

Best Friend to Husband?
Finding a Family Next Door

Also by Traci Douglass

Wyckford General Hospital miniseries

Single Dad's Unexpected Reunion
An ER Nurse to Redeem Him
Her Forbidden Firefighter
Family of Three Under the Tree

Boston Christmas Miracles miniseries

Home Alone with the Children's Doctor

Discover more at millsandboon.co.uk.

THE SURGEON'S RELATIONSHIP RUSE

LOUISA HEATON

A SINGLE DAD TO HEAL HIM

TRACI DOUGLASS

MILLS & BOON

All rights reserved including the right of reproduction in whole or in part in any form. This edition is published by arrangement with Harlequin Enterprises ULC.

This is a work of fiction. Names, characters, places, locations and incidents are purely fictional and bear no relationship to any real life individuals, living or dead, or to any actual places, business establishments, locations, events or incidents. Any resemblance is entirely coincidental.

This book is sold subject to the condition that it shall not, by way of trade or otherwise, be lent, resold, hired out or otherwise circulated without the prior consent of the publisher in any form of binding or cover other than that in which it is published and without a similar condition including this condition being imposed on the subsequent purchaser.

® and TM are trademarks owned and used by the trademark owner and/or its licensee. Trademarks marked with ® are registered with the United Kingdom Patent Office and/or the Office for Harmonisation in the Internal Market and in other countries.

First published in Great Britain 2025
by Mills & Boon, an imprint of HarperCollins*Publishers* Ltd,
1 London Bridge Street, London, SE1 9GF

www.harpercollins.co.uk

HarperCollins*Publishers* Macken House, 39/40 Mayor Street Upper,
Dublin 1, D01 C9W8, Ireland

The Surgeon's Relationship Ruse © 2025 Louisa Heaton

A Single Dad to Heal Him © 2025 Traci Douglass

ISBN: 978-0-263-32503-4

04/25

This book contains FSC™ certified paper
and other controlled sources to ensure responsible forest management.

For more information visit www.harpercollins.co.uk/green.

Printed and Bound in the UK using 100% Renewable Electricity
at CPI Group (UK) Ltd, Croydon, CR0 4YY

THE SURGEON'S RELATIONSHIP RUSE

LOUISA HEATON

MILLS & BOON

For Liss, Nathan, Lemoney and all the wonderful members of the Firefly Gang! Xxx

CHAPTER ONE

Ten years ago

THE FIRST SERIOUS Braxton Hicks contraction had happened at work. Practice contractions, her midwife had called them. The body getting ready for birth. She'd had a few tightenings before in the last few days. Nothing lasting more than a few seconds. But this felt different.

The café in which she worked, situated in the centre of the high street in a town in the Home Counties, was overrun. Customers were grabbing coffee and cake as a brief respite from their last-minute Christmas shopping. Christmas Eve was always a busy day, and Julia was carrying a tray over to table twelve. A pot of decaf breakfast tea. One cappuccino with chocolate sprinkles arranged in the shape of a snowflake. Two mince pies with brandy cream.

The first cramp hit like a bolt from the blue.

She'd gasped, surprised, then continued on as her abdomen relaxed, her gaze flicking to the large clock on the wall. Eleven minutes past twelve. It was gone as quickly as it started and she smiled at her customers as she placed their order down on the table, even though, internally, her heart had begun to pound.

The arrival of these first proper cramps signified that she was getting closer. Closer to becoming a single mother.

It was her due date, and she'd chosen to work right up to

her delivery. She needed the money. The tips she got from working, as well as her wages, if she was going to get by on her own.

The father, Jake, was *not* around. He'd once been a regular customer at the café. Coming in every day on his way to work at the bank, smiling and flirting with her until she'd agreed to a date with him. He had charmed her and let her fall in love with him. Then she'd announced the unexpected pregnancy and he had announced, also unexpectedly, that he was actually married. And had three children. Brokenhearted, she had decided to continue with the pregnancy. Jake had promised to provide financial aid, but nothing else.

As the rest of her shift continued the Braxton Hicks became more regular, and when the café had closed, and she'd helped clean up and mop the floor, her boss told her to get herself off home. She promised she would text him when she got home safely.

She was prepped and ready for anything. Her hospital bag was already in her car, alongside the child seat she would need when she drove home afterwards. The maternity hospital was only a twenty-five-minute drive away. She'd practised. She needed to be prepared for anything, anytime, especially as she was on her own.

And then it began to snow.

Julia smiled as she stepped from the café and turned her face up to the sky, her hands out to catch the softly falling flakes. This was perfect! Christmas Eve… Snowing… It was almost magical. Typically, the snow wasn't settling, as it had rained earlier, but that didn't stop the wonder of it.

As she got into her car, stretching out her seatbelt to fit around her abdomen, she hummed along to the Christmas music blasting from the radio and imagined herself telling her child, in the future, about how it had begun to snow the magical Christmas that he had been born.

She was trying to remain upbeat about the fact that she was going to do this alone, but as she drove through the busy streets, getting stuck in slow-moving traffic, she began to realise that her Braxton Hicks were more than just tightenings. They were beginning to hurt much more...like really bad period pains.

I think I might be in labour.

She tried to remain calm as she sat in traffic that was now at a standstill. Bumper to bumper. Her windows were beginning to fog. Was this truly happening? Now? Today?

Julia called her mum on her hands-free unit and explained the situation as another pain hit. And then another.

Her mum sounded so excited. 'It's happening?'

Julia smiled at hearing the excitement in her mum's voice. 'Yes, I think so. Pains are coming every few minutes already. Is that normal?'

At her antenatal classes the midwife had said first labours were long. Slow. Usually.

'There's no rulebook for babies, Julia. Is it safe for you to be driving?' asked her mum, clearly worried.

'I'm not driving right now. I'm sat here and I haven't moved in ages! Oh, God, what if I give birth in my car?'

'Is there a shortcut you can take?'

'Maybe...'

The next contraction hit hard whilst she was at a red traffic light. It hit like a vice, squeezing her, crushing her, making her gasp, and was just easing off as the lights went green and she found herself creeping forward at a snail's pace. It was rush hour, so traffic was to be expected, but the intensity of that last contraction had scared her.

She glanced ahead, trying to see past the cars. Was this just volume of traffic, or an accident, or what? This was the main route to the hospital, but what with the snow and all the shoppers it looked as if they were going nowhere, and it was starting to make Julia panic a little. She wanted to be moving. Wanted to be driving so that she could get closer to the safety of the hospital, its midwives and its medications.

She'd planned an epidural. At least, that was what she hoped for, if she needed it.

I could take that left turn up ahead. It would lead me down the country roads and through Weston, so I could get to the hospital that way...

Julia turned on her indicator and when the traffic had moved forward enough for her to take it she took the next exit and began to drive again, feeling good about her choice as the road here was clear. The wipers were dealing with the snow, and though the roads looked dark and slick she was doing okay.

She made it to Weston, drove through the village and out the other side and took the turning that would lead her to the hospital. She was doing great until she heard a strange bang, and then a *thud-thud-thud* with every rotation of her tyres and realised she'd got a flat tyre.

'No!'

Julia pulled over, switching on her hazard lights and getting out of the car to take a look. It was the back tyre, passenger's side, and if she wanted to change it—if there was even the possibility of changing it—she would have to do so from a ditch that was full of ice-cold muddy water and spiky brambles.

She cursed and grabbed her phone, but when she tried to dial for help saw she had no signal and no bars. This had to be a black spot.

She groaned and bent double as another contraction hit.

This one was stronger than any she'd had before and Julia sank to her knees from the sheer force of it, breathing it away as much as she could, the way she'd been taught in antenatal class. It seemed to last for ever, and just when she thought it was over, just when she thought she could breathe normally again, her waters broke and gushed down her legs.

'Oh...'

Don't panic. Don't panic!

But she couldn't help it. She was alone, cold and wet, and in labour. On Christmas Eve, shivering in the snow, with a flat tyre and no way nor ability to fix it and no phone signal.

I need someone to help. Is there a house around here?

She'd seen a house about a mile back, but she couldn't recall if there'd been lights on to show there was anyone there. If she turned back and everyone was out... Lots of people went out on Christmas Eve. To church. To parties. To visit family and friends.

As she got to her feet she thought she could see warm yellow lights up ahead. Something through the trees...

There was no other choice. She couldn't have her baby here on the road. Screw that midwife saying first babies took a long time to arrive. Her son seemed to be in one hell of a rush to be born.

Another contraction hit her, making her collapse against her car before she could get back to her feet and begin to stagger down the road. Julia kept trying to call her mum, or the emergency services, but now her phone seemed to have died, and she was beginning to think the universe was conspiring against her.

The lights were getting brighter, but she could see now that they were from a house set back from the road, up a long and winding driveway.

'You've got to be kidding me!' she gasped, and then another contraction hit, and towards the end of it she felt the urge to push. 'No. No, no, no, no!'

Her freezing breath billowed around her, but Julia got back to her feet and found from somewhere the strength to dig deep and keep on walking.

The house was right there in front of her. Getting closer. It looked like some kind of manor house, or something. It had a Christmas tree outside. Lit up by white fairy lights and topped with a giant silver star that drew her eye. Almost delirious, she laughed and wondered if Mary had felt this way in Bethlehem. Looking for a place to give birth and being guided by a star. Though there'd been no mention in the bible of her terrible contractions, and she'd managed to sit on the back of a donkey...

Ten metres.

Five.

Julia finally reached the door and reached up for the giant knocker, shaped like a lion's head. She rapped it as hard as she could, groaning against the wood.

'How are you doing now, Doe?'

Anthony Fitzpatrick, Duke of Weston, cradled his wife Yael's hand in his and looked up into her gorgeous big brown eyes.

He had begun to call her Doe because since her chemotherapy, and losing all her hair, her eyes had somehow seemingly become larger and more doe-like. They were beautiful, just as she was.

'I'm a little warmer.' Yale adjusted the oxygen cannula in her nose and pulled the blanket around her.

He knew she would like to get closer to the open fire he'd got going in the living room that had become their bedroom since she'd been wheelchair-bound, but he didn't want to risk it. Not now that she was permanently attached to her oxygen canister.

'Good. Can I get you anything? A hot chocolate? Cocoa?'

She smiled at him and shook her head. 'Just you.'

He smiled back. 'Always.'

Anthony laid his head upon her shoulder and stared into

the flames. He tried not to think about how many days they had left together. Two weeks ago the oncologist had told them that the cancer had now spread to her brain, liver and bones. The fluid on her lungs was getting worse, and he'd estimated that she had only weeks to live. Not months. *Weeks*.

This would be their last Christmas together.

Their last days together.

He wanted to make every precious moment count.

The orange flames licked at the fresh logs he'd only recently put onto the fire and his gaze lifted to the two stockings that hung there. They'd once hoped to add to the number of stockings on the mantelpiece, but cancer had put paid to that idea. Endless rounds of chemo, radiation, surgery, immunotherapy and clinical trials had ravaged his wife's body and dashed any hopes of fertility or children.

A rapid knocking at the front door made him lift his head from his wife's shoulders.

'Who's that?' Yael asked.

He laid his head back down again. 'It doesn't matter. Probably just carol singers.'

'Anthony! You should go and answer the door. If they've come all this way out into the country they've made an effort to sing for their duke.' She smiled at him and lifted a weary finger to stroke his jawline. 'The least we can do is give them an audience, and I think I'd like to hear them sing.'

'All right.' He smiled at her, once again amazed at his wife's boundless compassion and love for the festive season, despite all that was going on.

He got to his feet, made sure her blanket was tightly tucked about her, and then wheeled her through to the front hall, parking her just behind him so she'd have a good view of the carol singers, but not so close to the door that she'd feel the cold. The snow had become sleet now, and it was chilly out there.

Odd, though. He couldn't hear anyone singing. Did they wait these days for whoever was in to open the door before they started singing?

Anthony turned the key and swung the front door wide, forcing a jolly smile for whoever was out there. But as the door swung inwards it brought with it a woman, who sagged to her knees groaning, her long dark hair wet like rat's tails.

As she rolled onto her side he realised she was heavily pregnant.

And about to give birth.

A pair of strong arms scooped her up and then she was being carried. And although she longed to just close her eyes and go to sleep, another contraction hit.

'I need to push!'

'Don't push! Not yet!' the man carrying her said.

But it wasn't something she could fight. Her body began to push all on its own and she grunted as she bore down.

The man carried her to a bed and laid her upon it. She thought she heard the tell-tale snap of disposable gloves being put on. Where was she?

Julia opened her eyes briefly and glanced around. The room was a strange mix of palatial grandeur and hospital ward, and the man beside her, snapping on the gloves, was tall, handsome and darkly bearded.

'I need to examine you. Make sure you're fully dilated. But don't worry—I'm a doctor.'

A doctor? She glanced around for some sort of confirmation, but what she expected to see she wasn't sure. Was she hoping to see a certificate on the wall? Would that be enough to allow her to let this strange man remove her clothes and examine her intimately?

But then a woman wheeled herself into view. A frail woman. Young, but bald. A cannula in her nostrils was feeding her oxygen. Julia's first thought was that she must be a cancer patient. But the thought wasn't there for long. Another contraction hit and she gasped and sucked in air, ready to push once again.

'Okay. No time for that, I guess,' the man said, and she felt his hand rest upon her bump, almost as if he was measuring the strength of the contraction. 'Yael, can you pass me those clean towels over there? And I'll need those scissors.'

Julia heard packets being ripped open, things being placed beside her on a metal instrument trolley, and then the rest of the world disappeared as all she could feel was the pain and constriction of her latest contraction. She gasped and cried out, before sucking in more air so she could hold her breath and push. Push harder than she'd ever pushed in her life.

'That's it…you're doing great. I'm sorry, but I'm going to have to remove your underwear. Do you give me permission?'

She nodded furiously, not caring any more as she felt hands beneath her skirt and she lifted and twisted so that her knickers could be removed. Who cared what this strange man saw? Or did. Or touched. All that mattered was getting this baby out of her body. She felt as if she was on fire. As if she was being torn in two.

'Head's out! One more big push and you're done!'

The head was out! It was nearly over!

The thought gave her one last surge of energy—of strength—and she groaned and sucked in air for one final big push. And then, with a big whoosh of fluids, her son slithered out of her and was lifted onto her belly by the bearded man.

Julia looked down, crying, holding her son's hot, wet body as the strange man whose home she'd barged her way into began to rub her baby down with towels, clearing away blood and mucus and vernix, the natural white grease that coated a new baby's skin.

'Why isn't he crying?'

'He will. Give him a moment.'

She looked up at the man properly this time. She saw worry, concern, in his bright blue eyes, but he was staying calm, seemed certain of what he was doing, and she had no choice but to believe him.

To place her faith in him.

To trust him.

Not only with her life, but with her son's.

And then...

'Waah!'

The baby began to cry and she sobbed happy tears, holding her son to her, unable to believe all that had happened in the last hour or two. The tears combined with the relief that he was here and he was okay and she'd got through it all.

'Let me clamp and cut the cord,' the man said, before wrapping her son in another clean towel and putting him into her arms.

He was beautiful. Red. Plump. A button nose. A gummy mouth. Squinting every time he tried to open his eyes and look out at the world. He sneezed and looked bewildered, and Julia couldn't help but laugh at him before looking up at the man whose home she had invaded. At the bald woman in her wheelchair with her oxygen. They were both looking at her in awe and wonder.

'Thank you for letting me in. For answering the door. My name's Julia... Julia Morris.'

'And who's this little guy?' the man asked.

'I'm going to call him Marcus, after my grandfather. Marcus Arthur Morris.'

The man and the woman smiled. The woman in the wheelchair looked almost mesmerised by the baby.

'We never got a chance to be properly introduced, did we? My name's Anthony, and this is my wife Yael.'

Julia smiled and said hello, before looking down at her son again. He was so beautiful...

'I'll call for an ambulance. Get you both checked out.'

'There's no phone signal here,' Julia said.

'We have a landline.'

'Oh. Thank you.'

'You're welcome.'

The man removed his gloves and went to the opposite side of the room, where he picked up a phone handset, dialled and requested an ambulance. When he came back, he put on fresh gloves.

'For the placenta,' he explained.

'Oh, right. I forgot that part.'

'You'll hardly notice now you've got that little guy in your arms.'

He was right. She hardly did.

'The ambulance might be a while. It's Christmas Eve... they're busy. Can I get you anything, Julia? Water? Some tea?'

'Tea would be great, thank you. Thank you both for this... for going to so much trouble. I hope I haven't made a mess of your rugs or anything.'

Yael wheeled herself forward. 'Don't worry about that. Is...is he your first?'

Julia nodded, wondering whether she ought to try and breastfeed. 'Yes.'

'You'll always find Christmas special from now on.'

'I guess I will.'

His birthday was Christmas Eve. She'd never thought it would happen this way when the doctor had predicted her due date. 'First babies are always late,' she'd been told. He would more likely be a New Year baby. Or early January.

'He'll get two lots of presents,' said Yael.

She smiled. 'He'll get spoilt. My mother will go overboard, no doubt.'

'And his father? Will he be surprised?'

Julia turned to look at Yael. 'I'm not with him any more. He didn't want to know.'

'I'm sorry. I didn't mean to pry.'

'Don't worry. You didn't know.'

She looked around the room. Noted the opulent paintings. The long, heavy drapes. The expensive vases on the mantelpiece that was decorated with pine, fir cones and fairy lights. Two solitary stockings hung there.

'Do just the two of you live here?'

It was a big house. Huge for just two.

'Yes. We'd hoped to start our own family, but then this happened.' Yael fiddled with her oxygen tubing, looking embarrassed.

'Do you mind if I ask…?'

Yael shook her head kindly. 'Non-small cell lung cancer. It's metastasised.'

'Oh. And can they…do anything about it?'

Yael smiled. 'I'm fighting it. The doctors are throwing everything at it.'

'That's good.'

'Yeah. It is.' She looked down then, almost incredibly sad, and Julia wondered if the woman knew more about her condition than she was letting on.

Was the disease winning? Was it beating her? Was it killing her? She'd hoped to start a family with her husband—what was his name? Anthony? What if they couldn't? What if time was running out for them? What if this was Yael's last Christmas?

'Would you…like to hold him?'

Yael looked up, her eyes full of wonder and surprise. 'You don't mind?'

'Of course not. Here, come closer and I can pass him to you.'

Gently and carefully she passed her son down into Yael's waiting arms. She gasped as she took the baby, and looked at him so tenderly and with so much love he might as well have been her own baby.

'Tea.' Anthony came in bearing a tray, and suddenly stopped moving when he saw his wife cradling the baby.

Julia couldn't possibly describe the look on his face when he saw them. Gratitude? Happiness? Joy? Awe? Maybe it was all of them? And more. He placed the tray down on the table and then went to kneel by his wife's side. They held Julia's son together, as if he were their own. They looked like *they* were the new parents and she the surrogate. It made Julia's heart swell that she could do this for them.

'I can't thank you both enough for what you have done for me and my son tonight.'

Anthony looked up at her as he cradled Marcus's head. 'You're very welcome.'

'I was lucky to find a doctor, I guess.'

He smiled at her, and she had to admit that he was rather handsome. Yael had struck lucky in the husband department. It was ironic that Yael had something that Julia had hoped for and she had something Yael and Anthony had hoped for. Life was strange that way.

When the ambulance and the paramedics finally arrived and she was being loaded into the ambulance she waved goodbye to Anthony and Yael, thanking them one last time for all that they had done.

They stood in the doorway of their manor house and even though they had each other, Julia couldn't help but feel that they looked incredibly alone. Their arms empty of her son, they looked lost.

She could only hope, as she was driven down the long

driveway, that she had brought a little Christmas magic to their home. That they would always remember the Christmas they'd helped a stranger deliver her baby in their living room and that they would have many more Christmases together.

CHAPTER TWO

Present day

'HELLO? I'M LOOKING for the nurse in charge?'

Julia stood by the reception desk of the orthopaedic ward, smiling at the receptionist. The ID on a lanyard around her neck stated that her name was Mandy.

'And you are...?'

'Julia Morris. Newly qualified nurse. I start work here today.'

She beamed, still quite unable to believe she was saying it.

Newly. Qualified. Nurse.

It had felt incredibly strange going to university to study. Most of the rest of her class had been young girls. Teenagers, really. Eighteen years of age. Nineteen... She'd been about to turn thirty, but she'd not been the oldest by any means. There'd been one woman studying who'd just turned forty years old. She and Cesca had become really good friends, actually, which was nice, and Cesca was starting today, too, up on the Gynae Ward.

Julia's life had changed so much in the last few years. It had almost been a whirlwind. But now she was sure of her choices. She'd enjoyed her working placements on the orthopaedic ward where she'd trained, and she hoped she would enjoy it just as much here at London's Saints' Hospital.

'Oh, yes, I was told to expect you!' Mandy passed her a

sticky note with a number on it. 'Go down that corridor to the end and you'll see a sign that says *Staff Only*. Type in that number and it'll get you inside, where you can meet everyone for morning handover.'

'Thank you.'

Julia adjusted the backpack on her shoulder and headed down the corridor. It was bright here. Modern. The hospital had just had a major revamp that must have cost millions. She couldn't help but glance into the wards as she passed them by. Most of the beds were filled. Men in one ward. Women in another. She passed a door marked *Linen*, another marked *Utility* and then she was at the *Staff Only* door. There was a keypad on it, and she typed in the number and turned the handle, sucking in a breath for courage, knowing that she was about to meet the people who would become her work family for the next few years.

But as she turned the handle to push it forward the door was pulled back by someone exiting, and she bumped into a tall man by accident, backing away, blushing, full of apology... before she looked up to make eye contact and her heart almost erupted from her ribcage.

The man before her did not seem to have changed much since she had last seen him a decade ago. His hair was a little longer, but otherwise he looked exactly the same as when he and his wife Yael had waved her goodbye from the door of their home. Now he wore a slim-fit navy suit, with a white shirt and pink tie, a waistcoat rather than a blazer, and a stethoscope draped around his neck. His gaze grazed over her in an automatic apology, but then his eyes widened with recognition.

He recognises me. He remembers me.

'Anthony! Hello, again.'

He seemed to take a moment to think, and Julia stood

there, smiling, holding out her hand in greeting, as surprised as he to have remade his acquaintance.

'It's *Mr* Fitzpatrick,' he said, his voice gruff, and he avoided shaking her hand and walked straight past her, as if they had never shared something special at all.

Julia gaped after him, shocked and a little embarrassed at having been dismissed so easily.

Maybe he doesn't remember me?

But then a nurse dressed in a dark blue uniform, with white piping on her collar and a kind face, got her attention. 'Is it Nurse Morris? Come on in. Don't mind him—he's always grumpy.'

Julia turned to face the room and felt her cheeks flush even more when she realised that she seemed to be the last person to arrive and everyone had witnessed the interaction. The room was full of people in uniform. Nurses. Healthcare assistants. Student nurses. People whom she assumed were from the physio department, judging by their white polo shirts and navy tracksuits.

'Er...yes. Thank you.'

'I'm Maeve Booker, sister in charge of the ward. Come and take a seat. Sara? Can you budge over, so Nurse Morris can sit down?'

A young blonde nurse got up and moved, so that Julia could squeeze into the seat next to her.

'Thank you.'

'No problem.'

She was passed a handover sheet and she listened intently as a nurse ran through the patients from the nightshift, with a list of jobs that needed taking care of that day. Cannula insertions, medication requests, bloods... Which patients needed to get out of bed that day and ambulating around the ward, which ones were needing to be prepped for surgery, which ones were due to go home. She outlined overnight developments—who had slept well, who hadn't.

It was a lot of information for Julia to take in, but she was used to this. She'd sat in on many handovers during her placements as a student nurse. She scribbled down notes relating to each patient, so that she had a good idea of what needed to be achieved that day, and could try to understand the new problems and requirements that might crop up, or new patients who might arrive.

Afterwards, as everyone filtered out, Maeve grabbed her attention and waved her over.

'Do I call you Julia? Jools? What do you prefer?'

'Either is fine.'

'Okay. Obviously we need to orientate you, as it's only your first day, so why don't you work with some of the HCAs this morning, helping to get the patients washed and fed? That way you'll get to know who we've got and meet them all. Well, as many as you can get to. And then, later on, you can help with some of the duty list—how does that sound?'

'Perfect.'

'Great.' Maeve stood, pushing her handover sheet into her uniform pocket and looking at her curiously. 'You know Mr Fitzpatrick?'

She blushed again, not sure she wanted to share how exactly she knew him. 'Er...we met once. Years ago now. He probably doesn't remember.'

'Professionally? Or socially?'

'Socially.'

'Oh, okay... He's a great doctor. An orthopaedic surgical consultant. We all call him Mr Ice, because he keeps everyone at a distance. Never socialises. Never hangs around to gossip or chew the fat. He keeps himself to himself, to be fair.'

'So it wasn't just me, then?'

'No!' Maeve laughed. 'Definitely not. There are a lot of young nurses and other staff who wish he would be friendlier, though.'

Julia could understand why. Anthony was a very handsome man.

'Right, let's give you a bit of a tour. Show you where everything is.'

'Sounds good.'

She was raring to go and to put the discord of meeting Anthony—*Mr* Fitzpatrick...*Mr Ice*—to bed. This was a new start for her. The beginning of a brand-new chapter in her life. She wanted to do well, and her little faux pas with Anthony Fitzpatrick was not going to ruin that.

It had been a long nightshift and he'd been ready to go home. To sleep. To eat. To rest. He'd just been dropping off some surgical aftercare orders for an emergency that had come in through the London Saints' A&E department to Maeve before he went home. As he'd reached to pull the door open it had been thrust towards him, and then someone had run into his chest.

A nurse. Shorter than he was. With dark brown hair tied up in a bun.

When she'd looked up to apologise he'd recognised her instantly. No rat's tails of wet hair, no ruddy cheeks from the cold, cold snow, no pregnant belly and no baby about to make its entrance into the world. But of course he'd known who she was! Instantly. Because he'd often thought about that night.

Delivering babies wasn't in his remit at all, but he was a doctor, and he knew what to do, and he'd been so thankful that there hadn't been any complications. No postnatal haemorrhage or problems with the baby. But what he most remembered from that night was the gift she had given his wife. Letting Yael hold her son.

Yael had dreamed of having her own baby. Of carrying it in her womb, how the birth might be, how they'd be a little family afterwards and what great parents they would make. And Julia had allowed her a precious moment, a perfect Christmas gift, that Yael had spoken of many times after their surprise guest had been whisked away in an ambulance.

How she'd missed the feel of that baby in her arms. She'd allowed herself to imagine that the baby was hers. For just a little while. Knowing that it would be her only chance to hold a newborn baby like that. How perfect the little baby boy had been. How good it had felt to hold him. How it had lifted her heart and her mood after the news that they'd got a few days previously that she only had a few weeks left to live…

He'd not known Julia was a nurse. She'd never said. And he'd most definitely not expected to find her going into that staffroom. Did she work here now? Would he have to see her every day at the hospital?

The thought disturbed him.

She disturbed him.

He liked to keep his private and personal life away from work. He didn't need her blabbing about the incident to all and sundry. He'd have to have a word with her about it. Quietly. Somewhere private, where no one else could hear. The hospital grapevine was a vibrant, healthy thing. And she'd called him *Anthony*. In front of his colleagues. As if she knew him. Which she *did*. But he couldn't have her calling him by his first name here. It had felt…strangely intimate. A shock.

And had she always been that beautiful? Ten years ago he'd not really focused on her looks. Her long hair had been down, and loose, but it had been soaking wet, covering her face every time she pushed, her face squeezed tight, the skin flushed and red, wet from the cold, rounded with pregnancy.

Even after the birth, when she'd held her son in her arms, he'd never truly seen her real features.

Now her hair was swept up neatly, away from her face. Her eyes were a deep brown colour, large and wide—

Like Yael's.

The unbidden comparison arrived in his brain almost gleefully.

Doe.

But Julia's face was slimmer, her cheeks a soft, rosy pink. Her smile wide, her lips soft-looking. It had taken him a moment to recognise her, and when he had—when she'd used his name so easily—he'd felt so broadsided, so shocked, that he'd corrected her, not wanting their intimacy to be shared so publicly.

What am I going to do?

He would have to find a way to deal with working with her each day.

If I just treat her the way I treat everyone else then I can keep her separate and away from my life, like the other people I work with. It will be that simple.

Right?

The next day Julia was with her first patient, a Miss Tiffany Morello, who'd arrived on the ward from A&E that morning after falling. She had a broken tibia and fibula in her left leg that needed surgical plating and required the insertion of a cannula in preparation for surgery.

'What were you doing up a lamppost?' Julia asked as she swabbed the skin with an alcohol wipe. She'd already found the vein easily.

Miss Morello blushed. 'It was silly, I know, but I wanted to get a good view of Patrick Delacourt going into his hotel.'

'Who?'

'Patrick Delacourt. The actor. He's been in all those action movies…recently divorced and *single*!'

Julia smiled. She'd never heard of him. 'And so you climbed a lamppost?'

'I climbed a lamppost. I had no choice. I'd been waiting for ages, but all the paparazzi were there, and they had stepladders to see over each other and they blocked my view. So I thought, *I could shimmy up that lamppost and then I'll see him and maybe he'll see my banner.*'

'You made a banner?'

Tiffany smiled. 'It read *Patrick do you wanna court me?* And then my phone number.'

Julia laughed. 'Brave.'

'Or stupid. I thought I could hold on to the lamppost with one hand and wave my banner with the other when he arrived. But I slipped and fell and heard something snap.'

'Ouch.'

'Yeah…'

'Has he called?'

Tiffany pouted. 'No.'

'Maybe he'll hear about it and make a secret visit to you in hospital?'

Her patient suddenly brightened. 'Do you really think so? I should put something on social media and tag him into it!'

As her patient grabbed for her phone Julia heard the arrival of the doctors on the ward to do their round. She turned to look, as she cleared away after the cannula insertion, and noted Mr Fitzpatrick was leading the charge, surrounded by registrars and juniors.

He looked very commanding. An alpha male if ever there was one. And if she hadn't met him before, and seen his soft, encouraging side, she would probably have been a little afraid of him. But his bedside manner was amazing. She'd been on the receiving end of it, and she knew there was warmth within that Mr Ice personality.

'Who's presenting?' he asked his assorted juniors, without even looking at Julia. It was almost as if she wasn't there.

One of them raised a hand. 'Miss Tiffany Morello, twenty-two years of age, presented in A&E just after eight o'clock this morning after falling from a height of approximately eight feet. X-rays in the department demonstrated displaced fractures of both the tibia and fibula of the left leg.'

Julia watched as he was passed a tablet and he called up the X-ray images to examine them more closely.

Then he looked up at his patient and smiled. 'Miss Morello, I'm Mr Fitzpatrick, and I'm going to be operating on your leg later today. You've been told you need surgery?'

'Yes.'

'My plan is to do an open reduction and internal fixation of the bones. What that means is that we'll do an open surgery to realign and set your bones with screws and plates, to facilitate the healing and stability of the leg to bear weight for walking.'

'Will it be a general anaesthetic?' Tiffany asked nervously.

'Yes. An anaesthetist will come along shortly to talk to you about anaesthesia, but a general is the best solution with this sort of surgery.'

'Is it an easy fix?'

He nodded. 'Generally. Of course we can never know the true extent of an injury until we get inside, but it's usually a run-of-the-mill operation for us. I understand that it's not for you, and that you may have some concerns or worries. I'd be very happy to talk you through them, if you like?'

'I've had a surgery before. My appendix...' Tiffany explained, blushing.

Julia couldn't help but notice how Tiffany was looking at Mr Fitzpatrick.

'Good. You should also know that after this surgery it can take anything from six to eight weeks to heal. You'll be given crutches, and physiotherapy to assist you afterwards. Do you have family or friends who can help you?'

'I live with my mum and dad. Still.'

He smiled. 'Nothing wrong with that. Now, just promise me that you won't slack on the physio afterwards. It's a comprehensive programme that should maximise the effectiveness of the surgery and give you full function, reduce any pain or stiffness you might experience and enable you to go climbing again.'

Tiffany laughed. 'Oh, I won't be climbing any more lamp-posts, let me tell you!'

'Glad to hear it. Now, if you have any questions then...' he turned and finally looked at Julia '...Nurse...?'

'Morris,' she said, her cheeks flushing.

'Nurse Morris will be able to contact me and I'll try and come and talk to you again. If not, I'll see you after the surgery, all right?'

'Thank you, Doctor.'

He gave his patient a nod, briefly looked at Julia, then moved on to the patient in the next bed.

Julia felt utterly deflated. She had thought that he might find time to come and talk to her, since running into her yesterday, but she'd learned that he'd been on a nightshift and had gone home. She'd then had a sleepless night of her own, wondering what shift he was on today, before she came into work wondering if they would have time to talk. She dearly wanted to ask him how his wife was doing, though if she did that she knew she'd have to talk about Marcus...

But it would be nice just to have a moment with him. Check in with him...see how he was doing and what he'd been up to these last ten years.

Had his life changed as much as hers?

She'd often wondered.

The urge to talk to him now that she knew he was here

was strong. Although only a tiny part of Marcus's life, he had been there when she'd brought him into the world and that meant something. He'd saved her from having to give birth on a freezing wintry night in the middle of the countryside. Open to the weather. He'd brought her into his warm home and delivered Marcus safely.

They had a connection.

They would always have it.

And somehow him being here made her feel close to her son once again. She felt a wave of sadness slam into her, almost taking away her breath, but then it was gone.

But what about that moment before, when he'd turned to her and asked her surname as if he didn't know it? She'd told him all those years ago. He knew her last name. Why pretend he didn't? To show everyone else that he didn't know her all that well after she'd called him Anthony?

It's been ten years. Maybe he thinks I got married?

It was a possibility.

Julia watched as he went around the ward, finishing his round, and when he went over to the reception desk to write notes in a file she swallowed hard, gathered some courage and went to stand beside him, leaning on the counter and deliberately looking at him, waiting for him to notice her.

'Can I help you, Nurse Morris?'

He continued to write. Didn't even look up. Why was he acting this way?

'Yes, you can.'

He closed the file, handing it to the receptionist, and then turned to look at her, one eyebrow raised. 'How?'

Now she was flustered. They might have shared a very intimate moment—a gargantuan moment in her life that she would always remember—but it was over a decade ago now, and it wasn't as if they were friends. They'd never kept in touch. Though she'd always meant to. It wasn't as if they had any obligation to each other, but she couldn't understand why he was talking to her the way that he was.

'I just… We shared something. A long time ago, I'll admit, but we shared an amazing moment together. And you and Yael were so…welcoming and kind and warm. Yet now I'm feeling confused, because you're…'

Should she call him cold? Distant? Unapproachable? Terse?

Anthony glanced at the receptionist, whom she saw was thankfully on a call and not listening to them at all.

'We are at work, and work requires us to be professionals,' he said quietly.

'I know that. Lives are in our hands. But we can be professionals and still be nice to one another.'

'You don't think I'm being "nice"? When was I mean?'

'You haven't been. It's just…your tone,' she said awkwardly.

'My *tone*?'

'You know they all call you Mr Ice?'

'I do. It's respectful.'

'Is it?'

Or maybe it signalled the fact that they thought he was the most unapproachable person they'd ever met?

Annoyed, she began to walk away. Flustered. Frustrated. Angry. Why had she even thought that they could be friends? Clearly the warm, kind and wonderful man she'd met on Christmas Eve all those years ago no longer existed. Was it because of something bad? Had he lost Yael?

She stopped walking as her mind filled with the memory of Yael. Wheelchair-bound. Thin. Frail. Bald. Using oxygen for her non-small cell lung cancer.

Julia turned back to face him. 'I've been wondering… I've been worried. How's Yael?'

His eyes darkened and she saw a muscle clench in his jaw.

'She's dead.'

CHAPTER THREE

THERE HAD BEEN no time to explain more, so he'd taken her quietly to one side and told her he'd meet her in the hospital canteen at lunchtime. Her lunch was at one, so he'd got his consults finished by then and now he sat at a table, nursing a coffee, thinking about how he would tell Julia what had happened.

He'd not shared the exact details with anyone here. They knew, of course, that his wife had died ten years ago, but they didn't know more than that. His private life was exactly that, and he refused to be the subject of pity or sympathy. The only way he could get through each day was to work hard, ignore gossip and keep himself to himself. Build walls. Keep people out. Keep people from getting close. That was what worked, and it was what kept him strong. His patients—the people who needed him—were what kept him going. They were his focus. Not his tragic past. The fact that he was now going to share what happened with someone at work felt very strange indeed.

Why her?

Why was he willing to tell *her* the truth?

Because she'd met his wife? Because she and Yael had talked? Because Julia had known what was going on with her cancer? Or was it because of the baby? The happiness that Julia had given his wife that magical Christmas night. As if she had known it would be Yael's only chance to hold a newborn and she had given her that gift selflessly, even when she had probably been very frightened, exhausted and spent after the events of that evening.

He felt he owed her an explanation.

She deserves the truth.

He watched her as she entered the canteen, her eyes scanning the room, looking for him. Saw the way she smiled softly when she spotted him. She grabbed a coffee for herself, placing it on a tray with a couple of plates of food, paid for them and then made her way over to the table.

She passed him a plate with a ham salad on it and fries. 'I figured you hadn't eaten. One of the nurses told me you've only just come out of clinic.'

He smiled and accepted. 'Thanks.'

But he wasn't hungry. Apprehension had obliterated any hunger he'd felt earlier in the day.

She sat opposite him, adding a little salt to her own fries before she looked up at him and smiled. 'So...'

'So.' He watched her face. She looked confused. Concerned. A little curious. 'I apologise for the way I spoke to you when we met yesterday.'

'Oh. Right. Thank you.'

'You took me by surprise. I keep my private life and my professional life separate, and I've never had a nurse call me Anthony.'

'Well, you might have to get used to it. To me, you're Anthony. Not Mr Fitzpatrick. He sounds like a lawyer. Or a judge.'

'I have been known to be judgemental in my time.'

He was finding it difficult not to be abrupt. This was strange for him. Sharing. And it was surprising to realise that he did want to be open with her.

'I'm sorry about Yael. I didn't know,' she said now.

He thought about his wife's doe eyes, so similar to the eyes of the woman opposite. 'Thank you.'

'I take it the cancer…won?'

Anthony looked down at the table. Even after all these years it never got any easier to say it. 'Yes, it did.'

'When?'

'A few weeks after we met you.'

'Weeks?' She looked horrified. 'I'm so sorry!'

'Not your fault. We knew she didn't have long. Those weeks should have been terrible, but in actual fact they were anything but. Yael couldn't stop talking about you and baby Marcus. About how it had felt to hold your son in her arms and pretend for just a moment that he was actually hers. We spoke about you both a lot.'

He let out a breath and ran his hands through his hair, before reaching for his coffee and taking a fortifying sip. His gaze grazed over everyone else in the cafeteria, making sure that no one could see him lose his usual composure.

'I could see it in her eyes,' she said.

'What?'

'That maybe she didn't have long left. Her need to hold him. It seemed like such an easy thing to do…to help another person who was suffering.'

'You know I almost didn't answer the door?'

Julia almost laughed in disbelief. 'Really?'

'I thought you were carol singers. Yael was exhausted. We'd received bad news from her doctors that the latest clinical trial wasn't working and that her treatment cycle was over. I was in no mood to celebrate Christmas. But she—Yael—she wanted to hear some singing. Her last Christmas. She wanted to hear people sing carols.'

'And you got me instead.'

'Better for her than any carol singers, believe me.'

'I'm glad. She looked so happy with Marcus in her arms.

The way she took him from me…so reverently, like he was the most precious thing in the world.'

'He was.'

'Yes…' she answered sadly. 'Please tell me she went painlessly.'

'She did. She was on a lot of morphine at the end. Slept a lot. And then one afternoon she just stopped breathing.'

'It must have been hard.'

He nodded, thinking back to that day. That moment. Sitting by her bedside having watched her chest for hours, having listened to each agonal breath, and then… Silence. Stillness.

'As a doctor, you're so well-trained that when someone's heart stops beating you want to give CPR…you want to start pumping that person's chest to bring them back. But I knew I couldn't bring her back, even if I wanted to.'

'What day did she die?'

He looked up at her. 'February eighteenth. Four days after Valentine's Day.'

He didn't understand the shock that registered on her face.

Or why her hand trembled as she lifted her mug of coffee to her lips.

'What's wrong?' he asked.

How to tell him? How to tell him about Marcus?

Just say it? The way he had about Yael?

There'd been no messing around—*'She's dead.'*

Was it easier to say it if the person who had died had been an adult? Someone who had experienced life, who'd had cancer, so maybe it was expected and not a surprise? It was surely harder to say when the person who had died was still a baby.

'It's Marcus.'

Anthony frowned.

She pushed her plate away, no longer hungry, and took a sip of fortifying coffee. This news never got any easier to say, no matter how many times she had given it. She remembered that early-morning phone call to her mother, when she was still in hysterics. The awkward call to Jake who, even though he'd wanted nothing to do with his son, would still need to know.

'He's...er...passed, too.'

Anthony looked at her in shock. Stunned.

It had been nearly a decade. The pain should be easier to deal with. But there was no timeline on grief. No rule to say that the pain of it should lessen with time. It could still hit her with the ferocity of an explosion. A punch to the gut. A tearing apart of the heart. And she felt that right now. Because Anthony had been there. Anthony had brought her son safely into the world and she... She had lost him.

She felt guilt wash over her, as if she somehow had to apologise to him, even though she knew that feeling was a ridiculous one.

'He was a colicky baby. Had trouble sleeping at night. I didn't mind. He was a beautiful gift and I loved him, and I knew that at some point it would pass. Colic is temporary. But I had many weeks of disturbed nights, and most days I was like a zombie. But we got through them. And when he started smiling at me, at about seven weeks, I couldn't believe I was so lucky to have such a wonderful baby boy.'

That was the easy part. The happy part of her recollection. She needed Anthony to know that she had loved and adored her baby. That she would have done anything for him.

'I tried all sorts of tricks. Colic drops. Rubbing his tummy. Massages. Rocking him. Warm baths before bed. Nothing much worked.'

Anthony said nothing. Just continued to listen intently to

her. It gave her the strength to continue, let her know that this was a safe space in which to share her pain.

'The night of February seventeenth I put him down just before midnight. I normally put him to bed at around nine o'clock, but he'd already woken up a few times and I'd paced the house for ages. He seemed to settle then, and I kissed him on the forehead and lay him down in his crib. I fell into my bed without even getting undressed. I was shattered. I hoped to get an hour or so's worth of sleep before he woke up again. But when I opened my eyes the clock said it was six in the morning, and I can remember looking at it, marvelling for a moment. Happy that he'd slept through for the first time ever. And then... I got worried. I've never got out of bed so fast, and I rushed to his room.'

Her voice had begun to wobble. Tremors of emotion were catching in her throat. Tears burned the backs of her eyes. Her hand trembled as she remembered that morning.

'I ran into his room, terrified that something had happened. But another part of me, the logical part, was telling me that I was being ridiculous, and that I'd open his door and see him softly snoozing...all red-cheeked and his face swollen with sleep. But he didn't look like that at all.'

How long had she lingered in the doorway, looking at him? Seconds? It had felt like minutes, with her brain refusing to acknowledge what she could see.

'He was pale. Still. His lips already blue,' she whispered. 'I didn't know what to do! Clearly he wasn't breathing... I remember lifting him up and holding him in my arms, begging him to wake up!'

The tears flowed freely now as the memory of discovering Marcus in his crib came right back to her and placed her in that moment.

'They'd taught us a little infant CPR during our antenatal classes, so I placed him on the floor and tried to remember the right way to do it. Some voice was screaming at me to phone for help first, but I knew that if I did that I would have to leave him to get my phone. So I picked him up again and raced to my bedroom and dialled for an ambulance.' She paused to catch her breath. 'It didn't take them long to arrive, but those moments alone in my bedroom felt like centuries. Nothing I was doing seemed to be helping, and I thought I was hurting him. It killed me with every compression I made on his chest, hoping to make him breathe again. To hear him cry again. I would have given anything to hear him cry again.'

Her tears dropped to the table. Even went in her cooling coffee.

Anthony was pale and still as he listened. Eyes downcast.

'They said it was SIDS. Sudden Infant Death Syndrome. He died on the morning of February the eighteenth.'

'The same day as Yael,' he whispered, so softly she almost couldn't hear his voice.

'The same day as Yael,' she confirmed, as stunned as he by the tragic coincidence.

Yael and Marcus, who had met one amazing, snowy Christmas Eve. Marcus had given Yael one moment of happiness that she'd carried with her to the end of her days. And when she'd passed Marcus had gone too. Almost as if they were joined somehow.

'Maybe she's up there holding him?' Julia suggested, trying to smile through her tears. Trying to find something good in the terrible. 'Maybe she's looking after him for me until I get there, too?'

'I hope so.'

Anthony suddenly seemed to realise that at some point during the telling of her tragic tale he'd reached out and taken her hand. That he'd been leaning in, listening intently, staring at her for a long time. Suddenly he sat back and let go, as if he was aware again of his surroundings. That he was at work and that someone might have seen them together.

She felt his walls go back up, saw the professional mask appear on his face as if by magic. She looked around, too. No one seemed to have noticed them, partially hidden as they were by some fake Yucca trees.

'I met some wonderful nurses who took care of me at the hospital when I arrived. The paramedics must have known Marcus was gone, but they kept working on him until we got to A&E, where the doctors told me there was nothing they could do. Those nurses…they inspired me to become one. Not straight away. I had to process my grief. But eventually, when the time was right, I applied to university and completed my three years training. And here I am.'

'You created something good out of tragedy. You chose to help people.'

She nodded. 'If I can help one person feel better, the way those nurses helped me during my darkest times, then it will help me feel close to Marcus again. Somehow… It makes sense to me,' she said, shrugging a little with embarrassment.

'It makes total sense. You find the light in the dark.'

'That's absolutely it.' She smiled at him. It was a thank-you for his kindness whilst she told him about her son. 'It's strange to still feel like you're a mother when you have no one to care for. This job helps. My placements during training showed me that. Do you…?' She paused, wondering if her question would sound stupid. 'Do you still feel like a husband? Sometimes? Do you…forget?'

Anthony gave a small laugh. 'Sometimes. My mother, on the other hand, is forever reminding me that I am not a husband, and that I have a duty to my seat not only to find myself another spouse, but also to provide an heir.'

Okay, something didn't make sense...

Julia frowned. 'Your seat? An heir? What do you mean?'

Anthony looked at her. 'I'm not just Anthony Fitzpatrick, orthopaedic surgeon. I am also the Duke of Weston.'

'What?'

'It's true.'

'You're a duke?'

She wanted to laugh now. A duke? A real-life duke?

'I am. My mother feels that I have mourned my wife long enough and she is forever trying to set me up with various suitably titled ladies.'

'Wow...'

'I don't want to upset her, but she seriously needs to butt out.'

'So tell her.'

'You've never met my mother. The word *no* is not in her vocabulary.'

'Sounds like my mother...'

'Really?'

'She thinks that the thing to gladden my heart again is for me to get involved with another man. Her response, when she heard I'd got a permanent job in this hospital, was not *Congratulations* but *"Think of all those eligible doctors you'll meet!"'*

Julia laughed wholeheartedly, seeing the mirth in his eyes, too, until her consciousness happily reminded her that in actual fact she was sitting across from a most eligible doctor indeed.

A handsome one.

A widowed one.

A *duke*.

Her laughter died quite quickly and she looked away, hoping he didn't think that she was going to come after him romantically.

'How similar our lives have become,' she said, her voice quiet.

Anthony looked back at her. A strange look in his gaze. 'Indeed.'

CHAPTER FOUR

It had been a most enlightening conversation with Julia. But sad and unfortunate, too. Discovering that Marcus had died had made him incredibly sad, because he'd believed for all this time that the perfect little baby boy who had brought his wife such joy was still out there. Living his life. Being a boisterous ten-year-old. At school. Playing football with his friends. Getting excited about the latest computer game. Streaming. Having fun and laughing and being absolutely, vitally, *alive*.

But he wasn't. He had died the same day as Yael. The two of them somehow bonded together, almost as if they'd been unable to survive without the other. Connected by some strange cosmic cord that had pulled them both into the darkness.

Life was good at throwing curveballs. But he'd put up enough walls to assume that he could avoid any further ones. Just continue to live his life as a doctor. Operate. Help people. Stay professional. Not get attached to anyone or anything.

Mr Ice.

Of course he knew they called him that, and it was fine by him. The name created another wall, because people knew what to expect and not to try to push past it. The only people he remained attached to were his mother and his sister, but his mother was as strong as an ox, and would be around for ages yet, and his sister was newly married and healthy.

His mother was a woman who lived a full life and kept herself busy. Right now she was organising a charity ball at the family seat, to raise money for cancer research, and in six weeks' time she would be flying out to Australia, to visit her sister. Amelia had emigrated years ago, and started a new life in Adelaide. No doubt, though, in those six weeks his mother would still find the time to badger him into finding someone.

'I don't like seeing you alone, Anthony,' she would say.

'I'm not alone. You're here.'

He had moved out of the manor house where he'd been living with Yael after her death. It had held too many painful memories, so he'd moved back into the main house, where the Duke of Weston usually resided.

'You know what I mean...' A pause, then, *'I've invited the delightful Lady Annabella Forsythe for dinner this evening.'*

'Delightful' in his mother's language, meant *available*. Single. Looking to settle down and marry.

Bless her. His mother was a wonderful woman, but she despaired at his staying unmarried and, even though she respected the great love he had for his wife, she most definitely felt he ought to be settling down again. Putting his grief into the past, where it firmly belonged, and looking for something—*someone*—new. Her efforts had ramped up lately, and she'd told him in no uncertain terms that she expected him to bring someone to her ball and he was not to attend alone. That she couldn't bear the idea of leaving him alone when she boarded that plane to Australia.

He'd briefly considered defying her, just to see the look on her face, but did he really want her flying off to Australia angry? What if that was the last time he saw her? And their last words, their last feelings towards one another, were ones of anger?

No. He would have to find someone. But who? Who to trust to understand that it was simply an agreement and not the start of something? Someone who wanted the same thing as he did. To just get through the evening on the understanding that when they said goodbye at the end of the night the peck on the cheek would be a polite thank-you and not a prelude to something more promising.

These thoughts were running through his head as he approached his next patient. He'd performed a hip replacement that morning on Mr Johnathan Carver and he was now doing his post-op. As he approached the patient, he noticed that Julia was beside his bed, checking the man's blood pressure.

'Mr Carver, how are you doing?'

'Not bad, Doc. Bit of a sore throat, but apart from that I feel good.'

'Some people feel that. It's from the tube they use when you're under, and it should pass reasonably quickly. I thought you'd like to know that your surgery went very well. I didn't have any problems at all and you were a model patient.'

'That's good.'

'How's his blood pressure, Nurse Morris?'

She turned and smiled at him as she folded up the blood pressure cuff. 'One thirty over seventy-five.'

'Perfect. You're not feeling any discomfort from the hip?'

'Not yet.'

He smiled. 'We will continue to give you pain relief whilst you're here, and also painkillers to take home. Let me just check your drain.'

He lifted up the blanket to assess the drain. It was working well and had already drained off a little fluid. All looked good.

'Excellent. The nurses and the physios will be around to help you get walking as soon as possible and teach you how to use a crutch or a walking frame to get about. If everything goes well, we'll get you home as soon as we can.'

'Sounds good to me. When will that be, do you think? I'll need to tell my wife.'

'We'll definitely keep you here for the next day, and then we'll assess you again. Most of my patients go home two or three days post op. The physios will talk to you about how you can manage your daily activities and give you home exercises to keep the joint and your limbs supple. We don't want you to stiffen up or develop any other problems.'

Johnathan nodded.

'You know to expect some pain or swelling in your legs and feet?'

'This lovely nurse was just talking to me about that.'

Julia smiled at him. She had a lovely smile. Her brown eyes large and gleaming. He blinked, unable to speak for a moment, as he quizzed himself on why he should notice her smile. Or her eyes.

He cleared his throat. 'It should get better with time. Don't be alarmed by it, unless you think it's excessive. In which case contact my secretary and I'll get you seen. Otherwise you'll need to make an appointment with your GP surgery to get your clips removed in about ten days as long as the wound is healing well. Questions?'

'Will I need any further follow-ups after the clips have come out?'

'Yes, we'll send you a letter two or three months afterwards. But if you follow your instructions, do your exercises and keep moving, I don't see any reason why you should have any further problems. No driving for six weeks. And no sex for six weeks either.'

Johnathan blushed and gave a mock salute. 'Yes, Doc. Thank you.'

'Look after yourself. Nurse? Let's keep him on observations for the next twenty-four hours, please. Any problems, have me paged.'

'Of course.'

He headed over to the computer terminal to update his post-op details onto Mr Carver's file, but as he stood there, typing, he couldn't help but feel the pull of Julia's orbit as she moved about the ward. Talking to patients. Caring for them. He saw her lay a hand on a patient's arm. She tucked another one in. She gave another a tissue and laughed at something they said. She was brand-new at this, but was showing no nerves, finding ways to engage with people from all walks of life. Knowing when to laugh, when to just be quiet and listen. When to support. She got along with everyone.

Pity I can't ask her to come to the charity ball...

But then a thought assailed him. *Why* couldn't he? She'd be perfect. She wanted her family off her back, too.

The thought wouldn't go away. He tried to imagine himself walking into the ballroom with her on his arm and seeing the look of surprise on his mother's face.

'Nurse Morris?' he said.

She looked up at him, her face relaxing into a smile as she came over to him. 'Yes?'

'I've got a strange request to ask of you.'

'Oh?'

He didn't want to air it here on the ward. 'Can you meet me at the end of the day? It won't take up much of your time.'

She seemed to think about it, then nodded. 'Sure.'

They walked to a coffee shop just down the street from the hospital and settled at a table in the back. Anthony got them both cappuccinos and a chocolate chip cookie each.

He sat across from her, looking a strange mix of intrigued and aloof.

She had no idea what he wanted to ask her. A request, he'd said. A strange request. She'd mulled over it all afternoon and her brain had taken her to some weird places, but now here they were, and she had no idea if she could help him, but she was willing to listen. She'd like to think that she could help.

'Well, I'm here and I'm all ears,' she said.

Anthony let out a sigh, as if he couldn't quite believe he was going to ask what he was going to ask her.

His apparent nerves were making her nervous. What could it be? He looked…uncomfortable. Was he not used to asking for help?

'I was thinking about what you were saying earlier. About what we were *both* saying about the pressures we have from other people to start dating again.'

'Okay…' What was he going to suggest?

'In my situation, I have pressure from my mother. She keeps inviting prospective brides to the house all the time, in the hope that one will take my fancy. The young Lady Annabella Forsythe is particularly forward and has her sights set on me the way a dog wants a bone. Not that I'm saying she's a dog, but…'

He cleared his throat. Pulled at his collar. Clearly uncomfortable. Awkward.

'I've this big charity ball coming up in a couple of days and then my mother's leaving in six weeks to fly to Australia. She keeps telling me she'd like to know that she's leaving me with Annabella…and honestly…? I'm not looking for love right now. I'm not sure I'll ever be looking for love again. I couldn't help but remember what you said about how your mother is pushing you to date, too.'

Julia nodded. She was. Incessantly. She'd called Julia at home just last night, wanting to know if any of the doctors or other specialists had captured her eye yet.

'And I'm guessing you feel the same way? That you don't want to get pushed into anything before you're ready?'

'That's right.' Julia wasn't sure she would ever trust again. She had a history of getting involved with unavailable men.

Her father had let her down spectacularly. And Jake, Marcus's father. She'd tried online dating a couple of years ago and though the men she'd met had looked great, their behaviour had not been. Engaged... Looking for a bit on the side... It had been awful. Plus, she'd worked so hard to secure this career for herself. This new start. This new beginning. Her independence meant so much to her, and getting involved with anyone right now would be an utter distraction and stress that she didn't need.

'So what if I suggested a way to solve *both* our problems?' he said.

'How do you mean?'

'We pretend to be dating. You accompany me to the charity ball as my fake girlfriend who I met at work. We socialise together. Are seen together as the perfect couple. Happy... I get Annabella off my back. My mother goes to Australia happy. Your mother is happy, too... And you and I? We know the truth, have a bit of fun for a few weeks without any threat of commitment, and then we part ways, as friends and colleagues.'

He seemed excited by his idea. Julia was intrigued. It sounded like it could work.

'I see... But there would have to be rules, though, right?'

'Absolutely!'

'Like it would never actually *be* a relationship, so no physical stuff?'

She blushed at the thought of kissing him. Touching him. Being affectionate. He was such a handsome man, but in her own head she thought of him as still married. Still in love with Yael. Even though she knew that his wife was gone. They were both single. There was no reason, actually, why she shouldn't think of him as available. But...no. She was in no state of mind to look for a relationship either.

'No. Apart from perhaps the odd kiss to make it believable. Hand-holding. Dancing at the ball, obviously. Maybe we could even have cutesy nicknames for one another?'

'Like Mr Ice?'

Julia smiled but inside she was reeling. The *odd kiss*? She couldn't help but look at his mouth. At his lips. She'd never really noticed before, but they were perfect. His bottom lip looked ideal for biting. Or sucking. She laughed nervously as wicked thoughts rushed through her head, surprising her, because she'd not thought that way in such a long time.

'Well, not that,' he said. 'Not if we're trying to pretend we're into one another.'

Right. Sensible.

'Okay And how would we end it? What would we tell people?'

He shrugged. 'I don't know. That our love for one another burned too bright and too briefly?'

'Erm… That sounds a little cheesy. Too poetic for something that's only going to last for a few weeks.'

'That we just decided to part as friends, then? We realised that we didn't have enough in common?'

She nodded. 'That could work. Sounds more reasonable. We met at work and though we share the same passion to help our patients, it wasn't enough to hold us together?'

'Yes! And if we tell everyone at work that we're dating, too, then it gets everyone off my back there, as well. Though of course we'd maintain the necessary professional boundaries at work.'

Hmm… People knowing about them at work? She didn't like the sound of that.

'I don't think we should do that at work. It wouldn't be good for me or my career. Do you have problems with approaches at the hospital?'

'When you're an eligible doctor? A duke? People assume

I'm rich, and that can attract the wrong type of people—so, yes. I certainly get my fair share of offers.'

'*Aren't* you rich, though?'

He shrugged. 'Oh, definitely.'

She laughed at him. At the easy way he said it. As if money wasn't important. Only rich people thought that, she figured, thinking about how she worried about the cost of running her own car, and the fact that she'd been saving up for months just to be able to buy herself some new furniture. He really was from another planet.

'I don't know… It seems a lot. I don't like lying to people.'

'Neither do I. But it would really help me out, and I'd like to help you, too.'

'Can I think about it?'

'Of course! But just so you know…the charity ball is this weekend.'

'In three days' time?'

He nodded. 'And if you agreed you'd need a ballgown.'

A ballgown. That sounded expensive.

He must have seen the look of doubt on her face. 'I can refund any expenses.'

Julia thought hard. It was a strange proposal, after all! But…maybe it would be fun? Just to accept his offer and go with the flow? Experience Anthony's life a little bit more? He was a good guy, and he'd helped her all those years ago, letting her in to his house and safely delivering her son. She *owed* him. Even after all this time. And a ball sounded grand and fun. It would be nice to step out of her own life for a bit. Celebrate her new start. To get her mother off her back by dating a duke. And if he was willing to pay for it, then why not? And then, when it was over, it would buy her more time to *not* date. To say she was getting over Anthony, or something.

Who would it hurt?

'Okay,' she said, smiling. 'I'm in!'

CHAPTER FIVE

'Where are we going?' she asked, as he led her to a boutique dress shop in the heart of London. 'Aren't all the shops closing?'

It had taken them some time to negotiate their way through the capital's traffic. It was a busy Thursday evening and everyone was trying to get home.

'I called ahead and Celine is staying open just for us.'

Julia raised an eyebrow in surprise. 'Celine?'

'She is the most talented dressmaker I have ever seen. She's made outfits for royalty.'

'You know I could have just bought a dress from somewhere?'

'I'm sure. But if we're to pull off this illusion for my mother, I really need her to see that you're someone special. A reason that you, just a nurse, caught my eye when I could have had Annabella. Descended from royalty. A millionairess in her own right. Breeder of some of the finest racehorses in all of England.'

'Just a nurse? Right...'

'I didn't mean that in any derogatory sense. Nurses are what keep hospitals running. Without you, we doctors would be nothing.'

'How is your mother going to believe I could afford such a dress on a nurse's salary?'

'I'll tell her we went dress shopping together—which is

true. I'll tell her that you tried on many dresses—which will also be true. And that the dress you fell in love with looked so wonderful on you that I, as the perfect gentleman, offered to pay for it for you, despite your protests, because I thought you looked so beautiful in it. Which will also be true.' He smiled. 'All good lies work when they are bathed in elements of the truth.'

Anthony felt certain that their ruse would work on everyone. He would present Julia as a Cinderella. It would be a *fait accompli*. Everyone there would marvel. With the exception of Annabella, maybe. But they would all smile and nod, even if they wanted to grimace, because they would want to be seen as being happy for him after his tragic past.

He knew that those in his social circle talked about him as some tragic widower. *Poor Anthony Fitzpatrick. Heartbroken over the loss of Yael.* Another woman they'd never expected him to marry...

When you were a duke, there was an expectation that you would marry within your social circle. To another titled woman, perhaps? A lady. A viscountess. Yael had been someone he'd met on his travels. In Brazil, of all places. She'd been there on a gap year, working in a kitchen. She'd cooked his meal and when he'd asked to see the chef, to give her his compliments and appreciation, he'd been bowled over by her in an instant.

Coming home with a girlfriend on his arm—a girlfriend who was just a 'normal' person—had surprised everyone, but everyone had fallen in love with her the way he had. She'd just been that kind of lovely person who made everyone smile.

So Julia wouldn't be a surprise. He'd done this before. There was a precedent.

Celine's shop was situated in Mayfair. It had a simple, elegant exterior—dark blue, with her name in hand-scripted gold—and she welcomed him like an old friend.

'Anthony! Such an honour!'

He greeted her with a kiss on both cheeks, then turned to introduce her to Julia.

Celine looked Julia up and down. 'Exquisite! What a figure! Pleasure to meet you, my darling.'

Julia blushed. 'Er...thanks.'

'You said she was beautiful and you weren't wrong, Anthony. Can I offer you both refreshments? I have coffee... wine? Something a little more...celebratory?'

'Julia?' Anthony turned to her and could see that she was looking a little bewildered.

'Erm...would tea be okay?' she asked timidly.

'Of course!' Celine said. 'Black tea? Green? Peppermint? I've actually just this morning got in some salted caramel tea, which is delicious. You should try it!'

'Er...sure.'

He smiled, kind of enjoying her bewilderment.

As Celine disappeared to prepare their drinks he walked over to a dark green dress with a full skirt. He touched the silky fabric. 'See anything you like?' he asked.

Julia looked around her, her gaze sweeping over the shop, a smile settling onto her features. 'I see plenty, but...'

'But what?'

'I don't know what would be right.'

'Celine can help.'

'What about you? You sound like you've been to your fair share of balls. Which do you like?'

'They're all amazing. What I like isn't important. What is important is finding you a dress that makes you feel like a duchess.'

She turned to him. 'You really think we can pull this off?'

Anthony smiled. 'I do.'

Celine came back with a tray and placed it on a side table, pouring out two cups of tea and asking if they wanted sugar or milk. Once the drinks were sorted, Celine gave Julia another look over, turning her this way and that.

'Let me guess...you're a size twelve, right?'

'I usually buy fourteens...'

'But you hide within your clothes! Trust me, you're a twelve.'

Anthony sat down whilst Celine fussed and flitted about Julia and the shop, presenting dresses, holding them up to her to see if they were her colour, putting some to one side for trying on.

'And don't forget we can adjust any garment, add or take away embellishments, in time for Saturday evening.'

'You have so many beautiful dresses, Celine,' Julia said.

'Thank you. But what makes them *truly* beautiful is the woman wearing them!'

Julia walked over to a midnight-blue gown adorned with crystals. 'This is nice.'

'It is—but I think we could find a better colour for you, to make an impact when you enter the ballroom. You have gorgeous chestnut hair. Eyes like chocolate. I wonder if... Yes! What about this one?'

Celine held up a dress in a soft pink. Ballerina pink. With an asymmetrical neckline.

'I'm not sure I could carry that off...'

'Try it and see,' said Anthony.

He wanted to see her in it. And the realisation that he really wanted to see her in it intrigued him. Yes, he wanted that moment of walking into the ballroom with her, and for everyone to gasp in wonder at the mystery woman on his arm, but he also thought that she would look stunning in it, and he wanted that first view all to himself.

It was a thought process that both stunned and terrified him. He'd never thought he could feel this way again.

'Should I?' she asked.

He nodded and sat back in his chair as Julia and Celine headed to the changing room. As he waited, he pondered their plan. Wondered what Yael would have thought of it all and knew that she would have laughed and laughed and told him it was wonderful. A part of him felt that Yael would love that he was doing this with Julia. Because they'd often spoken of her in the weeks after she'd arrived at their house. Wondered about her. How her life was going. Whether they should have exchanged details and kept in touch…

'Ready?' Celine poked her head out from behind the changing room door.

'Absolutely.' His heart was actually thudding. He was excited.

And then he was gasping, getting to his feet as Julia stepped out from behind the door. Celine had done something to Julia's hair—taken it up in some kind of loose twist, exposing Julia's neck and allowing tendrils of curls to fall softly onto her shoulders. The dress itself had looked amazing on the hanger…but on Julia…

His mouth dropped open and he just *stared*. 'You look…'

'Is it too much?'

'No! You look out of this world!'

He barely noticed her blushes as she stood in front of the mirror to see for herself, checking it from all angles, watching as the soft tulle skirt, grazed the floor. Seeing the way the crystals on the bodice caught the light.

'The right necklace and earrings and no one will be able to take their eyes from her all night,' Celine said.

He couldn't take his eyes from her now. Something long dormant stirred within him and his mouth went dry. But then he forced himself to stop gaping as he remembered that this was pretend, and he wasn't looking for any complications right now. This was all about putting Annabella and his mother off the scent.

'Celine gave me these shoes too.' Julia lifted her skirt slightly to reveal a soft pink heel beneath, which arched her foot and shaped her calf muscle.

'This is the one,' he said.

Anthony dropped her back at her flat afterwards. She wondered what he thought of her rented apartment. It was not anywhere near as glorious as his home had been, and she could only assume the ducal seat, where the ball was going to be held, would be even more grand.

But she felt a lot more comfortable here as he helped her carry in the bags and boxes that contained her outfit for the ball.

'I will come and pick you up Saturday evening. Seven-thirty?' he asked at the door.

'Sounds great.'

'I guess I should have asked this before, but...you can dance, right?'

'I can body pop. Want to see my robot?' She smiled at him.

He laughed. 'You do the robot on the dance floor and everyone will most definitely notice you.'

Julia laughed. 'I can dance. I actually attended dance school for a few years as a kid. We did modern, tap, ballet... Waltz. Latin. I'm sure it's like riding a bike.'

'I don't think I've ever ridden a bike.'

She looked at him. 'You're kidding?'

'I rode ponies.'

Julia bit her lip, trying not to laugh at the disparity in their upbringing. 'Of course you did. So maybe I'll have to teach you one day. As part of our courtship.'

He smiled. 'It's a date.'

'It sure is.'

He didn't kiss her goodbye before she closed the door.

He didn't need to. There's no one here we need to pretend for.

But she still felt weirdly disappointed that he'd not even pecked her on the cheek. Why was that? Irritation because she was doing him a huge favour? This subterfuge was a very big deal. She didn't normally go out of her way to lie to people. She didn't like lying at all! But where was this disappointment at no kiss coming from? Was part of her dreaming that this could be real?

The confusion and puzzlement she felt was disconcerting. To distract herself, Julia picked up the phone and dialled.

Her mother answered almost straight away. 'Hi, honey, how did your day go?'

'Yeah, not bad. I got to see a really cool amputation today.'

There was a pause. 'You and I have different definitions for the word *"cool".*'

Julia laughed. 'I guess... How are you and what's-his-name?' Her mother had recently started seeing a guy she'd met at her book club.

'His name's Ray and he's fine. He's taking me out dancing this Saturday night. Some eighties theme night. So I get to dress up in crazy clothes and backcomb my hair. Or crimp it.'

'Oh. That's a coincidence.'

'What is?'

'Well... I'm going out dancing on Saturday night, too. With a guy.'

Her mother gasped in delight. 'Oh, my God! Tell me everything! What's his name? Is he a doctor? Is he handsome?'

'He's called Anthony. Yes, he's a doctor. An orthopaedic surgeon. But he's an ugly troll.'

'Of course he is. I bet he's absolutely gorgeous. A surgeon, huh? Is he rich?'

'Mum! That kind of thing doesn't matter.'

'Oh, doesn't it? Wait...wasn't that guy who delivered Marcus a doctor called Anthony?'

Julia gripped the phone tighter. 'Yes.'

'It's not the same one, though?'

'Actually...it is. He works on my ward.'

Her mother gasped again. 'But you said he had a wife with... Oh. I see.' Georgia Morris sighed. 'So where is he taking you?'

'There's a charity ball. To raise money for cancer research. He's taking me to that.'

'A ball? Sounds expensive. Do you have a dress?'

'I do. When I put it on I'll send you a selfie of me wearing it.'

'Do. What colour is it?'

'Pink. But not bubblegum-pink...more of a soft blush colour.'

'Sounds lovely. When did he ask you out?'

'I don't know... We've kind of been talking all week, really. Catching up with each other over what's happened in our lives over the years.'

'He knows about Marcus?'

'Yes.'

'How did he take it?'

'How does anyone take hearing that kind of news?'

'And he just asked you out?'

'Yes. Why? What's wrong? You've been going on at me for ages to start dating, and now that I am you don't sound happy.'

'I am, honey. Honestly. It's just a surprise, that's all. The connection.'

'He's nice, Mum. Really nice. And he's handsome and employed and decent. That's all you need to know.'

'And you like him?'

'Of course!'

She meant it, too. She did like him. How could she not like him? It was Anthony. He had delivered her baby. He had found room at his inn and let her in on Christmas Eve, when he'd had his own concerns and worries going on. And he had taken care of her. Her and Marcus. He might never have ridden a bike, only ponies, but she liked him. A lot. He was easy to talk to and he'd done his best to make her feel comfortable when they were at Celine's as they'd sipped salted caramel tea—which had been a revelation. And then the subtle way he'd passed Celine his card to pay for the dress, as if it were *nothing*. And she'd seen the price tag!

'Okay. Well...best of luck with it, then. And I might send you a selfie of me in my eighties gear.'

'I bet you still have it in your wardrobe. I bet you've not even had to buy anything for it.' She smiled, trying to bring a note of levity into her voice, to lighten the mood again.

'I may have kept a shoulder pad or two...'

For the first time since it had been announced Anthony was looking forward to his mother's charity ball. He would have gone anyway. After all, it was for a great cause, and they'd sold all the tickets. He would have gone in Yael's memory, but he wouldn't have enjoyed it. Simply because of the pressure from his mother and Annabella's constant presence at his side as she tried to be delightful. His mother had sent a lot of lovely young women his way, he had to admit, but no one with whom he had truly felt a connection. No one he wanted to get to know more or become intimate with. So he'd remained a widower and thrown himself into his work at the hospital, even become head of the department—because of his skill and dedication, rather than because of his title.

He had a good surgical list today. A fine way to end his

work week before the ball tomorrow, and another day to spend in the company of Julia.

He felt strangely relaxed when he was with her. His guard was down. Had been ever since they'd reconnected, really. There was something about the way her arrival in his life had shaped it and how he felt he knew her, even though that couldn't really be true. But he felt he had a new pep in his step as he entered Theatre to work on a scoliosis case.

Scoliosis was a condition in which the spine would twist or curve abnormally. Most cases were relatively minor, and people could live with it without surgery, but in some cases—like the one he had on his table this morning—it was more severe and the curvature was so bad it affected the lung capacity of the patient.

He was busy inserting a steel rod when the door to Theatre opened.

'Mr Fitzpatrick?'

He felt himself straighten at the sound of Julia's voice. Looked up. 'Yes?'

'One of your patients has come into A&E.'

'Which patient?'

'A Mrs Giger? You performed knee replacement surgery on her two weeks ago.'

'Is there a problem with it?'

'She's been in a car accident and the knee in question has been crushed. They're requesting you go down there to consult.'

'Thank you, Nurse Morris.' He refused to call her Julia in front of their colleagues. 'If you could let them know I'm in surgery, but I'll be down as soon as I can. Is Dr Manning, free?'

Dr Manning was one of his surgical registrars.

'He's on the ward.'

'Could you ask him to come in to assist?'

'Of course.'

She disappeared again and he refocused on the patient in front of him. Mrs Giger would have to wait for his attention, unfortunately. He owed it to the patient on his table to give him his full experience and attention.

He'd already got the hooks attached to the vertebrae, and now he could insert the rod to extend the hooks and therefore straighten the spine and create more stability, resulting in more room for the lungs to work effectively. Now he needed to perform the bone grafts to fuse the vertebrae and maintain the spine's new position. Once he was done, his patient would need to wear a brace for a few months to ensure the best healing.

'You needed me?' Dr Manning arrived in Theatre.

'Yes, I need you to check the autograft, please.'

In an autograft a surgeon used bone from the patient's own body, rather than cadaver bone. In this case the best place to harvest it was from the iliac crest on the rim of the pelvic bone.

He and Dr Manning worked well together, and when the complicated parts of the surgery were over Anthony stepped back from the table. 'Can you finish up for me here? I'm needed down in A&E.'

'Of course.'

He left Theatre, scrubbed out, and headed down to check on Mrs Giger. In Majors, he perused the scan results they had on the patient and saw that all the good work he'd done to replace her knee had been destroyed. Her patella was in pieces and she had comminuted fractures of both the lower leg bones.

'Is it salvageable?' asked the department head.

He sighed. 'Possibly. But it's going to take an awful lot of work—and even if we can help her she could still lose this leg if she develops complications.'

'She's diabetic,' he reminded Anthony.

'Which certainly adds complications...'

Diabetics often had problems with healing wounds. It was something he had discussed with Mrs Giger when he'd replaced her knee.

'I'll go and talk to her. Are her family here?'

'In the waiting room.'

'Put them in the family room. I'll speak to them after I've seen Mrs Giger.'

Anthony grabbed the phone on the desk and dialled up to his own ward.

'Orthopaedics. Nurse Morris speaking.'

He smiled. 'It's Anthony.'

'Hey.'

'Can you contact the admissions nurse and inform her that those patients arriving for my surgical list this afternoon will have to either see Dr Manning or be postponed? I've got an emergency that's going to take up the rest of my day.'

'Of course. Can I help in any way?'

'No, thanks. Oh, actually... I haven't eaten anything, and if I'm going to be in Theatre for a long time I ought to grab something. Could you pop into the hospital shop and grab me a meal deal?'

'Sure. What do you feel like nibbling on?'

He raised an amused eyebrow, surprised by the question, and laughed. 'Er...'

'Oh, wow. Sorry, I didn't mean it that way. I meant—'

She went into some explanation about how she'd just been talking to another nurse about their favourite nibbles, and the word was at the forefront of her mind. But all he could think of was nibbling her neck, which caused a rush of blood to head south so he had to clear his throat and his mind!

'It's fine. Anything will do. I'm not fussy.'

'I hope you didn't think that I meant...something else?'

He smiled. 'Of course not. It was totally innocent.'
'Yes. Good. Thanks.'
He just needed to tell himself that now...

It was the day of the ball and Julia felt nervous. Incredibly so. She sat on her bed, staring at the dress that was hanging on her wardrobe door in a protective cover, and all she could think about was whether they would be able to persuade Anthony's mother and everyone else he knew that he was actually dating *her*.

She'd thought that just mentioning Anthony would blow her mother away, and that she'd be so happy for her she'd get off her back. But instead, ever since her mum had discovered who her 'beau' was, there'd been doubt.

Would the same thing happen with Anthony's family? Would his mother be suspicious of him dating a mere nurse? Would she think of her as a possible gold-digger? A fake? They needed this thing to seem real to everyone else—which meant that a phone call telling someone she was dating was utterly different from *showing* people that they were dating. She could picture holding his hand. She could imagine dancing with him on the dance floor. But could she see herself kissing him? Being affectionate with him?

He was handsome, sure. Attractive, most definitely. And maybe if he'd been a perfect stranger and they hadn't had the history they had with one another, then, hell, yeah, she'd have noticed him in a bar. Maybe flirted a little.

But they did know one another. And that changed things.

It'll be okay. He's not looking for anything and neither am I.

She felt bad about lying to people, but who was it hurting? No one. It would make both their parents happy, their wider circle happy, and it would make *them* happy because everyone would finally be off their backs. There was no downside to it.

He was a friend—and besides, she really wanted to experience a little more of his life. Peep behind the curtain and see the Duke of Weston. Who wouldn't be curious? Seeing how the other half lived. How *he* lived. Since running into him again and getting to know him she'd been able to feel herself being drawn into his orbit.

Julia stood and unzipped the cover on her dress. Her fingers trailed down the soft pink silk and tulle as she imagined herself in it. Swirling around the dance floor in Anthony's arms with everyone watching. It was every little girl's dream to be the belle of the ball, and here was her opportunity. It was going to be amazing. And all she had to do to enjoy it was to relax into the idea and just accept it.

She started on her hair first. She liked the way Celine had twisted her hair up in the boutique and left little waves hanging, so once she'd washed and dried it she used a hot iron to add curls to the soft tendrils after she'd pinned up the rest of it with diamante hair slides. She kept her make-up minimal, creating a soft, smoky eye and a nude lip, and once she'd found the perfect underwear that would not show or ruin the line of the dress she slid into the ballgown, strapped on the heels and stood in front of the mirror to check her reflection.

I look like a fairytale princess.

She couldn't help but smile, and then laugh with delight. At heart, Julia was a romantic, and she'd grown up like most little girls reading stories about princesses who met handsome princes or were saved from dragons by knights, who whisked them away to their palaces for a happy-ever-after. And though Anthony was no prince, and he didn't have a palace, he was a duke, and he had a duchy, and he was going to dance with her at the ball and pretend to be in love with her. They would twirl and whirl around the ballroom, staring into each other's eyes, and...

And *nothing*.

She would not let herself be carried away by the fairytale. Life so far had proved to her that fairytales were nothing but myths. All she'd ever attracted were frogs.

A knock at her door had her gaze rushing to the clock. It was seven-thirty on the dot. Anthony was right on time.

She checked her hair and make-up one final time, then glided to the door and opened it.

Anthony stood outside, looking like the perfect gentleman. He wore a tuxedo, but instead of a black bow tie he wore one in soft blush-pink. Even his pocket square was the same colour, to match her gown. The suit clung in all the right places and in one hand he held a single red rose, which he proffered to her. In the other, he held two velvet-lined boxes.

Julia smiled and took the rose, pressing it to her nose to inhale the scent. It was long-stemmed and thorn-free, and its rich aroma filled her nose with a warm deliciousness that only roses could.

'Thank you. It's beautiful.'

'Not as beautiful as you.'

She blushed, feeling ridiculously pleased by his words, her stomach doing somersaults.

'There's no one here to hear that. Save your compliments for when we're there.'

But she liked it that he'd said it anyway. Almost as if he meant it.

He smiled. 'I have two other things for you.'

'Oh?'

He tilted his head. 'May I come in?'

'Of course!' She stepped back, closing the door behind him as he made her turn and face the hall mirror.

'Close your eyes.'

She felt excited. As if her whole body was humming with anticipation and thrill. She closed her eyes and listened intently. Heard him open one of the boxes. And then there was nothing—until she felt him drape something cold around her neck, fastening a clasp at the back.

'Open your eyes.'

Was this really happening? Smiling, she opened her eyes and then gasped out loud at the sight of the beautiful ruby and diamond teardrop necklace that he had placed around her neck. Set in gold, it glimmered and gleamed, catching the light as she moved.

'Anthony! This is...beautiful! Where did you get it?'

'It's been in the family for a while. It's nothing.'

'Nothing?' She wanted to touch it, but was almost afraid to. She could feel its weight, its history, its worth around her neck, but still she wanted to reassure herself that it was actually there.

'And these to match.'

He passed her the second, smaller box, and she opened it up to reveal ruby and diamond teardrop earrings.

'Oh, my gosh!'

'I thought they would look perfect with your dress. I hope you don't mind?'

'Mind?' Of course she didn't mind! She couldn't believe it. Never in her wildest dreams would she ever have thought that something like this could happen to her. 'Anthony, this is amazing. Thank you.'

'I just knew you'd look perfect in them.'

He stood behind her right shoulder, looking into the mirror at her. Admiring her. Smiling as if he was really happy. And she was, too.

'It will really help with our ruse if you're wearing the family jewellery.'

Of course. The *ruse*. She'd forgotten that for a moment, so caught up had she been in the fantasy. The disappointment she felt was sickening, but she reminded herself quickly that this was what it was all about. Being convincing to his family as well as hers. And this was what it would take to convince them.

'They know you're bringing me?' she asked.

'I've told them that I've been seeing someone quietly, yes. That I wanted to keep you to myself for a while. You know... like a good boyfriend would.'

'Of course.'

But she didn't want to be hidden. She wanted to think of him as shouting about her from the rooftops. Even if this was fake, she wanted that. To feel special.

'We should get going then, shouldn't we?' she said.

He checked his watch. 'Yes. I have a car waiting for us downstairs.'

He had a car waiting?

Anthony gave her his arm as they left her flat and she stepped outside to see a sleek, dark saloon car, with a chauffeur standing by the open rear passenger door. A *chauffeur*!

'Evening, ma'am,' said the man in a grey uniform and hat.

'Good evening. What's your name?'

'Mason, ma'am.'

She smiled. 'Thank you, Mason. Call me Julia.'

'Yes, ma'am.' He bowed.

Anthony caught her gaze and smiled at her.

Was this how the other half lived? Looked after? Served by staff? And yet Anthony worked. He worked hard. He wasn't waited on at the hospital. He had clearly gone looking for something fulfilling in life. He didn't just want *easy*. She admired him for that.

He took her hand as she got into the car. Helped her with her skirts as she sat down. Mason closed the door and Anthony got in the other side.

'Ready for this?'

'As I'll ever be. What does everyone know about me? What have you told them?'

'Your name.'

'That's it?'

'Like I said—I told them I wanted to keep you to myself for a little while. I've said they can ask you all the questions they want when they meet you.'

'And what do I say?'

'Tell them the truth.'

'That I'm a nurse?'

He smiled at her. 'Yes.'

'But won't they be expecting someone...*more* than that?'

'That's on them. Lying would make this more complicated than it needs to be. Let's just look like two people who are enjoying each other's company. We're still dating, remember? Still getting to know one another. Finding out how we might fit in with each other's family and friends.'

'And this is me making my debut?'

'Yes.'

'And doing it in style!'

He laughed. 'Yes! Are you nervous? Is there anything I can do to make this easier for you?'

As they drove through the city she looked out of the window at the ordinary people just walking by, getting on with their lives. Maybe coming home from work or going out for the evening to the local pub. And here she was, dressed up like a princess, in a chauffeur-driven car, about to be presented to dukes and earls and God only knew who else.

'Stay close?' she said.

Anthony smiled. 'I can do that.'

It took about an hour for them to drive out of town and reach the countryside where the manor was. Weston House looked imposing and regal, with a crenellated roof, a long sweeping driveway and high columns by the front door, where a butler waited with a tray of champagne to greet the guests.

The car swept right up to the doors and Mason got out and opened her door, standing back so that Anthony could take her hand and help her alight from the car.

Her stomach was filled with butterflies and she felt incredibly excited as well as nervous. Would her legs hold her up? They felt trembly. Weak. But as she took Anthony's hand and he slipped her arm through his, all the while smiling at her, she felt a strength begin to grow inside her. The feeling that with him on her arm she could do this.

Julia smiled back and even laughed a little.

'Your Grace...'

The butler nodded as they passed and stepped into a vast entryway that almost had Julia gaping. Twin staircases swept up on either side and the walls were covered in portraits of stern-faced men and imperious-looking women dressed in their finery, each one with a small brass plaque beneath, giving their name. The floor was marble, and over in one corner something caught her eye.

'Is that a suit of armour?'

Anthony nodded. 'Yes, actually, it is.'

'You have a *suit of armour*?' she asked again, just to clarify.

'I do.'

'Have you ever worn it?'

He laughed. 'No.'

'Maybe you should?'

She turned and winked at him, but he simply smiled and guided her towards the room where the music was coming from. It sounded as if an actual orchestra was playing, but she wasn't sure it was a real one until they got to the double doors of the ballroom and she saw the twelve-piece orchestra situated on a raised dais over to their left.

'His Grace the Duke of Weston and Miss Julia Morris!'

She'd not expected to be announced. Julia had kind of

hoped that they would just enter the room and slowly mingle, and she would get to know everyone one by one, but suddenly all heads turned and she felt the gaze of *every single person* in the room.

Oh, my God. What are we doing?

Her smile was frozen to her face and her hand clutched Anthony's arm tightly, but he was moving forward and she had no choice but to step with him as he walked her right onto the dance floor.

'Relax,' he told her.

'People are looking.'

'Of course they are. They're intrigued. I've not brought a date to any social event in the last ten years.'

'What if they hate me?'

'That's their issue, not ours.'

'But what if they tell me to my face?'

'People aren't that rude.'

'Clearly you never went to my kind of school.'

He looked at her then. Raised an eyebrow. 'People told you they hated you?'

'Shelly Radcliffe did. She hated me. Because I got to sit next to Danny Howard and he was my dance partner.'

'How old were you?'

'Ten.'

He smirked. 'Years ago. Kids can be brutally honest. Thankfully, we adults hide behind etiquette and masks.'

'So you're saying they might hate me, but they'll keep it to themselves?'

'Or gossip about you with their friends—but never to your face.'

'Oh, well, that's okay, then,' she replied sarcastically.

'Relax. I'll keep you safe. Just keep looking into my eyes.'

She could do that.

Anthony began to twirl her around the dance floor. A

waltz was playing and she tried to focus on her footwork and looking graceful, knowing that if she made a single mistake, like stepping on his foot or stumbling, then everyone would notice.

She had to be perfect.

For the next few hours and the next six weeks, until his mother went to Australia, she had to be perfect girlfriend material.

How hard could it possibly be?

CHAPTER SIX

As he'd expected, all eyes were on them. He saw questions in the eyes of many ladies. A raised eyebrow on the face of the Duchess of Denby. Even open jealousy on the face of Lady Annabella, whom he'd been forced to endure a lunch with two weeks ago—thanks, once again, to his mother.

But on his mother's face he saw a smile. Approval. Intrigue. He knew it must be killing her to wait whilst they danced, knew that she would want to take Julia aside and talk to her, ask questions and delve into her life like a bloodhound.

Well, she would have to wait. Because for now he was dancing with his beautifully stunning girlfriend. Dancing with a woman he was proud to be with and experiencing feelings and thoughts that he'd never expected to feel when he'd suggested this ruse.

He felt as if he'd won already. Outsmarting his mother. Letting Lady Annabella know that she was not his choice without saying so outright and hurting her feelings. And here he was. Dancing. With Julia in his arms. And it couldn't have felt easier.

He felt so comfortable with her. Maybe it was because they'd been bound together by that fateful night ten years ago? Whatever it was, he felt as if he could share anything with her and it would be all right. That she would keep any secrets if he needed. This ease he felt, though, he had to admit was slightly alarming. Unexpected. Concerning. He'd never thought he'd ever feel this way again. Protective. *Attached*.

By coming here with him she'd made herself a small fish swimming in a shark tank, and yet she didn't look perturbed at all. There was a sparkle in Julia's eyes. She looked happy. And he liked it that she was happy.

'How are you doing?' he whispered.

'All right. The dancing helps. Means I only have to look at you and not at everyone else.' She paused. 'Are they all still staring at us?'

He smiled back. 'Yes. Shall we give them a show?'

A wicked gleam entered her eyes. 'Lead the way.'

Smirking, he led them into a series of twirls and spins that caused her beautiful skirts to billow out around her. Clockwise. Anti-clockwise. They took up the whole floor. He worried that he might be making her feel dizzy, but she kept step with him and he saw the challenge in her eyes, felt the knowledge that anything he did she would be able to match.

As the music built towards its end he moved them to the centre of the dance floor and performed a standing spin, a ronde, a contra check, and then moved into another turn. But instead of looking past his shoulder Julia stared into his eyes, and he was hypnotised into looking back into hers. They were keeping each other strong, keeping each other safe...

When the music ended, the bubble was broken by the arrival of his sister Zoey. And he was grateful for the interruption. Because he could only stare into Julia's beautiful doe-like eyes for a moment and he was lost in them. And he didn't like feeling lost.

'Anthony! You really know how to put on a show... And here was me thinking that you were the family wallflower. Are you going to introduce me to this stunning woman who has finally brought you out of your shell?'

Zoey wore a royal blue dress, off the shoulder, and now she turned to gaze at Julia with a large, friendly smile.

'This is Julia. Julia—my sister Zoey.' He paused. 'She doesn't normally bite.'

Julia smiled. 'Pleased to meet you, Zoey.'

Zoey leaned in. 'Lady Annabella and our mother are on the prowl, so if you don't want to be gored by lionesses right away I can smuggle you into a corner where you can at least get a glass of champagne down you to fortify yourselves.'

'Oh, I'm sure they're not that bad,' Julia said.

Zoey raised an eyebrow and stared at him. 'Did you tell her nothing before tonight? Come on.'

Anthony followed as Zoey led them over to a corner behind the orchestra, catching the attention of a member of staff and asking him to bring them three flutes of champagne.

Once they possessed drinks, Zoey turned to talk to Julia once again. 'Your dress is stunning!'

'Thank you. I love yours, too.'

'This old thing? I wore it to the evening do of some politician's wedding.'

'Well, it's gorgeous,' Julia said.

'Oh, I love her already, Anthony. So, tell me...how did you two meet? Everyone is agog at the news that my dear, tragically single brother has finally found himself someone new.'

'We met at work.'

'You're a doctor?' interrupted a new, imperious voice before Julia could answer.

Anthony turned to greet his mother, whom he kissed on both cheeks. 'Evening, Mother.'

'Hello, dear. Zoey. Did you two really think you could hide away here? I've had years' worth of practice in knowing your hiding places.' She smiled at them both, letting them know that she could easily outwit them. 'Julia! How lovely to meet you at last.'

'Julia, this is my mother, the Dowager Duchess of Weston.'

'Your Grace...' Julia gave a small curtsey.

'My son has told me barely anything about you. And now, after that display on the dance floor, you'll be needing a long rest. Come with me and tell me all about yourself.'

He did not want his mother to monopolise her, or tear her from his grasp. 'I was about to give Julia the tour,' he said.

'Well, can't that wait? People are here to see *you*, darling.'

'No, they're here to raise money for charity.'

'I'm not a doctor,' Julia interjected, perhaps sensing an impending argument. 'I'm a nurse. A newly qualified nurse, actually. I work on the orthopaedic ward in the same hospital as Anthony.'

'Oh! But Anthony has always been against relationships forming in the workplace.'

Julia slid her fingers into his and looked up at him with a genuine heartfelt smile. 'Well, I guess when you know, you know.'

His mother looked from Julia to him and then back again. Considering. Weighing. 'What were you before you qualified as a nurse?'

'A waitress in a café.'

His mother smiled. 'Your life has changed dramatically, then?'

'Ever since starting at the hospital, yes.'

Anthony felt the warmth in Julia's smile as she gazed at him. Felt the squeeze of her fingers in his. Saw that she was totally assured in the face of his mother. He admired her for that.

'My son is a prime catch. What was it about him that made you interested?'

'His kindness. The welcome he gave me. His care and attention. The look in his eyes when he speaks to me. The way he makes me feel when I'm with him.'

Anthony looked at Julia, smiling broadly. Every word she spoke was truthful, even though this relationship was a lie. Nobody here would be able to pick it apart. By having Julia at his side he was a different man. It was as if he could feel himself coming back to life, unaware that he'd been drifting for so long. *Her* kindness, *her* welcome, *her* care and attention… She made him feel *alive*.

'She's going to make my head swell,' he said now. 'Julia, you remember I promised to show you the library?'

She nodded.

'Excuse us.' He draped Julia's hand over his arm and led her away. 'Well done,' he said quietly. 'Not everyone can stand up to my mother's interrogations.'

'She wasn't that bad. She's just looking out for you. She loves you and wants the best person for you. There's nothing wrong in that.'

'I know. I just sometimes disagree with her methods.'

'I like your sister.'

'Zoey? Yeah, she's good. She was my rock when Yael died. Came and called on me every day to make sure I was okay. Got me out for a walk around the grounds even when I didn't want to do anything.'

'It's good to have people like that in your corner. You have a strong, accomplished family. Maybe you should let them in more?'

He laughed. 'I must tell my mother you said that.'

'Why?'

'She'll love you for ever.'

Julia chuckled as he led her up a staircase and down a red-carpeted hallway hung with drapes and tapestries towards the library, his pride and joy. He hadn't promised to show her anything. The lie about showing her the library had simply slipped from his lips. It was really his desire to be alone. He'd never been fond of these big, social gatherings, and as an introvert he would often slip away to recharge his social battery. Tonight, the thought of being alone with Julia was overwhelming. He wanted a moment with her. A moment to breathe and gather himself.

As they reached the library he swung open the doors with a sigh of relief, stepping to one side to allow Julia a moment of seeing it. He knew it was grand. Impressive. He'd collected a lot of the books himself. Finding first editions of all his favourites. Amassing those that were rare. Signed editions. Folios. The most delicate were kept in sealed glass cases, away from dust and light. The carpet was a rich moss-green, the drapes a forest-green. The tall windows usually let in beams of sunlight to brighten the soft recliners, the comfortable chairs adorned with cushions embroidered with hares and stags. The library was his retreat.

'Anthony! This is…' Her voice trailed off in awe as she walked past a shelf, her fingertips trailing over the books.

'I know.'

'Have you read all of these?'

'As many as I possibly could. Perhaps thirty per cent are still unread. Do you like books?'

'Are you kidding me? They're my happy place.'

He smiled at that. Glad. Because they were his happy place, too. 'Good.'

She slid a book from the shelf and flicked through it. An eighteenth-century text adorned with drawings of botanicals. She marvelled at each sketch. 'Can we stay in here all night, instead?' she asked.

Anthony laughed. 'Unfortunately our presence will be required downstairs. The revelation that you used to be a waitress will be all around the ballroom by now.'

'Should I not have said it?' She turned to him, concern in her gaze.

'Of course you should! There is nothing wrong with being a waitress.'

'But a waitress who has nabbed a duke? That might not be going down very well.'

'I don't care what they think. I've never let their thoughts and opinions on such matters interfere with my life before. Yael was a cook.'

She smiled. 'Really? She was? That's good to know. I'd hate to think you were a snob. Especially since I'm going out with you.' She winked at him, and then he saw her notice that the book she held had an inscription: *With love, Yael x*.

She slid the book back upon the shelf. 'You must miss her so much…'

He nodded. 'Things happen every day that I think she would love to hear about. Sometimes I talk to her out loud. I've told her about meeting up with you again.'

'And what did she say?'

Julia came towards him, her skirts grazing the carpet as if she were walking through a forest.

'She was happy.'

'Good.'

She reached for his hand and held it in hers. Her soft touch was alluring. The comfort it brought made him realise just how much he'd missed that kind of casual touch.

'Well?' she said. 'Should we descend upon the masses once again? Show them my robot?'

She began making robotic dance moves, and in her elegant dress she made even that look amazing. He laughed, surprised at the way she could make him smile, but knew that they couldn't hide out here for ever.

'Sure. Let's surprise them even more.'

Julia giggled. 'Maybe I should keep that special dance move for your eyes only?'

'All right. If you say so. Come on. We'd better get back downstairs in time for the auction.'

'Lead on, my love.'

She slipped her arm into his and he led them both back towards the ballroom.

CHAPTER SEVEN

The ball had been a complete success, in Julia's eyes.

It had raised money for charity, Anthony had only had to dance with her, and his mother had had no reason to introduce him to any eligible young women—although Lady Annabella had looked particularly sour-faced and cheated.

She'd even made a new friend in Zoey, who'd given her her mobile phone number and promised to ring and arrange a meet-up for coffee. She sensed that Zoey could become a great friend, but knew that friendship would be threatened by their subterfuge. Guilt made her wonder if Zoey would still want to know her after the fake relationship with her brother was over...

'Did you have a good time?' he asked now.

'Despite the guilt? Amazing, thank you.'

'Not too stressful?'

'Actually, no. It went easier than I thought. People seemed to believe we're really into one another.'

'Yes.' He gave a small laugh and glanced out of the window before turning back to look at her. 'You know, if I haven't already said thank you for all of this, then I want to say it now. This may seem like a silly thing we're doing, but it means a lot to me. That you're willing to help me with this.'

'Hey, you're doing the same thing for me.'

'True. Do you have any family events coming up that maybe I ought to accompany you to?'

'My grandmother is having her eightieth birthday party a week tomorrow.'

'Next Sunday?'

She nodded. Her Gramma May was her only living grandparent, and she meant the world to her.

'I can make that, if you'd like me to come along?'

'It won't be as grand as your ball. It'll just be a small get-together in a council house. Sausages on sticks and trifle in the fridge...that kind of thing.'

'I love trifle.' He smiled.

Julia laughed. 'Okay! It's a date. No tux, though. Just casual.'

'You say that like I don't have any casual clothes.'

'I've only ever seen you in a suit!'

'And scrubs.'

'Well, yes, but they're work clothes. *Your* clothes look like they're all bespoke...made just for you.'

He looked embarrassed.

'Oh, my God, they are, aren't they?'

She laughed out loud and he began to laugh with her.

'I'll go and buy some jeans. Or some jogging bottoms.'

'And trainers—don't forget the trainers,' she joked.

'Yes, ma'am.'

He really was ridiculous! But lovely. Their worlds were so far apart, but she liked it that she could still reach him. That he was easy to be with. But she'd felt that way with Jake, too, at the beginning. And look at how that had ended up.

As Mason pulled the car up in front of her home she turned to look at Anthony. 'I really have had a wonderful night, tonight. Thank you. And thank you for this dress.'

'You're welcome.'

'I should give you these back.'

She began to remove the earrings and the necklace. She knew they weren't hers to keep. She'd just borrowed them for the night. For the ruse. But as she removed each piece she began to feel as if she was breaking their connection. Bursting the bubble. But still, it was important to be realistic, right? None of this was real, no matter how much she'd enjoyed it. Time to face reality, even if she wanted to hold on to the fairytale for a little bit longer. To feel special again.

Anthony almost looked reluctant to take them back, but he did so, laying them out in their velvet-lined boxes and staring at them glittering in the light from the street lamps overhead.

'You looked beautiful in them,' he said.

'Thank you. I felt beautiful.'

Mason opened the car door and she got out, fumbling in her small clutch bag for the keys to her flat.

Behind her, she heard Anthony get out, too. He stood behind her, as if he was guarding her, making sure she would get inside safely.

'You know that you don't need jewels to look beautiful. You were stunning without them.'

It meant *so much* that he thought that. For too long she'd felt like an afterthought. Second best. Not someone's first choice. 'You're very kind to say so.'

'It's the truth.' He shrugged and turned to look at Mason. 'Could we have a moment?'

'Of course, Your Grace.' Mason went back to the driver's side of the car and got in.

'May I kiss you goodnight?'

Julia's heart rate suddenly galloped ahead and she gave a nervous laugh. 'I guess…'

'I'm going to need a firm yes or a no.' He smiled, hands in his pockets.

A kiss goodnight? For whose sake? His family weren't around. Nor were her own. Mason would have heard them talking in the car, and surely knew about their secret, but as a member of Anthony's staff would keep his mouth shut in loyalty to his boss. And did he mean a kiss on the cheek? Or on the mouth? She'd not kissed him at all tonight at the ball. She'd held his hand, slipped her arm through this, smiled sweetly at him and gazed lovingly into his eyes.

But kiss him?

She had to admit, if she was being honest, that the idea not only excited her, but terrified her. None of this was real and yet...part of her wanted it to be. Part of her wanted him to yearn to kiss her. And those feelings were terrifying and thrilling in the extreme.

Cheeks burning, she gazed up at him softly. 'Yes, you may.'

Her heart pounded in her chest as he leaned towards her. Her breath was catching in her throat, her skin seemed alive, feeling every breath of wind that grazed her. Her senses went into overdrive as his face grew closer and closer. It was as if she could hear the hum of the streetlight above, could taste the aroma of fish and chips in the air from the takeout shop at the end of her road, could smell Anthony's cologne as he leaned in...

At the last minute his lips brushed her cheek and she closed her eyes to capture the moment.

And then it was done.

He was pulling back, smiling, walking away to the car, opening the door. 'Get inside, so I know you're safe.'

She nodded, blushing, glad of the darkness so he wouldn't be able to see the flush on her face. And then her hands were fumbling for her keys, and somehow she got the key into the lock without dropping them. She pushed open the door.

Had she wanted him to kiss her on the lips? Why? She reminded herself, cursing inwardly, that this wasn't real and she didn't need the complication of actually falling for him...

'See you at work on Monday,' he said.

'Yes. You too.'

Julia gave a wave and closed the door, locking it behind her, then frowned at herself. She groaned and headed up the stairs to get out of the dress and the heels and slip into something a little more comfortable.

Anthony couldn't wait to get into work on Monday morning. He felt light, happy—and, weirdly enough, when his mother had called to speak to him on Sunday, she'd told him that she liked Julia. That she seemed like a good fit for him—which had been surprising, but welcome.

He and Julia had certainly put on a show, and to be fair, his partner in crime had made it very easy indeed. The guilt he'd initially felt about fooling everyone had simply died when he'd walked into that ballroom with Julia dazzling in her gorgeous dress. Even Annabella's sour face hadn't ruined it. And the evening itself had been very successful—not just for him, but also for the charity, raising thousands of pounds.

He couldn't wait to see Julia again. Couldn't wait to see her smile and hear her voice and just be near her again. She'd made him feel so good. So relaxed. So happy. It had been a long time since he'd felt like that and it was all down to her. He knew he needed to rein his feelings in. Become Mr Ice again as he entered the walls of the hospital. But it was difficult when he felt so light. So free. These feelings she engendered within him were dizzying.

When he walked onto the ward and found her in the supplies room, collecting some dressings for a bandage change, a broad smile broke across his face. 'Good morning!'

'Morning!' she replied.

'How are you?' he asked.

'Great! You?'

'Amazing. Just thought I'd check in with you before I start my rounds.'

'Oh, okay. I'm just getting dressings for Mr Bundy's leg. He's soaked through them.'

'All right. Do you fancy meeting up later? For lunch in the cafeteria? Start the rumours here?'

She looked around them. 'Actually, like I said before, if you don't mind…can we *not* be in a relationship here at work? This is my first job as a nurse, and I don't really want people gossiping about me here and thinking that I'm anything other than good at my job. Is that okay?'

He'd not thought about that, and instantly felt subdued. 'Of course. You're right. I can continue to be Mr Ice here, at least.'

'You don't mind?'

'No. Of course not. Okay, well… I'll see you around.'

She smiled at him. 'You will.'

He left the room, cursing himself inwardly for not even thinking about her reputation here. Of course she would want everyone here on the ward and in this hospital to recognise that she was earnest and hardworking and good at her job, and not just here to bag a doctor. A lot of people assumed that about nurses—wrongly—just perpetuating a stereotype. She was right to say what she had and he admired her for that.

They needed to be sensible about this and not get carried away. This was where they both worked, and when this was all over they would still have to work together. Wouldn't that be easier if they didn't have to pretend to avoid each other after the 'break-up'?

Perhaps work was where they shouldn't pretend? Where they were just who they were?

And so he made his way through his rounds, behaving as he normally would, but he couldn't help but notice whenever Julia was around. It was as if his gaze was pulled towards her, like a moth hypnotised by a flame.

He didn't question it. He didn't worry about it. Supposed

it was natural after having spent some time together. Since she'd been on his arm in front of his family.

Because they were friends.

Partners.

He was extremely fond of her, and perhaps he was even feeling a little more than that—but it was only natural, considering how close they'd had to be. She was probably the only person in this whole hospital that he *was* fond of. Yes, he had colleagues. Acquaintances. Other surgeons he occasionally met up with to play golf, or have drinks at some kind of function. He was friendly with them, but would he confide in them? No.

I could with Julia, he thought. *In fact, I do already.*

But that reminded him that he also needed to keep her at arm's length, and that was welcome.

No point in getting carried away in their fiction.

CHAPTER EIGHT

How could a guy who looked so devastatingly handsome in a suit or a tuxedo look just as amazing in a distressed pair of jeans and a fitted black tee shirt?

When Julia opened her front door, she literally gasped. 'Oh, my God.'

Anthony looked down at himself, alarmed. 'Is it too casual?'

'No! No, it's…perfect,' she said, trying not to smile at the wave of attraction she felt for him.

This guy was hitting it out of the park, without even trying that hard! How could it be that, seeing him in tee shirt and jeans, she was more aware of every muscle he had? How broad those shoulders of his were… How his forearms—God, those forearms!—looked so fabulously sexy?

'I didn't know what to get your grandmother, so I did a little digging from the information that you've given me and I've paid for her to have a treatment day at her local salon. Hair, make-up, manicure, pedicure… Too much, or not enough?'

He genuinely looked unsure.

She laughed. 'Well, you've never met her before—she's a total stranger to you. So…yeah, that might be construed as a little bit too much. You could just buy her flowers?'

'Flowers. Right… We can buy some on the way.'

'But a *small* bouquet—not the entire shop. Or franchise.'

'Perfect.'

'What are you like?' She laughed again as she locked the door behind her and glanced out at his car. 'No chauffeur today?'

'Occasionally I drive myself, you know.'

'Good to know.'

She stood back as he opened the car door for her and then slid inside and waited for him to walk around and get in the driver's seat. As they drove out of London she reflected on their past week at work.

He'd kept his word and maintained his Mr Ice persona in front of other members of staff, but when they'd found themselves alone, his smiles and his inherent warmth had emerged, just for her. His friendship meant a lot to her, and she kind of liked it that they had this shared secret. This private agreement between them. When their gazes met, their shared secret felt like a small blaze inside her chest and she almost beamed with it.

As they pulled up outside a flower shop near her mother's house, she turned to ask him a question. 'Have you ever been to a float parade?'

'A float parade? No.'

'A street parade? Mardi Gras?'

'No.' He shook his head.

'There's one being held here this year. Some of my friends are making a float from scratch. The theme is heroes and heroines, and someone's got an old flatbed truck we can use. I said I'd help out. There's a prize for best float. Do you want to join us?'

'What would it involve?'

She shrugged. 'I don't know... Making things. Painting. Decorating. Building. It's all for a good cause, too. When you go through the streets people walk alongside with buckets and collecting tins.'

'Sure. Sounds fun. Just let me know where and when.' He smiled and looked at her. 'Are you going to be on the float?'

'Oh! No. I did that last year. The theme was animals and I wore a bird costume for the whole day... I've never sweated so much in my entire life. No, this year I'll be there with my collecting tin and that's all.'

'You? A bird?'

'My mum tried to set me up with a guy dressed like a parrot. Said we looked like a pair of lovebirds—can you believe it?'

He smiled. 'What would we do without our mothers?'

'Live peaceful lives?'

Anthony laughed as they stepped into the shop. 'We'd miss them. Even though she can poke her nose in where it's not wanted, I'm still going to miss mine when she goes to Adelaide.'

'How long will she be gone for?'

'Two months. What about those?' He pointed at a bucket holding miniature bouquets.

'Perfect.'

They pulled up in front of an ordinary terraced council house with a neat front garden. A small, square lawn. One flowerbed filled with roses. A pot with a dwarf fern in it either side of the front door, which was painted dark blue.

Julia rang the doorbell.

'When was the last time you saw your grandma?' he asked.

'Just before I started at the hospital.'

The door was opened by a woman who looked like the older version of Julia. Her hair was dark brown too, but shoulder-length and there was a grey streak at the front. Her smile was the same as Julia's and she greeted him with huge warmth.

'You must be Anthony! I've heard so much about you!' Unexpectedly she threw her arms around him and hugged him close, whispering, 'I've wanted to thank you for a very long time. For looking after my girl that night. And for Marcus.'

Julia had told him that her mother knew he was the same Anthony who had delivered Marcus, but that was all she had told her.

'Nice to meet you, Mrs Morris.'

'Georgia, please. Come in! Everyone else is here.'

He stepped into a room overflowing with people. At the heart of it was a little old lady, with silver hair and the same brown eyes as Georgia and Julia, sitting with balloons attached to the back of her chair.

'Gramma May! Happy Birthday!' Julia stooped down to give her gran a hug and a kiss and then stepped back. It was his turn.

'Hi. I'm Anthony. Happy Birthday.' He smiled at the older lady and passed her the bouquet.

'Roses! My favourite! How did you know?'

He looked at Julia. 'A little birdie might have told me.'

'Someone find chairs for these two,' said May.

Chairs were acquired and the three of them settled down together. Anthony had Julia to his left and Georgia to his right. He reached for Julia's hand to hold it. It felt easy, now he had already danced with her at his ball and held her close And it felt good to be touching her again. He saw the way she looked at him and smiled as he did so. Was she enjoying it, too?

'Would you like a drink?' Julia asked.

'Whatever you're having will be fine.'

'Won't be a minute.'

She released him and got up and headed into the kitchen.

'I've heard so much about you, of course.' Georgia leaned in when her daughter was gone. 'The way you helped my daughter that night… How you delivered Marcus… I've never been so grateful to a stranger in my entire life.'

'Anyone would have done the same.'

'I hope so. But she was lucky to find you and your lovely wife. I was so sorry to hear of her passing.'

'Thank you. And I was devastated to learn of Marcus's.'

'It was a very difficult time for us all, as I'm sure you can imagine. Well… You know grief, too.'

'Too much.'

He didn't like to remember those dark days after Yael's death. They'd been hard enough to live through. He didn't need to keep bringing them out and re-examining them. Why would he torture himself like that?

'So, to learn that you two were dating…' Georgia went on. 'Well, I was taken aback, at first, if I'm honest. But I've had time to think about it and it's nice to know that Julia's with a real man. The kind of man who can step up to the plate and be strong, you know? Be honest with her. She's been lied to enough, what with all that business with Jake, Marcus's father. Not that he deserves that title.'

Anthony would never want to lie to Julia. He would never want to hurt her.

'I'm an honest man. At least, I hope I am.'

'Good. I'm glad to hear it. I've worried about her being alone all this time. Oh, she'd hate knowing that I'm saying all of this to you, but she's my daughter, and I love her, and she's been through enough torment in her life. I only want to see her happy and no longer alone.'

'I understand. My mother feels the same way about me.'

'Your mother and I would get along perfectly, then!' Georgia smiled.

'I'm sure you would.'

He could just imagine Georgia and his mother sitting at

high tea, china cups in their hands as they discussed their children. They'd get along very well.

Julia arrived back then, with drinks, passing him orange juice in a glass, with ice. 'What are you two talking about?'

'You, of course!' Georgia laughed.

Anthony tried to keep up with all the different conversations going on in the room, but everyone was talking to each other at once so he sat and listened politely. Everyone was reminiscing. Recalling Gramma May stories. It sounded as if she was a really cool grandma, which was great. He had no memories of grandparents himself. They had died when he was very young. There were portraits on the wall, and occasionally his mother would mention her parents fondly, but she found it difficult to speak of them, so he never asked. It was the same thing with his dad. He'd died shortly after Anthony was born. Helicopter crash.

'I remember when Georgia came to visit and brought her new husband with her. I never much liked him,' Gramma May said. 'He seemed a little full of himself to me. Remember I told you that you were expecting, Georgia? You didn't even know you were carrying Julia.'

Georgia nodded. 'I remember.'

'And do you remember me telling you that you had nine months to sort that man out or he wouldn't stick around?'

'Yes, we all remember, Mum.'

'And I was right. He buggered off. Stayed for the cute stage...disappeared as soon as she hit the terrible twos.' Gramma May rubbed at her forehead as if she had pain or discomfort there. 'I remember s-s-saying to you...you look after that little...' Her voice trailed off as if she couldn't quite think of the word.

Girl. That was what she meant to say, Anthony knew, but his red flags had gone up. Was this just a normal glitch in an octogenarian's memory, or something more sinister happening before their very eyes?

'Gramma May?' Julia was frowning.

'I… I'm…'

And then he saw it. The droop to her face. She was trying to smile, but it was only happening on one side.

Both he and Julia rushed to their feet at the same time.

She had seen it too, for what it was.

Gramma May was having a stroke, right before their eyes.

'Somebody call for an ambulance,' Anthony instructed calmly, turning to look Georgia directly in the eyes.

'Why? What's happening?'

'I think your mother is having a stroke.'

'What? Mum?'

'Mum!' Julia interrupted. 'Call for an ambulance, now!'

Anthony knelt before Gramma May, and with a smile and in a kind voice asked her to smile. It was still lopsided. He asked her to repeat a sentence that he gave her. Her speech was slurred and her words incomplete. He asked her to try and raise her arms in front of her with her eyes closed, and although she could move both arms, one rose higher than the other.

He turned to Georgia, who was on the phone with the emergency services. 'Please tell them that she has a positive FAST test.'

Georgia nodded as Julia asked everyone, even though they were concerned, to stand back and give Gramma May some room to breathe.

He did not know what was going on in her brain. It could be a burst blood vessel, or a clot. There was nothing he could do but remain calm.

'We should give her aspirin or something!' someone called out.

Anthony shook his head. 'No. If she has a bleed on her

brain, that could make it worse.' He noted the time on his watch. They had an hour to help May. It was called the golden hour by medics because if a patient received definitive treatment within the first sixty minutes of an event then they were likely to have good results. As opposed to after that amount of time, when the risk of complications, deficits or even death might be higher.

'We have to do something!' said another voice. 'Aren't you a doctor?'

'I am. But there's nothing we can do until the paramedics arrive. Maybe someone could get her a blanket? A pillow for her head?'

Relatives rushed around trying to do something. He understood the urge. No one liked to feel helpless or impotent in the face of such upsetting events. Actually doing something, no matter how small, would help to make them feel better later. As long as there was a good result. A bad result would make them feel like they'd not done enough.

'You're doing great, May,' he said in a soothing voice, as he held the older woman's fragile, liver-spotted hand. 'Just breathe normally and soon we'll have help here, okay?'

'We've got you, Gramma May,' said Julia, helping to drape the blanket over her grandma's legs.

Gramma May looked upset. She tried to speak, but her words were still slurred and unclear. Her eyes looked frightened.

'Don't try to speak yet. Just breathe normally. We're all here for you,' he soothed.

It didn't take too long for the paramedics to arrive. About ten minutes. Anthony and Julia gave them the facts and the timing of the suspected stroke to pass along to the doctors in Emergency. The paramedics could only take one person in the ambulance with them, so Georgia went with her mother and Anthony told Julia they would follow behind in his car.

Gramma May went off with lights and sirens blaring, and Anthony and Julia left everyone else to clear up after the party as they headed off to the local hospital, promising to call the others with updates once they had them.

Anthony glanced at Julia as he drove and reached for her hand, squeezing it. 'Are you all right?' he asked. He knew what it felt like to feel as if you couldn't help a person you loved.

She nodded, biting at her bottom lip. 'She's just always been there, you know…?'

'I know.'

'She's always been a part of my life. I can't imagine her not being here.'

'She's strong.'

'Yes. I'm sure she'll get through this. The woman has nine lives! She was bombed as a child, you know, before she was evacuated out of London.'

'Yeah?'

'Yeah.' She squeezed back, gaining strength from his touch. 'She'll get through this, too. Nothing can stop her.'

'The Morris women are strong,' he said with a smile.

'We've always had to be.'

Sitting in the family room waiting for an update seemed interminable. Julia would pace for a little bit in the small area, then sit down. And then, when she got twitchy again, she would pace again.

'Do you want me to go and see if I can get an update?' Anthony asked.

'Would you?'

'Sure. Stay here a moment.'

When he was gone she began biting her nails, and she turned to look at her mum. 'Do you think Gramma May will be all right?'

'I don't know…'

'Tell me what happened again. When you arrived in the emergency department.'

'They took her off for a scan and someone brought me here. Said they'd fetch me when they could.'

'Okay.'

Julia began pacing again. She didn't like being in this hospital. The last time she'd been here, in this A&E had been when she'd lost Marcus. And even though she knew in her heart that Marcus had actually passed away at home, his death had been confirmed *here*, so she associated this place with dying. She couldn't lose Gramma May here, too.

The door opened and Anthony was there. 'We can go and see her now,' he told them.

When they got to her bedside Gramma May still wasn't able to talk, but a doctor in green scrubs was waiting to speak to them.

'We've had the scan results back and they show a clot in May's brain. We would like your permission to administer a clot-busting drug, which should work quite quickly and hopefully restore as much function as we can.'

'Then do it,' Julia's mum said.

The doctor nodded. 'You do need to be aware, however, of the risks in taking thrombolysis medication. It can very quickly dissolve the clot, and restore blood flow to the parts of your mum's brain that have been starved of it, but we need to check some things first. Has May any history of high blood pressure?'

'No. If anything she has low blood pressure.'

'Any bleeding issues? Or a head injury?'

'No.'

'Okay. This drug can cause a bleed in the brain within seven days of being administered, so you'll need to be on the lookout for any signs of that. I'll get the rt-PA if you're happy for us to proceed with this treatment.'

Rt-PA stood for recombinant tissue plasminogen activator, and was a standard treatment for dealing with ischaemic stroke.

Georgia looked at Julia. 'We are.'

'All right.'

They watched as the drug was administered.

'How long will it take before we see results?' Julia asked.

'It can be a couple of hours—or even a couple of days in some cases. We'll keep her here for monitoring initially, and then in a few hours we'll move her up to the stroke ward.'

'Can we stay with her?'

'Of course. Can I get someone to bring you a cup of tea, or anything?'

'That's very kind. Thank you.'

'I'll get it,' Anthony said. 'You guys are rushed off your feet.'

The doctor nodded and left the bedside.

'Georgia, why don't you sit down here,' Anthony suggested. 'And I'll grab another chair for Julia.'

'You're very kind, Anthony, thank you,' Georgia said.

When Anthony had disappeared, her mother sat down on the opposite side of Gramma May's bed, looked at Julia and smiled softly. 'You've got a good one there, Jools.'

Julia nodded. 'I have.'

'Don't let him go.'

'I'll try not to.'

She didn't know what else to say. It did feel amazing to have his support. For him to be by her side during this difficult time. In this moment she felt as if maybe she ought to just tell her mother the truth about her and Anthony. Come clean. But did she really want to declare all whilst Gramma

May couldn't speak? She and Anthony weren't important right now. Her grandmother was.

Anthony arrived back with another chair for her and she settled into it, and then he disappeared again to get them some drinks.

Her mum was right. He really was good. He'd only just met her family and yet here he was, taking care of them as if they were his own. Of course he was a doctor, and he knew how to speak to families who were worried and upset. He knew that they needed comfort and reassurance and he was trying to provide them with that. The way he'd taken care of May when he'd noticed the stroke happening a split second before she had had been amazing. He'd not panicked. He'd not tried to alarm anyone. He'd been calm and decisive and in charge. He'd stepped up to the plate and guided everyone, when the other guests had panicked and not known what to do.

She'd been most terribly glad that he'd been there to do that. Even though she was a qualified nurse herself, it was different when the patient was one of your own. It was harder to maintain the professional distance you used at work.

When he arrived back in the cubicle carrying a small tray of drinks, she was so thankful for him...so grateful.

She took her cup of tea with a genuine smile. 'Thank you.'

'No problem. She's still sleeping?'

'Yes.'

'Probably to be expected.'

'You don't have to stay here if you've got things to do.' Julia said, not wanting to take up his entire day. She'd only expected them to be at her grandma's house for a couple of hours, and they were way past that now.

'There's nowhere else I'd rather be,' he said, taking her hand in his.

She was confused. Was that for the benefit of her mother? Or actually for her?

Part of her—no, most of her—wanted it to be just for her. Wanted this affection not to be a ruse. Not part of the show. A boyfriend would try to comfort his girlfriend at a time like this, after all. Why couldn't she see his motivation in doing this right now? But he was a good friend. And he cared about her the way she cared about him. If this situation had been reversed she'd have been at his side, as well.

She decided that this part—him holding her hand—was real.

And it meant the world.

CHAPTER NINE

As soon as she walked onto the orthopaedic ward the next Monday, Anthony came to find her. 'How's May?'

'She's doing well. Her speech is getting better. They think she can go home soon, but they want to make sure a care package is in place.'

'Good. I'm glad to hear it. She had us all worried there for a moment.'

Us.

'How are you?' she asked. 'I'm sorry we took up most of your weekend.'

Anthony had dutifully called her every day this week, and driven her back and forth to the hospital. Sitting with her. Taking care of her. Asking her if there was anything she needed. She'd told him that he didn't have to do all that. That their pretence didn't have to go so far. Their relationship was meant to be fun pretend, not dutiful pretend. But he'd simply shaken his head and told her he was her friend, she was going through a tough time, and he would treat anyone the same.

Which was nice, but… She didn't want to be just anyone to him. She wanted—needed—to be more, and that was throwing her. Confusing her.

'I didn't mind,' he said now.

'What have you got on your list today?'

'Rounds…and then I've got a clinic.'

'No surgeries today?'

'Not unless they come through A&E. You?'

'The usual. Drugs round...dressing changes.' She shrugged.

'I'd better let you get on, then. Before Sister tells me off for delaying you. Fancy meeting for lunch?'

She did, but as she'd said before she didn't want there to be rumours about them at the hospital. 'We'd best not.'

He looked disappointed. 'Okay. Well, maybe I'll see you tonight? Let me take you out to dinner.'

'You don't have to.'

'I know. I want to. If you're free?'

'Mum's with Gramma May tonight, so...yes. Please. That'll be nice.'

'I'll book a table somewhere nice.'

Rosaria, another nurse, began to walk towards them, so Julia suddenly straightened and smiled. 'Thank you, Mr Fitzpatrick. I'll get that done right away.'

'Thank you, Nurse.'

And he walked the other way to gather his registrar and the junior doctors, and the medical students who would follow him around the ward. He cut a tall, lonely figure, but that of a man in charge. A man who knew he was valued and respected.

Had it always come so easy to him? she wondered. Was life gifted on a plate to some, while others, like herself, always had to fight for respect?

As a waitress, she'd often felt like a second-class citizen. Customers would be rude and take out their frustrations with their meals or the service on her. And as a student nurse she'd often felt that she was on the bottom rung of the ladder and that the climb ahead of her was long and difficult. Now, as a qualified nurse, she'd experienced, in these two short weeks, the way some patients would not listen to her advice, preferring to hear it from 'a proper doctor'.

The one time she'd felt powerful and respected had been

when she'd given birth to Marcus. She'd been recognised as a mother, a woman who had gone through the trials of labour and then birth. She had felt accepted by her peers. By the friends that she'd made in antenatal classes.

But where were they now? They'd sent cards when Marcus had passed away. One or two had phoned to check in on her. Brought flowers. Taken her out for coffee. But had any of them kept in touch since? It was as if losing her baby had somehow singled her out. As if they didn't want to associate with her. Didn't know what to say to her. She hadn't been one of them any more, and she'd so wanted to belong somewhere—which was why her university friends had become her new friendship group. Cesca, Yvette and Janine had welcomed her with open arms. They knew about Marcus, but it didn't change the way they felt about her.

She reached into her pocket, pulled out her mobile and texted Anthony.

Let tonight be my treat. I'll take you somewhere special. J x.

'Where are we going?' Anthony asked as he cycled alongside her that evening.

As promised, she'd decided to get him on a bike, and they'd rented a couple of the ones that were available all over the city. She'd expected a few false starts, but after an initial wobble he'd actually taken to it very quickly.

'It's a surprise,' she told him.

'I don't know of any decent restaurants down here.'

'Who said anything about a restaurant?'

She winked at him and laughed, then led him along until they turned a corner to reveal a mobile food stand. It was lit up with fairy lights and revealed a longish queue trailing around the square.

'Baked potatoes?' Anthony looked confused.

She laughed. 'It's the very best baked potato you will ever have in your entire life. Trust me!'

He looked doubtful.

Julia grinned, enjoying the look on Anthony's face. 'Haven't you ever eaten from a food truck before?'

'Of course I have!'

'Where? When?' she asked.

He shrugged. 'Well, it might not have been a truck *per se*...more of a pop-up restaurant.'

'Serving?'

'Oysters.'

'Hah! I knew it! And I bet they cost a small fortune?'

'It was very reasonable,' he argued with a smile.

'"Reasonable" to you would probably mean a mortgage to me. Trust me—this grub you're about to eat will blow those oysters out of the water. No pun intended.'

'How wonderful can a jacket potato be?'

'Have you not seen the queue? That's how good.'

'You know I could have taken you to a wonderful little place with fine wines and a river view?'

'I don't need fine wines or a river view. Not when I can eat food out of a cardboard container whilst admiring this lovely view of a city square and a water fountain.'

'My place has a piano.'

'There's a violin player over there, busking.'

'It serves the finest spatchcock chicken you have ever seen.'

Julia shrugged. 'This has pigeons.' She laughed as she cycled through a flock of them, causing them to leap into the airs, wings flapping.

'Okay, you win.'

'I'll win once you taste the food.'

'You're promising big, Morris! This had better deliver.'

'It will!'

They parked their bikes and got into the queue. The busker was playing a recent hit from the charts and Julia found herself swaying and bopping to it, much to Anthony's amusement.

They finally reached the serving hatch.

'What can I getcha?' asked the man behind the counter.

'Do you trust me to order?' Julia asked.

'Implicitly.'

'We'll have two of your finest jacket potatoes, both with chilli beef and cheese, please.'

'Coming right up!'

The aromas from the food truck were tantalising, and after a long day at work Julia was starving and ready to eat her fill. Their food was passed over, steaming hot, and they walked over to a low stone wall, near where they'd parked their bikes, to eat with the water fountain behind them.

She could barely see the potato. It was all chilli beef and melted cheese. She dipped in her wooden fork and pulled out a forkful, watching the cheese stretching between the fork and the food in her hand before she placed it into her mouth.

'Oh, my God! Just as I remember! What do you think?'

Anthony's eyes were wide in surprise as he ate some of his own. 'I don't think I've eaten chilli this good in my entire life!'

'I told you!'

'Okay, okay. You're right. From now on, you can choose all our eateries, if their food tastes this delicious.'

'Well, I can't promise five-star food every time, but this place certainly hits the spot after a long day. How did your clinic go?'

He nodded, swallowing. 'Good. I had an interesting case come in.'

'Can you tell me about it?'

'It's a young man who's been brought over from Africa by

a charity. He's had polio and his legs are malformed. We're looking to see if we can help him.'

'Really? Wow… Well, I hope you can. That could make a big difference to his quality of life.'

Anthony nodded. 'It was just an assessment today. I've arranged for up-to-date scans and we'll go from there.'

'Are his parents with him?'

'No, he's an orphan.'

'Poor kid…'

'Hopefully we can make a difference.' Anthony swallowed another mouthful of potato, then looked at her carefully. 'Can I ask you a personal question?'

'Of course.'

'Do you ever think about having kids again?'

And there it was. The question that haunted her. The question that her mother had asked her multiple times. The question that made her uncomfortable and desperate to avoid it. She wasn't sure she could answer him, so she did what she always did. Deflected.

'What about you? Do you see yourself having children one day?'

'I've always hoped to be a father. I wanted it to happen with Yael, but obviously that didn't work out. And I don't want to enter a relationship and have a child just to fulfil some destiny and heritage decreed by my birth and title. I'd want a child because I was in a serious, committed relationship with someone. A child born from true love and for no other reason.'

'So you can envisage yourself marrying again?' she asked, curious.

He shrugged. 'I don't know. Yael told me to find someone to be with. To not be alone. To find someone who makes my heart lift the way she did. But I'm not sure I'd ever be brave enough to put myself out there and risk having my heart broken again if I were to lose them.'

'It's difficult, isn't it?'

She understood his pain and reticence. Becoming a mother had been everything. To lose Marcus had ripped out her heart. Sometimes she yearned to have a baby to hold. To watch one grow. But could she do something that would terrify her?

'You and I are so different, and yet so similar in many ways. Maybe it's because I'm a dreamer and a romantic. I want a *guaranteed* happy-ever-after.'

'Life doesn't give guarantees, though,' said Anthony.

'No, it doesn't. So maybe we both need to just grasp true moments of happiness when we can? Not to expect a happy-ever-after, where we head into the sunset, knowing that everything will be perfect. Instead, we should grasp and keep hold of the small moments, and hope that by the time we're old and grey—if we're lucky enough to get old and grey—we have enough happy moments to make us smile each time we remember them?'

Anthony smiled. 'Sounds lonely, though.'

'We're not alone. We've found each other, after all these years, and we're doing something to help one another. I don't know about you, but that makes me smile. And no matter what happens…no matter which direction our lives take us in, even if they take us to opposite ends of the earth… I will always look back on our time together and be grateful for it.'

'To friendship?' He lifted a fork filled with potato and chilli.

'To friendship!' She touched her fork to his and felt a warmth inside her heart at having found herself a true friend. Someone who understood her fears. He didn't dismiss them, like her own mother sometimes did, telling her that she'd find someone one day and everything would be okay. He just accepted them.

And that was all she needed, she told herself.

She hoped it was the truth. Because no matter how wonderful Anthony was, he could not offer her what she needed—and she couldn't give him what he needed, either.

When they'd finally eaten their fill, and could eat no more, Julia turned to look at the fountain. There were some kids playing in the water on the other side of it because it was such a nice, warm evening.

She turned back to look at Anthony's feet.

'What?' he asked.

'You ever gone paddling in a fountain?'

Anthony gave a half-laugh and looked behind him. 'Isn't that...er...illegal?'

'I don't see anyone arresting those kids.'

'I'm not sure we should.'

'Come on! Live a little! Break a rule and be happy.'

Julia began to reach down for her own shoes, slipping them off her feet and removing the little anklet socks that she'd got on underneath. Then she stood and stepped over the rim of the fountain and into the water, gasping at the coldness.

'It's fun! Come on!'

He looked at her and laughed. 'Okay, but if we get arrested I'm telling the judge that you drove me to it.'

'Fine.' She held out her hand once he'd slipped off his brogues and peeled off his dark socks.

He shook his head, almost as he couldn't believe he was going to do what she was encouraging him to do, and then took her fingers in his.

She felt a frisson of something tremble up her arm at his touch, the feel of his hand in hers bringing an awareness that went beyond mere friendship. The shiver was from the cold water, though. Surely?

'See? It's fun,' she said, trying to distract herself from the feeling of needing more.

'It's freezing—and there are pennies in here.'

'Not pennies. *Wishes.*' She laughed, suddenly nervous.

He was still holding her hand, still gazing into her eyes as with his free hand he pulled a coin from his pocket. A five pence piece. Small and silvery.

He passed it to her. 'Make a wish!'

Julia shook her head. 'It's your coin. You make the wish.'

'All right.'

'Close your eyes,' she said, watching as he stood still and slowly closed his eyes. Then with a flick of his finger the coin spun high into the air and came splashing down into the water between them. 'What did you wish for?'

Anthony smiled. 'That would be telling.'

Julia knew what she would have wished for as she gazed at his handsome, smiling face and her gaze dropped to his lips...

'Nurse, if you could change Mrs Mackie's dressing, please?'

'Yes, Mr Fitzpatrick.'

Mrs Mackie was an outlier patient who had been brought to the orthopaedic ward because there'd been no room for her elsewhere in the hospital at the time. She was an elderly woman, in her seventies, who had come into A&E after trying to break up a fight between two of her cats, using her stockinged foot. Her foot had been ripped to shreds by cat claws, and her thin, friable skin had developed an infection. They were treating it with larvae therapy, in which maggots would eat away at the dead skin and keep the wound clean.

'How is it feeling, Mrs Mackie?'

'A little sore, but I think better. These tiny pets aren't causing me any issues.'

'So no increased pain? That's good.'

Anthony watched as Julia cut away most of the bandaging and then, as she got closer to the biologics, slowed to make sure she didn't aggravate the wounds. The last layer was a piece of gauze soaked in sodium chloride, which she peeled off slowly, revealing the larvae bag, which she removed.

He bent over the patient's foot to examine it and smiled. 'Well, they've certainly done a very good job. You see how all the dead and infected tissue has been eaten away?'

Mrs Mackie nodded, intrigued.

'I think Nurse, that we can now move on to normal dressings—if you could get that done for me?'

Julia nodded to him and smiled. 'Yes, Mr Fitzpatrick.'

'I should imagine if you continue to heal without developing any further infection we can get you home soon. I'm going to arrange for the physios to come and give you some exercises you can do, and someone from Occupational Health to come and talk to you about how to manage at home.'

'Home? How soon?'

'Maybe in a couple of days? I just want to keep an eye on these wounds…make sure they start closing up properly on their own.'

'All right. Thank you.'

'You're welcome.'

'What will happen to them?' Mrs Mackie asked.

He had to admit he was a little confused by her question. 'What will happen to whom?'

'The maggots?'

'They'll be destroyed.'

'Seems such a shame when they did such a good job.'

He smiled and moved on to the next bed.

Patients never failed to surprise him.

'I have news!' Julia said as she swung open her front door.

'Hello to you, too,' Anthony said, as he leaned in to drop a kiss onto her cheek.

As excited as she was to share her news, she still felt a

blush fill her cheeks with an enticing heat at his kiss. She wondered how it might feel to kiss him on the lips…

'I have news,' she said again.

'What is it?'

'Gramma May is doing so well they're talking of letting her home in a couple of days. Her speech is much better, and she's gained strength back in her affected arm.'

'That's fantastic!'

'I know! I told you she had nine lives.'

'I'm really happy for you.'

'Thanks. Now, are you ready for this?'

'As ready as I'll ever be.'

They were going to start work on the float for the parade. Her friend Paulie owned a large garage and they'd all agreed to work there.

'I think you'll get on well with Paulie,' she said.

'Have you known him long?'

'Quite a few years. He's the local mechanic and he fixed my tyre and collected my car that night when I got stranded near your place.'

'Sounds a good guy.'

'He is.'

'Who else is going to be there?'

'I think Janine. She was at university with me and now works in the critical care ward of St Agatha's Hospital in Surrey. Then there's Yvette, Paulie's wife. She's been sewing drapey curtains to hide the wheels all around the truck to make it look like it's floating.'

'What's the float going to be?'

'Castle in the sky. So we're going to be making clouds and a castle, with platforms for all our heroes and heroines to stand upon.'

'Great!'

'You're sure you're up for this? I'd hate to get any splinters in those surgical hands.'

'Splinter-schminter. I want to help. I'm *happy* to help.'

'Okay. Let's go!'

It wasn't far to the garage. About a twenty-minute drive. When they arrived everyone else was already there. Yvette and Janine were working out how to attach the drapes to the truck, whilst Paulie was sorting out wooden batons to construct the castle.

'Hi, guys. I've brought reinforcements. This is Anthony.'

The others stopped what they were doing to say hello, and there was a little bit of a chinwag for a while, and then they began working.

Julia was soon helping Anthony and Paulie to construct the base for the castle. 'A bit more over to the left, Anthony? About an inch?' she asked.

'Yep, that's it.'

Paulie had a power drill and connected two batons with a screw. 'Now the other end,' he said.

Essentially, they were constructing a rectangular base that would fit on the truck bed. They wanted to build two small rectangles to go on top of that, so the castle was tiered. With Paulie's tools, they made short work of it.

'Okay, we need to put this sheeting on the top of each layer. Ant, can you give me a hand carrying it over?'

Julia noticed that Paulie had started calling Anthony 'Ant'. He didn't seem to mind, and she had to admit she liked seeing Anthony fit in with her friends, getting to know them. She also liked watching his muscles flex as he carried things and hammered things. The look of concentration on his face… the easy way he fitted in with everyone.

'He's a good guy,' Janine said as they stood in the small kitchen to make tea for everyone.

'He is,' Julia agreed.

'Handsome.' Her friend raised an eyebrow.

'Yes.' She blushed. He *was* very handsome.

'What's he like?'

Julia frowned, not sure what she meant. 'How do you mean?'

'You know!' Janine grinned. 'In bed!'

'Wow.' Julia laughed nervously.

She'd stopped short of trying to imagine what he might be like in bed. She'd thought about kissing him passionately, and what that might feel like—of course she had. For their plan to work there might be an occasion when they needed to be seen sharing 'a moment', and she'd wondered where that might possibly lead. If his hands might wander a little bit. But she'd always stopped short of thinking beyond that. The excitement of it thrilled her in a way that scared her. But she kept telling herself it was pointless—because that would never happen between them, even though she liked him very much. Their relationship was pretend.

But, as a hopeless romantic, of course she'd thought of what it might be like to be his girlfriend for real. Wouldn't anybody? And she'd seen sometimes that he looked at her in a certain way, so she could never be quite sure if he was attracted to her too, in some small way. But it would have to be a small way, because surely he wasn't really interested in her?

'We've...er...not gone that far yet,' she answered, being as honest as she could, considering the situation between them. 'We're taking it slowly.'

'Oh... I was hoping for a few juicy details!' Janine grinned. 'Being single myself, you know I like to live vicariously through others. What about you, Yvette?'

'I've been married for years—what do you think?'

Janine shrugged. 'I don't know. Does Paulie still drive you wild?'

Yvette laughed. 'He has some skills.'

'Yes! Tell me his best move.'

Julia laughed and picked up the tea tray to take it out to the two guys still working hard in the garage. She didn't need to hear about Paulie's 'best move' to thrill his wife in bed.

'Tea break.'

Paulie and Anthony had worked hard to create the basic structure, and now they were using the hammer gun to attach the second base onto the largest rectangular structure.

'Perfect,' Paulie said. 'No biscuits?'

'I can get some if you like?'

'No, it's fine. I'm watching my figure.' He winked, rubbing at his slight paunch. 'Yvette wants me beach-body-ready for when we hit Jamaica later in the year. You ever been there, Ant?'

'No, actually, I haven't.'

'You should go, mate. Amazing people...beautiful beaches. It's got this vibe, you know?'

Anthony smiled. 'I'll add it to my bucket list.'

'So! You two been going out long?'

'About a month?' Julia looked to Anthony to clarify.

'Something like that, yeah. It's hard to know exactly when it started, what with us working together.'

'And how is that? Dating and working together?'

'He hasn't got sick of me yet.' Julia laughed.

'Well, why would he?' Paulie asked, slurping at his mug of tea and slapping his lips together in appreciation. 'You've got a good one here, Ant, mate. You take care of her, all right?'

'I will.'

Julia looked at Anthony and smiled at him. Was this a moment to kiss him? Should she do that? She felt that a real couple would at this point.

But her hesitation made her miss the moment. Anthony just smiled at her and sipped his tea, unaware of the turmoil of her thoughts.

'When you find the right woman you just know, don't you?' Paulie continued. 'Look at me and Yvette. Everyone said we wouldn't work out, because we were so different, but look at us now. Married nearly ten years and happy as Larry.'

'Congratulations,' Anthony said.

'Cheers, mate. Well, I think we should call an end to this for the day. Next time we can make the remaining platform, stick it all together and then start painting—what do you say?'

'Sounds like a plan to me,' Anthony said.

'Yeah. Great,' Julia said. 'Though I'm not sure if Anthony will be able to make it to all these sessions.'

Anthony turned to her. 'I'll make it. I like spending my time with you.'

She blushed, not sure what to say.

But Paulie was. 'Aww…you two lovebirds. Makes me happy to see Julia smiling again.'

CHAPTER TEN

Anthony was escorting Musa, the young man who'd come over from Africa to have his legs operated on after suffering polio. He'd spent hours in Theatre with him, lengthening the tightened ligaments and getting rid of deformed muscle. Musa had also needed a total knee arthroplasty in his left leg—a knee replacement.

The surgery had gone very well indeed. But, as with most of his paediatric patients, Anthony liked to sit with them in Recovery and then escort them back to the ward. It was just a thing he did.

As he walked along the corridor with Musa, he spotted Julia at the reception desk.

'Nurse? Which bay for Musa?'

He saw Julia wipe at her eyes before turning round. 'Bay fourteen, please.'

Had she been crying? He felt his stomach lurch, not knowing why she was upset, but he knew he needed to get Musa settled first. Then he would come and see her.

Once he had Musa in his bay and comfortable, and had promised to check on him in another hour or so, Anthony went to find Julia. He saw her go into the utility room, and glanced around to make sure no one was watching before he went in.

'Are you all right?' he asked.

She gave a short, embarrassed laugh. 'Yes! I'm fine!' she said, as she bent down to look for something on a shelf.

The shelf was filled with a variety of linens that were used to make up the beds. Sheets, blankets, pillowcases... There were also pyjamas and dressing gowns for those patients who didn't bring in their own, or those who arrived in A&E and were brought up to the ward not knowing that they would be kept in.

'You look upset,' he told her.

'It's fine. Honestly. You should go before people find us in here together.'

The tone of her voice told him something. That this was the thing that was bothering her.

'Has someone said something to you?'

She stopped. Straightened. Closed her eyes, then nodded.

'What's been said?'

'Another nurse said that she's noticed our interactions are different to anyone else's. That she can see that something's going on and that she expected better from a newly qualified nurse. She said that if I was sleeping with you, I ought to be ashamed.' She began to cry. 'This is exactly what I was trying to avoid!'

He felt incredibly guilty, then. He'd not thought they would hurt anyone with their ruse, and he'd honestly tried to treat her like everyone else at work, but maybe he hadn't? Maybe it had been clear to anyone with eyes that Mr Ice's interactions with Nurse Morris were different. Softer. Kinder. Maybe his gaze lingered too long upon her? Maybe he smiled too much when he spoke to her? Maybe he called on her to assist him more than any of the other nurses? His preference to be with Julia had obviously created a bias and others had noticed. And rather than tell *him* about it, they had gone to the one with less power. The easier target.

And all because he'd wanted to get his mother off his back for a few weeks. He should have been better. A better Mr Ice.

He'd never wanted to hurt her professionally. It had never crossed his mind that he would.

Without thinking, he stepped towards her and pulled her into his arms. At first he felt her resistance, and he was about to let go, not wanting to make things worse, but then she relaxed against him and put her arms around him too, snuffling into his shirt. And even though she was upset, it felt really good to have her back in his arms. Pressed up against him. He was just holding her. Comforting her. It felt right. As if she was meant to be there. And it was his damn right to be able to do this for her.

Anger stirred within him at the unknown person who had upset her and the urge to go out there and defend her name washed over him briefly, before he let the anger go and just relaxed into the hug. He would stand there with her for hours if need be.

'Do you want me to talk to them? Put them straight?'

She shook her head.

'Who was it?'

'It doesn't matter.'

'You shouldn't be bullied.'

'It wasn't bullying. She said it like she was really disappointed in me, and it stung a bit. My reputation is very important to me.'

She didn't need to tell him that she'd hate anyone thinking she was just trying to land a doctor. That that was all she was here for. He knew she wanted to help people. She wanted to be respected. She'd come to this career later than others...

And then she seemed to realise what she was doing, and she let him go and stepped back, wiping her eyes. 'Better not. Anyone could come in.'

'Do you want me to leave?' He wanted to go on holding her. To comfort her.

'I want you to treat me like everyone else.' She looked him in the eye, her voice hard.

'I've been trying.'

'Try harder.'

And that was when he saw her strength. Her determination. And he knew then how she'd managed to get through those dark days when she'd lost Marcus. Because Julia was made of stern stuff. She had a steel core. A determination to make things right. Look at how eventually she'd turned her life around. Knowing that something needed to change. Taking on a new career path. Going to university as a mature student. Getting through her nursing education and passing all her modules with distinction. He could do nothing but admire her fortitude and bravery—if anything, she could only go up in his estimation.

'It's going to be hard to pretend that you're just anyone when you mean so much to me.'

She looked at him, then, with warmth and appreciation in her eyes. Her voice softened. 'You mean a lot to me, too.'

He was glad. That made him feel good. That it was reciprocated. 'I'd better go, then.'

'Yes...'

'I've just brought Musa down from Theatre.' It seemed best to change the subject.

'The boy from Africa?'

'Yes. His surgery went very well, but he won't have many visitors, so if all the staff could make an extra effort to look after him...make him feel that he's not alone?'

'Of course.'

He turned to go, his hand on the door handle, but then he stopped. 'If anyone says anything else to you I want you to come to me and let me know. We're in this together, you and I. You shouldn't bear the brunt of any accusations.'

Julia nodded.

Satisfied, he left the room. Her words had made him feel sickened. That another nurse should say that to her... His eyes scanned the ward, looking at the other nurses he could see and wondering if it was one of them?

She would never tell him—he knew that—but he wished he knew.

Because right now he felt as if he would go to the ends of the earth to protect her.

Back at Paulie's garage, the construction of the castle had been completed and now everyone was wielding a paintbrush to decorate the float. Julia had a light blue paint, which she'd already managed to get on her hands and her clothes, and opposite her, at the far end of the truck, was Anthony. He had a white colour that he was using to paint the fake clouds that Paulie had carved out of thin MDF boards.

Today's accusation from Rosaria had stung.

Julia had been feeling so good beforehand. She'd just managed a difficult cannulation on a patient who'd kept pulling out her tubes and had earned a promise from her that she wouldn't do so again. She'd been tidying up and putting the rubbish into clinical waste when Rosaria, an older and more experienced nurse, who had worked on the ward for ten years or more now, had come up to her and said those words that had upset her quietly into her ear.

She'd thought Rosaria was a friend. She'd thought the senior and much-respected nurse respected *her* in turn. She'd said those words about her sleeping with Anthony as if she'd been giving her a warning, and when she'd protested that she wasn't sleeping with him, the older woman had simply rolled her eyes and said, *'Protest as much as you like, love.*

It's obvious there's something going on between you two. A man doesn't look at a woman like that unless something's going on.'

Her protests had fallen on deaf ears, and the more she'd protested her innocence, the more Rosaria had looked disappointed in her for lying, and after that Julia hadn't known how to feel. She'd been so upset she'd had to take herself off to an empty room for a cry, hiccupping and gulping her way back to normal.

Wiping her eyes when she'd emerged from the room, she'd hoped no one would be able to tell that she'd been crying. And she thought she'd done okay until Anthony had seen her.

Of course he'd noticed. She'd tried to downplay it. She didn't want Rosaria to get into trouble. Julia hadn't been in her position long enough to feel that she could openly challenge a popular nurse with over a decade's worth of experience on this ward.

She gazed at Anthony now, across the other side of the float structure. He was smiling, listening to Paulie as he told him some story about a holiday he'd taken with his wife Yvette.

Anthony was really concentrating on his painting. He'd told Julia on the way over that he'd never painted a thing in his life and hoped he wouldn't do a bad job, and here he was anyway. Concentrating hard. Eyes focused. Carefully applying his brush strokes as if he were a master artist working on a portrait, or something. He'd begun to fit into her life so well. Her friends loved him. Her family loved him—especially for helping Gramma May. He'd tried to protect her at work, and she loved how thoughtful and kind he was, wanting to look out for her like that. But was this getting too complicated?

She'd not meant to start developing feelings for him, but if she'd been looking for a relationship to get into, he'd be just the kind of guy she'd go for. Forget that he was a duke.

Forget that he was a surgeon. Those titles didn't matter. It was who he was as a person that she liked very much. Kindhearted. Loving. Funny. Generous.

Loyal.

She realised, as they sat there painting, that she truly felt she would be able to trust him, and that was a big thing for her. She'd trusted Jake before she'd learned the truth about him already being married. And he hadn't been prepared to leave his marriage even though she'd been pregnant with his child. He'd made her feel that she didn't matter. That she and the baby weren't enough. Other guys she'd met through dating apps had been all shades of wrong, too, making her feel like something to be used. And yet she didn't feel like that when she was with Anthony.

What would it be like to date Anthony for real?

Perhaps all men seemed perfect until you got to know them better.

The thought of being with him, though, sent a shiver of excitement through her. She could do it, couldn't she? She could pretend that it was real and experience it through the safety net of their pretence to their families. The fact was that this wouldn't last. It was only for a few weeks more. His mother would be flying to Adelaide soon. Perhaps if she was more physical? A touch? A kiss? Not just those pecks on the cheeks they'd been doing, but actually going in for a real kiss? On those delicious-looking lips of his? Nothing too prolonged. No tongues—nothing like that to begin with. Not unless he responded, of course, and they both got carried away in the moment…

He would be shocked, no doubt, but they had already told one another that they would kiss each other if the situation required it. They just hadn't done it yet. How would she be able to engineer the occasion? Or should it just come naturally?

Julia licked her own lips in anticipation of the idea of kissing Anthony and looked away. Her paintbrush had dropped away from the wood and more paint had dripped onto her trousers. She could imagine it. Picture it. The press of his lips. Would he sigh with pleasure? Would she?

'You're making a right mess there,' Yvette said, laughing. 'The paint's meant to go on the wood—not you.'

'Sorry!' Julia blushed. 'I was daydreaming.'

'Yeah...and I think I know what about.' Yvette winked at her and then looked knowingly at Anthony, before laughing again and leaning in quietly. 'It's okay. I remember that first flush of love, when he can do no wrong. I used to daydream about Paulie like that.'

'You don't daydream about him still?'

'Oh, yeah! But now my fantasies revolve around whether he'll get that kitchen tap fixed, or whether he can push the vacuum around whilst I read my book.'

Julia laughed. 'You love him still!'

'Yeah, he's not bad.'

'What made you fall in love with Paulie? What was it about him?'

'He could make me laugh. And he was very good with his hands!' She wiggled her eyebrows suggestively and laughed at herself. 'Most of all it was because he made me feel safe. Made me feel like I could just be me and he'd adore me for it. I didn't have to put on a mask to be with him. He just loved me...warts and all.'

Julia smiled. That sounded exactly like the type of relationship she would love to have. And she could have it. A ruse within another ruse. For a measly few pretend weeks and then it would be gone.

Who could it hurt?

What if the experiences they had together made them see that there could be something for them after this? A relationship? That they worked well together and it all made sense?

Anthony wasn't hiding anything about who he was with her. She knew his past and he knew hers. They both knew how the other one had been hurt, and knew they didn't want to feel that pain again. They were each other's safety net, weren't they? And wasn't that what Yvette had said about Paulie? That he made her feel safe?

'Anthony?'

'Yes?' He stopped painting to look at her, warmth and kindness in his eyes.

'After this, maybe we should go for a walk along the river. It's such a nice night... I think it will be great.'

He nodded. 'Sure!'

'You guys could go now, to be honest with you,' said Paulie. 'There's not much more we can do tonight, before letting all of this dry.'

'I'll just finish this last baton, then,' Anthony said.

It was lovely and cool down by the river. There were people out on the water—some kayaking, one or two paddle boarding. Couples and families were sitting on the concrete steps just watching the world go by.

Anthony couldn't ever remember walking by a river like this. He'd been by lakes, salmon fishing. He'd crossed oceans on cruise liners. But this river—the River Tamblin, which was near Paulie's garage—he'd never walked beside. He'd not even known it existed. But apparently it meandered along the edge of the town and even had areas for paddling.

'We should do that,' Julia said.

'What?'

'Go paddling.'

He didn't understand. 'Why?'

'Because it's nice. Because it's fun. Like at the fountain.'

He had fond memories of that. Yes, it had been fun to paddle in the water—but it had been more fun to hold her hand and listen to her laugh and splash each other.

'Have you got a thing for messing about in water?' he asked, and smiled to show he was joking.

'I find it calming after a long day. Come on!'

'It's not clean...'

'You think the fountain was clean?'

He shrugged.

'Take off your shoes and socks. Roll up those jeans. It's soothing. Come *on*!'

Anthony marvelled at her. Sometimes it was as if she had the innocence of a young child. She loved puddles, she'd once told him. She could remember as a child walking up the street to her school in bright red wellington boots, holding her mother's hand whilst she splashed in the puddles that had gathered near the kerbs and gutters.

She'd splashed around in that water fountain the other day, and when she'd made him close his eyes to make a wish, her face turned up towards his, he'd thought how easy it would be to kiss her. Only he hadn't. Because he was a gentleman, and he would never do anything like that without her consent. And besides, they were only pretending to be in a relationship. They weren't actually in one.

And now she wanted to splash around at the river's edge... Why not?

So he bent down once again, removed his shoes and socks, and walked out into the water with her, holding her hand to keep her steady. He didn't want her to slip or fall, after all. This was a safety issue, he told himself.

He could feel mud beneath his toes, squelching through the gaps. Cold and soft. And although the sensation was incredibly weird to begin with, after a while he actually began to like it.

'You see?' she said.

'How often do you do this?' he asked. 'Mess about in water?'

'As often as I can. It makes me feel… I don't know…kind of free. Kind of empty of all my woes and worries for a little while.'

He nodded. 'It's relaxing for you?'

'Yes. You can't imagine how many times I did this when I was studying to be a nurse. I'd take exams and then, instead of waiting at home, worrying about the results and whether I'd passed, I would find somewhere to paddle. You can forget about being an adult for a while. It's good for you.'

'Why don't you just go swimming at a leisure centre?'

She stopped to look at him. 'Because that would be too busy. Too loud and echoey. Out here, I can be in nature. Birds singing. Blue skies…'

'Muddy water?'

Julia laughed and turned back to look at him. Then she looked down at their hands, still holding one another. 'Have you thought about us kissing?' she asked suddenly, looking serious.

He hoped his cheeks didn't colour and betray him. Because of course he had! He'd thought about kissing her for real every single time he'd leaned in and dropped a kiss on her cheek. He'd dreamed about kissing her every time she'd looked at him and smiled. There was something in the way that she looked at him… It went straight to his heart.

But surely she didn't mean that? 'You mean to help the illusion we're creating with our families?' he asked.

She shrugged. 'Sure.'

'We do kiss. We've done it in front of them.'

'Pecks on the cheek. Polite kisses. I mean…' She seemed to swallow. 'Proper kisses.'

His gaze dropped to her mouth. 'On the lips?'

'Where else?'

'How...how do you mean?' He wasn't sure what to say. What to admit to. What was she actually asking him, here?

'Well, if this ruse is going to work properly, I think that, on occasion, we may have to kiss each other on the lips the way a proper couple would.'

'Right...'

'And we don't want that to be awkward, do we? We want it to look...natural.'

'Comfortable?'

'Yes.'

Her gaze had dropped to his lips. Ever so briefly. Then she met his gaze again and her cheeks were flushed with a rosy glow.

'What do you propose?' he asked.

She laughed and looked away, her gaze taking in the couples, the families, a dog splashing into the water, chasing after a ball that had been thrown for it to retrieve.

'That maybe...maybe we ought to practise? So that it looks natural for us.'

He realised her tone was trying to make her suggestion sound as reasonable and as logical as possible.

'We don't want to kiss and look awkward...or clash teeth or anything...'

He thought about what she was suggesting.

Practice-kissing.

She did have a point. They'd need to look as if they'd kissed before. Many times! And if they practised, then that would be true, right?

'All right. Seems sensible.'

He tried to sound as if it was simply a sensible idea. A logical idea. When in reality his heart was pounding as if he'd run a marathon. Was she truly just being sensible about this? Or did she really want to kiss him? A part of him wished for the latter—even though that, in itself, would be terrifying.

She looked at him. 'Yeah? Okay… So, maybe we should do that?'

He looked around them. 'Here?'

'No. Not here. Not with an audience like this!' She laughed.

'Somewhere private?'

Julia nodded.

'Back in the car?'

His heart was thudding. He was imagining himself in such a small, confined space with Julia. Kissing her.

'Sounds as good a place as any.'

'Okay.'

'Okay…'

They stood there in the water for a little longer, not saying anything.

'When do you want to…?' he asked.

'Let's go and do it now,' she said, blushing madly.

He nodded. 'No time like the present,' he agreed, trying to sound reasonable.

CHAPTER ELEVEN

They walked in silence back towards the car, the air between them heavy with intent and expectation.

Julia had not expected him to agree to her suggestion so easily. Or so quickly. Had she expected him to laugh it off? Say it wasn't necessary? Or maybe even say that he would feel weird doing so? But perhaps he was keen to kiss her too? No, most likely he wanted their fake relationship to look real. He'd already told her he wasn't ready to be in another relationship. It was the whole reason they were together in the first place.

Would she be the first woman to kiss him seriously, since Yael? Surely not? Surely a guy like Anthony would have had many opportunities?

But he hadn't laughed it off. He'd seemed keen, too. Perhaps he'd even thought of this issue himself, but hadn't known how to raise the subject? Maybe he was glad that she had done so instead?

They were here. They'd arrived at the car park and she found herself going round to the passenger side of the car as Anthony went to the driver's side and unlocked the doors. She gave him one lingering glance before she got in, encouraged to see that he seemed as nervous as she was.

Julia slid into her seat and closed the door with a sense of finality. She rubbed her hands along her thighs, in case they were damp—which they were not.

She sucked in a breath and gave a small laugh. 'How do you want to do this?'

'Well, why don't you tell me how you would like this to proceed? Maybe establish a few ground rules? A safe word?'

She nodded. 'Good. Yes. Okay. Maybe our safe word ought to be something one of us would say a lot…so maybe something from work?'

He nodded. 'So it would sound like we were talking about a case? What word would be good? But also sound like a way to tell the other person to stop?'

Julia thought. 'How about *patient*?'

Anthony smiled and nodded. 'Perfect.'

'Okay. Safe word chosen. Ground rules…'

'I never thought I would ever have to have ground rules for kissing,' he said.

'No, nor me. But in this situation it might make us both feel a little better about doing it,' she said, as if kissing Anthony was going to be some sort of chore. She strongly suspected that it would not be, but you never could tell. Not until you did it. 'I honestly don't know where to start.'

'Well, what about my hands? Where would you be happy with me placing them?'

She could feel her cheeks colour as she imagined all the places he *could* put them. But they had to be sensible here, and remember the impression they would give others.

'I guess we have to think about what other people would expect to see. Maybe around my waist?'

He nodded. 'I could do that. What about…' he turned in his seat to look at her properly '…if I cupped your face? Like so?'

Her lips parted and her breathing increased as his hands came up to cup her jawline. Softly. Reverently. His wonderful touch was, oh, so gentle.

'Would this be all right?' he asked, looking deeply into her eyes.

It meant she was staring deeply into his too. Not trusting herself to speak right then, all she could do was nod.

'Could my fingers go into your hair? Push back a strand, like this?'

She felt his fingers deftly delve into the hair at the nape of her neck. Felt a finger from his other hand tidy away a strand behind her left ear before he cupped her face again. She could imagine his fingers trailing elsewhere. Touching. Feeling. Exploring.

She gulped. 'That…that would be fine,' she managed, her voice croaky. His eyes were *so blue*. Like small oceans with hidden depths of beauty if only she cared to dive deeper.

'And when I kiss you…'

'Yes?'

'Closed mouth or…more?'

Had his voice grown hoarse too? Her gaze dropped to his lips. Parted, like hers. How would she like him to kiss her? Softly, yes. Tenderly. What would he taste like? He was asking her permission to be able to taste her, too, though she couldn't imagine they'd be doing any full-on snogging in front of his mother…

'Either's fine.'

It was all she could think of to say. She was imagining it. Imagining his tongue delving deep into her mouth to find hers and entwining with it. She wanted it all! Wanted to try all of his kisses and pretend they were real. But she had to pretend that this was pretend! To maintain the pretence!

I'm going to die.

'Okay…' he breathed. 'I guess those are the rules.'

She nodded, though her head was still held within his gentle grasp.

'I guess all that's left to do, then, is…kiss.'

'I guess so.'

Her heart was pounding out of her chest. Thudding and

thumping like a wild animal madly trying to escape her ribcage. Her face felt hot, her skin tingling. She tried to slow her heartbeat, to remain in control. To act as if this was nothing. Because she couldn't let him know how badly she wanted this to be real.

He leaned in. Slowly. She could feel his breaths—rapid, like her own—and she wondered if he was craving the kiss as much as she was.

'Wait!' she said suddenly.

'What is it?'

'We haven't come up with your rules.'

'Oh. Right.'

She smiled shyly. 'Where can I put *my* hands? Here?' She leaned in and gently placed her hands upon his chest. She could feel his heart pounding beneath her fingertips.

He nodded.

'Okay.'

'Okay. You ready?'

'Yes. Are you?'

'Yes.'

'Okay…'

Anthony leaned in again. Slowly. Inching forward. Making sure that she still wanted this.

She wanted nothing more. She'd been craving his kiss for so long now she couldn't quite believe that it was about to happen. At long last.

She closed her eyes as his lips met hers and her world imploded. The kiss was sensuous, hot, and it thrilled her every sense and nerve and heartbeat. His tongue met hers in a warm embrace and time grew still as if only they existed and only they moved…as if they were an anomaly compared to the rest of the universe. Julia felt dizzy, as if she needed to come up for air, but strangely *he* was her air, and her oxygen, and she felt that she could stay kissing him for ever.

It felt perfect. It felt right. It felt...hot! Tantalising... erotic. Her body came alive at his touch and she felt the desire to pull open his shirt, rip away those buttons, to find her hands touching his skin, his flesh, feeling the heat of him, the strength of him, those muscles... She wanted to trail her fingers down his chest, across his abs, lower...lower...and then...

And then the kiss was over, much too soon, and he pulled back slightly to look at her with glazed eyes.

'Was that all right?' he whispered softly.

All right?

Was that *all right*?

It had been more than all right! She was out of breath, stunned by everything she had felt and amazed she could even make her brain work enough to form a coherent response. It wasn't enough. She needed more. To see that it wasn't just a fluke, but that it would feel like that with him every time!

'Yes. Should we...do it again? Just to...you know...feel *really* comfortable?'

A small smile curved the corners of his beautiful, delicious mouth. 'One more time, then. For good luck.'

And he kissed her again.

Anthony totally forgot that this was just *practising*. That this was just a *rehearsal* in case they had to do the real thing in front of people one day in the next few weeks. To look *authentic*.

Kissing Julia made him forget the world. Made everything else simply melt away at the feel of her lips upon his. She was warm, and she tasted of mint, and of orange from the juice that she'd had at Paulie's. His hands were in her hair and, by God, he had to fight the urge to let them wander.

He was sorely tempted, but she'd not agreed to his hands

going anywhere apart from where they were and on her waist, and if he let them explore...let them touch, feel, stroke...then she would stop the kiss. She would say *patient*, their safe word, and he did not want to break her trust. She'd already explained to him how she felt she couldn't trust men, not after what Marcus's father had done to her, and she was trusting him to stick to their ground rules. So he would.

But...

He'd not kissed a woman like this for a very long time, and his senses were going into overload. His body was afire with need and desire after being starved of affection and touch for so long. His head felt scrambled and stunned.

When they broke apart she gazed at him uncertainly, and then leaned back into her own seat, her fingers touching her lips, before she smiled at him. She looked so beautiful in that moment—so shy, so innocent... Even though that kiss they'd just shared had been nothing like innocent.

He cleared his throat. 'Well, I think we've got that covered, don't you?'

Julia nodded. 'I thought it was very convincing.' She gave a strange sated smile.

'Me too.'

What were they supposed to do now? Act as if nothing had happened?

'Shall I take you home?' he asked.

She glanced at her watch. 'It is starting to get late...and we have work tomorrow.'

He started the engine as he tried to cool down. It felt weird that he wanted more. He'd not felt this way in a long time, and he'd never imagined he would find a passion for someone like this ever again. The idea that he might have a fulfilling life after Yael had seemed impossible. And yet here he was. Considering it.

But no. This is all just an illusion. She didn't mean any of what we just did. It was just acting. And I'd do well to remember that.

CHAPTER TWELVE

Rosaria looked up at Julia as she came onto the ward the next morning. She'd been on a night shift, and would be doing the handover for the day shift.

'Morning, Rosaria!' said Julia. 'How was last night?'

'Well, I hesitate to use the Q word, but it actually was.'

Quiet. She meant quiet. They tried not to use that word to describe a shift, because the second they did, usually all hell would break loose.

'Great. See you in a few minutes.'

'Yes, you will.'

Julia disappeared into the staff room. She hung up her things in her locker, and then took her water bottle and placed it in the fridge before going to make herself a quick cup of tea.

Other staff arrived in dribs and drabs.

'Hey, Jo.'

'Debs! How are you?'

'Living the dream.'

'And experiencing a nightmare?'

Julia smiled at the familiar start-of-shift banter as she took one of the handover sheets, grabbed a pen from her top pocket and waited for Rosaria to come in and begin.

The older nurse came in and stood at the front of the room, waiting for the hustle and bustle to die down, and then she began.

As she'd said, it seemed the orthopaedic ward had had a

quiet night. Most of the patients had slept soundly, with only bed three needing an extra dose of painkillers as he wasn't coping with his pain levels. Musa, the young man who'd had polio, was recovering well and had begun to eat again after feeling sick for a few days after the anaesthetic. And they'd had a new patient arrive from A&E, who had fallen down the stairs in the middle of the night and fractured his back as well as his arm. He would be going down for surgery this morning, to be put back together again.

There were no outstanding jobs to carry over onto the day shift so they had a fresh start, when all they had to do was get everyone washed and dressed, if they could be, then fed, and then do the drugs round, before their new patient got called for surgery.

'That's it! Best of luck!' Rosaria said, and they all began to file out and take over from the night shift staff. 'Julia? Could I have a quick word?'

Julia started, and then nodded.

Oh, no. I hope she's not going to say something else about me and Anthony.

Because if she did, her blushes from the knowledge that she'd now kissed Anthony passionately would probably overwhelm her.

Julia waited for the room to empty, then turned to the older nurse. 'Everything all right?'

'No, it's not.' Rosaria gave a sigh. 'I need to make an apology to you.'

'Oh, there's no need to do that!'

Because you were right.

'There is. I was out of line the other day, suggesting that there was something going on with you and a senior colleague on the ward without direct evidence, and I said some unkind and unfair things. I was particularly tired and stressed that day, and I took out my frustrations about things going on in my life on you, which I know is no excuse. So, I apologise.'

Julia was shocked. She'd not expected Rosaria to apologise at all. And honestly there *was* something going on between her and Anthony—just not what Rosaria thought. Julia felt guilty that she had to hide it from her colleague, but it was important for her to be seen as a professional—especially since she was only just starting out as a nurse and this job was very important to her.

She wanted to be like those nurses who had helped her after Marcus had passed. She wanted to provide the warmth that she'd received then. And if she helped just one person walk away from this hospital feeling that they were important, and not just another patient, then she would have achieved that. She was here for her patients. Not for anything else.

If something were to develop between her and Anthony… something real…then she would tell her colleagues. But only if it developed into something serious, like an engagement or a marriage. And she really didn't think that would happen. Anthony had made no suggestion that their kissing had changed anything for him. All they'd been doing was practising. Even if, for her, the kissing had been out of this world.

'I appreciate that, Rosaria, thank you,' she said quietly.

'So, we're good?'

She nodded. 'We're good.'

But she still felt guilty. As if she'd somehow made Rosaria apologise for nothing.

Julia was on the drugs round that morning. She donned a tabard that said *Do Not Disturb. Drug Round in Progress* on the back, and began taking the drugs cabinet from bed to bed, issuing medication to patients and marking the drugs issued on the patient's records. It was very important not to be disturbed whilst performing this task. It was so easy to make a mistake, to be distracted, and also, walking around with a cabinet filled with medication was a hazard. A risk. Medication was counted and had to be accounted for, and it was a job that each nurse took seriously.

As she went from patient to patient, saying good morning, asking them how they'd slept, issuing prescriptions, she noticed Anthony and his horde of junior doctors arrive. Instantly she felt her heartbeat escalate. How could she not? Those kisses of his had burned into her lips and her memory, and she'd gone to sleep that night dreaming of him.

'Morning, Nurse!' said her next patient, Thomasina Young, who was on the ward with a broken pelvis and neck of femur after a cliff fall.

'Morning, Thomasina. Sleep well?'

'Not really.'

'Oh, I'm sorry to hear that? Could you just not sleep? Or were you in discomfort?'

'Flashbacks to the fall. Every time I closed my eyes I kept experiencing it.'

Julia gave a sympathetic smile to her patient. She understood that. She'd experienced the same thing in the first few months after Marcus's passing. If she'd got to sleep, then she would suddenly wake with a start, heart pounding, fearing something was wrong. She would go rushing to his room, only to find it empty, all silent, and each time, it would break her heart. She'd been too late. Why hadn't she woken with a start the night he'd died?

Because I was exhausted. I hadn't slept properly for weeks.

She would stand in the doorway of his room and remember that moment. The moment she'd entered his room that fateful morning and seen him lying peacefully in his cot. The realisation as she'd stared at his face and known that something had gone terribly wrong.

'Maybe I could ask the nurse in charge if you could have

a sleeping tablet tonight? It's very important for you to get some decent rest after an injury like this.'

'They already offered me one, but I refused.'

'Why?'

'I think it's important for me to understand where I went wrong. If I keep reliving it, maybe one time I'll see my mistake.'

'You shouldn't let yourself be tormented like that.'

'Maybe, but it wasn't just me that got hurt. My fall hurt my friend. She got sent to another hospital and I'm responsible for that.'

'It sounds like you feel guilty.'

'I am.'

'But it was an accident. Accidents happen. You can't foresee everything that is going to happen.'

It was something she'd struggled with in the early days. Blaming herself. And though she'd hated it every terror-stricken time when she'd rushed to her son's room to check on him, she also, weirdly, hadn't minded it. Because in those few precious moments between her waking and arriving at her son's bedroom door in her mind there had been the possibility that he was still alive. That he was still with her.

Eventually, her doctor had prescribed sleeping tablets, which she'd begun to take, knowing she couldn't carry on the way she had been. Everyone had begun commenting on her appearance. How haggard she looked. The size of the bags and dark circles beneath her eyes. The sleeping tablets had helped get her back into a healthy sleeping pattern, but she'd still felt guilty every time she'd woken up without him.

'I'm sure your friend doesn't blame you,' she said now.

'She doesn't. I've talked to her on the phone. But that doesn't stop me from feeling guilty.'

'It'll pass. With time, it'll pass.' She didn't want to tell

Thomasina that actually the guilt would remain...it would just get easier to carry.

That didn't sound half as good.

But it was the truth.

She would always feel that way about Marcus. If only she hadn't slept through... If only she'd gone and checked on him. Maybe he would still be here today and her life would be totally different. She wouldn't have become a nurse. She would never have met Anthony again.

A warm feeling spread through her at the thought of him, and she completed her drugs round in a very good mood indeed.

When she was done, she felt her mobile phone vibrate in her uniform pocket, and checked it to see an invitation from Zoey, Anthony's sister.

It's my birthday tomorrow and I'm inviting the family. Do say you'll come! Seven p.m., Clareleas House. Zoey x

Of course. By dating Anthony, she was now considered *family*. She and Zoey had not yet made it out for that coffee they'd promised each other, but a birthday invitation was just as good, and she'd not seen any of his family since the ball. She knew she would need to talk to Anthony about it first, though, and if she was going she needed to know what kind of present to buy.

At lunchtime, she noticed Anthony in the cafeteria, eating his lunch. She wanted to go over to him, to talk about Zoey's invitation, but two tables away from Anthony, sat a group of nurses, and she didn't want to provoke more rumours. So she grabbed her own lunch and sat on the opposite side of the room and texted him.

She watched as he reached for his phone and pulled it

from his pocket, and then she saw the delightful way his face brightened when he saw the text was from her.

It made her smile. He was unobserved. He had no way of knowing that she was watching him from afar.

Pretty soon, his answer arrived.

Sounds great. I'll pick you up at six-thirty. Smart casual will be fine. I'll buy her favourite perfume. A x

Julia loved it that he'd added a kiss after his initial. And the way he'd smiled at seeing her name on his phone. After the kissing, she felt that something had most definitely changed in her feelings for him, and she hoped that he'd felt the genuine change in her affections too.

It felt nice...what they had going on. Surprising. Unexpected. When he'd first suggested this ruse, to get their respective families off their backs, she'd never expected that her feelings might change. That she might come to hope for more. That she might want their feelings to become real. Because she'd never expected to trust a man ever again. She'd never expected to feel safe with a man who would not disrespect her in any way. And even though she'd hoped that in the future she wouldn't be alone, she'd not expected to feel so strongly for someone yet.

That it had happened with Anthony was truly lovely. Because she felt as if he'd been with her since the start of her story, all those years ago—when she was a waitress, and pregnant, and not only full of baby, but full of hope that she would forge a bright future for herself and her son. Her last decade had been spent in a grey fog, but since meeting Anthony again that fog had drifted away and she felt that her life was sunny again.

All because of how being with him made her feel.

From her table, she watched him get up and return his

tray. He stopped briefly to converse with another surgeon. She thought he was from neuro, maybe. Anthony laughed, and the way his smile brightened his face made her smile, too, as the two men shook hands and parted ways.

Julia's gaze went to Rosaria, and she blushed when she realised Rosaria was watching her.

Clareleas House was a large new-build house constructed to look as if it had been built in the Georgian era. Brick-built, with symmetrical sash windows and a side gabled roof, it sat at the end of a long driveway bordered by dwarf willow trees.

Zoey and her husband Michael were there to greet Julia and Anthony as they arrived at the front door.

'Julia! How lovely to see you again! I adore that dress—whose is it?' Zoey asked, as if Julia was wearing some designer outfit.

She blushed. 'Oh, no one special. Off the rack.'

'Well, you look stunning in it—doesn't she Anthony?'

He had to admit that she did. But lately he'd begun to believe that Julia could wear a potato sack and still look amazing.

'Yes, she looks beautiful,' he agreed, leaning in casually to drape an arm around Julia's waist.

'Don't worry, brother dear, you look handsome, too,' Zoey said, dropping a kiss onto his cheek. She turned then and grabbed her husband's hand. 'Julia? This is Michael, my hubby. He couldn't come to Mother's ball. He had a situation at work that needed his attention.'

'Pleased to meet you, Michael.' Julia shook his hand.

'You too. Always happy to meet another victim willing to get involved with the Fitzpatrick family.' He laughed.

Anthony laughed, too. 'I think that says more about you than it does about us.'

'Oh, I don't know, old boy. Come on in! Everyone else has

already arrived and your mother is making her way through my wine collection. We need to get some food into her sharpish.'

Ah, he thought. *One of those evenings.*

When his mother's desire for grandchildren became overwhelming, because unhappily none of her children had yet produced heirs, she got a little tipsy as she turned to wine to make her feel better. His mother was no serious drinker, by a long shot, but every now and again she'd get maudlin about the fact that she had no grandchildren to spoil. And it seemed that today was going to be one of those days when she did.

'Let's hope Zoey hasn't sat you next to my mother at the table,' he whispered into Julia's ear, unwittingly inhaling her floral perfume and apple-scented shampoo.

He was thrown by the sensory overload, and the desire it prompted within him not to head to the dining room, but to a bedroom instead. Where he could explore all her other scents.

He honestly didn't know what was happening to him. Since meeting Julia again, his world had turned on its axis. Tilting wildly. Throwing all his expectations of what his life was going to be like into the air. And since the kissing practice he'd begun to feel a hunger for her that consumed him daily.

He was amazed he could feel this way. After Yael, he'd never thought he could have such strong feelings for another woman. But his connection to Julia was unlike anything he'd ever had before. Different from Yael. Different from anyone. He burned to be with her. He looked for her at the hospital. Just getting glimpses of her as she went about her work was enough and could make him smile. And the instances in which they could talk to one another, unobserved, brightened his day considerably. And when he couldn't see her or be with her he thought about her constantly.

These feelings, these desires, had come so fast, so intensely, that they worried him. What did it all mean? This wasn't a permanent thing. It was only for a few weeks. His mother flew to Adelaide soon, and would be gone for two months. As soon as she got on that aeroplane this illusion that he and Julia had created could stop.

And what would that feel like?

To return to normal?

Did he even *want* normal?

In the dining room, they greeted everyone. His mother, who dropped kisses on their cheeks, Zoey's friend Simon and his wife Harriet, Xavier and his fiancée Anna-Louise. And his mother had brought her friend Francesca, who was Zoey's godmother.

He could feel everyone's eyes on them as they moved around the room and he introduced Julia to them all. He kept a tight grip on her waist, taking reassurance from having her at his side. Normally at these events he would turn up alone and endure comments from everyone about how he needed to find someone and to settle down. How wonderful being part of a couple was. How no Duke of Weston had ever remained single and that he had a duty to provide an heir.

He would have loved to have a child with Yael, but they hadn't even got close to that goal. They'd had fun practising, though… In the early days, when they'd not known anything malignant was growing within her, they had been happy, carefree, fun. The hopes and possibilities for the future had seemed bright and available to them. As if the whole world could be theirs if they just reached for it.

And then cancer had reared its ugly head. Non-small cell lung cancer. Filling her lungs with fluid, metastasising to her brain and her bones and her liver. Into her lymph nodes. She'd fought so bravely, and for so long, holding on to hope each time she was given chemotherapy or immunotherapy or a new clinical trial when all the other possibilities had run out.

Yael would have made an excellent mother.

And now he was here, with Julia, his body craving her, his mind awash with her.

They'd barely sat down before the questions began.

'So how long have you two been together now?' his mother asked.

'Only a few weeks,' he said, hoping that such a short amount of time would be regarded by everyone else as not long enough to start asking them the heavy-hitting questions, like *Have you thought about getting engaged?* or *How many kids do you see yourself having?*

'Tick-tock, Anthony, darling. Tick-tock!' His mother laughed and sipped at her wine.

'Maybe you should make that your last glass, Mother, and move on to something more suitable. Say, black coffee?'

'Nonsense, darling! The night is yet young!'

Zoey made a motion to her staff to indicate that they ought to serve the first course and their plates arrived perfectly in time with each other. Smoked salmon with Greenland prawns, on a bed of salad with aioli sauce.

'This looks lovely, Zoey,' Julia said.

'Thank you. They're all my favourite dishes tonight, so I hope you like seafood?'

'I do. It's a favourite of mine, too.'

Zoey smiled. 'Tuck in, everyone.'

The first course went pleasantly enough. Anthony had Julia opposite him, his mother on one side and Zoey on the other. The three most important women in his life all around him. It would have been nice, if he hadn't felt so on edge.

'I know it's early days, Julia, and obviously you're a young woman with your career ahead of you, but do you ever think about the future?'

'Mother...' he warned.

'I'm just asking a simple question, darling.'

'Of course I do,' Julia answered diplomatically. 'I often wonder what it will hold.'

'Have you ever foreseen children as part of that future?' his mother persisted, determined in her line of questioning.

Julia blushed and sipped at her water, dabbing at her mouth with her napkin.

Of course his mother did not know about baby Marcus. That a child had already been a part of her life.

'Yes. I would very much like to have children in my future,' she answered, smiling.

Was she saying that because she was playing her part? Proving to his mother that he was in a relationship that might lead him the way his mother so desperately wanted? Or did she actually mean it?

Losing Marcus would have knocked her sideways. He couldn't imagine how it had affected her. After losing Yael, he'd felt he couldn't function without her in those early days. He'd wished he could have her back. Was Julia brave enough to go through all that uncertainty and fear if she had another child? She was indeed the bravest woman he knew, if that was the case.

Or maybe she didn't really want kids. He couldn't imagine being brave enough to take that on again. The fear would be unimaginable. And if she didn't want any more kids, could he still imagine a future with her? He'd figured he'd have them one day…just not on his mother's timeline, that was all.

'Excellent!' His mother took another sip of wine. 'Hopefully you can persuade my son to feel the same way at some point. He seems quite reluctant on that front.'

Julia glanced at him, and there was a warm, loving smile on her face as she reached for his hand upon the table, for everyone to see, and said, 'I respect Anthony enough to know he'll make up his own mind on what he wants and when he wants it. Especially after all he's been through. I don't believe in forcing anyone to do anything they're not ready for.'

He smiled back at her. No one had ever stood up to his mother like that before. They'd all been too polite to say anything that might upset the Dowager Duchess, who was a true force of nature.

Even his mother looked surprised. 'I know he's been through a lot, but he needs to move on. He can't stay single for the rest of his life—and it has been *ten years*,' she said, as if time somehow played a part in his decision.

Julia smiled. 'Grief has no timetable,' she said. 'Having children, getting married…these are all huge life changes. They don't always go smoothly, and your life is changed irreparably. Especially having children. They become your everything. They change who you are. Your outlook on life. They take up all of your time…your thoughts.'

'I know that, Julia!' his mother responded rather sharply. Too sharply. 'I have a son and daughter right here. And, forgive me, but you've never been a mother, so I'm not sure you have the right to sit there and tell me what sacrifices you have to make as a parent.'

Anthony felt Julia's grip on his hand tighten. He was going to speak, to try and smooth things over, but Julia spoke first.

'But that's where you're wrong, Your Grace. I am a mother. I am mother to a beautiful little boy called Marcus, who passed away ten years ago. I know about motherly sacrifice and worry. I know about how a child takes up your every consuming thought. He may no longer be here, but I am still Marcus's mother.'

Julia got up from the table and rushed away. All the other guests looked on, shocked, then turned to look at him, as if to confirm whether he knew about Marcus or not.

Anthony stood, dabbed at his mouth and stared down at

his mother. 'You really need to think before you speak sometimes, Mother.'

As he stood, so did Zoey laying a hand upon his arm. 'I'll help you find her.'

'No. You stay here. Look after your guests. I'm sorry if we've spoilt your birthday.'

'You haven't.' She dropped a kiss upon his cheek and gave him a sympathetic smile.

Anthony left the dining room, trying to decide which way Julia might have gone.

A member of staff was just closing the front doors.

'Can I help you, sir?'

'Yes, I'm looking for Julia. The young lady I arrived with.'

'She's gone out to the rose garden, sir.'

'Thank you.'

The rose garden was beautiful, with a gentle scent in the air from the smorgasbord of blooms. Soft pinks, blood-reds, butter-yellows and creamy whites. In the centre of the garden was a circular wooden bench, enveloping the trunk of a large tree, and it was there that Julia sat, cursing softly at herself for allowing Anthony's mother to wind her up so badly.

Yes, the older woman had been drinking, and Julia should have taken her words with a pinch of salt, but the woman was pushing her son so hard that he'd had to invent this situation that they were in just to get the woman off his back for a few short weeks. He needed a break.

Julia couldn't imagine that she would ever have treated Marcus in such a way, if he'd have been so lucky to have reached adulthood.

The Dowager Duchess's children were a gift, and she was treating them like commodities to be shown off and sold and bred. It was all about her. What *she* wanted. What *she* needed. She was not letting her children just *be*. And Julia refused to be steamrollered by her.

'Are you all right?'

She turned at Anthony's voice and looked up at him guiltily. 'Yes. I'm sorry I caused a scene. I must go back in and apologise to Zoey.'

'You don't have to do that.'

'I do. This is her birthday dinner and I've caused a scene. With her mother, no less.'

'Probably the most excitement that's ever been experienced at one of our dining tables. I'm sure Zoey loved it. Especially you putting our mother in her place.'

'I suppose I ought to apologise to her, too.'

'Don't you dare.'

He settled onto the bench next to her. She felt soothed by his presence. His solidity. The fact that he'd come out to check on her.

'I was rude, though. I should never have told her about Marcus. Does that ruin the ruse we've created?'

'No. Absolutely not. I'll tell them I already knew about Marcus because that's the truth. All you've done is tell them the truth. We've just left *other* bits of the truth out.'

She smiled and laid a head upon his shoulder. His comfort meant a great deal to her. 'Thank you.'

'What for?'

'For being you. For not being mad at me.'

'I could never be mad at you,' he answered softly.

She turned to look at him, then. Looked up into the soft blue eyes that looked darker in the shade of the tree and the dimming light. Looked at the way the darkness of his short trimmed beard framed his jaw. Looked at his mouth. Those lips she had kissed. Lips that she knew brought both comfort and tremendous pleasure.

She wondered if she could be brave enough to kiss them again...

Could she? There was no excuse here about how she thought they ought to practise kissing in case they needed to do so in front of their families. So it looked natural. So it looked as if they'd been kissing each other that way for some time and felt comfortable doing so.

This bit was real. What she felt for him she knew was real. But how could she tell him that? His love for Yael had been complete, and there was no way she could compete with that. She was just a convenience. And he didn't want a relationship—that was why he was faking one. She'd merely agreed to help him out for a few weeks. She couldn't tell him that, for her, the rules had changed. That everything had changed.

Even though she was terrified by what she felt, something about him made her feel as if she wanted to rush headlong into whatever whirlwind of feelings and emotions she could find with him.

She knew he liked her as a friend. As a colleague at work. Knew they had a bond that could never be broken, thanks to her son. Thanks to his being the house she'd found all those years ago, in her time of need one Christmas Eve.

'I'm so glad we met again,' she said.

'Me too.'

'I never imagined when we did that we would end up here.'

'In a rose garden?' he asked jokily.

'Hiding in a rose garden because I called out your mother. Oh, my God, she's a duchess... I called out a *duchess*!'

'She needed to hear it. We've all tiptoed around her for so long. No one ever challenges her. I mean, look at what we're doing. Creating a fake relationship just so I don't have to listen to her go on and on. Maybe I should have just told her straight, so that I didn't need to drag you into my mess and make you feel this way.'

He reached up with his hand and wiped away the wetness from her cheek. She hadn't even noticed that she'd been crying.

'I needed you too. Don't forget *my* mother in all this.'

'Do you think this means we need to be firmer with our families? Tell them to butt out, because we'll live our lives our way?'

'Maybe we should...' She tried to imagine saying that to her mum. The look that would appear on her face.

They sat in silence for a moment, contemplating.

'But that would mean ending this,' he said. 'I'm not sure I'm ready to do that.'

She smiled. 'Just go back to being colleagues? Friends? I don't want that, either. Yet,' she added, feeling it was sensible to say that.

'Yet.' He nodded, agreeing. 'So, we continue?'

'We do. As agreed.'

'But the second my mother gets on the plane we go back to our own lives.'

She nodded, not trusting herself to speak as she imagined that moment. What would she do if her feelings for him continued to escalate? Would she walk away? Or would she say something?

Her gaze dropped to his mouth once more. Tempting her. The problem was, she knew how great kissing was with him. And he was so close. Right there. And they had privacy here... No one would know except them. And even if someone did see, they'd just think Anthony was consoling her. That they were having a moment.

She so very badly wanted to press her lips to his once

again. To breathe into him. To lay her hand upon his chest once again and feel the rapid beating of his heart, the heat of his skin, the feel of his chest muscles beneath her touch. To feel him breathe into her as they kissed, the tickle of his beard against her skin. The taste of him...

She leaned in a little closer, daring herself to try.

Maybe if he felt the same way as her he would kiss her back, and then she would know that this thing between them went beyond their ruse. That what she'd been feeling was real because he felt it too.

All they had to do was be brave and breach that gap between them. Move from the pretend to the real...

'Found you!' said a voice.

Zoey's voice.

Julia jumped back, blushing madly, heart pounding, unsure if she could see regret in his eyes or embarrassment that she'd been about to kiss him.

Oh, God! Did I read this all wrong? Is he embarrassed for me?

'I've looked all over for you both. Are you all right?'

Julia stood up, blushing again, as if they'd been caught doing something they shouldn't. 'Zoey! Yes, I'm fine. I'm so sorry about earlier...making a scene.'

Anthony's sister waved away her apology. 'Mother had it coming. Believe me. Always acting like she's the only person in the world ever to be a mother.' She smiled, then took a step closer towards her, reaching for her hands. Holding them. 'I'm so sorry to hear about your son. Such a horrible thing for you to have gone through. If you need to talk—ever—about him, or my brother, or my mother...' She laughed. 'You call me. Any time—you hear?'

'Thank you.'

'Now, come on. We can't serve the main course until you

two come back, and the chef is worried the monkfish will dry out.'

'Well, we can't have that!' Julia laughed.

'And don't worry about Mother. I've had a word with her and she won't give you a moment's more trouble. In fact, I've persuaded her not only to start on the coffee early, but also to give you an apology.'

'Oh, there's no need…'

'There's *every* need.'

As they followed Zoey back towards the house Julia risked a glance at Anthony and saw he looked quite disturbed. Confused? Surprised?

The idea that she'd been about to kiss him had clearly appalled him!

CHAPTER THIRTEEN

'You don't have to walk me to my door,' Julia said later, as he dropped her back off at her flat.

'I don't mind.'

'No, honestly! It's fine.'

Julia had appeared to be quite flustered for the rest of the evening after her set-to with his mother. When they'd gone back inside the house she'd barely spoken a word to him, engaging with the other guests for most of the night. Actually, for that he'd been grateful—because there'd been a moment in the rose garden when he'd been sorely tempted to kiss her.

Not to convince anyone they were in a relationship. Just to kiss her. Because he'd wanted to. Because the urge to do so had built so strongly and so overpoweringly that he'd thought he was going mad.

They'd certainly had a moment—that was for sure. It had been nice to sit outside with her on that bench, surrounded by the scent of roses. Just talking. Just them. No pretence. Just being who they were.

There'd been a moment when she'd laid her head upon his shoulder and he'd wanted to lay his head against hers. To just be with her. To maybe reach up and stroke her face. But then she'd turned and looked up at him with such a look in her eyes... It had gone straight to his heart and something had bloomed within him. A madness. An insanity. A desire to kiss her because he wanted to, because he desired to, because he *needed* to.

He'd actually begun to lean in, because he'd thought that she'd been about to do the same thing, too. But that was crazy. Because Julia knew the parameters of this illusion, and the rules were keeping them both safe. He couldn't break them! He shouldn't step over that line.

How would she have reacted if he had? They worked together, and her job was very important to her. Her work relationship with her colleagues was incredibly important too. Was he willing to ruin that for her by overstepping the mark? She'd have said their safe word, and he'd have stopped, and then he'd have felt guilty and...

He had to get a grip on these feelings he was having for her. His future was in a direction that would require too much from her if he involved her in it. Assuming she wanted to be in it... Becoming a duchess was more than just using a title. She'd become a part of his official family history. And, despite him trying to put off his mother's wishes, she was right. He *did* need to produce an heir at some point. And Anthony did not want to put Julia through something that he knew would terrify her.

'Thank you for a lovely evening. See you at work, yes?' she asked now.

'See you tomorrow.'

He leaned in, as usual, to drop a polite, friendly, innocent kiss upon her cheek.

She smiled briefly, but it was an embarrassed smile, and she got out of the car quickly, opening her door and closing it again in seconds.

He felt a bloom of guilt wash over him. She was embarrassed for him. Embarrassed by what he'd done...trying to go in for that kiss. She had noticed. And she didn't know how to tell him to back off without hurting his feelings, no doubt.

Had he ruined this?

Had he ruined their wonderful friendship?

Anthony was furious with himself as he drove away from her place. Fuming, in fact. He'd been such a fool. Such a ridiculous romantic to let his feelings run away with him.

He'd thought this plan was perfect, but he'd never actually expected any feelings to come along with it. The connection that they would build. And now, rather stupidly, he'd started to believe that maybe this thing he had with Julia could lead to a happy-ever-after, perhaps?

Of course not. This is real life, and real life doesn't work that way.

'Thank you for meeting with me.'

Cecily Fitzpatrick, the Dowager Duchess of Weston, Anthony's mother, sat opposite Julia in the hospital cafeteria, nursing a large cappuccino as Julia sat down for her meeting with her.

Julia held her own large mug of tea, feeling nervous. She still felt awkward about her verbal bout with the Dowager, even if she had felt, at the time, that it was justified.

'No problem at all,' she said.

'How long do you have for your break?'

'Twenty minutes.'

'Right. Well, I'd best get to it, then. First of all, I wish to apologise for my remarks at Zoey's birthday dinner. One often forgets one should not take people at face value. I had no idea of your past, *your son*, and I am upset that I may have caused you distress. That was not my intention. Maybe I let the wine go to my head, making me…presumptuous.'

'You couldn't have known.'

'No, but still… I'm nervous about going to Australia and leaving Anthony alone. It troubles me. I've been trying to ensure that I leave him with someone, so that I can go without guilt. As mothers, you and I should have stood united. I'm afraid that the concern I have for my son's well-being sometimes means that I overstep and say things I should not.'

'You're a mama bear,' Julia said with a smile. 'I understand. You love him and care for him and you want to advocate for him. I remember how I felt that first day I brought my son home from the hospital. I wanted to protect him from everything. Sitting with him in that taxi, in his car seat, I was absolutely terrified and amazed at how all the other drivers drove so badly when I had my precious son in the car. And after that I spent every day just…trying to protect him from everything.'

'May I ask how…?' Cecily Fitzpatrick looked uncomfortable.

'How he died? It was SIDS. Sudden Infant Death Syndrome. I put him down at his usual bedtime, and when I woke in the morning he was gone.'

Cecily looked down and then reached for Julia's hand. 'I'm so sorry,' she said, with such feeling and empathy it brought Julia to tears. 'I can't imagine for one moment… If that had happened to Anthony or Zoey…'

The older woman blinked and wiped at her eyes, and Julia could see just how much her children meant to her.

'I don't worry so much about Zoey. She's happy. Settled. But Anthony… Well, you never stop worrying, do you? I wasn't sure that Yael was right for him in the beginning, but then he showed me how much he loved her, and how much she loved him. What she had to go through…what they *both* had to go through…broke my heart.'

'It must have been difficult.'

'It was. I did what I could, but I was helpless in the face of cancer. All I could do was hope the doctors could make it right.' She paused. 'Yael fought. She fought hard. I was so proud of her. She told me once that she wished they could have had a child before the cancer came to steal that chance away. She was upset for Anthony, you see? He really wanted children. But it never happened.' Cecily took a sip of her coffee. 'When she died, he was bereft. I thought I might lose him, too. He cut himself off from everyone...would disappear for weeks at a time. Sometimes I thought that he might do something... Well, you know.'

Julia nodded.

'But eventually he came back, and then I just wanted him to be happy. I hated seeing him alone...knowing how much being with someone would bring him happiness. And now...? Finally I can go and visit my sister without worrying about him. I can see how much he loves you. How much he cares for you. I can go, knowing that he won't be alone.'

Julia blushed and cast her head down, feeling ashamed of the lie that had been concocted for this woman who had been through so much. To worry about her son like that must have been awful. Yet this ruse was giving her peace of mind, so Julia wasn't sure exactly *how* to feel. Good or bad?

They must have been truly convincing if Cecily thought that her son loved her. But Julia knew differently. He'd been embarrassed that night in the rose garden, when she'd leaned in for a kiss. Thank goodness they'd been disturbed!

'He'll be okay. I've got him. I'll look after him for you,' she said, wanting to ensure that the Duchess, as a fellow mother, would feel some peace of mind.

She could give her that for now. Even though by the time Cecily arrived back home she would have learned that Julia had broken that promise, having split up with her son whilst she was away. What would the Dowager think of her then?

Cecily beamed, eyes gleaming. 'I know you will.' She patted Julia's hand and let out a big sigh. 'I'm glad we could have this talk. Mother to mother.'

'Yes. Me too.'

* * *

Anthony loved being in Theatre. Despite the intensity of the situation, and the laser focus of concentration that was needed, it was the place in which he felt most at home. There was something reassuring about it. The sterility, the orderliness, the beep and rhythm of the machines. The bright lights shining upon the stage that was the patient, immobilised and anaesthetised on a bed. And as for the surgery itself... From the most complicated reconstruction to the simplest fracture, he loved every procedure. They all allowed him to retreat within himself and switch off his thoughts about the world. To focus on the job in hand.

He had a full list today, and he was glad of it. Glad of the chance to not be on the ward, where Julia would be. Glad to be free of the turmoil of his mind with regard to her. Glad of the chance to hide for a little bit without having to answer questions.

His first patient of the day was a hip replacement. Trevor Godwin, sixty-nine years of age, had always been a runner, but he had experienced pain in his left side for so long now he hadn't run for months and months, and it was making him miserable.

Anthony understood the agony of not being allowed to do the thing you wanted to do. He couldn't imagine someone telling him he couldn't operate any more. Or could never kiss Julia again.

No. Must stop thinking about her like that. We're just pretending and that will be over soon.

'Okay, everyone. Let's change a life,' he said, holding out his hand for a scalpel from his Theatre nurse, Liv.

They'd offered Trevor the option to have a spinal block and be awake during the surgery, but Trevor had requested a general anaesthetic.

Anthony made a minimal incision and then made his way

down to the hip joint, to expose the full ball joint and socket. Trevor's hip was definitely in a bad way. The damage caused by advanced osteoarthritis could visibly be seen, and Anthony was glad he'd decided to perform a total hip replacement today.

'Look at that...' Liv said.

'Amazed he could still walk,' Anthony agreed as he began to remove the femoral head.

Some of the other specialists called this kind of work carpentry. Joints. Sockets. Screws. Hammers. Some surgeons looked down on orthopaedics. But where would anyone be without a working skeleton to support the body? Without bones, people would be nothing more than gelatinous bags of skin on the floor. Anthony knew how important his work was, and how much the surgeries he performed improved lives.

'Let's prepare the bone for the insertion of the artificial hip.'

He began to remove part of the bone, shaping the interior of the femur to fit exactly the stem of the hip replacement. Once that was done, he prepared the socket in the pelvis. With the stem inserted into the thigh bone, and sealed into place with a specialised cement, the ball joint was placed on the end and fixed into the socket.

'Looks great,' Liv observed, as Anthony checked the movement of the leg, this way and that.

'Should get him back on the trails soon enough, don't you think?'

'Definitely.'

'Okay, let's close up. Pete? Can you phone through to Recovery to let them know we'll be bringing Trevor down soon? And let the ward know that I can do my next patient at about ten o clock?'

Pete was one of the Theatre technicians. 'Sure thing,' he

said, and picked up the phone as Anthony began to staple the small incisions that he'd made.

Once he was done, he pulled off his gloves and gown and reflected on a good couple of hours' worth of work.

'There are some blood and urine results waiting for you on Mrs Tucker,' Pete said, popping his head into the scrub room.

Mrs Tucker had been unknowingly suffering from a UTI when she'd come into hospital for her surgery. Thankfully it had been picked up on admission, and she'd been given some specific antibiotics to deal with the situation. No one wanted to operate when a patient's system was already stressed from fighting an infection.

'Thanks, Pete. I'm going to grab a quick bite to eat and then we'll go again.'

'Yes, boss.'

Once he'd scrubbed out, Anthony headed off to check on the blood results, expecting to use the computer to do so.

Julia was waiting by the computer terminal. He paused when he saw her, and knew she saw him pause.

She coloured and looked away as he approached.

'Morning.'

'Good morning,' she said, looking up at him and smiling. 'How are you?'

'Yeah, I'm good. Just checking on some results. You?'

'I had to bring down some notes for Dr Howard. I'm just heading back to the ward now. You're in surgery all day?'

'Yes,' he said.

'Great. I met up with your mum the other day. We had a chat.'

That was a surprise. His mother hadn't mentioned anything.

'Oh? Everything okay?'

Julia smiled. 'Yes. We talked about Marcus and then

about you. About motherly worry about our sons, no matter their age.'

Well, she didn't look upset, so that was good.

'In fact, I think she saw me properly for the first time. Said she was happy to go to Australia now that she could see that you were settled with someone you...' She paused, looking uncertain.

'That I what?'

'That you love. She said that she could tell how much you loved me by the way you were looking at me.'

Was she trying to work out how badly the ruse had gone? he wondered. How far off the rails he'd gone with his feelings? Well, he would do his best to reassure her that he was bringing himself back into line.

'So our ruse is working well, then?'

She nodded quickly. Beamed a smile that went as quickly as it arrived. 'Yes.'

'Great! Well, I've got to...er...get on. I won't keep you. See you later,' he said, bending down to tap his details into the computer and access the results he needed for his next patient, dismissing her with the action.

He became aware of her hurried steps as she walked away from the station. He was groaning inwardly at how stupid he'd been to believe that she was feeling something for him. Clearly, she was not. Hopefully he had somewhat reassured her, now, that he would not embarrass them again by going in for an unwarranted, unwanted kiss.

He looked up to watch her go...felt a pang in his heart that somehow he'd screwed this up, too. He didn't want to ruin their connection. It was special between Julia and him. He'd brought her son into the world. They'd shared that magical Christmas Eve. She'd given Yael the best gift of her life. One that even he could not have given her. And for that he would be eternally grateful. He would hate himself if he screwed up their friendship.

'Julia?' he called out, before realising he was actually going to.

She turned around, a query in her gaze. 'Yes?'

He wanted to ask to meet her for coffee. He wanted to ask if he could take her out to dinner. He wanted to ask if he could dance with her, kiss her, paddle in more water with her—all of those things. But he didn't want to ruin things with her.

'Do we…er…need to go back to Paulie's soon? Do any more work on the float?' He knew there were a few little bits of construction that needed finishing. Tiny things, that clearly wouldn't need more than one of them—but, hey, no harm in asking, right? Because this wasn't for *them*…it was for the float.

'Erm… I think it's all finished.'

'Oh. Right. Okay, then.'

He smiled at her and watched her disappear through the double doors at the end of the corridor. Then cursed silently as he punched in his password to bring up the urinalysis and blood results. The infection had been cleared and Mrs Tucker was ready for the arthroscopic surgery on her knee.

He double-checked the details, just in case. He didn't want his frustration to result in any silly mistakes.

A doctor slumped into a chair next to him. Dr Howard—a young registrar with a bit of a reputation for dating the nurses.

'Hey, do you know her?' he asked.

'Who?' Anthony was distracted.

'That nurse you were talking to. Joanne? Julianne?'

'Julia.' He was annoyed that Dr Howard couldn't even get her name right. 'Yes. Why?'

'She's cute… Know if she's single?'

And even though he knew he ought to give Julia the opportunity to make her own mind up about people, the opportunity to find a real relationship, he couldn't help but steer her away from this guy.

'No, she's involved with someone.'

Technically, he reasoned, it was true.

'Oh. Shame. She's hot.'

Anthony gave him a withering stare.

CHAPTER FOURTEEN

I'M DOING IT AGAIN, Julia thought. I'm falling in love with an unavailable man.

Her own father had never been emotionally available. Jake, Marcus's father, had not been available at all, and had left her to deal with their child's death alone. And now she could feel herself pining for a guy who was in a fake relationship with her and who would dump her the moment his mother boarded an aeroplane.

He would do it nicely. It wouldn't be like the break-up with Jake. Knowing Anthony, he would be kind, gracious... maybe buy her some flowers, drop a kiss onto her cheek and wish her the best. But then it would all be over and she would have to watch him walk away.

They would just be friends after that. Because he wasn't ready. He'd told her that right at the beginning.

Just like I told him the same thing.

But her feelings had changed the more she'd got to know him. The more she'd got to experience his life. The more he'd shared hers. Her mother adored him, her friends loved him and so did she.

Was she ready to deal with yet another broken heart? Or should she try to be brave enough to tell him that her feelings had changed?

How can I? If he is where I think he is, he's going to turn me down—and then work will be awkward.

Look at how their conversation had gone when she'd repeated to him his mother's words about the way Anthony looked at her. Told him that Cecily had said she could tell he loved her. What had he answered with?

'So the ruse is working, then?'

Like a dagger to her heart.

More than anything, she didn't want that feeling. She wanted to keep Anthony's friendship, the connection they had. So maybe, instead of being awkward with him and uncomfortable since that near-kiss, she ought to be friendly and return to the parameters that they had set earlier, to keep each other safe?

Unable to find him on the ward, she texted him, asking for a minute to talk to him. When he arrived, still in his scrubs, tired from a long day in surgery, she hurried to his side with a beaming smile.

'Can I talk to you about Mrs Tucker, Mr Fitzpatrick?' she asked, in a tone that should imply to anyone listening that their chat was work-related.

'Is there a problem?'

She guided him over to one side of the room. 'Mrs Tucker is absolutely fine. I just wanted to talk to you.'

'Oh. Okay.'

'You asked about working on the float?'

'Mm-hmm.' He smiled at a nurse who passed by, holding refills for the glove boxes at the nurses' station.

'We could go out and do something else, if you wanted?'

'Like what?'

She shrugged. 'I don't know... But until your mother goes away I think we ought to be seen still doing things that suggest we're in a relationship. What about going for coffee? Or maybe dinner? Somewhere we might be seen by your family or mine?'

He smiled and nodded. 'Sure. When?'

'Your mother leaves in a couple of days…which means we don't have much time left together. Maybe we could go out and celebrate a…a job well done?'

'Well, actually, my second cousin Tobias is having a dinner dance thing at his place the night before my mother leaves. We could attend that?'

It sounded perfect. One last hurrah with him that she could treasure for ever. Because she didn't want to end things on bad terms. She wanted to remember this time fondly.

'Do I have to get another dress?'

'Probably. But I can reimburse you for any expenses.'

She smiled. 'No need. This one's on me.' She looked about them…saw the nurse with the gloves looking at them. 'I'll get to that right away, Mr Fitzpatrick. Thank you,' she said loudly as she walked away from him, nodding at the nurse with a smile as she passed.

She felt better.

She'd made things right.

Even if it was going to break her heart.

He texted her with more details later, and she sent him pictures of possible dresses and asked which he thought might suit her best.

Anthony thought she would look beautiful in any of them, but refrained from saying so, instead stating they were all lovely. She sent back a reply saying that she would surprise him, then.

The fact that her awkwardness with him had gone gladdened him immensely. He'd not been able to bear the disruption between them, and because of that he knew he had to harden his heart immediately. He'd let his emotions run away with him. Had let his hopes grow when reality was showing him that he needed to rein them in.

And so, when the night arrived for Tobias's dinner dance,

he put back up all the walls that had surrounded him since Yael's passing, knowing that he needed to do so in order to cope with the moment when the illusion ended and he and Julia would shake hands and part as friends.

He stood on her doorstep, waiting for her to answer the door, taking deep breaths, hardening his heart. He was ready for the reveal, determined to be polite, to compliment her and say she looked beautiful, but to do so in a way that was detached. Polite. Non-committal.

He heard her footsteps and got a flashback to the dress she'd worn at his mother's charity ball. That blush-pink number that she'd looked so stunning in. No dress was going to be better than that, surely?

But when she opened the door and revealed herself wearing a body-hugging dark purple silk number, which hugged her in all the right places, he had to fight to stop his jaw from hitting the ground.

'Wow! You look…amazing.'

'Is it all right?' she asked, turning so that he could view it from all angles.

He loved the way the silk curved over her backside… how most of her back was exposed, revealing an expanse of tempting flesh…how her legs seemed to go on for days through the split that began at mid-thigh. He saw the glint of an ankle bracelet…her painted toes peeking from matching high heeled shoes. The urge to reach out, to touch, to glide his fingers up the length of her legs, trace her spine, her neck, her lips, was just *overwhelming*.

Instead he stepped back, creating more space between them, and produced the politest smile he could, nodding. 'It's perfect.'

'Great. I wasn't sure.'

He opened the car door for her. No chauffeur tonight. He made himself look away as she settled into the seat and then swung those endless legs inside the vehicle, smoothing her skirt and placing her small clutch bag on her lap. Once she was in, he closed the door and walked round to his own side, giving himself a pep talk, telling himself he could do this. It was just Julia. His friend, his colleague.

But his brain wanted to tell him so many other things. She wasn't '*just* Julia'. She was the woman he had come to care for greatly. The woman he would go to the ends of the earth to protect. The woman who had brought happiness back into his life. Wonder. Joy. The ability to laugh again and not feel guilty. The woman he thought about constantly. The woman he knew Yael would have loved, too.

The woman he *desired*.

But he could not have her. She had made that plain. She had told him she wasn't ready for a relationship. Had looked embarrassed when he'd leaned in for that kiss—had been so uncomfortable with him that they had avoided each other for a little while and he'd hated that.

As he drove towards Tobias's house he tried to act relaxed. Nonchalant. But his body was thrilled by the proximity of her. By her perfume in the small, intimate space of the car. In his peripheral vision his gaze caught glimpses of diamante in the dress he hadn't noticed before, glittering in the moonlight. Caught the way the dress shaped her delicious curves. A hint of cleavage. His physical attraction to her was threatening to burst forth from behind walls that already had huge cracks in them.

'One last hurrah,' she said.

'Mm...' he said, not trusting himself to speak yet.

Part of him wanted this night to go on for ever. For it never to end. But he knew that time would go by in an instant. At some point he would drive her home and say goodbye and that would be the end of their ruse. Their illusion. He would take his mother to the airport tomorrow and wave her off, knowing he was alone even if his mother thought differently. He would wait for her return in a couple of months before letting her know that he and Julia had not worked out.

And somehow he would have to see her at work every day and deal with that.

'I've had a great time doing this—just so you know,' she said. 'It's actually been fun. Almost a life-swap. Like you see on those shows on television.'

He smiled and glanced at her briefly, torturing himself with her beauty.

'I guess I just want to say thank you, too,' she went on. 'It's been nice not having people going on at me about finding someone to be with.'

'Me too.'

It had been nice. But what had been nicer were the conversations he'd had with people who had met Julia. Zoey. His mother. His friends. All of them telling him how they made such a great couple. How they were so perfectly suited.

Soul mates.

In the beginning, he'd simply smiled and nodded, pleased that they had managed to convince entire swathes of people that they were in a real relationship, but now that he was deeper into it he hated that he couldn't have it for real.

What would they all say when he declared it was over? Would he have to deal with their pity? Their sympathy? Their disbelief?

Maybe I should go away for a bit? Go travelling, or something, to avoid all that?

'It's going to be strange when it's over,' she mused.

'It is,' he replied. 'I was just thinking that I might go away for a bit afterwards. You know...to avoid the pity party when people find out that we're not together any more.'

'Great idea. I might do the same thing.'

'Maybe stagger our vacations, though. Make sure people don't think we're together.'

'Where would you go?'

He shrugged. 'Not sure. Lake Garda? Cannes?'

'Wow. Okay... I was thinking about Scotland.'

'You like Scotland?'

'I've never been. But there are so many places that look interesting and beautiful up there. I've always wanted to go.'

He'd been to Scotland and she was right. There was the beauty of Loch Lomond. The historical city of Edinburgh. The amazing Isle of Skye. Glencoe. Iona. Orkney. He could imagine taking her to all those places. Watching her eyes brighten with delight as she visited them. Holding her hand as they walked. Maybe paddling with her in Loch Ness...

'I can recommend a few places for you,' he said.

'Great.'

They were quiet as he pulled to a stop outside Tobias's place. He walked around the car to open her door and held out his hand, gazing at her with adoration as she alighted from the vehicle and adjusted her dress.

He felt so lucky that she had come into his life—even if it had been just for such a short while. He would remember his time with her fondly. Never forget.

He could hear music playing as they neared the house. They were presented with drinks as they entered. He saw faces he knew, and faces he didn't, and they were soon met by members of his family. He introduced Julia to those who had never met her before, and said hello to those who had.

Tobias clapped him on the back and gave him a huge hug, before turning to Julia, taking her hand and kissing the back of it. 'Nice to meet you at last, Julia. I've heard all about you!' he said.

'Nice to meet you, too. You have a beautiful home.'

'This old thing? Needs redecorating, but it'll do.'

He was being self-deprecating. Anthony knew Tobias had taken on this old house about eight years ago, renovating and restoring it to its former grandeur. He was an architect, and it had become a passion project. Anthony knew how much work and investment had gone into it, despite the way Tobias was playing it down.

'Well, I think it's lovely,' said Julia.

'And so are you. Do you mind if I have this dance?'

Tobias held out his hand towards Julia. She glanced at Anthony before turning back to his cousin.

'Of course.'

Anthony didn't examine his feelings too closely as he watched Julia being led onto the dance floor by Tobias. He felt a little bit of everything. Envy. Loss. Reluctance. But most of all he found himself sneaking the opportunity to just look at her whilst she moved across the floor in Tobias's arms.

This is what it will be like, he thought. *When she finds someone else.*

She was smiling at his cousin. Laughing at something Tobias was saying. Tobias was a funny guy, quite the charmer, and he had always been successful with the ladies before settling down with his sweetheart. Anthony wondered where Tobias's wife was. What she thought of her husband dancing with Julia.

Probably nothing at all. I'm just feeling jealous.

Julia's eyes gleamed, her smile was broad, and the way that dress skimmed her body, accentuating all those sumptuous curves and softness, made his heart pound.

But she was not to be his.

And no doubt she would be glad when this was over.

He accepted another drink from a passing member of staff.

When the music finished, Tobias escorted Julia back to him. 'Your turn, I think.'

'Thank you. I was wondering when I'd get to dance with the lady *I* brought to the party.'

Tobias mouthed a word at him. *Stunning.* Then slipped away to attend to his other guests.

Julia turned to look at Anthony. 'He's quite a character.'

'Mm… He is.'

'Wicked sense of humour!'

'Yes, he has. I hope he wasn't too rude?'

'Far from it.'

'Would you like a drink?'

She looked up at him. 'No, I want to dance. I want us to dance the night away. Make it memorable, seeing as this is our last time.'

Did she look sad?

No. It was his own wishful thinking. It had to be. And she was right. This would be their last night together. There was no reason for them to spend their leisure hours with each other ever again.

He took her hand and led her back to the dance floor as a slow and dreamy number began to play. They'd begun this at a dance. It seemed only fitting that it should end this way, too.

He tried to keep his thoughts and his feelings straight as he pulled her close, but the way she was looking into his eyes as they began to move was making that extremely difficult.

'Are you looking forward to your mother going away?' she asked.

'I'm happy that she's going to get away for a bit. She hasn't had a break in years—so, yes, it will be good for her.'

'What are you going to do whilst she's away?'

'I haven't really thought about it. Maybe just chill. Read.' He met her gaze. 'When are you going to tell your family that we've split up?'

She looked away, eyeing the other couples on the dance floor. 'I don't know. Maybe in a few weeks?'

He nodded. 'Will they be okay with it?'

'They'll be disappointed... But hopefully they'll be pleased that I've dipped my toes back into the dating waters.'

He smiled, remembering those times she'd taken him paddling. The water fountain. The river. The delight it had given her.

'You've made me dip my toes into water, too.'

She smiled shyly back at him. 'We had fun, didn't we?'

'We did.'

'We made a pretty convincing couple.'

He sighed. 'Yes.'

'Did you ever...?' She stopped and blushed.

'What?'

'Did you ever think what it might be like for real?'

His heart almost leapt from his chest. Could she feel it pounding through his jacket? Could she see his pulse thrumming in his throat? Feel the soaring of his temperature?

The urge to tell her the truth overwhelmed him. This way he could actually explain how he'd been feeling! 'Of course I thought about it!'

But then his throat closed up as her eyes widened and he hurried to say more, looking away from her. It was the only way he could gather. Regroup.

'What we were doing lent itself to those kinds of thoughts,' he said. 'But... I never took it seriously,' he lied.

She nodded. 'No, nor me,' she said quietly.

He continued to lead her around the dance floor, unable to look her in the eyes. If this relationship had been real, they would never have made it away from her flat once he'd seen her in that dress. He'd have taken her hand and raised it above her head. Made her give him a turn. And then he would have begun kissing her. And they'd have gone back inside. And then he would have helped her remove it...

I can't keep thinking like this!

But he couldn't stop the thoughts. They bombarded him.

If they'd been in a real relationship he would have looked at the split in her dress in the car and he would have placed a hand upon her knee as he drove, unable to not touch her. He would not have let Tobias dance with her. He would have held on to her and maybe found an empty room somewhere, where he would have kissed her like she'd never been kissed before. Perhaps he would have been dancing with her like he was dancing with her now, but he would be looking deep into her eyes and telling her silently of all the things he wanted to do with her when he got her home.

But most of all he would have been enjoying his time with her guilt-free. He wouldn't be hiding his real feelings from her. She would know them. He would be able to tell her how much she meant to him. Sit with her on her couch and watch trashy television. Make her tea. Treat her like a queen. Wake up with her every morning and thank the heavens that his life was so blessed after he'd begun to believe that it could never be blessed again.

The bombardment of his feelings left him feeling dizzy.

'Excuse me a moment,' he said, letting her go and walking off the dance floor to find a bathroom.

He needed to splash some water on his face and regain some sort of bloody control.

Julia felt bewildered when Anthony suddenly left her in the middle of the dance floor. Had she said something wrong? She didn't think so. All she'd done was agree with what he'd said, even though it had been painful to lie.

Of course she'd had thoughts about them being a couple for real.

But she'd never thought that in creating this ruse for others she would have to lie to *him*, too.

How had it got so complicated?

The sooner I'm out of this mess, the better!

Embarrassed, and hoping no one had noticed, she headed over to the side of the room, to hide amongst the assembled guests. But no sooner had she arrived than someone was touching her arm.

'Julia!'

She turned. Cecily Fitzpatrick. Anthony's mother.

'Cecily! How are you?'

'I'm fine. Is Anthony all right? I saw him leave you just now. He looked...ill, or something.'

Julia knew she couldn't muck up the plan now. Not when they were so close to the end. The whole point of this was so that his mother could fly away like a little bird and not worry about her son for two months whilst she enjoyed Adelaide with her sister.

'He was a little hot. I think he said he was going to splash some water on his face,' she said, hoping it sounded convincing.

'Yes, it is warm in here, isn't it? That dress you're wearing is divine!'

'Oh, this? Thank you.' She didn't want to say that she'd actually got it for a very reasonable price from a high street store. 'Are you excited for tomorrow?' she asked.

'Absolutely! I haven't seen Amelia for ages, and it will be nice to catch up with all my nieces and nephews over there. Do you know, my sister became a grandparent for the fourth time last month?'

'No, I hadn't heard that.'

'I can't wait to hold the little one. You don't mind me talking about babies?'

'Of course not! They're a joy.'

Cecily beamed. 'I knew you'd understand. And one day, I'm sure, you'll hold another one of your own. Maybe Anthony's! I know that he'll make a wonderful father.'

Julia believed her. 'I'm sure he will.'

'You know, when I get back you and I should meet up. Go out for dinner together, or something. Perhaps with Zoey. Just us girls.'

'That would be lovely,' she said, knowing it would never happen.

She would never be one of *'us girls'*. She wasn't now. It was all just pretend. It was as if she'd been in a dressing up box and was now playing a role. Anthony's girlfriend.

It would have been a nice romantic story for her and Anthony to have fallen in love for real, though. She could picture it so easily... And she loved everyone that she'd met in his world. They were not pretentious, and they all had Anthony's best interests at heart. They loved him.

And so do I.

'I'll ring you when I get back,' said his mother. 'Oh, there's Jasmine! I simply must go and talk to her about her interior designer... Excuse me.'

And then Cecily was gone. Like a force of nature. Cutting a swathe through the guests to arrive at the side of a middle-aged woman in a red dress.

Julia watched them embrace and drop air kisses either side of each other's cheeks.

'Sorry about that.'

She turned. Anthony was back, looking a lot more composed than earlier. Maybe he really had gone to splash water on his face.

'Everything all right?' she asked.

'Absolutely. I saw you talking to Mother.'

'She wants us to meet up when she gets back from Australia.'

'Oh. You didn't say anything?'

'Of course not!'

'Good. The quicker this is all over, the better.'

CHAPTER FIFTEEN

'THE QUICKER THIS is all over, the better.'

Anthony had driven her home and now he sat in the driver's seat, not really looking at her. He'd been strange all evening, and she wondered if someone had said something to him that had upset him.

'Are you all right?' she asked.

'I'm fine.'

'You've been weird all night.'

'Have I?'

'Yes, you have. I thought tonight would be…joyful. That we'd both be thrilled with our success. But you don't seem to be.'

'The quicker this is over, the better.'

She was trying her best not to let his words rend her heart in two, but it was difficult.

Anthony bit his lip before speaking. 'I am thrilled. Of course I am. And I'm very grateful that you've done all that for me.'

'But…?'

He looked as if he was going to say something else. She hoped that he would. That he would say something along the lines of *I've made a mistake. I don't want this to be a lie. I want this thing between us to be real.*

But he didn't. Of course he didn't. That was just her allowing her romantic illusions to break through her logical reasoning. Things like that didn't happen to her. Julia Morris was not a woman who ever got a happy ending. She was doomed to live her life on the edge of disappointment, letdowns and broken hearts.

This situation was no different. No matter how much she wanted it to be otherwise.

'But nothing,' he said. 'I'm not sure what you want me to say.'

'I want you to say…' she began, her voice raised. But then she was stopping herself. Because if she begged him to tell her that he wanted this to be real and he laughed at her, or said something that broke her heart for real…

Julia didn't need to hear him actually *say* it. Tell her that they couldn't be anything more than friends. Because that would truly break her heart. So it was easier not to push for it.

'I want you to say that we've had a good time and that it was fun. And for you to sound like you mean it. Not be in this…this weird mood you're in. It can't end with this mood. I know you want all this to be over now, but could you at least sound like you had a good time?'

Anthony looked down for a moment, then turned in his seat to look at her, his eyes gleaming in the dark shadows of the car's interior. 'I've had an amazing time with you. Like I could never have imagined. It's been the most fun I've had in years,' he said, reaching for her hand and squeezing it.

And…?

'That's it?' she demanded.

She yearned for him to say more, but he remained quiet. Just sat there, holding her hand. And even though she longed to stay like that for ever, she knew she had to end this. He was never going to say what she truly wanted him to say, and she was too scared to say it herself. So instead she just raised his hand to her lips, kissed the back of it and whispered goodbye, alighting from the car and walking to her door without looking back. Because she knew that if she did it would break her heart.

Unlocking the door, she slipped inside and closed it behind her, tears stinging her eyes as she heard his car drive away. The realisation that it was all over was just too much for her damaged and fragile heart to handle.

Anthony stayed at the airport long enough to watch his mother's flight take off. He stood there for a long while, watching the aeroplane disappear into the distance, hearing his mother's last words repeated over and over again in his mind.

'You look after Julia, do you hear? She's everything.'

She was everything.

He hated it that his mother was right, but what could he do? He wasn't able to admit out loud that Julia had brought him more happiness in the last few weeks than he'd ever thought possible and it was now over. They had to go back to just being work colleagues. It didn't sit well with him at all.

All of last night he'd lain awake, his brain presenting him conflicting images and emotions. Tobias taking Julia's hand and leading her onto the dance floor. Dr Howard ogling Julia in the hospital and asking him if he knew if she was single. One day that would be real…her being with someone else.

It felt wrong.

But there were other, happier memories. Seeing her in that dress she'd worn for his mother's charity ball. Listening to her laugh as she painted wood for the float, a smear of paint across her cheek. Watching the delight on her face as she encouraged him to paddle with her in the river. The jacket potato stall in the square. Twirling around the dance floor with her in a waltz. Seeing the way she'd looked into his eyes. The way she'd looked at him as she'd laughed at his jokes. The way she'd held his hand and how that had made him feel.

Those practice kisses…

They'd been so convincing, his mother had questioned him on the way to the airport. She'd asked if their relationship was serious. If he could imagine himself popping the question to her one day.

He'd made non-committal noises. Changed the subject. But now he thought about those questions. Questions he'd never allowed himself to think about before.

Because he *could* imagine it. He'd dreamed about her saying yes to him. And now he'd left her in such a way she could say yes to someone else—because he was too damned afraid of her saying no to him.

And if she says no…? Yes, it'll hurt like hell. And we'll have to find a way to carry on working together so that it isn't awkward. I could check the rota. Stay more in Theatre. Get my registrars to do the rounds and report back.

But he knew he would never do that. That wasn't the kind of doctor he was. He was hands on. He was involved. He liked to reassure patients himself, if he was the one doing their surgery, and he liked to check on them afterwards. Answer their questions as only their surgeon could.

He and Julia were both adults. They would find a way to put it all behind them for the sake of their jobs.

But what if she didn't say no…?

If those kisses were real…?

If she wanted more but was also afraid to say it…?

Hadn't she asked him often enough? Hadn't she given him ample opportunity to say something? Perhaps tell the truth?

Anthony looked up at the sky, at the clouds his mother's plane had disappeared into. Had he missed all the clues? Had he been so afraid of rejection he'd missed the subtle signs she'd been giving him? Imagine if he had… What if he didn't have to continue the ruse with his mother because he and Julia really were going out with each another?

Then those kisses would be *real*!

He glanced at his watch. He knew where she would be. It was the float parade that afternoon. She was going to watch it. Cheer her friends on. Rattle a bucket.

He could meet her there!

Or am I being totally crazy?

Julia so wanted to enjoy the float parade. So she pushed her heartbreak to one side and forced a smile onto her face as the floats passed, trying her damnedest not to think about all those hours spent with Anthony, helping make the float with Paulie, Yvette and Janine.

She could see their float coming. Janine was driving the truck and Paulie and some of the others were dressed up in superhero outfits. Yvette was dressed as a princess. She could see them waving at the crowds, as a band played pop music on a float nearby, blasting the sound from speakers.

The crowds were loving the parade, waving banners, holding balloons. Kids sat on the shoulders of their parents as they waved and licked ice creams. She imagined what it would have been like to stand here with Marcus. He would have loved this. At least she hoped so...

But as her friends' float got closer she could see another figure standing in the castle with them. Somebody dressed as a knight in full armour.

Whoever he is, he must be hot.

Odd, though, that none of her friends had mentioned there was going to be a knight on the float. Perhaps it wasn't anyone she knew?

But she waved anyway as the float grew closer, beaming a smile, showing her support and her joy to her friends, even though inside she felt so sad she'd almost not come.

I promised, though.

And she'd also had wanted to see the full effect of the castle after all those hours of work.

Janine waved at her from behind the wheel, then stopped the float in front of her.

What are you doing? Julia mouthed to her friend, not sure what was going on.

As she watched, Paulie and Yvette blew her kisses. And then the knight, in his armour, descended the steps at the back of the faux castle and got off the float.

Janine began driving again, waving goodbye, and Julia frowned in confusion. The knight was coming towards her, his armour actually clanking, a sword at his hip, sheathed in a scabbard.

What is this?

There was something familiar about him... but she couldn't think too hard about it because the knight was reaching behind his breastplate for something and when he removed his gauntleted hand, he held a piece of pink silk and proffered it to her.

All around her, the crowd was clapping and cheering. Julia took the kerchief, remembering where she'd seen in films knights offering their tokens to princesses before they went into battle.

And then the knight reached up to his helmet and removed it. And before she knew it she was looking at Anthony. It was *him*. It was *his* suit of armour that she'd recognised. The one that had been at his house.

'What are you doing?' she asked, laughing, so pleased to see him she'd forgotten all her woes. Their parting. Her heartbreak.

'My lady.' He gave a bow. 'Julia... As a man, I was not brave enough to ask for your hand. But as a knight of the realm...' he smiled as he patted his chest '...and with my heart protected by armour plating, I ask you for it now.'

'Anthony!'

Was this a joke? More of the role-playing they'd been doing?

'You are my heart. You have become my everything. I ask that you consider becoming my lady for life. Fear not saying no. I will survive it. But know ye that if you say yes, then I will spend every day of the rest of my life being proud that you are my lady and proclaiming our happiness to the world. What say you?'

Julia half gasped, half laughed at the incredulity of the moment. 'Are you asking me to be your girlfriend?'

'No. I'm asking you to be my *wife*.'

She needed someone to pinch her. Was this truly happening? Was this really Anthony? Being her knight in shining armour? This was crazy!

But it was also everything she'd ever wanted. For she could see a future with him. Had dreamed of a future with him. And she would accept his love, his ring, without a second of doubt.

She took his hand in hers. 'I accept.'

Around them, the assembled crowd went crazy as Anthony scooped her up and twirled her around before kissing her.

One kiss. Two. Three. She didn't want it to stop.

Real kisses. Not pretend. And she felt his love in every one of them.

Becoming his duchess would be far better than becoming his lady.

EPILOGUE

'I CAN'T BELIEVE it ended like that!' Julia cried, reaching for a tissue from the box and dabbing at her eyes as the final credits rolled on the movie she and Anthony had been watching at home.

'Are you crying because of the happy ending, or crying because of the baby?' Anthony asked, smiling at his wife where she sat on the couch, her feet on a footstool, because she'd learned that it helped with her swollen ankles towards the end of the day.

Julia was at full term and their baby would come any day now. They were both so excited, and they had no idea what they were having as they wanted it to be a surprise.

'I don't know! Both!' she said, hiccupping a laugh as she dabbed at her tears and rubbed her belly at the same time.

'Baby kicking?' he asked.

'No. I feel crampy.'

'Labour crampy?' he asked, sitting forward.

Technically, she was two days past her due date. She had an appointment in three days' time to see the midwife and have a sweep of her membranes done, if she wanted to.

She looked at him, suddenly nervous. 'Maybe? I don't know.'

He understood. He knew she was anxious about having this baby, and they'd waited a long time before deciding to try for a child. He'd wanted Julia to be ready. Not to feel forced into doing something that he knew terrified her. But they'd spoken to lots of doctors. Lots of specialists. And they'd had counselling. They'd been reassured, also, by buying lots of equipment. Video monitors. Oxygen monitors. They were both medically trained and they would do absolutely everything they could to avoid anything bad happening.

Julia had not wanted to live in fear.

'I nearly lost you because I was afraid,' she'd told him in those early days. *'And now look at how happy we are. If I can be brave enough to try again, imagine how happy we would be!'*

And they were. Extremely happy. Happier than any two people had a right to be.

They'd come clean to both their families. Told them about the ruse. Everyone thought it was a cool story, thankfully. Something to tell their children. And their grandchildren, one day.

Most people at work had not been surprised. And Rosaria hadn't even said anything mean. She'd just chuckled and said, with a big smile, *'I knew something was going on!'*

Julia got up and began walking off the cramp. He walked with her, holding her hand.

'How long did that one last?' he asked.

'Only about thirty seconds. Not long.'

'I guess we wait to see if you have another?'

'Yes.' She nodded, stopping, turning to look up into his eyes. 'I love you.'

'I love you, too. Both of you,' he said, laying a hand on her bump, feeling her skin tighten beneath his fingertips. 'Is that another? Already?'

She laughed. 'Yes!'

The contractions began to come thick and fast. They paced. They sat. They paced some more. And when her waters broke they phoned the hospital and made their way in.

It felt strange to be going into a hospital as patients and family, rather than as doctor and nurse, but the midwives there made them feel they were special, and they'd organised a private room for Julia to labour in.

She was monitored, briefly, to check her contractions and monitor the baby's heart, and they joked with each other about what the birth weight might be.

'About seven pounds?' Julia guessed.

'I'm thinking more like nine pounds,' said Anthony. 'I was a big baby.'

'You still are,' she joked—before another contraction hit and she had to breathe her way through it.

He held her hand. He coached her. Stroked her when she asked for it. Dabbed her forehead with a cold, wet flannel when she needed it. And before they knew it she was fully dilated.

'I'm scared,' she said, reaching for his hand.

He kissed her, pressed his forehead to hers and looked deep into her eyes. 'I know. But we can do this, you and I. We're in this together. And, actually, you're the bravest woman I've ever known.'

'But what if...?' She couldn't finish her sentence, and her eyes filled with tears.

He reached into his pocket, pulled out his phone and brought up the photo she'd shared with him of Marcus, smiling into the camera. 'He's going to look after us. He never left you. He's in there.' He gestured at her chest. 'In your heart and mine. And no matter what, he always will be.'

She nodded. It was what she needed to hear as she began to push.

Anthony watched the woman he loved and adored battle her way through the intense contractions, pushing hard, breathing heavily. The look of determination on her face never faltered. Never wavered.

She was a mother.
She had never stopped being a mother.
And now she was going to make them a family.

*****

*If you enjoyed this story,
check out these other great reads from
Louisa Heaton*

Finding a Family Next Door
Best Friend to Husband?
Resisting the Single Dad Surgeon
A Mistletoe Marriage Reunion

All available now!

A SINGLE DAD TO HEAL HIM

TRACI DOUGLASS

MILLS & BOON

For all the misfits.

For all those who are afraid to be
who they are meant to be.

For everyone scared to tell their truth.

I see you. I feel you. I support you. I love you.

Just as you are. <3

CHAPTER ONE

I CAN'T BELIEVE I'm back here again.

Dr. Devon Harrison's footsteps squeaked on the shiny linoleum floor as he walked down the corridor to Minneapolis Medical Center's emergency department, the heart of this busy teaching hospital. With each step, a sense of déjà vu coursed through him, bringing back memories of his time here as a resident, fresh out of the classroom and stupidly optimistic and trusting, ready to conquer the dreaded disease that was cancer, one tiny patient at a time.

He still wanted to cure as many kids as possible, but his ability to trust adults, especially when it came to himself, had shattered for good the year before and wasn't ever coming back. God, he still berated himself for being so naive. Why hadn't he seen the signs of betrayal, when looking back now they were so glaringly obvious? Well, he wouldn't make the same mistake again. He wouldn't trust his emotional instincts since they clearly didn't know what they were doing. Logic and reason and facts were his North Star in all things from here on out.

A set of automatic glass doors whooshed open in front of him, and he stepped into the controlled chaos of the ER. Nurses and techs bustled around, carrying equipment or tablets displaying digital charts, and orderlies wheeled patients around to their designated areas. The air vibrated with a constant low thrum of adrenaline—punctuated now and then with a pulse of urgency—tinged with the familiar scent of antiseptic. He'd been gone from this place for nearly a decade, completing his pediatric oncology fellowship in California where he'd moved with Tom—his now ex-husband—never imagining setting foot here again.

But life seemed to have a funny way of knocking you for a loop when you least expected it, at least it had in Dev's case. He stepped aside to allow a fast-moving gurney pushed by two paramedics to pass him, taking a moment to collect his thoughts. He'd been in town three weeks now since moving home while he waited on the final divorce papers and getting settled at his mother's house while he searched for a place of his own. His mother needed more help now since her MS was worsening and she was wheelchair bound, so it worked. Plus, staying busy helped distract him from the fact that other than his mother, he had no one now. Back in medical school he'd had a few close friends—well, one really close friend—but they'd lost touch after a falling-out before the wedding. A warning, really, about Tom that his friend had given him. A warning that Dev had been too besotted at the time to heed.

Boy, did he regret ignoring it now.

He wondered if Val was still around. Most of their class had scattered across the country after graduation, taking positions at different hospitals and medical centers or going into private practice, depending on their specialties. But the last he'd heard Val was still in Minneapolis. The last update Dev had gotten from his mother was after Val's sister's passing almost two years prior…

Dev honestly wasn't sure he wanted to see his old friend again. Not after everything that had happened. It would be beyond awkward, seeing the man who'd claimed Dev's fiancé had tried to sleep with him less than twenty-four hours before the wedding. Even now, Dev's gut tightened in response to that last fight with Val. He hadn't wanted to hear it, hadn't wanted to believe that the man he'd cast his usual caution aside for and gone all in on was not the person he'd thought he was. Back then, Dev had had too much time, too much emotion invested in the idealized future he'd planned with Tom to see the truth. So he'd gone through with the wedding and followed Tom to California, leaving Val and his accusations behind. He'd been wrong about Tom and Val had been right. Which Dev only interpreted as more proof that his own instincts and emotions were not to be trusted.

Better to keep to himself now. Safer that way.

Even if it was a bit lonely.

With a sigh, Dev stared at a large whiteboard on the wall behind the nurses' station, scanning the information there to find the room his consult was in, but with so many people running around and scribbling orders everywhere, in the end the most expedient route was to just ask someone. He approached the central hub, noticing a small group of scrubs-clad staff gathered there, laughing and obviously friendly with each other. The kind of social group Dev had always yearned for growing up, but had never really figured out the knack of being part of one himself. Crowds tended to make him self-conscious and nervous, so he'd invariably close in on himself, making him appear aloof and unfriendly. But honestly, he was just painfully shy. Years of working with patients, and children in particular, had helped ease that social anxiety a bit, thankfully, but he still wasn't great at meeting new people. Especially now that he was on alert for possible deception everywhere he looked.

As Dev got closer to the desk, several members of the group parted, revealing the man at the center of their orbit, his toned physique filling out a set of faded blue scrubs to perfection. His back was to Dev, so he couldn't see the man's face, but based on the tingling in his bloodstream, he didn't need to. It was the tawny hair and wide, confident stance that did it. He'd recognized those details anywhere.

Guess that answered his question.

Dammit. He did not need this today.

Dev stopped where he was and turned away fast, but not fast enough, apparently.

"Is that you, Dev?" Val said from behind him, a touch of the same astonishment in his voice that Dev felt inside at seeing his old friend again. "I'd heard you were back in town, but didn't know you were starting here today."

Throat tight, Dev took a deep breath and turned slowly. Best get it over with now. He gave Val a curt nod, taking refuge behind his professional facade. "Dr. Laurent."

If Val was surprised by Dev's formality, he didn't show it, other than a slight quirk of one brow. Then again, Val always handled himself well in social situations. He'd been Mr. Popular during medical school. Everyone liked him. Given the coworkers flocking around him now, it seemed nothing had changed there since they'd last seen each other. Dev had never really understood how'd they'd ended up friends in the first place, other than maybe Val had felt sorry for him and taken him under his wing. And on paper, they did have a lot in common. They were both born and bred Minneapolitans, both queer, both determined to be the best physicians they could be and help as many people as possible along the way. But despite their different temperaments—or maybe because of them—as they'd spent more time together during marathon study sessions and brutally long residency hours, they'd become best friends. Val had been the closest person in the world to Dev back then. The one with whom he'd shared his deepest wishes and most outlandish dreams.

And for Dev, who'd always secretly blamed his own personal shortcomings for his own father leaving him and his mother behind when Dev was five, having Val's friendship had felt like the sun coming out after a long, cloudy day. Dev had basked in that golden light, letting down his guard and opening himself up to new experiences, new emotions for the first time in his life. And maybe that's why he hadn't seen Tom coming. With the razzle-dazzle and potent sexiness of a rock star, Tom had swept Dev right off his feet and deftly dodged any concerns Dev might have had through sheer charisma. He'd invested fast and fully in the fantasy, thinking they'd live some kind of magical life together in southern California and any issues would vanish like a rabbit in a top hat. They were in love. What could possibly go wrong? And sure, deep down, Dev had inklings that maybe not everything was as it seemed with Tom. He'd seemed cagey about where he had gone when Dev couldn't get a hold of him. His stories of busy schedules and late-night meetings with his venture capital clients didn't always ring true. It was fine, Dev had told himself. He and Tom were in love and that meant they trusted each other. He was making problems out of nothing. He needed to lighten up, as Tom constantly reminded him. Dev was too uptight, too controlling, too suspicious. Just relax and go with the flow and everything would be just fine. Stop worrying. Then Val had come to him the night before the wedding saying Tom had tried to sleep with him, saying Tom had come on to him at the bachelor party.

Dev, of course, had played it off. Said it had to be a joke. Said that maybe Tom was drunk. That he hadn't meant it. Maybe Val needed to lighten up too, just like Dev. Of course he was still going through with the wedding. They had people coming. They had paid for everything. They were going to get married and have a wonderful life together. If Val couldn't get on board with that, then maybe he shouldn't come at all.

In the end, Val had attended, sitting in the back row of their outdoor ceremony and leaving before the reception. Dev hadn't seen him again until now.

He hid his cringe at those painful memories, barely, and gritted his teeth as some small part of him pinched with bittersweet yearning for the friendship they'd had and lost, for the innocence that was gone forever, for the ease they used to share together.

All of that was gone.

They were virtual strangers now, and Dev was fine with that.

He wasn't interested in new relationships of any kind now, thanks to Tom. He'd rebuilt the walls around his heart high and strong and never planned to let them down again. The risk of allowing people close to you, of allowing his emotions to override his common sense, was not worth it.

He was better off alone.

Val continued to stare at him as Dev stepped up to the counter and cleared his throat to catch the attention of a nearby nurse. "Excuse me. I'm Dr. Harrison. I was called down for a pediatric oncology consult. Can you tell me which room it's in, please?"

"I requested the consult," Val said, and Dev's stomach sank to his toes. Of course he had. That just seemed to be the way this day was going. At least Val's brisk voice was all business now as he grabbed a tablet computer from the counter and handed it to Dev before starting off down one of the halls without waiting to see if Dev followed.

After a moment, Dev hurried down the corridor after him, doing his best to study the updated lab results on the tablet instead of remembering all the times he and Val had seen patients together back in residency. Back when everything had been fresh and new, and the possibilities limitless. Nostalgia threatened to overtake him before Dev shoved it firmly aside. The sooner he started treating Val like any other work colleague, the sooner they could put the past behind them and move on.

They reached the last trauma bay on the right, and Val pulled aside a curtain to reveal a teenaged boy on the bed with his mother sitting in a chair beside him. The mother looked understandably worried, given her son's symptoms. Dev had seen the file upstairs in his office before coming down and it could be serious. The monitors hooked up to the patient beeped rhythmically, flashing the teen's vitals in neon green against a backdrop of black as Val made the introductions.

"This is Matthew Warden. He's sixteen and a running back on his high school football team. He presents to the ER today with extreme fatigue, unexplained bruises that aren't sports-related, and a persistent fever not responding to OTC meds…"

As he continued, Dev became acutely aware of Val's warmth beside him, penetrating through the material of Dev's lab coat, and with each inhale, he caught a hint of soap from Val's skin.

What the hell?

He didn't want to notice anything about Val other than his medical evaluation of the patient before them. Certainly not how he smelled or felt.

"And this is Dr. Harrison, one of the pediatric oncologists. I've called him in to consult as a precaution, pending the results of the blood work we're running," Val said.

As Dev leaned in to shake hands with both the patient and the mother, his arm inadvertently brushed against

Val's and caused an unwanted wave of tingles up the side of Dev's body.

Stop it.

Dev adjusted his glasses and inched away from Val, doing his best not to stare at the dusting of hair on Val's bare forearms. Throat constricted, he asked Matthew, "Have you had any night sweats, Mr. Warden?"

"No. And call me Matt." He crossed his arms over the sheets. "I'm hoping it's just mono."

For Matt's sake, Dev hoped that as well, but he suspected more. "How's your appetite been?"

Ms. Warden answered for her son this time. "He normally eats me out of house and home, but he hasn't been doing that the past two weeks. One of his friends on the team had mono about a month or so ago, so that's why we're hoping it's just that. I know it can be super contagious and Matt said they shared a water bottle after a game."

"That could do it," Val confirmed. "You need to come in contact with their saliva. That's why they call it the kissing disease."

Great. And now Dev had images of kissing Val in his head.

Flustered, Dev stepped over to the bedside to put even more space between him and Val. This was not like him at all, and he needed to get himself under control this instant. He focused on the case and not his racing heart. "Based on the exam results and his history, I'd rather be safe than sorry. I'd say go ahead and isolate him and let's schedule a bone marrow biopsy as well, to cover all our bases."

Val nodded then left to presumably take care of that while Dev pulled on some gloves. "Matt, if you don't mind, I'd like to do a quick exam myself to confirm Dr. Laurent's findings."

"Sure," the kid said, shrugging. "Whatever will get me out of here and back to football practice."

"We'll need to discharge you first for that, and we've still got more tests to run, but I promise we'll do everything we can to get you back to your life outside of here as quickly as possible, Matt." Dev smiled. "Ready?"

Matt nodded.

Dev started by palpating the teen's abdomen, and Matt winced as he pressed lightly over the upper left side of his abdomen just below his rib cage, confirming an enlarged spleen. Next, he checked Matt's ears for signs of infection, but they were clear, as were his throat and lungs. Finally, Dev checked Matt's neck and found several enlarged lymph nodes. Of course, none of those things on their own were proof of anything more serious than mono, but they also didn't rule out acute lymphoblastic leukemia, also called ALL. Only biopsies would do that. He made a mental note to add the lymph nodes to that order.

Finished with the exam, Dev removed his gloves and washed his hands before turning to the patient and his mother, giving them his most comforting smile. "As I said before, we're going to run a few more tests to figure out exactly what we're dealing with here, then we'll know the best treatment for you."

Matt nodded, looking uncertain for the first time since Dev had arrived. "Will that biopsy hurt?"

"It can be a little uncomfortable, yes. But probably nothing worse than you've already experienced on the football field. And we'll do our best to make sure you're as comfortable as possible throughout, okay? We'll take a couple of samples from your neck as well." Dev placed a hand on Matt's shoulder. "We'll take good care of you, I promise."

"Thank you, Dr. Harrison," the mother said, her voice tremulous as she shook Dev's hand again.

"I'm here to help." Dev squeezed her fingers. "I'll review the test results as soon as they become available and keep you both and Dr. Laurent informed of any changes we find. I know the waiting is scary, but I'm committed to getting to the bottom of this."

She smiled, her gaze weary. "I appreciate that, Doctor. My Matthew's been so healthy his whole life. We're not used to spending this much time in hospitals."

"Well, try not to worry," Dev said, giving her as much comfort as he could. Channeling his emotions into his patients and their families was a much safer alternative for him and made him better at his job too. Win-win. "We'll talk again soon."

After leaving Matt and his mother, Dev went to find Val and make sure all his orders were in place, and found him back at the nurses' station. "I confirmed Matthew's spleen is enlarged and tender, as are the lymph nodes in his neck, but his throat, lungs and ears are clear. I'd like to add lymph node biopsies and a lumbar puncture to rule out ALL," Dev told the nurse, then checked his smartwatch before turning back to Val. "I need to get back upstairs to see another patient, but please keep me updated on the results when they come in and we'll go from there."

"I had them schedule an MRI for Matt as well," Val said as Dev headed toward the automatic doors.

"Good." Dev nodded, not turning back for fear of getting lost in Val's blue eyes again. Whatever this ridiculous, odd reaction was, he needed to get it under control before they saw each other again. "Monitor his temperature and blood counts closely. We don't want to miss anything. We'll reconvene after the biopsy results come in."

The doors swished open in front of Dev and before he exited the department, he hazarded one last glance back at Val, only to see him on the phone, bits of his conversation filtering over to Dev, even though he was doing his best not to eavesdrop.

"Hey, Nancy. How's Cam? Still running a fever? Okay." Val ran a hand through his hair, disheveling it, a familiar gesture Dev remembered him doing a lot in residency—a sign he was stressed and trying to hide it. Which made Dev wonder who this Cam person was. Was Val married? Engaged? In a committed relationship with someone? Though he didn't remember seeing a ring on Val's finger.

Not that that meant anything. Doctors frequently removed their rings while treating patients, so...

"Well, make sure Cam stays hydrated, and if his temperature goes up again, call me immediately, okay?" Val continued as the alarm buzzed on the automatic doors and Dev finally stepped out into the hallway, where the elevators were located. The last words that drifted to him before the doors closed again were "Thanks, hon. You're a lifesaver."

Val ended his call and glanced over at Dev through the glass, and Dev looked away fast.

Why am I standing here gawking at the last man on earth I should be interested in?

As he rode back up to his office on the third floor, Dev still felt discombobulated by the whole encounter. He huffed out a breath as the glowing numbers above the door ticked upward, his determination to put it behind him growing as the seconds passed. Whatever strange things seeing Val again had stirred inside him, he needed to deal with because they had a patient to work on together now. And given that they were in the same hospital, Matt wouldn't be the last either. They were both professionals. They could do this, no matter how awkward. He'd come home to focus on his career again and that's exactly what he intended to do. Not get wrapped up in the past. It was all over and done with. The sooner he remembered that, the better.

Val stood at the nurses' station after Dev left, still a bit stunned. When he'd called for the oncology consult, he hadn't paid much attention to who was on call for that department—he just knew he needed one stat for Matthew. So when he'd turned around and saw Dev again after all these years, it had been a real gut punch, to say the least.

Before he got back to work in the ER, Val pulled out his phone again to see a text update from the nanny, Nancy. Cam's temperature was holding steady now and she'd gotten some soup into him, which was good. A bit of the tension in his back eased as he adjusted the stethoscope slung around his neck and made his way back into the fray of the busy department. He still had a few hours left on his shift before he could leave to personally check on his son.

Scanning the list of waiting patients, Val's gaze snagged on Matt's name, then Dev's now listed beside it as consulting oncologist. He'd heard through the grapevine that Dev was back in town, but hadn't expected to see him so soon, and it still seemed unreal. Once upon a time, they'd been about as close as two people could get without sleeping together. He still remembered seeing Dev sitting there at his desk on the first day of medical school, looking so shy and nervous that Val had yearned to make him smile. He'd never imagined that first encounter would lead to years of friendship, nor how it would all end. But even now, he wouldn't have done anything different. He'd been compelled to warn Dev about Tom and the fact he'd come on to him, and he'd do it again, even though it now made working together akin to navigating a minefield of old hurts and resentments.

An image of Dev's face as he'd finally faced Val again after all these years flashed in his head.

He looked good. A bit thinner than he'd been when he'd left ten years ago, but good. Same dark hair and eyes, same lithe build and Tom Ford glasses. There was a new wariness though, a sense of guarded detachedness that Val was sure was meant to keep people away. It only intrigued him more.

Not that he'd indulge that curiosity anytime soon.

Dev had been extremely clear during their last fight that he wanted nothing more to do with Val, and until he heard differently, he had no intention of trying to mend that fence.

Working together on cases would be enough interaction for now.

And, speaking of new cases, he moved between trauma bays over the new few hours, concentrating to keep himself busy and stop worrying about Cam. One of his greatest strengths—or weaknesses, depending on who you asked—was how quickly he connected with people. It had always been something that came easily to him. His sister, Vicki, used to tease him that he could talk to a post, and it was true. He thrived on relationships, felt things deeply. So the last year and half had been especially hard on him since Vicki had died of ovarian cancer and he'd adopted his only nephew, Cam, as his son. Cam's biological father had left shortly before Cam was born, never marrying Vicki or accepting any responsibility for his own child. Val knew from his own childhood growing up in a household with neglectful parents that the world often wasn't fair, but he didn't want that for Cam. The boy was the most important thing in Val's life now and his only family left alive.

For months now, his grief and raising Cam had taken up all his time outside of work, so Val hadn't been connecting socially like he used to, and he missed it. And when he did have time to relax and hang out, the only person he usually did that with was Alex, his late sister's fiancé, who understood what Val and Cam had been through, so it made it easier to not have to explain it all again. There was absolutely nothing romantic between them. Alex was straight. But they were good sounding boards for each other, and had helped each other and Cam through the worst times after the funeral.

Huh. He hadn't really thought about how isolated he'd become, which for an extrovert like him was difficult.

Maybe that's why he was so curious about Dev now, despite knowing that he was off-limits.

And why, when he remembered how close they'd once been, his chest ached for the friend he'd loved like a brother. Sure, if he was honest, he'd always harbored a bit of a crush on Dev, with his whole sexy nerd vibe going on. They'd never crossed that line, but…

Val shook off those inappropriate thoughts and entered a new trauma bay.

Dev could barely look at him today, let alone do anything else.

He needed to keep his feelings to himself.

Waiting for him was an elderly woman named Doris, who'd been brought in by one of the local assisted-living homes. She was complaining of abdominal pain, blood in her stool and weight loss. After running tests to rule out other causes, he got an ultrasound that showed a fecal impaction that both an enema and digital manipulation of the blockage should handle. And that honor fell squarely with one of the new residents. In fact, catching all the fecal-related cases was a rite of passage for the med students around here. Lord knew Val had done his share during that time. He was ready to pass the duty on to the next generation. As he made notes in the patient's chart on his tablet, a nurse poked her head in.

"Dr. Laurent, we need you in trauma bay three," she said.

"On my way." Val turned back to pat Doris's frail hand with a sincere smile. "Don't worry, Mrs. Carson, we will get you feeling better again soon. Is there anyone we can call for you?"

"My son, please," she said. "He's working downtown. Thank you."

Val got the information and passed it on to someone at the desk before heading to the next case—a twenty-two-year-old man named Bo with a broken arm. After examining the X-rays, he applied a cast with practiced ease, talking the patient through his at-home care as he went. "You'll need to wear this for four weeks, then follow up with Orthopedics. Barring any unforeseen circumstances, you should be good as new."

"Thanks, Doc," Bo said, flashing a relieved grin. "Got to be ready for snowboarding season soon."

"Well, be careful," Val warned as he washed his hands. "Don't want to end up back in here again."

With half an hour left on his shift, Val went to the break room for a bottled water, and the calm between storms allowed thoughts of Dev to creep back in again. He hadn't realized until today how much he'd actually missed the guy until seeing him again. Ten years seemed like a lifetime ago now, and as he bought an energy bar from the vending machine, Val wondered what had brought Dev back home now. Which then led to thoughts of Tom. Ugh. *There* was someone Val would be more than happy never to see again. But if Dev was here, then his husband must be too, right? Though he'd noted Dev hadn't had his wedding ring on today either.

He sat down at a table to eat his quick snack, pondering the situation despite his earlier promise not to. Mentally, he was running on fumes at this point, so he needed to cut himself some slack. Last he'd heard, Tom was running his own successful venture capital company in San Diego, but with the volatile economy these days, maybe something had gone wrong, and the company had folded. Not that he wished anyone ill, but he couldn't imagine it happening to a better guy than Tom. Tom had somehow managed to fool Dev all those years ago, but Val had seen through his phony act from a mile away, especially after the bachelor party.

But if Dev was happy, then that was all that mattered.

The potential what-ifs and what-might-have-beens left Val feeling charged up as he finished his break. He had more than enough on his own plate these days—with Cam sick again and bills to pay and general life stuff as a single dad—than to waste time thinking about things that were none of his business, but still. Whatever this weirdness was between him and Dev, they both needed to get past it if they were going to make this work. For his part, Val was more than ready to move past the awkwardness and back to some semblance of civility.

He stood, yawning and stretching before making his way back to the ER. At thirty-six, pulling these back-to-back twenty-four-hour shifts was getting old. He still had twenty minutes left before he could leave, and he intended to use those to process his day so he didn't take the stress home with him. Cam needed him to be strong, focused and present during their time together, not worrying about the past.

But as soon as he walked back into the department, those plans were shot to hell because a nurse stopped him with an urgent "Dr. Laurent. We need you in trauma bay one."

With a sigh, Val grabbed his tablet from the nurses' station and brought up the patient's file, slipping back into the role he knew best. He followed her down the corridor, donning a fresh gown on the way. "Coming."

CHAPTER TWO

Dev unlocked the front door of his mother's house that night and walked inside his childhood home. It had been a long, unsettling day, and he wanted nothing more than some peace and quiet to clear his head. Unfortunately, he'd barely made it across the living room when his mother called from down the hall, "Devon, sweetheart. Is that you?"

"Yes. Hi, Mom," he called back, not bothering to mask the weariness edging his voice.

"The delivery service dropped off an envelope for you," she said as she rolled her wheelchair into the room and pointed toward the coffee table. "Looks important. Has a fancy law firm listed as the return address."

"Great." Must be the final divorce papers. Considering how the rest of his day had gone, he probably should have expected they'd show up today. One thing he hadn't really thought through before moving back here was how this place would remind him of his father walking out on them, and how the ones you loved could hurt you, which only made the pain of the divorce sharper. And while his father had never specifically blamed Dev for his leaving, Tom sure had. He'd claimed Dev wasn't giving him what he needed emotionally, and that's why he'd had to seek comfort and solace elsewhere. But it wasn't like he didn't know who Dev was before he'd married him. Hell, before the wedding, he'd actually teased that one day he'd crack Dev's shell. Well, he'd sure done that, Dev supposed. Just not in the way he'd expected. Dev had felt completely shattered after the divorce, but instead of wallowing, he'd quickly reassembled the pieces and sewn them back together stronger and harder than ever. No one was getting into his heart again. No matter how attracted to them he might be, he added, after an image of Val from earlier in the day flickered through his mind. Nope. He was done with romance.

Scowling, he scrubbed a hand over his face, then snatched the envelope off the table and started toward the hallway leading to his old bedroom. "Just what I needed. Thanks."

"Honey, I'm sorry things didn't work out with Tom." His mom watched him as he passed, her expression concerned. "But I hope you don't—"

"Don't what, Mom?" he snapped before he could stop himself. And now he felt worse than before. It wasn't her fault all this was happening. "Don't get angry because he lied and cheated on me? Don't get bitter because it was my own fault for not seeing what he was from the start? Don't close myself off and stop trusting people? Too late for that, Mom. I should have known better. End of story. I won't make the same mistake again. Now, if you'll excuse me."

"Sweetheart—"

"Mom, I really don't want to talk about this tonight, okay?" He stopped at the entrance to the hallway, head down, more exhausted than he could remember in a long time. "Look, I'm sorry I snapped at you. Today has been a lot. I'm going to take a shower then sort through the mess in this envelope. I'll talk to you in the morning."

"I made dinner," his mother called after him. "Yours is in the fridge when you're ready."

"Okay. Thanks," he said. "But I'm not very hungry."

Dev held his breath until the bedroom door closed behind him, then exhaled slowly as blessed isolation wrapped around him like a shroud, a welcome barrier against the world that seemed too loud and too confusing and too cruel for his taste.

Eventually, he shuffled over to the twin bed and sat on the edge, looking around at the space where he'd spent so much time as a kid, building toy models and dreaming of better things. His mom had redecorated in here after he'd married Tom and left for California. The old blue walls were now painted a soothing cream color, and his childhood dark wood furniture had been replaced with light oak and white. Outside the window across from him, autumn leaves rustled in the wind and the old house creaked as if in answer. Then he caught his reflection in the mirror above the dresser, and his sense of failure came roaring back. Dammit. For once, he'd acted recklessly, letting his emotions lead. And look where it had gotten him. Right back where he'd started. The lesson he took from all of this was that love was not worth the risk. He stared at the envelope in his hands and shook his head. More proof of just how blind he'd been about the man he thought he'd loved. Even after Val had tried to tell him. Which only proved he was even more of a fool to trust his own instincts when it came to his feelings. They never led anywhere but trouble for everyone involved. Tom. His dad. Val. If he'd only kept his feelings out of it, things would've been fine. Or at least no one would've been hurt, especially himself.

With a sigh, he closed his eyes and took a deep breath, pushing his glasses up the bridge of his nose and forcing his tense shoulders to relax. Okay, fine. He honestly couldn't say that if things would've been different, he'd have stuck to cool aloofness, but at least he wouldn't have cared so much when it all fell apart. No. Always keep your armor on was the takeaway here, and he intended to follow that rule going forward. Life was much safer that way.

He blinked down at the envelope in his hand, willing himself to feel nothing. "You were a liar and a cheat, and you cost me everything. Good riddance to you."

The words echoed in the quiet, shadowed room, so different from the home he'd had with Tom in California. Their beach house had always seemed filled with people and light. That was gone now though. He'd let Tom keep the house and all his San Diego friends, in exchange for what he hoped would be peace and quiet, and time to heal back home in Minneapolis. And now that's what he had. Sort of. If he could just get his overanalytical brain to shut off, he'd be all set. He flopped back on the bed to stare up at the ceiling. Things were fine. Or they would be. Just as soon as he got settled and got his head right again. Which meant getting used to having Val around, at least professionally.

A soft knock on the door was followed by his mom

poking her head into the room. "Can I come in for a minute?"

Dev shoved the envelope under his pillow, then sat up as she came in with his dinner on a tray across her lap. There were also two mugs of chamomile tea—his favorite—one for him and one for her. The sight of it made a fresh wave of nostalgia squeeze his chest. "Mom, you didn't have to do this. I really am sorry about earlier. I so appreciate you for letting me stay here until I find my own place in town."

"Of course you can stay here, honey. For as long as you need." She smiled as she passed him the tray, minus her own mug. "And it's nice for me to have some help again. Now eat before it gets cold. You're getting too skinny."

He smiled, doing as he was told. Her meat loaf was just as delicious as he remembered growing up. He couldn't remember the last time he'd had a home-cooked meal like this. Tom was out a lot of the time for dinner with clients and Dev didn't really see the point of cooking for one, so he'd ordered in most nights. As he ate, he said, "It's been a long day, and I wasn't expecting to get the divorce papers today. Moving back here has been challenging. Seeing all these reminders of the past."

"You're not having second thoughts, are you?" His mom frowned at him over the rim of her mug. "About Tom, I mean."

"No. God, no." Dev chewed and swallowed another bite of food. With so many things up in the air right now, ending his marriage was the one certainty he had. "I couldn't trust him anymore, Mom. He lied to me repeatedly, from before we were even married. Can't stay with someone after that. Toward the end, the fights... the silence... It was awful." His throat tightened over the last word, and he gulped some tea to ease it. *Awful* was an understatement. *Excruciating* was more like it. All the constant doubts, fears, never knowing who Tom was with or where he was, what to believe. "Like I said, I learned my lesson. I won't make that mistake again."

"Oh, honey." His mother patted his knee. "I'm sorry you had to go through that, but it seems I passed that legacy on to you."

"Legacy?" he asked, frowning as he looked up from his nearly empty plate to her.

"Of dysfunctional relationships." She gave a small shrug. "And you had a hard enough time opening up to people already. I just hope you don't close yourself off completely."

"Why not?" he countered. "I'm perfectly fine on my own. I have a good job, good family. What more do I need? Once I find a place of my own, I'll be set here. Besides, my instincts and emotions are not reliable. That's what got me into this situation in the first place. Better to lead with my head and not my heart, I think, going forward."

A beat passed before his mom responded, watching him. "Sweetheart, I just want to make sure you understand that feeling things is a part of being human. And closing yourself off isn't any safer or healthier than being too open and vulnerable. You have to find the right balance is all. And the right person. Contrary to what that big brain of yours might be telling you, it's not a weakness to trust others, Dev. It's courageous, especially when you have no idea what the outcome will be. Sometimes it works out, sometimes it doesn't. But that doesn't mean you should stop trying." He gave a derisive snort, and she sat back, looking resigned. "Well, whatever happens, I'm just glad you're home, honey. Give yourself some time to heal and relax before you make any big decisions, eh? Because those walls you build around yourself don't just keep out the possibility of pain. They also keep out the possibility of joy. Of love."

Dev put his empty plate and silverware back on the tray, followed by his empty mug after draining his tea in one last, long gulp. Then he stood and headed for the door to take it all back to the kitchen. His mother followed him down the hall. After rinsing his dishes and putting them in the dishwasher, he turned and bent to kiss her cheek. "Thanks again for dinner and the talk, Mom. Now, I need to take a shower and get in bed before I fall over. Good night."

"'Night," she called after him, and he headed back to his room.

The long, steamy shower helped ease away some stress. Afterward, he wrapped a towel around his waist and stood at the sink to brush his teeth, staring at himself in the mirror. Dark eyes lined with stress, stubble-covered jaw, shadows under his cheekbones. His mom was right. He was too skinny.

It's not a weakness to trust others, Dev. It's courageous, especially when you have no idea what the outcome will be.

Maybe she was right, but it didn't feel like that right

now. In fact, Dev wasn't sure he'd ever let go of that tight control over his emotions again. He wasn't sure he even knew how.

Across town, nestled in a cozy bedroom painted blue, Val sat propped up against a mountain of pillows with a well-worn copy of *The Velveteen Rabbit* in his hand and his son curled beside him beneath a heap of blankets. The boy's eyes were wide and attentive, despite the pallor of his cheeks. His cold seemed unchanged from the last time Val had checked him.

"Does it hurt?" Cam asked, his voice small but earnest. "Being real, I mean?"

Val paused, considering the story's deeper meaning. Since Vicki's passing, it had become Cam's favorite, so he wanted to choose his answer wisely. "Sometimes. But being real is also worth it. Because when you're real, authentic, you can truly love and be loved in return. And that's worth any risk."

Cam seemed to take a moment to process that new information. "What about when someone dies? Do they stop being real?"

Val's heart clenched. Hard as it had been for him to lose his older sister, poor Cam had lost his mother and no amount of love and connection from Val could ever fill that void, though he tried his best. One of the reasons he'd gone ahead and adopted Cam was to give him a sense of stability and to reassure the boy that Val had no intention of leaving him anytime soon. "No, buddy. Those who pass on will always be real, and the love we have for them stays with us forever. That's the magic part—you carry them with you for eternity."

"Mommy is here with me now then?"

"Always, buddy." Cam's hopeful tone pinched Val's heart and he pulled the boy in for a hug. "She's always with you."

"Okay." Cam snuggled beneath the covers then, his eyelids slowly lowering as sleep beckoned. "Love is forever."

"Forever and ever." Val set the book aside and extricated himself carefully, smiling as he kissed his son's forehead, then shut off the light, the soft glow of the night-light casting soft shadows across the room. "Now, get some sleep. You need your rest to heal."

He was almost out the door when Cam asked quietly from behind him, "Do you miss her a lot?"

"Every day, buddy," Val said, his voice rough. Vicki had been the center of both of their lives since Dev had left. She'd been so vibrant and full of life right up until the disease took her too soon.

"Does it get easier? The missing?" Cam peeked out from under the blanket to meet Val's gaze.

Chest tight, he swallowed hard, trying to figure out the best way to talk about grief with a child. "It changes," he said finally. "Like…carrying a pebble in your pocket. At first, it feels heavy, and you're aware of it constantly. But over time, it just becomes a normal part of you. Then you don't notice the weight as much, but you never forget it's there."

Cam nodded, looking solemn. "I know you said she's

here, but I wish I could see her again, even for a little while."

"Me too, buddy," Val said from the doorway. "But we still have each other, right?"

"Yeah," Cam said. "You won't leave me, will you?"

The question, laden with the fear of further loss, was another stab in Val's heart.

"I don't plan on going anywhere, Cam. Promise," Val vowed "We have each other. Nothing will change that, no matter what happens."

"Good," Cam murmured, closing his eyes at last. "'Night, Uncle Val."

"'Night." Val hesitated before closing the door, watching over the boy who'd become his world. As the night settled, his thoughts snagged on how quickly time passed when you weren't paying attention, how precious the moments were, how quickly they could slip away.

He walked through the quiet house, checking the front and back doors to make sure they were locked. As he flopped down on the couch in the living room to watch TV, he realized how lonely his life had become. For a guy who'd always been surrounded by friends, it was a bit disconcerting. It wasn't like he didn't go out sometimes after work, have a casual drink or a dance. And, of course, Alex still came over once in a while when he wasn't traveling for his job to spend time with Cam and check in on Val. But honestly, other than Vicki, no one had ever been as close to him as Dev…

God, Dev.

He wondered what Dev was doing right now. Was he sitting alone too, thinking about Val? He snorted and shook his head. Given how cold Dev had been toward him earlier, that was probably a no. Which meant he needed to face facts. It might be too late to change things between him and Dev, and the sooner Val accepted that, the sooner they could all move on.

Now, if he could just get the message through to his heart to stop caring, he'd be all set.

CHAPTER THREE

"We've got one more patient, Dr. Harrison," the nurse said as Dev washed his hands.

"Great. Tell them I'll be right in," Dev said over his shoulder. When he'd taken the position at the MCC, part of his responsibilities was to volunteer in the staff clinic once a month, and tonight was his night. It was a nice service the hospital offered their employees and their families, and most of the cases he saw were kids needing shots or school physicals, with the occasional cold and ear infection thrown in for fun. It was nice to keep his skills sharp and see patients with less ominous diagnoses than were usually on his roster.

He dried his hands then picked up the tablet the nurse had left for him with the patient's file without glancing at it, and headed into the next room. It was in a corridor that had formerly held a private practice that had since been vacated and was now used for the monthly clinic. A check of his smartwatch said it was almost closing time, so once he finished with this case, he could go home and rest.

"Hello, I'm Dr. Dev Harrison," he said as he opened the door. "How can I—"

Dev stopped in his tracks at the sight of Val sitting there beside a small boy with the same tawny hair and blue eyes on the table. Stunned speechless, he just blinked at them both until Val finally broke the silence.

"Uh…hi," Val said, standing and rubbing his palms on the legs of his jeans. He must not have worked today, Dev thought absently. "Cam here is on his third cold in a month and a half and while the OTC meds have helped, I'd just like to have him checked out by a fresh set of eyes to make sure he's good to go back to school tomorrow."

"Are you a doctor like Uncle Val?" the boy asked, finally snapping Dev out of his stupor. Uncle Val? Right. This must be Vicki's son. He'd been born after Dev had moved to California, but his mom had mentioned him in her emails. The boy must be living with Val now after Vicki's passing.

Dev cleared his throat and finally looked at the file. Cameron Laurent. Seven years old. According to the file, the boy had had several colds over the past few months but was feeling better now. Vitals were normal and he had no complaints today. Good. That was good. Because it meant Dev could hopefully get this exam finished quickly and get out of here because he could feel Val watching him like a physical weight on his shoulders. Gah. Despite his wishes, he was still far too aware of the man than he wanted to be.

Get a grip. Get this over with. Get out.

Dev turned away to set the tablet aside and pull on his gloves, affixing his most professional demeanor to hide the swirl of disorder inside him. When he turned back, he was all business, ignoring Val completely to focus on his patient. "Yes, I'm a doctor. But I'm a pediatric oncologist."

The boy scrunched his nose, continuing to play with the toy he'd brought with him, a Lego figurine of a Transformers character, if Dev wasn't mistaken. He kept abreast of the latest toys as much as possible for relating to his young patients. Plus, Lego sets were just cool. "What's that?"

"I normally treat children with cancer," he said, stepping closer. "But today I'm volunteering down here in the clinic. Cameron, do you mind if I examine you?"

"No," the boy said, glancing up at Dev. "And people call me Cam. My mom had cancer."

"Okay, Cam," Dev said, cringing inwardly at his blunder. Normally, he had way more tact, but he felt knocked off-kilter by Val showing up again so unexpectedly. "And I'm very sorry about your mother. I knew her and she was a great lady."

"Everyone says that." Cam frowned down at his toy. "I miss her a lot sometimes."

"I bet you do."

Cam nodded. "She always made me laugh."

"Me too," Dev agreed. Vicki had always been so full of energy and light.

"So, how'd you know my mom?" Cam looked so much like Val that if Dev didn't know better, he'd think the boy was his biological son. Same tawny hair, same blue eyes, same disarming smile. "Was she your friend?"

"She was," Dev said, his voice turning gruff again before he swallowed hard. "I spent a lot of time at her house during medical school."

"Then you were friends with Uncle Val too?" Cam asked, looking back up at Dev again before he turned to his uncle with an excited grin. "Are you guys friends too?"

"Oh…uh…" Val said.

At the same time, Dev said, "We used to be."

"Let's get this exam done then, shall we?" Flustered, Dev pulled an otoscope from his pocket and focused on his patient instead of Val, who stood to the side, close enough that Dev was aware of his every movement. Or at least it seemed that way. His pulse tripped before he forced himself to calm down. "Ears look clear," he said to no one in particular. He grabbed a tongue depressor from a canister on the counter. "Say *ah*, please."

Cam did so and Dev checked the boy's throat next. "Throat clear as well."

"Like I said," Val said into the uncomfortable tension between them as Dev palpated the lymph nodes in Cam's neck. "He's had a couple of colds, and I just wanted him cleared before I send him back to school tomorrow. Nancy's been watching him all day and said he's been fine, but I wanted fresh eyes. My shift ended a few hours ago, so I ran home and changed and brought him back here to the clinic, thinking it would be faster than trying to get a last-minute appointment with his regular pediatrician, so…" Val's voice trailed off as if he realized he'd been babbling. "Anyway, thanks for seeing him."

Dev took the stethoscope from around his neck to listen to the boy's breathing. Clear as well. Cam seemed good to go. Dev documented it all in the file, then told Val as much.

"Do you like Lego, Dr. Harrison?" Cam asked as Dev took off his gloves and washed his hands again.

"I do," Dev said, grabbing several paper towels from the dispenser, glad for something to concentrate on beside Val. "I used to love them as a kid too, but they weren't as fancy as the one you have there. Is that a Transformer?"

"It is!" Cam unfolded a set of wings from the back of the toy. "These have to be strong enough to fly through space."

"Very true," Dev said, knowing that play was an important part of healing for many grieving young patients. "Strong wings for a strong journey. Do you have a favorite Lego set?"

"I like anything space!" Cam said. "I'm just starting the new Mandalorian N-1 Starfighter Microfighter set now. Uncle Val says I go through them too fast. He says I'm going to bankrupt him one day." Those sets could be very expensive, sometimes upward of several hundred dollars for the collector sets, so Dev couldn't help chuckling at that. His laughter ended abruptly at Cam's next words. "You should come over to our house and help me build it. Can he come over, Uncle Val?"

Both men looked at each other, then away fast.

"Okay, buddy. I'm sure Dr. Harrison is way too busy to build toys with you right now," Val said, picking up the boy and setting him on his feet on the floor. "I think you've got a clean bill of health to return to school in the morning. Why don't you go out and play in the waiting room, Cam, while I finish up with Dr. Harrison."

"Okay," the boy said agreeably. "And don't forget to ask about coming over! Bye, Dr. Dev. Is it okay if I call you that, Dr. Harrison?"

"Uh, sure," Dev said, resisting the urge to run a finger under his collar. When had it gotten so hot in here? "That's fine, Cam."

"Okay. Bye, Dr. Dev!" Cam took off then, leaving another awkward silence in his wake.

Alone with Val again, Dev turned back toward the counter to type his notes into the chart on his tablet while Val shuffled from foot to foot beside him, looking about as uncomfortable as Dev felt.

"Look, I didn't plan this at all, I swear. I had no idea you'd be manning the clinic tonight," Val said. "Like I said, I just thought it would be easier bringing him here."

"It's fine." Dev finished his notes then scribbled a quick note of clearance for Cam to take back to school with him the next day, praying for a swift escape. "Have a good night, Dr. Laurent. Oh, and I'd suggest getting a humidifier for Cam's room with the drier winter air coming."

He turned on his heels then and walked away, only to find Val following him. The man had always been persistent. Dev finally stopped at the empty nurses' station and turned back to Val. He needed this to be over so he could collect himself again. Spending too much time around Val was dangerous to his plans to stay distant. "Was there something else you needed?"

Val huffed out a breath then scrubbed his hands over

his face. "Look, Dev. About Tom. I know you didn't want to hear it, but now that we're working together again, I really think we should clear the air once and for all. I'm sorry about how things ended between us all those years ago. When I told you about Tom coming on to me, I wasn't trying to hurt you. I was just trying to look out for you. I hope that you and Tom can forgive me, and we can all move on from here."

Oh, God.

Dev realized that Val didn't know about the divorce. And how would he? They'd barely spoken to each other since Dev's return to Minneapolis and, even then, only about the cases they were working on together. Right. Jaw tight, Dev forced out the words. "Not that it's any of your business, but Tom and I are divorced. I just sent the signed papers back. He cheated on me during our marriage. Repeatedly. Congratulations. You were right about him all along."

All the shame and embarrassment curdled inside him like sludge as he steeled himself for Val's I-told-you-so reaction. Dev should have known. Should have listened. Would have saved himself a lot of pain, but he'd been in love. Or what he'd thought was love. *Never again.* But when he finally hazarded a glance at Val, all he saw was sympathy.

"Oh, no. I'm so sorry, Dev."

"Yes, well. It's over and done now. Water under the bridge. I've moved on." Dev turned back around and sucked in a breath, wishing to God that was true. But maybe if he willed it enough, it would become so… "And apology accepted. I should have heeded your warnings back then. Would've saved me a lot of wasted time."

Val just stood there, looking like he wanted to say more, but wasn't sure if he should. Finally, he sighed. "For what it's worth, I'm glad you're home, Dev. And I hope we can start fresh now. Thank you again for checking on Cam. I know he's in good hands with you."

Dev only nodded then, not trusting his voice as he pushed his glasses up the bridge of his nose again, memories of the past lingering like a fine mist between them. "Thank you."

Neither of them moved, eyes locked, until a small voice called down the hall.

"Uncle Val, can we stop for ice cream on the way home? I ate all my peas at dinner. Ask Nancy."

Val finally tore his gaze from Dev's and called back over his shoulder. "All right, buddy. You've been a good patient tonight, so…" Then he turned back to Dev with a twinkle in his eye. Dev hadn't realized how much he'd missed seeing that mischievousness until now. He tamped that down fast. He had no business missing Val or his twinkle. "If you're done here, do you want to go for ice cream with us? I know a place that has the best Moose Tracks in town. My treat. Consider it a peace offering."

"Oh, I…" Not expecting the invitation and not sure what to say, Dev checked his smartwatch, more to give himself a moment to think of a way to get out of it than anything else. It was going on 8:00 p.m. He could claim his mother needed him for something, or that he had an early call in the morning. But when he opened his mouth, what came out was "Okay."

What the hell is wrong with me?

Val gave him a bright grin then and the whole room seemed to lighten around Dev. Which was just plain ridiculous. He scowled, annoyed with himself for getting himself in this situation. "I'll need to finish up here first."

"Don't worry, Doc," said the nurse who'd been giving shots all day as she walked out of the room Dev had seen Cam in. "I've got everything cleaned up and ready to go for next week. You go ahead. I'll lock up here."

Perfect.

Teeth gritted, Dev gave a curt nod. "Guess I'm ready to go then."

He pulled on his coat then followed Val out to the waiting room, where Cam cheered with excitement when he found out Dev was going with them for ice cream. They walked outside into the chilly night air, Dev grateful for the coolness on his heated skin. "Where is this place?"

"Not far. Do you want to ride together?" Val asked as they stopped near a shiny new SUV.

"No," Dev said. It was one thing to suffer through a quick snack with Val. Riding in a confined space with him would be entirely too much for Dev at this point. His stupid insides were already quivering in anticipation for some reason that Dev didn't want to think too much about. "I'll drive too. I can't stay long."

"Okay," Val said agreeably. "Where are you parked?"

Dev pointed to the gray sedan he was renting until

he got settled and bought something permanent. "I'll follow you."

A few minutes later, they pulled up outside a nondescript white building on Upton Avenue and parked at the curb. Cam was the first out, hopping on the sidewalk, while Val and Dev locked up their vehicles then followed him inside the local shop. From all the signs, Dev gathered they made homemade ice cream in unique flavors, along with specialty coffees and baked goods. The air smelled of sugar and waffle cones, and a scattering of round tables filled a brightly lit area with people laughing and chatting over their desserts. Dev didn't remember the place from before his move, but he'd been gone a while, so…

"What flavor are you getting tonight, buddy?" Val asked Cam, holding him by the shoulders in front of him as they stood looking up at the handwritten menu boards hanging behind the counter.

"Oreo!" Cam clapped excitedly. "In a chocolate cone, please."

"Did you get that?" Val asked the guy at the register, who nodded and grinned at Cam. "And for you?" the cashier asked Val.

"Moose Tracks in a plain waffle cone, please," Val said, then looked back at Dev. "What about you?"

Dev read all the selections, and they all sounded good, but he decided to indulge his chocolate cravings tonight. He chose the one listed as being filled with fudge, truffles, chunks of Heath Bar and a dash of sea salt. He deserved it after all the stress he was putting himself through here. "A scoop of the Nicollet Avenue Pothole, please. In a waffle bowl."

"You got it, sir," the cashier said, then rang up the order for Val and directed them to the other end of the counter to wait on their orders. They stood in line and soon carried a tray with their goodies to a table in the far corner.

Once they were all seated and had their ice cream, Dev sat back and ate, listening in as Val and Cam chatted about their days, zoning out a bit as he went into a chocolate coma from the most delicious ice cream he'd ever had in his life. So much so that when he did manage to tune back in to the conversation, he found both Val and Cam looking at him expectantly.

Whoops. They'd obviously asked him something.

"Sorry, I didn't catch that," Dev said, sitting forward to finish his dessert.

"I asked where you were living," Val said. "Cam and I are in Vicki's old place."

"Oh. I'm staying at my mother's right now until I find someplace."

"How is your mom?" Val asked. "I haven't seen her since the funeral."

"Good," Dev said, glad for a neutral topic to discuss. "Her MS is under control right now, though she's in a wheelchair, as I'm sure you saw. She's still upbeat and positive though. She's glad to have me back in town to help out when she needs."

"I'm sure she is." Val smiled. "You know, I still keep in touch with some of the old gang from medical school who are in town. We try to get together at least once a month for dinner and drinks. If you're interested, I can let you know the next time we go out. I'm sure everyone would love to see you."

The last thing Dev wanted to do was spend an evening answering a bunch of uncomfortable questions about things he was trying to forget, so he kept his response as noncommittal as possible. "I'll have to check my schedule. Things are a bit chaotic right now, schedule-wise."

"Understood." Val reached for a napkin from the dispenser in the center of the table at the same time Dev did, and their fingers brushed, the slight contact another unwanted jolt of awareness up Dev's arm. He pulled back fast, frowning. The ink was barely dry on his divorce papers. He didn't want to get involved with anyone again, let alone Val. He needed to stop this nonsense before it got out of hand.

He mumbled an apology and waited for Val to get his napkin before reaching for one himself. He wasn't sure exactly why Val was affecting him this way now, but he didn't like it. Not at all. It made no sense. They'd been friends for years before the falling-out and not once had he been attracted to Val like this. What was wrong now that this was happening? Had something short-circuited in his brain after the divorce? Had Tom permanently broken him? Or, worst of all, was he actually interested in Val that way? No. No, he couldn't be. He'd vowed never to get involved with anyone like that again. Never to let anyone close like that again. Must be his wonky instincts again, leading him down the path to rack and ruin.

Thankfully, both Val and Cam seemed oblivious to Dev's inner turmoil as they continued chatting about some project Cam was working on at school. Dev was glad for the reprieve, watching them interact from beneath his lashes. Val seemed like a good parent, attentive and sweet, ruffling the boy's hair when Cam said something funny, valuing his ideas and opinions. Dev would've given anything for a dad like that at Cam's age…

"Dev?" Val asked, pulling him back to the present again as Cam slid off his stool to take their empty tray back to the counter. "Everything okay?"

"What?" Devon frowned down at the table. He'd devoured his edible bowl while he'd been lost in his thoughts and didn't even remember eating it. "Sorry."

"Don't apologize," Val said, standing when Cam returned to the table. "I just asked if you needed anything. I know it can be a lot, starting over again. And with the crazy schedule you mentioned, if you need help with anything, just let me know."

They all pulled their coats back on and headed for the exit. This hadn't been as horrible as Dev had expected. Not that he planned to repeat it or anything. "I really do need to get home now. Thanks for the ice cream."

"My pleasure." Val held the door for them, then stood on the sidewalk outside with Dev as Cam climbed into the SUV. "I'm glad we cleared things up."

"Me too." Dev turned toward his car. "Good night. Bye, Cam."

"Bye, Dr. Dev," the boy called before closing the door on the SUV.

"'Night," Val called from behind Dev, then added, "Hey, if you're not busy next weekend, I've got season tickets to the Timberwolves. It's their home opener. I have an extra ticket this time, so if you want to come with me and Cam, I'm sure he'd love it, and you'd save the ticket from going to waste…"

It sounded like an innocent enough invitation. Practical too, since season tickets to an NBA game were not cheap, but Dev had to stick to his plans. Still, he didn't want to be rude after he and Val had just reached an accord, so he went with his usual nonanswer. "I'll have to check my schedule."

"Great," Val said, waving as Dev reached his car at the curb. "I'll text you the details just in case."

City lights blurred past as Dev drove home, the hum of the car's engine soothing away a bit of the tension that had lingered within him ever since he'd left San Diego. Even though this evening hadn't gone the way he'd expected at all, it had been oddly relaxing. In the months since he and Tom had separated, he'd been so guarded, losing himself in work to avoid dealing with the loss of the future he'd thought they'd have had together. But tonight, something had shifted a little inside him, making him think that perhaps he would be okay on his own after all.

He stopped at a red light and glanced up at the night sky through the window. The stars were pinpricks of light against the vast darkness, and for the first time in a long time, Dev allowed himself to just take it in, to let go of his tight control. Not all the way, never all the way, not anymore, but a tiny crack appeared in his walls just the same.

Dev was still contemplating it all when he arrived back home at his mom's. He walked in to find her watching a special celebrity prime-time episode of *Jeopardy!*, calling out answers to the people on screen as she worked on her knitting. He took off his coat and sat on the couch, not quite ready to go to bed.

When a commercial break came on, his mom glanced over at him. "How was your day, honey?"

"Interesting," he said, distracted.

"Interesting good or interesting bad?" she asked over the steady *clack-clack* of her knitting needles.

"I'm not sure yet. I volunteered at the staff clinic tonight and Val showed up with his son, Cam. Did you know he'd adopted Vicki's boy?"

"Of course." His mom smiled. "He couldn't have a better father."

Dev frowned. "And you didn't think to mention it to me?"

"I guess it never came up," she said, shrugging slightly. "Why? Is it important to you?"

"No." He scowled. "Yes. I don't know. It would have been nice not to be blindsided is all."

His mother raised a skeptical brow at him. "Sure. Okay. And how was it seeing him again?"

Wasn't that the question of the night? Dev exhaled slowly. "Fine. We'd actually worked on a case together in the ER, so it wasn't like we haven't talked at all since I've been back. And Cam is a very sweet boy. He reminds me a lot of Vicki." Dev found himself smiling. "He loves Lego."

"Sounds like someone else I know when he was that age," his mom said, echoing Dev's own thoughts. "I know you can't tell me specifics, but I hope Cam is okay?"

"He's fine," Dev said, staring at the TV screen where the new host was talking to the contestants about the charities they were supporting with their winnings. "We went for ice cream afterward."

"Really?" His mom stopped knitting and leaned forward, her sudden interest making his cheeks heat. "And how did that go?"

"Fine," Dev snapped, more annoyed with himself than anything. For some frustrating reason, he couldn't seem to stop himself from becoming a blushing schoolboy now whenever he discussed Val. It was embarrassing. "I'm a grown man," he said, as much for his mother's benefit as his own. "I can certainly handle myself through a brief encounter at an ice-cream parlor."

"Glad to hear it," his mother said, chuckling as she sat back and resumed her knitting. "Where'd you go?"

He gave her the name. "I don't remember it from when I lived here before. So much has changed in the city since I've been gone."

"You can say that again." She grinned. "I'm glad you're starting to get out again and explore it all. Sounds like having Val back in your life is good for you."

"I don't know about that," Dev argued, agitated by the spike of adrenaline in his bloodstream. Yes, he'd enjoyed their trip to get ice cream. Didn't mean he planned to repeat it.

Do I?

No. That would just be asking for trouble, and Dev had had enough of that for a lifetime.

Still, he couldn't seem to stop himself from mentioning, "He invited me to go with him and Cam to a Timberwolves game this weekend."

"Excellent." His mother grinned wider. "I went to one last season with my church group, and it was great fun."

"I'm not going," Dev said, steadfast in his decision. He had no business continuing to socialize with Val and Cam when it would never come to anything. "I'll probably be on call anyway."

He wasn't on call. The schedule for his practice had already been posted earlier that day, and Dev had Saturday off. But it sounded like as good an excuse as any.

"Well, if you're not going, I'd seriously consider it. Those tickets are hard to come by and I think you'd really enjoy yourself. Get you out and about again. Do you good. And you don't know many people in town yet. Val is nothing if not social. He could help you meet new people."

Dev couldn't argue with that. Val had always been the extrovert friend he'd relied on back in medical school to drag him out of the house and to whatever events were happening. He'd almost always enjoyed himself when he got there, and he would have missed it all if Val hadn't brought him along.

He took a deep breath. As part of his hiring into the hospital, he'd promised not only to volunteer at the staff clinic but also to volunteer at other community events and charities to help promote the practice's health-care initiatives, so maybe his mother was right. Maybe Val could be his first step into that world. And yes, it would mean controlling his errant reactions for another evening, but then Dev had had a lot of practice doing that, didn't he?

Still, he wasn't quite ready to commit yet. He needed to consider it more beforehand. He pushed to his feet and headed for the hallway. "I'll think about it."

"Hey," Val said, stepping aside and holding the front door open for Alex, who walked in holding a large pizza box with a two-liter bottle of soda balanced precariously atop it. As he passed, the air filled with the delicious scents of baked cheese and veggies, and Val's stomach growled loudly. "Smells great."

"I know, right?" Alex said, hiking his chin toward the bottle. "Can you grab that?"

Val shut the door then did as he'd been asked, carrying it to the kitchen table where plates and napkins had already been set out in preparation for their meal. As he got out glasses and filled them with ice, Alex set the pizza box in the center of the table. Val called down the hall, "Dinner's here, Cam."

The next few seconds were filled with an excited seven-year-old racing down the hall and into Alex's arms, and Alex swinging him around like he weighed nothing. The guy was a salesman but built like a lumberjack, big and burly with the beard to match.

"Hey, kiddo," Alex said, setting Cam down at last. "How goes it?"

Cam proceeded to fill Alex in on basically everything that had happened to him that week while they all took a seat and filled their plates with pizza and Val filled their glasses with soda. He'd just come off another twenty-four-hour shift and he appreciated not having to worry about dinner more than he could say. When Alex had called earlier and asked if tonight was good for him to stop by for their monthly meetup, Val had jumped at the chance.

"So," Alex said once Val had taken his seat and was pulling his first slice out of the box. "What was it like seeing your old friend again?"

Val had been trying to answer that himself in the days since the clinic and the ice cream afterward. He still hadn't landed on a clear answer yet, so he went with a shrug and a "It was nice."

"Nice?" Alex gave him a flat look. "That's it?"

"What do you want me to say?" Val asked after swallowing a large bite of deluxe pizza. "It was fine. We haven't seen each other in ten years and we've both changed a lot, so it was a little awkward at first, but we're both adults and we dealt with it. And we'd already worked on a case together at work, so it wasn't like it was the first time we had seen each other again, so it wasn't a big deal. End of story."

If only that were true...

"How'd you meet, Uncle Val?" Cam asked, a big dollop of sauce dripping off the pizza in his hand and on to the front of his shirt. "Oops!"

Val reached over with a napkin to clean him up. He'd have to mention that stain to Nancy when she did laundry next time to make sure she soaked it. Hopefully tomato came out. That shirt was brand-new. "We met in med school," Val said, as he dabbed at the stain with his own napkin wet with his spit. "On our first day. I walked in and saw Dev alone in the corner and felt sorry for him, so I made it my mission to be his friend. Just like I told you to do at school. Not everyone is as comfortable socially around other people as we are, so we need to meet them where they are and help them be comfortable."

"That's how I met Benjamin," Cam said, nodding. "He's a good friend."

"He is." Val sat back, giving up on the stain for now. He smiled at Cam then turned back to Alex. "Seriously. It was just a nice gesture to help ease the awkwardness between us after what happened."

"What happened?" Cam asked innocently.

"Nothing you need to worry about, kiddo," Alex intervened, ruffling Cam's hair. "Tell me about your new Lego set."

That, thankfully, set Cam off on a whole other tangent, going on and on about Microfighters and *Star Wars* and the next show that was coming out soon on streaming. Val had a hard time keeping up with it all and didn't try. He loved sci-fi as much as the next person, but Cam took it to a whole new level, so he just indulged his son and loved that he loved it all so much. He wouldn't be surprised if Cam walked on Mars someday, he was that focused on science and space. And he was happy to encourage that in whatever way he could.

By the time they finished the meal and Val cleaned up then got Cam ready for bed, Alex was sitting in the living room, having picked up and put away all the scattered toys from earlier. He really was a good friend. Val sank down tiredly on the other end of the sofa from him and rested his head against the cushions.

"So, now tell me how it really was, seeing this guy again," Alex said. "And don't give me that 'nice' BS. That won't cut it."

"Honestly? I'm still trying to figure it out myself," Val said truthfully. He and Alex talked regularly about everything they were going through. It was a bond forged when they'd gone through it all with Vicki together, and one they still treasured now as they ventured back out into the world post-loss. Alex was dipping his toe back into dating again after more than a year, and Val helped advise him with that as best he could, since he hadn't really dated anyone since Vicki's passing himself. He was too busy with work and Cam and adjusting to life as a single dad. But sometimes just having fresh eyes on things helped, and Val was happy to be that for Alex— and hoped for the same in return now. "I told you about the fight we had after Dev's then-fiancé came on to me at the bachelor party. Back then he didn't believe me. But I'm pretty sure he does now, since they're divorced. He said Tom cheated on him. Repeatedly."

"Oh, wow." Alex's eyes widened. "And what did you say?"

"That I was sorry. Which I am. I'm sorry Dev had to go through all that. Tom never deserved Dev, and I hope the guy is attacked by a swarm of killer bees for hurting Dev."

Alex snorted. "Tell me how you really feel."

"The bee-nado didn't cover it?" Val laughed. "Enough about that a-hole though. He doesn't deserve the attention. It's Dev who's important now."

"How important?" Alex pushed. He'd never let Val

off easy before, so he knew better than to expect it now. "You said it was awkward seeing him again. Do you want to reconnect?"

"I do," Val said without reservation. "After what he's been through, I'm sure he could use a friend."

"And that's all it is? Friendship?"

"Of course." Val frowned. "What else would it be?"

"I don't know. That's why I'm asking," Alex countered, looking innocent enough, though Val suspected more beneath that question.

Or maybe that was just him reading more into it than he should, a frequent problem he had. Reading more into things, feeling things more deeply than he should, caring too much. He liked to genuinely connect with people, that was all. It was the same with Dev. He'd missed that connection, and he wanted it back. That was all. And if some tiny part of him might wish for more, well, that was too bad. Dev was clearly avoiding anything like that, and Val would honor those boundaries. Period.

"Just friendship," he said, as much for Alex as himself. "I invited him to the Timberwolves game Saturday, since you bailed on me."

"Hey, I can't help it if work requires me at a conference in Las Vegas the next day." Alex shrugged. "Did he take you up on your offer?"

"Not yet." It had been three days since the ice cream encounter on Monday night, and each time Val checked his messages on his phone, there'd been nothing—despite him sending Dev the details on Tuesday. It was okay, he told himself. Dev would let him know when he was ready. If he was ready. He wasn't holding out hope though. "If he doesn't want to go, it's fine. I wanted to offer though. He hasn't been back long and probably doesn't know many people here now, so I wanted to make him feel welcome."

"Uh-huh." Alex snorted. "Whatever."

"What?" Val sat up and smacked his friend with one of the throw pillows between them. "I'm a friendly guy."

His phone buzzed in his pocket then and he pulled it out, expecting an update on one of his patients from the ER. What he saw onscreen though froze him to the spot.

Alex paused midretaliation with a throw pillow in his hand, noticing how still Val had gotten. "What? Something wrong?"

"Uh…no. I don't think so," he said, unable to keep the astonishment from his voice. "Dev just texted me back. He's going to the game on Saturday with us."

"Wow." Alex barked out a laugh and set his throw pillow aside. "Well, that's good news then, right?"

"Sure," Val said, still a bit dazed. He'd basically given up on the invitation, but now, his heart was racing a million miles a minute even though he knew it shouldn't be. It was just a game, just an evening between friends, as he'd told Alex. So why did it feel like more? "It's good."

Saturday late afternoon found Val standing in a large crowd, entering the Target Center arena beside Dev, still stunned the guy had actually shown up. Sure, he'd texted Val and told him he would, but they hadn't had a chance to talk in person since, and Val had half expected that Dev would cancel at the last minute. But he hadn't, and sure enough, when he and Cam had arrived at their appointed meetup spot, Dev had been waiting there, early as always, looking as uncomfortable as a fart in church, as Vicki would have said. Cam had been thrilled to see Dr. Dev again, of course, and had rushed to hug Dev's legs. The kid had inherited Val's gift of the gab and collecting people, it seemed, and he made friends wherever he went. Plus, after Dev had confessed to a love of Lego too, he'd become Cam's new favorite obsession, apparently. The kid hadn't stopped talking about this game since Val had told him the news that Dev would be joining them this morning.

And speaking of obsessions…

Val glanced over at Dev for the umpteenth time as they now made their way inside with the rest of the throng of Timberwolves fans, like he still needed proof this was really happening. And yep. It was. The clamor of excitement reverberating through the stadium matched the zing of electricity inside Val's own bloodstream. Chances were slim that even though Dev had finally accepted his apology the other night, they'd just fall back easily into the friendship they'd had before. But if they could at least keep things lighter between them now, Val would be grateful.

He'd had enough darkness since the funeral to last him a lifetime.

Cam, who stood between him and Dev and clasped each of their hands to avoid getting lost, stared around them with wonder at the sea of blue jersey-wearing fans milling around. He'd been too young to bring here when Vicki was still alive, and then after she'd passed, the timing hadn't been right. Tonight was Cam's first time at a real NBA game, though he watched them on TV with

Val when they could. He'd even bought them each a new official jersey to wear today. He would have gotten one for Dev too, but he wasn't sure of the size or if he'd even want one so... Dev wore his usual jeans and sweater, an island of calm amidst the frenetic energy of game night, and damn if he still didn't have his whole sexy nerd thing going on, even after all these years, which had always hit Val's sweet spot, even though they'd never crossed that line.

And wouldn't now, he reminded himself.

This was about friendship, like he'd told Alex. Showing Dev around. Nothing more.

Besides, even sixteen months later, Val still felt like he was processing his grief over losing his sister and adjusting to his new life with Cam. Most of the time, he barely had time to breathe, let alone the time for a fling or anything more. And sure, sometimes he missed having that close connection with someone, a special person who knew him better than anyone else and loved him anyway, but he wouldn't trade his life with Cam now for anything in the world. He had Alex, sure, but some small part of him still yearned for more... And if he was lonely, well, he'd get over it.

"Look, Uncle Val! There's Crunch the Wolf!" Cam's voice cut through his thoughts as his son pointed to the team's mascot bouncing between laughing, cheering fans.

"You want to say hi to him?" Val asked, crouching beside the boy. Dev watched them, his dark gaze lingering on their interaction, a ghost of a smile tugging at the corner of his lips as something flashed across his features, so quick Val couldn't quite read it, but it made his chest pinch anyway.

"Yes, please!" Cam jumped up and down, obviously feeling better than he had the other day.

By the time they got through the line to greet Crunch, then made their way into the arena itself to find their seats, the pregame festivities had reached a crescendo. Val settled into one of their three hard plastic chairs, with Dev on the other end and Cam sandwiched between them. Several people around them nodded and smiled, one lady cooing about how cute Cam was.

"This place is packed," Dev said as he shrugged out of his jacket and scanned the crowd. "Is it always like this for games?"

"Yep." Val grinned as he inhaled the smell of popcorn and beer. He hadn't been to a game since the funeral, and he'd missed them. Vicki had been a die-hard Timberwolves fan, and he'd often come with her and Alex. But Alex had been too busy with his job recently and Val didn't like to come alone, so…

A vendor passed by, and Val stopped him to buy each of them a drink. The knot of tension that had been present since he'd gotten the text Thursday night was easing. This would be fine. They'd have a good time here, and maybe they could leave all that unresolved baggage that still lingered between them like an overloaded laundry line behind. No more awkwardness. That was Val's greatest wish at this point. It made everything harder, and he longed for the ease they'd once shared. And sure, Dev had to have some scars left behind from his divorce from douchebag Tom, but if they could just move past all that, it would be such a relief. And if they could somehow recover some semblance of their old friendship, that would be even better. With Vicki gone, no one knew his past better than Dev now, and vice versa. Dev knew about his deadbeat parents, and why Val was so outgoing was partly because he wanted people to like him. Because if people liked you, they treated you better. And he knew all about Dev's triggers too—the abandonment by his father, the misplaced shame and embarrassment of thinking that he was somehow responsible for his dad leaving. It had had nothing to do with Dev and everything to do with the man's own issues and selfishness. He'd missed being able to talk to Dev, knowing that Dev would understand when almost no one else would.

Before he could get too lost down that path though, the announcer thankfully drew him back to the here and now by asking everyone to stand for the national anthem.

Soon, the game got underway, and the roar of the crowd surged like a wave as the Timberwolves claimed possession, and Val and Cam got swept up in the collective excitement, jumping to their feet and cheering whenever their team scored. Dev remained seated, more reserved as always, clapping but not going overboard. Val had to chuckle. Even now, he'd never met anyone more in control of his emotions than Devon Harrison. It was one of the things that had drawn Val to the guy from the start and something he still admired, since he tended to be too emotional himself sometimes. Having grown up surrounded by such chaos, never knowing what he'd get at home from his alcoholic parents, Val found that being around Dev, who always came across as so calm and collected, had been a true revelation. Not that it wasn't challenging too sometimes, when he wished Dev could get upset more, but the only time that had ever happened was the night of the bachelor party when he'd told Dev about Tom…

Wincing slightly, he hazarded another glance Dev's way, hoping he hadn't noticed, but Dev seemed totally engrossed in the action on the court, his jaw shadowed by a hint of dark stubble that Val had a sudden urge to lean over and lick just to see what Dev would do and…

And what the…?

Stunned at himself, Val sat back and swallowed hard. Where the hell had that come from? He'd been telling the truth the other night when he'd told Alex that this was about friendship. That was all. He'd never wanted to cross that line with Dev, never wanted to push the well-established boundaries they'd set for themselves all those years ago, so why the hell was he suddenly having these thoughts now? The connection they'd had and lost, but might have again if he was careful, was too precious to risk the possibility of more.

Isn't it?

"Go! Go!" Cam shouted as the Timberwolves scored another basket against the opposing team, jarring Val out of those dangerous thoughts. No. He didn't want to get involved with Dev like that now. Sex made everything more complicated, and they already had enough issues between them to deal with.

Thinking about wanting Dev that way was stupid. Ridiculous. Absurd.

Then Dev glanced over at him and a fresh shot of kinetic attraction shot straight through Val, making his knees wobble even though he was sitting down, and that's when he knew.

This was going to be a problem.

He had to hide it, had to keep it to himself until he could move past it. To that end, he stood and hoisted Cam onto his shoulders and moved down to the railing for a better view, and as applause erupted around them, he put as much distance as he could between himself and the man who suddenly filled him with a need that threatened everything Val had said he wanted. His heart felt like it would pound out of his chest. Maybe he was taking the coward's way out, but at least Dev would never know because he'd never tell him.

Unless he asks...

Because he'd also vowed after the fight they'd had that he'd always be truthful with Dev.

The guy deserved that after all the lies he'd been fed by his ex-husband.

But is the truth best about this?

Val was still pondering that conundrum as the first quarter closed and the buzzer blared. He took Cam to the restroom, waited in line there, then caught another vendor on the way back as the next quarter started to buy more drinks and popcorn. As they took their seats once more, Dev still sat there, looking at least a bit more relaxed than before, which was good. Not wanting to disturb that—and to cover his own inner turmoil over his newly discovered desire—Val tried making small talk, pointing down to where the players were currently huddled around their coach courtside during a time-out.

"Quite the game, huh? Remember those charity matches we used to play during residency?"

"I do," Dev said, watching a replay of the last call on the overhead screen. "You always played a mean offense."

"Only because I knew your defense tactics by heart." Val snorted.

"True," Dev conceded. "You were always good at reading people, on and off the court."

"I try," he said, feeling some of the tension ease between his shoulder blades. Maybe it was just an isolated thing, that hot stab of want he'd felt toward Dev. It had been a long time since he'd gotten laid. Too long, probably. That had to be it. Yep. "That group of friends I mentioned from medical school still plays on the weekend sometimes. I'll let you know the next time we get together. We also play board games too. Trivial Pursuit, Pictionary, Cards Against Humanity. Though that last one can get kind of brutal. Hilarious, but brutal."

Dev chuckled. "I don't think you want to go against me at Trivial Pursuit. Did you know I once auditioned for *Jeopardy!* while I was living in California?"

"No way." Val straightened, forgetting all about his desire now as he learned this new important information. That had been their favorite show back in medical school. "How far did you make it?"

"All the way up to the in-person audition with the producers. I was so excited because I thought maybe I'd finally get to meet Alex Trebek, but then I messed up what should have been the easiest answer ever because of my nerves."

Val frowned. "What was it?"

"Who was the king of the Zulu Kingdom from 1816 to 1828?" He cringed. "I meant to say 'Who is Shaka Zulu?' But what came out instead was 'Who is Chaka Khan?'"

Val couldn't contain his laughter, especially when the DJ at the arena chose that moment to play Ms. Khan's eighties megahit "I Feel for You" after an impressive three-pointer by the home team. Soon Dev was laughing too, and it was like the years disappeared. Cam ignored them both, too enthralled with the game to pay either of them much attention. The moment lasted a few seconds before Dev returned to his usual contained self and focused on the game once more, but it was enough to confirm to Val that he'd made the right choice to ignore his new feelings toward Dev. That glimmer was enough to convince him that a return to their old connection might be possible after all.

The game continued with a spectacular score from a Timberwolves star player, causing the crowd to erupt into raucous cheers. Val gave it a standing ovation, grinning over at Dev, who was on his feet too, while Cam did a little victory dance between them. The Timberwolves were so far ahead now that it would be virtually impossible for the other team to win as the clock ticked down in the final quarter. The air felt electric as the last few seconds ticked down on the clock and the Timberwolves point guard launched one final shot. As the basketball arced as if in slow motion toward the basket, a hushed whisper took over the arena as every eye followed the ball. When it kissed the rim then fell through the net, the home crowd erupted in triumph. Val picked up Cam and put him on his shoulders again as elation surged between their trio. "Did you see that?"

"Yes!" Dev grinned, his usual reserve giving way to genuine awe. "Unbelievable!"

Eventually, the crowd began to dissipate, and they made their way out of the stadium. Val's arm occasionally brushed Dev's as they weaved through people, sending forbidden tingles through him before he shoved them down. Cam couldn't stop talking about the game and the kid was practically floating with energy now. Val was glad the next day was Sunday, since he'd bet good money his son wouldn't fall asleep for a while, and there was no way he'd get up for school.

They reached Dev's car first. They stopped at the rear bumper to part ways. "Tonight was fun. Thanks for inviting me."

"Thanks for accepting," Val said, meaning it. "I'm glad you enjoyed it, and I hope it won't be the last time."

Dev nodded then stared down at the keys in his hand. "My mom thinks you can help me get out more."

"She's right." Val rocked back on his heels. "I'm happy to show you around again, if you want."

"We'll see," Dev said noncommittally, then transferred his attention to Cam. "How are you feeling?"

"I feel great!" Cam said, then yawned. "Good night, Dr. Dev."

Dev smiled, causing Val's heart to flip over before he scolded himself. "Good night, Cam."

Both men hesitated, one beat stretching into two, until finally Val picked up his son. "Well, I'll see you around the hospital, then."

"Yes, you will," Dev said. "We're still consulting together on Matt's case, since his results came back ALL and not mono. And let me know if you ever need me to check Cam again. Clinic or not."

"Will do. Thanks." Val backed away, waiting until Dev had gotten in his car and started the engine, before turning toward his SUV parked down the same row. It was a generous offer on Dev's part, and one Val might take him up on, if needed. They could do this. He could do this. Put Dev firmly back in the friendship category and be happy about it. He'd get over this weird new desire and things would get back to normal between them. He'd have the connection he wanted back in his life.

And maybe, if he told himself that enough times, he'd believe his own nonsense.

CHAPTER FOUR

When he'd offered to check Cam again if needed, he'd hadn't expected a text from Val so soon. But here he was, parked outside of Val's house this time, ready to go in for what Val had called a "final check." Of course he'd said yes, because he considered Cam one of his patients now and because, well, he'd missed the boy. Missed Val too, if he was honest, even though it had only been a few days since the game.

Dev had never allowed himself to need a lot of other people around, so it was odd, honestly, missing them. Usually, he enjoyed his alone time. Even with Tom, he hadn't questioned how little time they had spent together because of their crazy schedules. In hindsight, maybe if he'd paid more attention then, he would've saved himself a lot of heartache.

Scowling, he got out and grabbed his medical bag, then walked up to the porch to ring the doorbell, ignoring the sudden thrumming of his heart against his ribs and nerves sizzling through him. Then the door opened to reveal a dark-haired woman with a kind smile.

"You must be Dr. Harrison," she said, holding out her hand. "I'm Nancy, the nanny. Please come in." She gestured him inside then took his coat. "I'll let Val and Cam know you're here. The kid hasn't stopped talking about that game. He's really taken a shine to you."

"I've taken a shine to him too," Dev said before she disappeared down the hall. While he waited, he sat on the sofa and glanced at several completed Lego structures stuck amidst the books on the built-in shelves along the walls, and the various colorful drawings strewn across the coffee table in front of him. He'd received his fair share of pictures from his patients over the years, so he considered himself a pretty good judge of talent, and Cam's were good.

Once upon a time, a home like this was all young Dev had dreamed of. Not that his mom hadn't done her best, but she'd had to work two jobs to keep a roof over their heads, and there was many a night when Dev had been left to his own devices. He hadn't thought about that in years, his loneliness back then, but being here reignited the pull of those old cravings for companionship. Except now he knew the price of letting someone that close and how badly you could get burned if you were wrong.

Before he could get too mired in the past, however, Cam raced into the living room in his stockinged feet, his blue eyes bright with excitement, looking about as healthy as a kid could get. "Dr. Dev! You're here!"

"I am," Dev said, his own smile matching the boy's enthusiasm. "Your dad asked me to come by."

"Cool!" He scrambled up onto the sofa next to Dev. "Did you save any kids today?"

Dev chuckled as he pulled on a pair of gloves from the medical kit. "Well, I met a little girl who loves dinosaurs as much as you love Lego." He held a digital thermometer against Cam's forehead. Ninety-eight point six. "We talked about triceratops while I gave her the medicine she needed."

"So you're a dino doc too?" Cam's eyes widened as Dev checked his pulse and respirations, then listened to the boy's lungs with his stethoscope. "That's so amazing!"

"Talking to her was pretty awesome," Dev agreed as he finished rechecking Cam's ears and throat. All clear. "Did you know that when I was your age, I wanted to be a paleontologist?"

"A pale what?" Cam scrunched his nose. "I don't know what that is."

"Paleontologist. They study dinosaurs for a living," he told the boy as he palpated the lymph nodes in Cam's neck and found them slightly swollen, but nothing unexpected after recovering from a cold as Cam had. They should be back to normal soon enough. "Did you know I used to dig in my backyard when I was your age, hoping I'd find a dinosaur bone?"

Cam gaped. "Did you ever find one?"

"No," Dev sighed, pulling off his gloves and returning them to his bag along with the rest of his stuff. "All I ever found were some plain old rocks, but I pretended they were fossils. My poor mom went along with it too to keep me happy. She used to say it was all about imagination."

"Uncle Val says that too!" Cam said, his gaze intent.

"What do I say?" Val asked, emerging from the hallway. "Sorry I was delayed—had to deal with a call from the ER. What did I miss?"

"That life is about imagination," Dev said, smiling at Cam. "We were just discussing dinosaurs."

"Dr. Dev said he dug in his backyard when he was my age. Can I do that too, Uncle Val? Please?"

"Uh…no." Val shook his head and walked over to sit in an armchair across from them, looking far too relaxed and delectable for his own good. Not that Dev noticed. Nope. "I think you have more than enough hobbies to keep you busy right now, don't you? Between Lego and soccer and drawing and Star Wars?"

"I guess," Cam sighed, then jumped off the couch. "Wait here, Dr. Dev. I'm gonna get the new Lego toy I built to show you."

He sprinted off down the hall again, leaving Val and Dev alone in the living room.

"I examined him as well, while we talked, and he's one hundred percent healthy. As if his energy wasn't enough of a sign," Dev said.

"Good, thanks." Val sat forward. "I got that humidifier you recommended too, and it seems to help."

"Excellent. Glad to hear it."

"I'm leaving for the night," Nancy said, reappearing with her coat on and her purse over her shoulder. "Unless you need anything else, Val. Nice to meet you, Dr. Harrison."

"You too," Dev said. "And please, call me Dev."

"Good night, Nancy. Thanks for everything."

"Sure thing." She gave them a little wave. "See you in the morning."

After she left, the ensuing moments stretched taut and the silence grew uncomfortable. Dev finally stood.

"Well, I should probably get going then too. Unless you need something else from me."

"Dr. Dev! Look at this!" Cam ran back in and thrust an oddly shaped blue building up at him. "Isn't it cool?"

"It sure is," Dev said, doing his best to look suitably impressed, even though he had no clue what the thing was. "It's very…blue."

"It's Stark Tower," Val supplied helpfully, humor edging his tone. "You know, from *The Avengers*."

"Oh, right." Dev nodded, shooting Val a grateful glance. That movie was from a while ago, so it had slipped his mind. "I loved *The Avengers*."

"Me too," Cam said. "I'm gonna be Iron Man one day."

"Really?" Dev crouched to put himself and Cam at eye level. "You have to be really brave for that."

"I can be brave, Dr. Dev!" Cam placed his hands on his hips in a superhero pose. "See?"

"I do see," Dev agreed, straightening and ruffling the boy's hair. "Very brave indeed."

"You're brave too, Dr. Dev," Cam continued, patting Dev's hand. "Saving people."

Considering how his life had gone the past few years, brave wasn't a word Dev would've used about himself. But now, looking back, maybe it had taken some courage to walk away from the life he'd planned with Tom in California and return to Minneapolis. At the time, he'd just wanted to get as far away as possible from all that pain, but perhaps some small part of him had also sought the comfort of the only place that had ever felt like home. He managed to say, "Thank you, Cam. That means a lot."

Thankfully, if Val noticed the crack in Dev's voice at those words, he didn't mention it.

Lord, what was happening to him? He'd gone from feeling nothing to nearly crying when a kid paid him a compliment. Maybe he was more tired after a long day than he'd thought.

Cam clambered back down the hall again, presumably to grab more toys for Dev to admire, and Val clapped Dev on the shoulder, making him jump. He hadn't even seen Val move because he'd been so focused on the boy.

"He'll keep you here all night showing you his stuff, if you're not careful," Val said, chuckling as he headed for the open kitchen behind them. "He's got a ton of Lego."

"Oh, well," Dev said, grabbing his medical bag, more flustered from that brief touch than he cared to admit. "I guess I'd better get going then."

Before he made it back to the foyer, where Nancy had hung his coat earlier, Cam was back. This time with a toy Dev recognized. "I finished my Microfighter too! See?"

"Oh, wow, Cam!" This time Dev didn't have to pretend to be impressed. It was a complicated and difficult build and Cam had done it in just a few days, apparently. The last time he'd heard the boy talk about it, he'd just started the new set. He took the model gently from Cam's hands to admire it up close. "This is amazing."

"Thanks. I can't wait to take it to school tomorrow and show my friends. I have lots of friends," Cam said, looking proud of himself. "My mom always said I could make friends with a tree."

"You take after your uncle." Dev grinned, glancing over at Val, who was watching them from behind the island. "Being sociable can be a good thing though. Helps you meet new people and learn new things. You can adapt easily and make life an adventure."

"Yes! I love adventures." Cam grinned over at Dev before growing serious again. "Did you have a lot of friends growing up, Dr. Dev?"

By now he should be used to children's astuteness. Back when he'd been doing his pediatric oncology fellowship, one of the first things his mentor had told him was to always be truthful with the children under his care, because they would see through a lie in a second. He'd always kept to that rule over the past eight years, and it had never steered him wrong. Tonight would be no exception, even though telling the truth left Dev feeling far more exposed than he'd like. He gave a curt shake of his head. "No. I wasn't as sociable as you, Cam," he answered honestly. "I did have this stuffed bear I'd take everywhere with me when I was your age. He was like a friend who never left my side."

"I never knew you had a bear," Val said quietly from the kitchen. Dev didn't dare risk a glance at him, afraid those sturdy walls he'd built around himself might take another hit.

"Did your bear have a name?" Cam asked.

Dev's answer sounded gruffer than intended. "Sir Bearington."

"Like Mr. Trunks!" Cam said, rushing to a corner of the living room to pick up a well-loved elephant plushie. "Before I started school all day, he went everywhere with me. Now he stays home." Unexpected warmth spread through Dev's chest, and he resisted the urge to rub the area over his heart. "Sometimes I still talk to him about stuff though…like how I miss my mom, or how I worry about Uncle Val working too hard."

"That's good. Talking helps," Dev agreed, thinking back to the long nights he'd spent confiding in his own stuffed bear. "After my father left, I used to talk to Sir Bearington about things too, like how I felt lonely."

Val came back into the living room to crouch beside Cam, looking concerned, and Dev's pulse took another tumble before he stepped back, away from temptation.

"You think I work too much, buddy?" Val asked. "I don't want you worrying about me."

Cam shrugged, setting the plushie aside. "I just don't want to lose you like I lost my mom."

"Oh, Cam," Val said, pulling his son into a hug. "You know I'll never leave you if I can help it."

Things had gotten very emotional very fast, and Dev felt adrift in a treacherous sea that could easily overwhelm him. He needed to get out of here now before he did something silly like end up in a huddle hug with Val and Cam…or just Val. And the thought of being that close to Val, pressed against him, feeling his heat, surrounded by his clean, citrusy scent, was too much. He cleared his throat and turned back toward the door again. "I'm going to go now."

Val glanced at him from over the top of Cam's head and frowned. "Please stay for dinner. It's the least I can do to repay you making another trip over here."

"Yes, Dr. Dev!" Cam chimed in, racing over to grab Dev's hand. "Please stay for dinner!"

"Oh, I don't think—" Damn. He didn't want to disappoint Cam. And with things between him and Val finally approaching something close to normal, he didn't want to backslide into the frozen tundra their relationship had been before the basketball game by insulting him. And, well, he hadn't eaten all day, and the smells now drifting from the kitchen from whatever Val had put in the oven smelled delicious. Besides, he was a grown adult. He could get through one dinner with Val without revealing his troublesome feelings to him. Lord knew he'd become a master of hiding his emotions over the years. He could do it again here. "Well, if you both insist. Thank you. Dinner sounds great."

"Awesome!" Cam clapped and jumped around, as if this was the best news ever.

"The lasagna has about five more minutes to reheat," Val said, checking the oven again. "Cam, can you set the table, please?"

While the boy did as he was asked, with a stack of mismatched plates and silverware that Val had handed him, Dev stood there wondering what to do with himself. So, he took a seat at the table and waited until the oven timer went off. Cam soon climbed onto the chair across from him as Val carried in a steaming pan of what looked like Vicki's old homemade lasagna recipe. He dished up generous portions for each of them, the aroma of tomato sauce and garlic and baked cheese making Dev's stomach growl. He hadn't eaten since grabbing a quick energy bar for breakfast at his mother's house that morning. Val returned to the kitchen for a basket of breadsticks, then sat down as well.

While they ate, Cam kept up the conversation. "Did you save any lives today, Uncle Val?"

"Don't talk with your mouth full, buddy," Val chided him gently, undermining it a bit by laughing. "And no. Today was just the usual ER stuff. Broken arms and cuts and bruises. What about you, Cam? Any superhero feats in school today? How'd your test go?"

They chatted about their days as Dev nearly died from food ecstasy. He'd forgotten how good this recipe of Vicki's was and ended up stuffing himself full of carbs, which was good because it left little room for all the confusing emotions he'd been dealing with earlier. By the time they finished eating and cleaning up, and Val sent Cam to his room to get ready for bed, things almost felt comfortable.

Dev took this as the perfect time to leave before things got sticky again. "Thank you again for dinner."

This time, Val didn't stop him, following him to the door instead, a sheepish grin on his face. "I'd invite you to stay longer, but I owe Cam story time before he'll go to sleep, which can take a while depending on the book, so…"

And damn if Dev's throat didn't tighten with yearning over picturing Val and Cam snuggled in bed, cozy and secure.

What the hell is happening to me?

He'd never had an issue keeping his walls high and strong, but the more time he spent with these two, the more difficulty he was having keeping them in place. It was terrifying and thrilling all at once.

Val reached past Dev to open the door, putting them even closer. "Thank you for coming by to check on Cam again, and putting an overprotective new dad's mind at ease. I really appreciate it, Dev."

Their eyes met then, and as if drawn inexplicably by some invisible cord, Dev found himself leaning toward Val. He wasn't sure what he intended to do, maybe hug him or clap him on the shoulder as Val had done to him earlier, but then something changed in the air between them. Something charged and sparkling, volatile and electric. As if in a daze, he whispered, "Cam's lucky to have you."

"We're lucky to have each other," Val replied, his voice equally low and sincere as his gaze flicked to Dev's lips before returning to his eyes again. "He's become my anchor."

And in that moment, Dev couldn't have moved if he'd tried. He was held in place by the craving inside him to kiss Val, even as the shadows of old fears urged him to run far and fast from the feelings that could destroy everything he'd thought he'd wanted.

Blood pounded through his body with the force of a drum. They both had so much to lose if they crossed this line—Dev's new life and career and Val's role as Cam's sole parent. Neither of them could afford to screw those things up.

Go. Now. Before it's too late.

Somehow, Dev found the strength to break the spell woven around them and hurried outside, his breath rough from the dance of desire and trepidation twirling through his body, leaving him dizzy. He fumbled his steps, stumbling over his words. "I… I'm sorry… I really need to go."

Val blinked at him, looking as confused as Dev felt as he fled into the night. What had almost happened there was a mistake. An aberration. And it couldn't happen again. Dev couldn't allow it to happen again. Because he'd been down that impetuous road before, letting his emotions rule over his head, only to discover too late he'd been wrong.

He wouldn't make the same mistake again.

The answer was simple. Get some space and distance and it would all go away.

CHAPTER FIVE

It didn't go away.

In fact, the more he tried not to think about Val and what had occurred between them at that doorway, the more he couldn't stop those thoughts from flooding back. Over the past two days, he'd replayed every second of that almost-kiss, over and over, desperate to understand why it had happened, and most importantly, how to ensure it didn't happen again. Because he and Val were finally back on cordial terms again and he didn't want to ruin that by bringing anything more complicated into that mix. And if he woke up at night, hot and sweaty, blood thrumming, well, that was his problem to deal with—in an icy cold shower.

And deal with it he did, because it wasn't like they could avoid each other. They had to work certain cases together, like Matt Warden's. Which is what had Dev worked up this morning. Not that things had taken a turn for the worse with their young patient. On the contrary, all the test results showed that Matt was responding well to treatment and making steady, gradual improvement with his leukemia. No. It was the fact that Matt and his mother were coming in for a follow-up that morning and it would be the first time Dev saw Val after the night at his house.

He'd come in early for his shift after a sleepless night, and now sat in his office in the oncology department, nursing a cup of strong coffee. He already felt wired enough from nerves to power the entire state of Minnesota, and was staring at a lab report he'd already memorized of the results for Matt without really seeing it, because his mind continued to churn with anxiety over how he'd handle seeing Val again. His current mood hovered between dejected and determined.

Determined to stay professional and on track during the follow-up, because Matt and his mother deserved his very best care and that's what they'd get from him. Dejected, because he couldn't understand why he failed to control his emotions where Val was concerned. He'd tried everything he could think of to jar himself out of it—remembering the worst few weeks after the breakup of his marriage, when he'd felt lost and adrift in a sea of hurt and self-recriminations; when he'd sworn never to end up there again in his life, no matter what it took—but nothing seemed to do the trick.

It was maddening. It was alarming. It was also oddly energizing, challenging him to do better.

And Dev had always relished a challenge.

And speaking of challenges, a glance as his smartwatch said it was time for the consult with Matt and his mother.

With a sigh, Dev closed the laptop on his desk and stood, smoothing a hand down the front of his pristine white lab coat before heading out of his office and down the hall that led to the busy nurses' station out front. Shoulders squared, he reminded himself of his professional duty, his years of practice and his expertise. He'd remain aloof and focused, and everything would be fine. Chances were good that Val wouldn't even remember their encounter by the door that night. Just because Dev couldn't seem to get it out of his mind didn't mean Val was fixated on it too…

Gah. I'm being ridiculous.

Frustrated with his own inability to get past this, Dev grabbed his tablet and headed for Matt's room. Val was mostly likely already in there, so hopefully they could get this done quickly. As he opened the consultation room door, Dev flashed his most professional smile at Matt and his mother. "Good morning, Matt. Ms. Warden." He hazarded a brief glance at Val, who stood off to the side, arms crossed, stretching the blue scrubs he wore enticingly over the muscled torso beneath. Dev swallowed hard and diverted his attention fast to the screen of the tablet in his hand, mumbling, "Dr. Laurent."

Dev took a seat on a stool across from the patient and his mother, and got down to business. "Well, the good news is that your white blood count is coming up, Matt, which is exactly what we want to see after this initial round of chemo. We still have a way to go, but things are headed in the right direction for now."

Val nodded. "Dr. Harrison is right. I had a look at your results down in the ER myself and you're doing great, Matt. And you're in the best hands for care. Keep fighting, and we'll have you back playing with your team before you know it."

"Thanks." Matt flashed a tired smile beneath the blue knit cap that covered his balding scalp. "That's really great news."

After a brief chat to discuss treatment plans going forward, answer questions and recommend several natural supplements to help Matt with energy and brain fog, Dev shook their hands then headed back to his office to dictate his notes from the consult, using the new secure app on his phone the hospital was trying out with the physicians on staff. But before he could start, the phone buzzed in his hand and his mother's face popped up on the caller ID. He took a seat behind his desk and answered.

"Mom, everything okay?" he asked, concerned.

"Everything's fine, honey. I just wanted to remind you to stop at the store on your way home and pick up the basil I need for dinner tonight," she said. "Maybe another bottle of white wine too, since I'll use up what I have in the recipe."

Dev leaned back in his chair and took off his glasses, then massaged the bridge of his nose between his thumb and forefinger, eyes closed. Now that the nervous energy he'd been running on prior to seeing Val again was gone, his lack of sleep was catching up with him. He yawned, then said, "I won't forget, Mom."

"Is that Elaine?" Val asked from the doorway, making Dev bolt up in his seat and nearly drop his phone on the floor.

"Uh..." he said, shoving his glasses back on, glad for the desk between them as a smiling Val stepped into the office and seemed to take up all the space available. "Yes."

"Who are you talking to, honey?" his mother said from the other end of the line. "Is that Val?"

Crap.

"Tell her I said hello," Val said, sitting down in one of the chairs across from Val, looking far too relaxed for Dev's comfort. Was he really oblivious to the sizzling chemistry between them that was driving Dev nuts? Apparently. When Dev didn't respond, Val called, "Hi, Elaine!"

"Honey, put me on speaker so I can talk to him," his mom said.

Reluctantly, Dev did as she asked, wondering who exactly in the universe he'd annoyed that they seemed to be conspiring against him now. He set the phone on his desk and Val leaned forward, his grin widening. "It's so good to hear your voice again, Elaine. How are you?"

"I'm good, Val. How are you? Still holding in there?" His mother's tone turned concerned. "How's poor Cam?"

"Cam is great, thanks for asking. We're doing okay. It's an adjustment but were getting through it. Also thank you for the flowers at Vicki's funeral. I never got a chance to say that personally and I'm sorry. Things were so crazy there for a while."

"No worries at all."

While they chatted, Dev turned his attention on sorting through his email on his laptop and ignoring the fact that with Val so close, he could catch the scent of soap and clean, warm maleness from his skin. Which only made the unwanted, simmering need low in his gut kick up a notch closer to full boil.

Enough.

He finally picked up his phone again, intent on ending this torture. "Right. If you two are caught up, I do have other work I need to attend to. Mom, I will pick up the things you need at the store and see you tonight when I get home."

"Val, I'm making chicken cacciatore, your favorite," his mother said before Dev could shut off the speakerphone. "Why don't you and Cam come over and join us if you don't have other plans? I'd love to meet Cam and see you again, and you can both get a good home-cooked meal."

"I'd love that, Elaine," Val said, grinning over at Dev. "What time should we be there? And can I bring anything?"

"Seven, and just yourselves," Elaine said. "Can't wait to see you both then."

"Same. Thanks again." Val sat back at last as Dev ended the call before fate could taunt him anymore. Val's grin slowly faded as he looked at Dev. "I hope it's okay that we come. If you don't want me to, I won't."

Great. Now Dev was stuck between a rock and a hard place. If he said no, that it was fine, he'd have to endure a whole night of sitting beside Val, thinking about their almost-kiss and how that could never ever happen again. If he said yes, then that made him sound petty and mean. And he would like to see Cam again. The kid was like a walking, talking ray of sunshine.

In the end, there wasn't much of a choice. "It's fine,"

he said curtly. "Now, if you'll excuse me, I really do have work to do."

"Sure." Val stood and walked back to the door, stopping there to look back at Dev. "Listen, about the other night…"

Oh, boy.

Dev squeezed his eyes shut and took a deep breath, fearful that Val would read too much in his eyes. "What about it?" he said, hoping to sound as detached as possible. "We had a nice dinner and some conversation. That's it."

Val just stood there, the weight of his stare heavy on the side of Dev's head. "Seriously?"

Exasperated and feeling trapped, Dev finally opened his eyes and threw up his hand as he looked at Val. "What? What do you want me to say? That we almost kissed by the door?" With the door open, he made sure to keep his voice low enough that his personal life wouldn't become fodder for the hospital gossip mill. "It was a mistake. I'm sorry. I don't know what I was thinking. Let's just forget all about it, all right?"

At that moment, Dev wished for nothing more than for a hole to open beneath him and swallow him completely— at least then, he could escape the embarrassing shame spiral he now found himself in.

Instead of leaving, Val stepped into the office and closed the door behind him, causing Dev's already-racing heart to triple its speed. "Dev, forgetting about it won't help. We can work through this."

Dev snorted. Sure. He knew firsthand it wouldn't be that easy. "I don't have time for this right now."

Val blinked at him. "Like I do?" He shook his head, hands on hips as he stared down at the floor. "Look, we might not know each other that well now, but you were the closest friend I had for years, and I'd bet good money you've been overanalyzing everything since that night."

Dev resented the fact that he was right. "I'm not sure what that has to do with this…weird thing…between us."

"It's not weird, it's attraction. And it's normal." Val watched him closely for a beat or two, then sighed. "Doesn't mean we have to act on it, okay? I just want things to be good between us again. Cam really likes you, and I don't want him hurt in all this because we decided to do something foolish."

"I like Cam too. He's a great kid." Forcing himself to breathe, Dev swallowed the lump in his throat. "And I don't want him hurt either. So, like I said, we forget all about the other night and move on like it never happened. Agreed?"

"Agreed. I need to get back downstairs. The ER was slammed when I left." Val opened the door and stepped out into the hallway again, sending Dev a last dazzling smile over his shoulder. "See you at seven."

Dev just sat there for a full minute after he left, wondering how the hell he'd ended up here in the first place—and more importantly, how he was going to get through the night ahead without getting close to Val to keep his sanity. They'd agreed, after all, and Dev knew then he was in big, big trouble.

After his shift, Val ran home, showered and changed, then stood before the mirror in his bedroom, adjusting the collar of his white dress shirt for the umpteenth time. The expression staring back at him looked more like a man gearing up for battle than one preparing for a casual dinner at a friend's house. Which was ridiculous. This was dinner with Elaine and Dev. Back in the day, he'd gone over to their house a couple of times a week for study sessions or just to hang out. It wasn't a big deal.

Except it sure felt like it was.

Despite the agreement he and Dev had reached in his office to not pursue things between them.

Because he knew he hadn't misread things the other night in the foyer. That if he'd just leaned in a little more, he and Dev would've kissed, and Val would've loved it. At first, his reaction when thinking about kissing Dev had taken Val by surprise, but he'd since come to terms with the fact that he wanted Dev as more than a friend now. Maybe it was a side effect of losing him for so long after the wedding, then getting him back unexpectedly, but this felt like a second chance and Val knew how rare those were. He didn't want to let this one slip through his fingers. And if Dev only wanted to be friends, that was fine. He'd deal with it. He'd take whatever he could get with Dev, honestly. For so long, he'd feared their cherished connection had disappeared forever, so an opportunity to revive it now sounded like the best idea in the world to Val, however that looked for them. It would be fine. Val would make sure of it. For himself and for his son too, since Cam had taken to Dev so quickly.

Just keep yourself grounded and take it slow.

He took a deep breath and gave up on studying his own reflection. He walked down the hall to Cam's room instead to make sure he was ready to go. Cam had insisted on wearing his new Timberwolves jersey, the one they'd bought for the game, despite the fact it was too big for him. He'd barely taken it off all week, so rather than argue, Val let him. Picking your battles was an essential rule of parenthood.

"Do you think Dr. Dev will let me see his models?" Cam asked as Val made sure the kid's sneakers were tied. "Did they even have Lego when he was a kid?"

Val bit back a laugh as he ruffled the boy's hair. "Yes, they had Lego back then. How old do you think Dev and I are?"

"Old." Cam tugged on his jacket as he raced for the front door.

The drive over to Elaine's house was uneventful, with Cam telling Val the whole way about his day at school. Val nodded or responded at the appropriate times, though his mind was only half on the conversation and half on seeing Dev again soon.

He'd meant what he'd said earlier, about wanting things to be good. And if that meant forgetting all about whatever this thing was that was developing between them, well, Val was okay with that too. Yes, he was attracted to Dev, but he would never act on it unless he got a clear signal from Dev that that's what he wanted too. And of course, there was Cam to consider as well. He didn't want to ruin the budding friendship between those two either, and if he and Dev did get involved, then it could get messy if it all went off the rails. Sex would only complicate that situation further.

When they finally pulled into the driveway, a jolt

of nostalgia ran through Val. The ranch-style suburban home looked just as he remembered, with its warmly lit windows and manicured lawn. He and Cam got out and walked up to the front door, but before he could knock, the door swung open, and there was Elaine in her wheelchair, her kind eyes and gentle smile calming all Val's nerves.

"Valentine Laurent, it feels like forever since I've seen you," she exclaimed, pulling him down for a hug before turning her attention to Cam. "And Cameron. It's so nice to meet you in person finally. I knew your mom well."

Cam tilted his head, studying her. "I remember the flowers you sent to the funeral. They were the biggest ones there."

Elaine hugged him too. "Precious boy."

She waited until they were inside before whispering to Val once Cam was busy searching for Dev. "I know my son is probably too stubborn to say this himself, but I'm really glad you two found each other again. I know he could use the support after everything that happened out in California, and I'm sure you could too, raising Cam on your own now. I think you both need each other."

"I'm glad too," he said, bending to kiss her cheek again. "And thank you for caring."

While she returned to the kitchen to check on dinner, Val took off his coat then grabbed Cam's from where he'd tossed it on the sofa, and hung them both up in the closet. There was no sign of Dev yet, and Val wondered where he was. Then Cam raced out of the kitchen, laughing, followed in short order by Dev, who was wiping his hands on a dish towel. He'd changed out of his office attire and now had on jeans and a sweater, looking sexier than anyone should be allowed to. He adjusted his glasses and raised a hand in greeting to Val. "Hi. Can I get you anything to drink? Dinner should be ready soon."

"Water would be great, thanks," Val said past his dry throat. Dev seemed more relaxed now that he was home, his normally neatly combed hair slightly ruffled and his cheeks flushed from cooking at the stove. The scent of tomato sauce and cooked chicken had Val's stomach rumbling. He hadn't eaten all day because the ER had been slammed again. Then his eyes locked with Dev's and a hunger of an entirely different kind took over.

Whoa there, cowboy.

He needed to remember their agreement. This was just dinner amongst friends, nothing more. And the sooner his libido got that memo, the better, because right now, all he could imagine was walking over there and diving his fingers into Dev's dark hair and finishing that kiss they'd almost started the other night, witnesses and agreements be damned. And that was a problem.

Thankfully, Cam interrupted, basically throwing ice water over the heat threatening to become a wildfire in Val's blood by asking, "Dr. Dev, can I see your models?"

"Sure," Dev said, tearing his eyes away from Val and tossing the dish towel on the table. "A few of them are still in the den. This way."

"Cool!" Cam said, skipping beside Dev down the hall.

"Here's that water you asked for," Elaine said, returning to the living room.

Val thanked her, then sank onto one end of the sofa and took a much-needed breath. Maybe keeping to that agreement wouldn't be as easy as he'd thought, based on his reactions just now.

"So, tell me what you've been up to lately?" She parked her wheelchair beside an armchair perpendicular to him and smiled. "Chicken still has about five more minutes before it's done."

"Not much, other than working," Val said, some of the tension inside him dissipating. "The ER really doesn't have a downtime. People are always getting injured somehow. What about you?"

They chatted about her church group and bridge club, then moved on to Cam's school activities. Finally, Elaine circled back to him and Dev again. "I'm so glad you're here tonight, Val. Dev's kept himself so isolated since the separation and divorce. He could really use a friend like you right now, even if he'd never say it himself."

Val took another sip of his water to dislodge the lump that had formed there at the thought of Dev being so lonely. "I'm sure he'll settle in and make new friends here."

Elaine gave him a look. "Now, you know as well as I do that my son isn't good with people, outside of his patients. He's not a social butterfly like you." She shrugged. "My hope is coming home can be a new start for him, and I think regaining that close friendship with you might be the beginning he needs."

Dev returned then, sans Cam, and took a seat on the other end of the sofa from Val. "He's busy checking out my old models. That'll keep him occupied for a while." He flashed Val a shy smile that set his traitorous heart racing again.

"I'll go check on that chicken again. Should be close to done by now," Elaine said, excusing herself, leaving him and Dev alone in the living room.

"The house looks the same," Val said, feeling tongue-tied for the first time in recent memory. Man, he was nervous, like a blind date before prom. Then Dev started fiddling with his glasses, a familiar sign that he was nervous too, and that knowledge put Val a bit more at ease. "It's good to be back here. Lots of great memories."

Dev huffed out a breath. "I didn't want you here."

Val looked over at him, speechless. "Why?"

"You know why." Dev sat forward and hung his head, hands dangling between his knees. "I can't get involved with anyone again, I'm sorry. But if that's what you want, I need to be clear about that upfront, Val."

"That's why we have an agreement," Val said, confused. "You know you can trust me to keep it."

"That's the problem though." Dev gave an unpleasant laugh. "Trust. I don't trust anyone anymore. Not even myself. And it's my fault. I should have listened to you back then." His tone turned weary as he met Val's gaze, his dark eyes fathomless behind his glasses. "My biggest regret now is that I didn't. I could have saved everyone a lot of heartache. But instead, I blamed you and ignored the warning signs right in front of me. You were right and I was wrong. And it makes it harder because I'm torn between this unwanted attraction to you and the fact you're also a constant reminder of my own failures."

Stunned by this new information, Val scooted closer to him, wanting so badly to touch him, but knowing it would be unwelcome, even as a gesture of comfort.

"Dev, I'm sorry about how things went down with us after the bachelor party, but we were both doing what we thought was right at that point with the information we had. You can't blame yourself for that. You were in love. Love makes people do crazy things, against their better judgment. And sometimes those choices don't work out, but it doesn't mean they're a failure. Especially if you learned something from it." Val huffed out a breath, staring down at his hands in his lap. "And if we're taking blame here, I could have done better too. The way I told you about what had happened at the party that night was so abrupt because I was angry on your behalf that Tom would've tried that with me, knowing you were my best friend, knowing I would tell you…" He shook his head and told him something he'd never spoken out loud before. "It was almost like Tom wanted me to tell you, like maybe he wanted to get out of the wedding but didn't know how, and I was scared for you. I knew how deeply you were invested in a future with him, so that fear spilled over into our argument too. But a day hasn't gone by since then that I don't wish we could go back and change it."

One silent beat stretched into two as those painful memories filled Val's mind, crowding out everything else until he reminded himself that things were different now. They could make them different, if they both wanted to. "We have a second chance here, Dev. To start over, to start fresh. To leave the past behind and move forward as friends. Maybe not the same as before, but just as good. Is that what you want?"

Dev hesitated before shaking his head and scrubbing his hands over his face. "I don't know what I want anymore."

"Dinner's almost ready," Elaine called from the kitchen, and before Val could respond, Dev was up and walking away again. "I need to help her get things on the table."

Val watched him go, worried he'd said the wrong thing. Again. To distract himself, he picked up a photo album off the coffee table in front of him and flipped through it, looking at pictures of a young Dev—probably around Cam's age, if he had to guess—laughing, his messy hair covered in mud. He wished that his Dev of today could get some of that carefree exuberance back again, then stopped short.

My Dev?

Restless, he put the album down. Okay, looking at those photos wasn't the distraction he wanted. He got up and went to fetch Cam for dinner.

Soon, they all sat around the dining room table, piles of hearty chicken cacciatore over pasta filling their plates. Everyone dug into the delicious food while Cam answered Elaine's questions between bites.

"So, what things do you like to do after school, Cam?" she asked.

"Well, besides Lego, I like soccer." Cam's face lit up. "I scored two goals last game!"

"Fantastic!" Elaine exclaimed, matching his son's enthusiasm.

Val and Dev shared fleeting glances across the table, Dev's statement from earlier lingering between them like a dark scowl. Did Dev really not know what he wanted?

That seemed hard to believe, given how logical and decisive he'd always been. No. What Val suspected was more likely that Dev knew exactly what he wanted; he just didn't want to want it.

Does he want me?

"Can we go white water rafting, Uncle Val?" Cam asked, jolting him out of his thoughts. "Please?"

"Oh. Uh…maybe? When you're big enough," Val said, trying to pick up the thread of conversation he'd dropped completely. "Why would you ask about that, buddy?"

"I saw it on a TV show last week and it looked so cool!" Cam said.

"Maybe you can go next summer," Elaine offered. "When you're a little bigger, if your Uncle Val says it's okay."

"Yes! I'd love that!" Cam bounced in his seat. "I hope I grow ten feet by then!"

"I don't, buddy. I'm going bankrupt keeping you in clothes as it is."

That even got a bit of a laugh out of Dev, and some of the stress sizzling in the air between them cleared. If only they could get back to being this easy again. The rest of dinner passed without consequence, and soon they were all stuffed and staring at empty plates.

"Thank you for dinner, Elaine," Val said. "It was delicious as always."

He nudged Cam's foot under the table. "Yes, thanks, Ms. Harrison. It was so good!"

"Glad you both enjoyed it," she said, pushing away from the table. "I hope you both won't be strangers from now on. And Cam, I'll try to make it to one of your soccer games soon. Now, if my son and new houseguest would like to earn his keep by clearing the table, that would be great."

"I'd love for you to come to my games!" Cam got up and ran around the table to hug Elaine while Val helped Dev carry the dirty dishes to the kitchen. Dev then washed while Val dried, a welcome lull in talking between them as they worked. By the time it was all cleaned up, it was time to go.

Val walked out into the living to find Cam and Elaine going through the same photo album he'd been looking at earlier. "Okay, buddy. Go get your jacket on. It's past your bedtime."

After putting on his own coat, Val hugged Elaine again at the front door and thanked her for inviting them, just as Cam returned and Dev emerged from the kitchen at last, looking troubled and uncertain. Val wanted to hug him too, but knew that wasn't allowed.

"Uncle Val, can I go with Elaine to see her garden gnome before we leave?" Cam asked, shuffling his feet. "She said he's really cool!"

"Uh…sure," Val said as Elaine winked at him. "As long as she doesn't mind."

"Not at all. Give you boys a chance to say your goodbyes." She opened the door and rolled out onto the front porch, followed closely by Cam. "We'll meet you at the car."

They disappeared down a paved path around the side of the house, leaving Dev and Val standing at the door alone again, just like the other night. Usually poised, Val wasn't sure what to do with his hands all of a sudden, where to look, what to say. He ended up with a lame "Well, good night, then."

"Good night," Dev murmured, still looking all dark and broody and so hot Val was surprised he wasn't scorched just from being in his vicinity.

Heart racing, Val tried to look anywhere but at Dev, but somehow his gaze ended up on Dev's mouth, his lips slightly parted as he took a hitched breath. Yeah, he needed to get out of here before he couldn't anymore. "I'll…uh…see you later then."

Val started to turn away, only to feel a hand on his arm, tugging him back around and into Dev's chest. Then Dev's mouth was on his, just a hesitant brush of lips, like a question asked and answered all at once, but everything else faded away. Their agreement. Their past. Their other responsibilities. Val wasn't sure what had changed between them, only that it had, and he couldn't regret it. Then Dev pulled back slightly, his stubble-covered jaw scraping against Val's skin. "I don't know why I did that."

Dev looked flushed and feral, his dark eyes sparkling with heat and hunger, and Val's fingers itched to dive into the man's perfect hair and muss him up a little more as he swayed toward Dev again. "I do."

Then they were kissing again, fiercer now, tasting, teasing, tempting…

"Uncle Val, I'm ready to go," Cam called from the side of the house as he and Elaine returned.

Val and Dev flew apart as reality crashed back down around them, the cold night air jarring after the fiery heat of their kiss.

Lips tingling, Val felt dizzy. He'd gotten so lost in the moment that he'd forgotten all about Cam. That had never happened. Never. He fumbled back a step or two, trying to sound normal and failing miserably as he stumbled over his words. "I…uh…we…uh…thanks again for dinner."

For his part, Dev looked equally flummoxed, clearing his throat to croak out, "Sure… Anytime…"

It felt like an eternity before he and Cam were back in the car and heading home, Val's pulse still jackhammering and his mind spinning. He wasn't sure exactly what that kiss had meant, just that Dev had initiated it, and Val had to figure out where to go from here, because their chemistry was off the charts and if it happened again, Val wasn't so sure they'd stop next time, agreement or not.

CHAPTER SIX

DEV SPENT ANOTHER sleepless night replaying that kiss and was awake before dawn, staring at the ceiling.

What the hell was I thinking?

The problem was he hadn't been thinking at all. He'd allowed his emotions to take over again, and now look at the mess he'd made. For weeks now, he'd been doing his best to deny the growing attraction between him and Val, hoping it would just go away, but that kiss had shown him that wasn't possible anymore, because the rational part of his brain had short-circuited when it came to Val, and now he couldn't forget that kiss.

It had been good. Better than good. Better than even his fantasies. Sweet and sexy and hot with just the right hint of wicked. Dev had sensed Val's surrender in that brief kiss too and maybe that's what had got him in the end.

Or it was Val's smile? Or his sexy voice? Or…

He groaned and covered his face with his hands.

Somehow, without him knowing it, he'd become so lost in his need for Val that he wasn't sure how to find his way back again. Val had seemed right there with him, eager and willing. And if he was truthful with himself, that was what had ultimately pushed him over the edge and made him lose control.

And that loss scared him more than anything else.

Because this deep need boiling inside him for Val was unlike anything he'd ever experienced before, even with Tom. It had felt like home. But home had a way of lulling you into letting your guard down, then hitting you so hard your universe blew apart.

No. They needed to reestablish their agreement as they'd planned. Last night was an aberration. Eventually, things between him and Val would cool off again and they'd forget all about this pesky attraction that threatened everything he was working hard to rebuild in his life. Safety. Security.

Resolved, he got up, got ready, then headed into work early, his analytical mind continuing to churn through possible solutions and outcomes to the situation with Val as he drove on autopilot.

But about a block away from the medical center, sudden gridlock made him pay attention. Traffic that early in the morning was unusual, which meant there must be another cause for it. An accident, maybe?

After forty-five minutes of no movement at all, Dev decided to take matters into his own hands and check what was going on himself. Besides, if there was some type of medical emergency, it was his professional duty to help. He pulled over to the curb and parked, then shut off his engine and grabbed his medical bag from the back seat. He locked up the sedan before walking toward what looked like a scene of complete carnage about half a block away from the medical center entrance.

Red-and-blue emergency lights flashed atop the numerous squad cars, and there were multiple ambulances and emergency fire vehicles surrounding the wreckage of several piled-up cars. First responders and hospital personnel were on scene, darting between smoking piles of crumpled metal as the acrid scent of burning oil and rubber filled the air. Amidst the cacophony of sirens, the occasional pained scream of a trapped victim echoed.

From somewhere close by, he heard a familiar voice call, "Help! I need help over here!"

Val.

Heart in his throat, Dev dove into action, adrenaline coursing through his veins. Had Val been involved in this horrible event? God, he hoped not. He had to find him, make sure he was okay. He frantically scanned the faces of several rescued victims as he rushed deeper into the chaos. There had to have been at least six vehicles involved, maybe more. He looked for Val's SUV but couldn't see much past the haze of smoke that was growing denser around them. At least they were close to the hospital, so even the most critical patients could get treatment quickly if needed.

"Over here!" Val called again, snapping his attention to a vehicle on the far side of the scene, sandwiched between a large box truck and another compact car, the hood grotesquely twisted from the impact. An insidious hiss echoed from somewhere near the gas tank of the crushed vehicle, and it only fueled Dev's desperation to find Val. And what about Cam? Had he been involved too? Were they both trapped, unable to move, bleeding out? Dying?

Oh, God. Please let them be okay.

Then, as if on command, the smoke parted enough for him to see a flash of blue scrubs standing on the other side of the crushed car, and his stomach went into freefall, especially as he got closer and saw the streaks of blood on Val's clothes. He broke into a run, dodging firemen and pieces of jagged metal, until he was standing on the sidewalk, staring down at a sweaty and grime-covered—but apparently unharmed—Val. No sign of the boy though. "What happened here? Where's Cam?"

Val swiped the back of a hand over his forehead, leaving a black streak of grease behind. "Cam's fine. He's home, getting ready for school with Nancy. I'm not sure what caused the accident, just that we all heard the commotion and rushed out to help anyway we could." He pointed to the crumpled vehicle beside them. "There's a woman trapped in there and they're going to have to cut her out."

"Help me, please!" the woman called from inside the wreckage.

"From what I can see, she's trapped by the steering column and the gas tank's leaking," Val said. "If they don't get her out soon, the whole thing could blow. I've been trying to flag one of the firefighters down but I'm not sure they can see me through all this smoke. Can you go get them and tell them what's going on here? Have them bring the Jaws of Life."

Dev set his medical bag on the sidewalk, then jogged back the way he'd come to find firefighters to help. By the time he'd flagged one down, who then got his superior involved as well, several minutes had passed before they got back. Dev found Val crouched near what was left of the vehicle's front bumper to peer inside the shattered passenger side window.

"Ma'am, my name is Dr. Laurent. I'm here to help you," Val called inside the crushed car to the trapped woman, his voice soothing despite the danger surrounding them. "The fire department will cut you out of here, but until then, keep talking to me, okay? Can you tell me your name?"

"Patty. My name's Patty," she panted.

"Nice to meet you, Patty. Can you tell me if you're hurt?"

"My right leg hurts."

"The firefighters are here, Val," Dev said, still trying to process what he was seeing. He'd chosen the slower pace of pediatric oncology for a reason. The immediacy of trauma was nonstop stress, but Val was calm like the eye of the storm.

"Can you move that leg, Patty?" Val asked. "Or is it trapped under something?"

Patty cried out again in agony. "No, I can't move it. I'm stuck. Please help me!"

"Doctors, you'll need to move back," one of the firemen said as a team moved in to stabilize the vehicle before they cut the woman out of it. "Wait over there, please."

He and Val stepped under a line of yellow tape blocking off the sidewalk nearby as the firefighters started up the Jaws of Life. The roar of its engine was like a chainsaw, and made it impossible to talk, but when Dev hazarded a glance at Val beside him, he found the same concern and relief he felt inside himself reflected back at him. It took several minutes for them to pry open even a partial section of the crushed vehicle. Enough for the firefighters to be able to see Patty's face and talk to her at least.

"Stay still, ma'am," one of the firefighters said as they peeled back another section of roof. "We'll have you out of there in a—"

The rest of his words were cut off by a loud screech as the wrecked vehicle tipped precariously despite the firefighters' best efforts, and Dev reached over and grasped Val's hand without thinking. Val squeezed Dev's fingers back as they both watched the race to free the woman from the car.

"Gas line's compromised," one of the firefighters called, just as the driver's side door finally came free. Paramedics quickly moved in and managed to get Patty out of the car and onto a bodyboard, then whisked her away to the ER before firefighters moved in with a huge hose to smother the entire vehicle with a flame-retardant foam to prevent an explosion.

By the time it was all over, Dev felt like he'd gone ten rounds with a heavyweight champion boxer. Val wasn't in much better shape, from the looks of him. As more hospital staff flooded the area to help the injured, they stood there, still holding hands. Neither of them ready to let go yet. When he'd left his mother's house this morning, Dev had intended to keep his distance from Val until he could be rational about the situation between them, but now he knew he had to face it head on.

Val finally looked down at himself and laughed.

"Looks like I need to go back home and take another shower."

Dev nodded, staring down at their joined hands. "Looks like it."

"Either you're going to have to let me go—" Val smiled "—or you're going to have to come with me."

"Oh," Dev said, snapping out of his daze, lost in Val's eyes. He let him go fast. "Sorry. I need to get up to my office to see patients. I have a full schedule today."

A hint of disappointment flashed across Val's face, so fast Dev would've missed it if he hadn't been paying such close attention. "Right. Sure. Um…maybe we could talk later?"

Dev's phone buzzed in his pocket and he pulled it out to see his practice's number on the screen, probably calling to find out where he was. "I need to take this. Text me and we'll set it up."

He grabbed his medical bag and headed inside, phone to his ear as he rode the elevator up to his floor. He'd go down later and move his car, but for now, he had patients waiting.

By the time he had enough time between appointments to take a break and check his messages, it was well into the afternoon. Val's shift ended at eight that night. He wanted to talk then.

Dev's first instinct was to say no, but he knew it was best to get this over with, so he told Val he'd meet him downstairs outside the ER entrance at eight fifteen.

The rest of his day passed in a blur of busyness and nervous tension, until finally Val found him waiting outside in the crisp night air right on time.

"Would you mind going to my house instead of a bar? That way I can let Nancy leave for the day and check on Cam too?"

"Fine." As they walked to their cars, breath frosting the air, Dev asked, "How's Patty?"

"Better. Badly broken right leg that required surgery, but she should make a full recovery."

"Good to hear."

They each climbed into their vehicles parked in the half-empty lot. Dev followed Val home. It was fine. It was just a simple talk. Nothing to be nervous about, he told himself, even as a small tremor of anticipation shimmered through him.

By the time they reached Val's house, Nancy was already waiting at the door and Dev felt like his skin was too tight for his body. Stepping into the quiet living room, nothing about this felt simple. It felt complicated and fraught with the previous night's kiss dangling tantalizingly between them like forbidden fruit. While Val went to check on Cam, Dev took off his coat then sent a quick text to his mother, letting her know where he was so she wouldn't worry.

She texted him back telling him to have fun.

Fun wasn't how Dev would describe the conversation they were about to have.

After the kiss, it felt like they were playing with fire and Dev didn't want to get burned again. And this was Val, a man who'd once been his closest friend and confidant. He couldn't relax, couldn't forget his decision to stay alone, stay safe. He was just so tired. Tired of being lonely. Tired of wanting things he couldn't have.

He closed his eyes and rested his head back against the sofa cushions, closing his eyes for a second, his mom's words reverberating in his exhausted brain.

Have fun.

If only it were that simple. Honestly, Dev couldn't remember the last time he'd done something just for fun, and not out of a sense of duty or responsibility or guilt. Even during his marriage, there'd always been something that had held him back from truly letting go. But something about seeing Val again seemed to have knocked his inner barriers loose, and now Dev felt far too exposed, all these dangerous emotions roiling inside him—desire, fear, need, hesitation. Because all of it was building up inside him like a powder keg.

And his undeniable chemistry with Val might just be the spark that would make him explode.

Val thanked Nancy and watched her leave, then went to check on Cam. His son was sound asleep, and as he closed Cam's bedroom door quietly and headed back toward the living room, his heart cartwheeled in his chest. It was just him and Dev now. The man he'd kissed last night. The man he hadn't stopped thinking about since they'd been reunited weeks ago. He ran a hand through his messy hair then called down the hall, "I'm going to hop in the shower quick and clean up. Make yourself at home and help yourself to anything you like. I'll be right out."

"Okay," Dev called back from the living room, his deep voice only making Val's adrenaline surge.

He hurried through a scrub down and shave, then

changed into comfy sweats and socks before hurrying back out to make sure Dev hadn't suddenly decided to make a run for it while he'd been gone.

Nope. He was still there, sitting at the kitchen table with two plates, each with a sandwich on them, and a bag of potato chips between them. At Val's surprised look, Dev smiled. "What? You asked me to make food and since I'm not a cook like you, I took the easy route. PB and J and chips. Not exactly a nutritional bonanza, but enough to fill us up for now."

Touched by the thoughtfulness, Val took a seat at the table. It had been a long time since someone had taken care of him like this. Usually, he was the caretaker, which was fine. He liked being needed, but having Dev care for him in this small way was nice too.

"Thanks," Val said, taking a sip from the glass of water Dev had set next to his plate. He really was starving, so dove into his food. Dev did too, and soon they were both happily eating away in companionable silence. It wasn't until they were both done and cleaning up that the old uncertainty reared its head again inside Val. He'd invited Dev here to talk about things. About that kiss specifically and what, if anything, they wanted to do about it. But now that the moment was upon them, he wasn't sure how to start. "Quite a day, huh?"

"Yep." Dev was rinsing their plates before putting them in the dishwasher. He was turned away from Val, allowing him time to admire the man's taut butt in those black pants he wore. Dev was built like a runner, which he was, or a racehorse—all sleek lines and lithe strength. Val swallowed hard, imagining those long, lanky limbs entwined with his amongst the sheets of his bed, breaths mingled, lost in passion and promise...

Oh, boy.

"So..." Dev finally shut the dishwasher and turned to face Val, who looked away quickly, face hot. "About that talk."

"Yeah." Val pulled two bottles of ale out of the fridge, handing one to Dev before leading him into the living room where they took a seat on the sofa. Val steeled himself for the necessary conversation ahead. He knew he wanted Dev, but he also knew that Dev was an emotional minefield right now too. Capable of blowing all the progress they'd made toward repairing their connection sky-high if Val made one wrong move at this point. So, he intended to let Dev take the lead here. Tell Val what he wanted and needed, and Val would do his best to fulfill that, whatever it was. As long as he continued to have Dev in his life, that's what mattered. He took a deep breath and twisted the cap off his ale, took a long swig, grateful for the cold liquid to soothe his burning throat as he said, "How do you feel about what happened?"

Dev's dark brows rose as he looked over at Val. "How do I feel about it?"

"Yes." Val nodded, feeling like the next few minutes would affect everything going forward. "You kissed me. Why?"

"Jesus, Val." Dev took a long swallow of his own ale, his normally neat hair disheveled after what was probably hours of running his fingers through it anxiously, if Val had to guess. After the accident, and what had happened last night, Dev had to be turning it all over in his head. Even jittery and brooding, every cell in Val's body was vibrating like a tuning fork at Dev's closeness now, and he craved more of him, as much of him as he could get. He couldn't remember ever being so attuned to someone before, or wanting them as much as he did Dev. But he wouldn't touch him. Not yet. Not until he made it clear what he needed. Val had to be smart about this to avoid ruining everything. And not just between him and Dev, but there was Cam to consider too. Cam really liked Dev, and the boy had already lost someone he cared for. He didn't want his son to experience that again, if he could help it.

Dev frowned, fiddling with his glasses again as he cleared his throat, looking so flustered that Val wanted to hug him and tell him it would be okay, but didn't dare. "I don't know how I feel about it," he said finally. He took another long gulp of ale before cursing under his breath. "No. That's not true. I feel scared about it. Because I never wanted to need anyone like this again after what happened with Tom. And I certainly never expected it to be you, Val." Val got that. All this had caught him by surprise too, but he knew it went deeper for Dev, with what he'd been through. "It shouldn't have happened. There are so many reasons why we should never do that again. You have Cam to worry about and a life here that I know nothing about. And I'm not sure I can ever open myself up to that again. We're so different Val. We always were."

"Is that what you want? To stop it now?" Val leaned forward. "It's your call, Dev. I don't want anyone to get hurt here, including Cam. That's why I wanted to talk about it now, before we did anything else." He glanced at the hallway then sat back again. "Tell me how you're feeling."

Dev shook his head, looking painfully confused. "That's the problem. I don't want to feel anything."

Val squeezed his eyes shut, knowing what it took for Dev to admit that after what he'd been through. "I get that. I think we've both experienced way more heartache than any person deserves in our lives. Especially the past couple of years."

"Exactly." Dev stood then, pacing the living room. "I don't trust emotions, don't trust myself either, after Tom. I never want to feel that raw and helpless again. I can't risk putting myself through that again."

Val understood where he was coming from, but that didn't lessen his disappointment that the possibility of more between them was over before it started. He should be happy about it. Keeping things strictly in the friend zone between them made life a lot easier. No worries about Cam losing his new friend Dev. No risk that Val wouldn't be able to stop his own emotions from crossing the line from casual to complicated, which would be so easy for him where Dev was concerned. It was good. It was fine. He shrugged and forced a half-hearted smile because it didn't feel good at all. "So that's it then."

Dev stopped near a window across from Val, and stared out through the blinds and the night sky beyond, his back to Val. "Today, at the accident scene, when I first got there and I heard your voice calling for help, I panicked. All I could think about was what if you were in one of those cars, hurt, trapped? What if it was Cam in there?" He huffed out a breath, his shoulders sagging. "I'm not sure what I'd do without you. And it terrified me, Val. Because I don't want to need anyone like that again. Not after what my dad did. Not after what Tom did."

Val set his ale bottle beside Dev's on the coffee table, then got up and walked over to stand beside him, wanting to be near him, lend support, but still not quite touching. "I get it. I thought about Cam too. About you. What I'd do if I was one of those poor victims. What I'd regret in my life if it was suddenly over."

"And what would you regret?" Dev asked quietly, still staring straight ahead out the window.

For a quick second, Val thought about lying, but tonight was all about being honest, and Dev deserved the truth after enduring so many lies in his past. "You. I'd regret not being with you, in any way I could."

The embrace was so fast that even looking back later, Val still wasn't sure how it had happened, but next thing he knew, he was in Dev's arms, his face buried in the side of Dev's neck, inhaling his good Dev scent—soap and fabric softener and a hint of spice. Dev held him tight, like he'd never let him go, like he needed Val so desperately, and Val just held on, needing to be needed, needing to fix whatever was wrong inside him, to protect this connection from harm.

Eventually, Dev said into the hair near Val's temple, "I shouldn't do this."

"What? Need comfort?" Val said against his skin, resisting the urge to nuzzle him.

Dev pulled back then, his dark gaze hot behind his

glasses. "It's not just comfort, Val. Never has been for us. Not now."

The words hung there, glowing like a beacon between them. Or a warning of danger ahead.

Either way, they both stood there, in each other's arms, gazes locked, frozen, as if caught between a bad decision and a worse need. Finally, Dev squeezed his eyes shut and whispered, the words ragged and so quiet Val had to lean in closer just to hear them, "If we do this, it can't mean anything more than sex, Val. That's all I can give you."

Val took that in, nose to nose with him, blood pounding through his body, every fiber of his being screaming for more, for release, for Dev. If no strings, no emotions, were the rules Dev needed to make this happen, Val would agree, because he wanted Dev. Period. More than his next breath. So, he'd do it, keep his heart out of it. Val wasn't sure how exactly, but he'd figure it out. Because staring up into Dev's huge, dark eyes, seeing his lips wet and parted and so close Val could almost taste them, all that strength and warmth and hardness right there against him, he would've promised just about anything to have more of it, more of him. "I'll take it."

Then they were kissing again, Dev's hands clenched in Val's hair, pulling him in tighter as his lips devoured Val's. By the time they pulled away again slightly, they were both breathless.

"What next?" Val growled, leaning in for a second round, only to be stopped by Dev tightening his fingers in his hair, stopping him. Val was a switch in bed, taking either role depending on who he was with—sometimes dominant, sometimes submissive as the mood suited. And Dev needed the power here too. He was fine with it—in fact, it turned him on even more. Val would happily be Dev's fantasy all night long if Dev was there with him. His slow, wicked smile grew. "Tell me what you need."

Dev cursed again, a muscle ticking near his tight jaw, his hot gaze searing Val from the inside out. "You. I need you."

"Then have me," Val teased, relishing the pull on his scalp that earned him.

"And you're good with casual," Dev growled. "Nothing more here than sex?"

In answer, Val ground against him, letting him feel just how all right he was with it. "I am."

"Good." Dev picked him up then, carrying Val down the hall, saying against his lips, "Which room?"

"Last one on the left," Val murmured into his mouth, not wanting to break contact for a second. He kissed along Dev's jaw, knocking his glasses askew, but it didn't matter. Nothing mattered except the fact they were inside Val's bedroom now. Dev shut the door and locked it. Val took off Dev's glasses and set them on the dresser for safekeeping, turning back around to find Dev watching him in the moon-shadowed darkness.

This time their kiss went deeper, flared brighter. They shed their clothes, then moved together onto the bed, each moan and groan caught and swallowed in each other's mouths to avoid detection. Sweet torture, especially as Dev's hands moved lower, with careful intention, exploring the landscape of Val's body as if memorizing it for the first time. And as much as he didn't want to rush, to take this first time slow, it had been far too long for Val, and he doubted he could last.

For so long, Dev had been an untouchable dream, so self-sufficient and contained. An enigma. But tonight, Val saw beneath the facade. With each stroke and caress, every lick and nip, Dev allowed Val closer, deeper, until there was nothing left between them but the truth of their desire. He wished it could go on forever. He was afraid it would disappear too soon.

Then Val surrendered to Dev, to sensation, exploring, tasting, teasing, moving together as the pressure built until they both went over the brink, finally collapsing on the bed, spent and sated.

Afterward, Val lay cocooned in Dev, limbs tangled in the quiet night, filled with the blessed satisfaction of finally getting exactly what he'd needed. Finally, he found the strength to move slightly and whisper in Dev's ear, savoring his slight shiver when Val's lips grazed the sensitive skin there. "All right?"

"Yes," Dev whispered back, voice gruff, smiling against Val's cheek. "Can't remember the last time I've been this relaxed."

"Same." Val grinned, feeling inordinately proud of himself for giving Dev that gift as they both gave in to sleep. For now, anyway, everything felt right with his world. And if complications arrived later, well, he'd worry about those then.

CHAPTER SEVEN

DEV FUMBLED WITH the bright blue Frisbee before tossing it into the open sky.

It had been a little over three weeks now since their first night together. They were into November now and… well, he was still trying to figure it all out. They'd both agreed to keep things friendly regardless, especially for Cam, who'd grown even more fond of Dev it seemed. And so far, so good.

They were spending a lovely fall Sunday in a field in Minnehaha Park, playing sports, though in general that was not his strong suit. He'd always been the kid who was happier figuring out the season stats for teams while Val was the star player. Still, they'd meshed well together.

Both in and out of bed...

Distracted now by the thought of them in bed together the night before, Val beneath him, around him, calling out Dev's name as he climaxed, he threw the Frisbee way too wide. Val leaped for it anyway, missing and tumbling to the ground. He got right back up again, running to get the errant Frisbee from where it had landed near a tree, Cam sprinting after him—taking after Val in his athletic abilities, apparently. Dev watched them from a safe distance, glad to be out of the fray.

"Show-offs," he called, as Val and Cam ran toward him, grinning. He enjoyed spending time with them both, and they were settling into a nice, comfortable ease. Not that he was letting himself get too used to it. They'd agreed to keep it all casual, no strings attached, which meant no emotions, no binding attachments. So far, so good. And the sex…well, that was amazing. Val seemed to sense what he needed before Dev could even ask for it, their yin and yang opposition translating well there too.

Sometimes, Dev worried that Val was giving more to make things work than he was, but he never complained and seemed happy just to have more time with Dev. And Dev was happy to have their friendship back too, and a new bond with Cam, so it worked out well for him. Cam reminded Dev so much of himself at that age in so many areas—the boy's interest in science and space, his love of building models—though Cam was much more outgoing than Dev ever was or would be.

And if, occasionally, Dev's old doubts and fears surfaced because things seemed to have fallen into place so easily, maybe too easily, well, he just needed time to adjust, he told himself. That was all. Easy wasn't something he trusted, among other things.

"I thought you might break something going after that Frisbee," Dev said to Val as he and Cam reached him on the field.

"Hey, I'm thirty-six, not three hundred and six," Val teased back as he stopped a few feet in front of Dev, his blue eyes sparkling with mirth as he handed the Frisbee to Cam. "Ready to eat now, buddy? I'm starving!"

"Yes!" Cam yelled, racing for the blanket they'd spread out on the ground under an ancient oak tree. Bright yellow and orange and red leaves scattered the ground, and the whole scene felt cozy and comfortable and—even Dev had to admit—pretty damn perfect.

You convinced yourself things were perfect with Tom too...

Dev shoved that unwanted doubt aside as they all settled on the blanket and began unpacking the basket of food Dev had ordered from his favorite local deli. He checked the label then passed Val a sandwich wrapped neatly in parchment paper. "Turkey and Swiss with all the trimmings, your favorite."

"You remembered?" Val asked as he took it, looking a bit astonished.

"How could I forget?" Dev snorted. "You ate those things every chance you got back in med school." He forced his gaze away from Val's now-beaming face, his chest squeezing with affection and something more he didn't want to think about too much right then. *Feeling more* wasn't allowed here, per his own rules.

Next, he pulled out a PB and J for Cam. "Crunchy with homemade strawberry preserves."

"Yum! Thanks, Dr. Dev!" Cam beamed too as he grabbed his food, and this time Dev couldn't help grinning right back, giving himself more emotional latitude there. He was used to relating to his young patients, forming a bond with them to allow for the most effective treatments. He'd trained for this, used his skills for this, so it felt safer to him. That's how he rationalized it to himself anyway.

"Oh, my God, this is so good," Val said around a hearty bite of his sandwich, giving a deep groan of pleasure that should have been illegal in all fifty states because of the effect it had on Dev's body. Then Val gave him a covert wink. "You're amazing."

Dev averted his gaze, hiding his heated face by digging out his own food—chicken salad on whole wheat bread with all the trimmings. The first delicious bite was just as good as he remembered from his med school days. As they ate, he avoided making eye contact with Val by watching a pair of squirrels chase each other across the field.

Cam finished first, as usual. For such a small kid, he could pack away food like no one's business. He scrambled to his feet to throw away his trash in a nearby can, then bounded back to the blanket with the relentless energy of childhood. "Can we play basketball now, Dr. Dev?" He pointed to the empty court a short distance away. "Please?"

Glad to have something to do besides sit there and lust after Val, Dev devoured the last bite of his sandwich then climbed to his feet to throw away his own trash. "Sure. But I have to warn you, I'm not very good."

They shot some hoops for a while, or at least Cam did. Dev basically ran after the ball when he missed. After that, he and Val pushed Cam on the swings, higher and higher, until the boy's laughter filled the air like music. Dev couldn't help noticing Val's muscles ripple as he guided the swing. The man was beautiful, no other way to describe it. His heart squeezed a little harder.

Mine.

Oh, no. No, no, no. Dev froze at the sudden rush of forbidden possessiveness that filled him as panic sank its teeth in around his edges. They were friends. Good friends. Friends with benefits. That was what he'd wanted, what Val had agreed to. He didn't want more than that, wasn't ready for more.

Am I?

He stumbled back a step and caught himself with a hand on the swing set. Val gave him a curious glance, but thankfully didn't mention anything about Dev's odd behavior.

Dev wasn't ready for another relationship. Not with Val, not with anyone. And yes, they'd agreed to a no-strings-attached fling, but he also didn't want to ruin his second chance at a great friendship with Val. He wasn't in love with the one person who knew him better than anyone—the good, the bad and the downright ugly—and supported him anyway. Val was light and optimistic and a steady shoulder to cry on. What he and Val had now was…indispensable to him.

He refused to screw that up by getting emotions involved.

Then there was Cam. He'd grown close to the boy too, treating him like the son he'd never had. He wouldn't risk the bond they'd developed by screwing up things with Val by doing something stupid, like getting his heart involved then having to walk away when it all fell apart, because love always fell apart. Usually at the worst possible time. No. This was all sex, no emotion. Exactly what he was looking for. He took a deep breath and steeled his resolve to maintain their agreement, remain friends, remain constant in each other's lives from here on out and not get the L-word involved at all.

They could share their bodies without their hearts messing it all up.

Easy-peasy. For a logical guy like himself, he should be able to detach at the drop of a hat.

No fuss. No muss.

"Higher, Uncle Val! Dr. Dev, look!" Cam shouted, kicking his legs out to touch the puffy white clouds above.

"Be careful," Dev called back, trying for a playful tone. But the sudden gruffness in his voice made the words sound more like a dire warning. Mainly for himself.

Keep it light. Keep it fun. Keep things easy.

It was getting late now, and streaks of orange and pink began to creep over the horizon as sunset grew closer. It came earlier and earlier this time of year. Another warning that time was fleeting. *Don't screw this up.*

Flustered and frowning, Dev checked his smartwatch. "We should head back home soon."

"Sure," Val said, glancing at Dev curiously as he scooped Cam off the swing and into his arms. "Everything okay?"

Dev nodded, not trusting his words at that point.

On the way home to Val's, they stopped to pick up a few essentials at a local grocery store, the fluorescent glow of the overhead lights a stark contrast to the gathering twilight outside. The trio navigated the aisles together, Val grabbing milk and bread while Cam directed from his seat in their Racecart—a shopping cart made to look like a racecar with the basket in the front—pointing out his favorite snacks with the glee of a tiny emperor.

For some reason, shopping together felt strangely intimate and domestic, but Dev was grateful for the distraction as he continued to process what had happened back at the park. His panic had subsided at least, allowing him to think more clearly about the situation. It wasn't like he didn't care for Val at all. He did. They'd known each other a long time. Of course he cared for him. For Cam too, since the two of them were now a package deal. Perhaps that's where the surge of protectiveness had come from, he reasoned. Yes. That sounded totally natural and normal. No need to go overboard and push things to the next forbidden level. It wasn't love. Nope. It was kinship, deep and abiding. That was all.

Satisfied now that he'd found a plausible explanation for his irrational deviation from their plan, Dev turned his focus back to the new things Val had added to their cart. Potatoes, bacon and a package of steaks for the grill. An old memory from their med school days rose, making Dev chuckle. "Remember when you nearly set your apartment on fire trying to make filet mignon in the oven?"

"Hey, I was following a recipe from the Food Network. I couldn't help it if the butter browned quicker than I expected." Val shook his head, his laugh reverberating deep inside Dev. "And there was never an actual fire. Just lots of smoke that set off the alarm." He shrugged and added a bottle of spices. "That's why I grill them now."

"Can I get some of this, Uncle Val?" Cam asked, pointing at a box with a neon green monster on the front. "Please?"

"You have cereal at home, buddy." Val reached forward to ruffle Cam's hair. "Maybe next week."

As they approached an open checkout lane, the cashier smiled. "What a lovely family."

Dev and Val froze midway through emptying the cart as Cam answered. "Oh, we're not a family. Not yet anyway. Right, Uncle Val?"

Val recovered first, placing the rest of the stuff on the counter while Dev escaped to the far end of the lane to bag up their purchases. Cam continued to chat to the cashier, completely oblivious to the fact he'd just blown all Dev's perfectly rational explanations clean out of the water, because for just a second, he'd wished it was true. That they were a real family.

Oh, boy.

This was bad. So, so bad.

Dev swallowed so hard it clicked. Cam's answer had been completely honest. They'd both been careful not to give him any impression that they were together as a couple. To Cam, he and Val were just good friends, which was why Dev had spent more time at their house over the last few weeks. They'd thought they were handling it well. That no one would get hurt here when it ended. But Cam adding on those last three words—*not yet anyway*—made it clear that he hoped for more. Which was a problem, because whatever this was between him and Val would eventually end. Things like this always did. And when Dev was gone, Cam would be hurt and that was the last thing Dev wanted.

As he shoved items into the cloth bags they'd brought in with them, he continued to berate himself for not sticking to the plan, for thinking somehow that this arrangement would work out in everyone's favor just because they'd made some stupid agreement. He obviously wasn't ready for this. Maybe he never would be, given how his marriage turned out. And yet, he'd gone ahead with Val, knowing it was a risk. Knowing it could all go sideways again. Knowing it could go too far.

Driving home passed in a blur of self-recriminations, and next thing Dev knew, they were carrying the groceries inside Val's house.

The soft hum of the refrigerator cycling on echoed through the silence as Val put away the groceries and Cam went to his room to get ready for bed. They were all still so stuffed from lunch that no one had wanted dinner. Dev had no appetite anyway, too full of stress for much else—or at least he thought so, until Cam raced back into the kitchen a few minutes later to let Val know he was ready for his bedtime story. Instead of going back to his bedroom though, the boy ran over to Dev and hugged his legs. "Goodnight, Dr. Dev. I love you!"

Dev gripped the edge of the counter and reminded himself to breathe, throat tight and heart thundering. Yep. Things had definitely gone too far, and it was up to him to put on the brakes before it was too late.

After tucking Cam in for the night, Val joined Dev in the living room. He could feel the tension radiating off

Dev from the other end of the couch, and saw the slight sheen of sweat on his forehead. Yep. He was flipping out, probably because of Cam's sudden proclamation of love earlier. Honestly, Val had been a little shocked by it too, but knew emotions of any kind were touchy, scary subjects for Dev, so he tried to hide that as much as possible. They'd agreed to keep things light, easy, and make sure Cam wasn't hurt by any of it. So his son dropping the L-word was a bombshell, to say the least. And while he fully supported Cam in feeling his feels, Val was also trying to teach him that not every emotion needed to be expressed as you were having it.

Sometimes it was better to wait for the perfect time and place.

Or never, in Val's case, considering the agreement they'd made.

So, even if he did want to do what Cam had done—wrap his arms around Dev and tell him he loved him—he wouldn't. Especially right now, with that haunted, shell-shocked look on Dev's face. Instead, Val sat cautiously and tried to think of a way to avoid the gravity threatening to pull them both under by downplaying the importance of Cam's statement. "You know, he told his teacher last week that he loved her too."

It was true. Cam was still the happiest kid Val had ever met, despite what he'd been through. And that joy had just grown since Dev had spent more time at their house. For Val too, and the last thing he wanted was to ruin the wonderful thing they had going and scare Dev away by confessing feelings he wasn't supposed to have. He'd known the rules going into this, and had promised to keep his heart out of the mix. At the time, he'd honestly thought he could, but he just wasn't built that way.

Neither was Cam. Must be genetic, getting attached to people so deeply.

Dev finally turned toward Val, frowning, as if he'd just realized Val was there. "Cam told his teacher he loved her?"

"Yeah." Val sighed and stretched his legs out in front of him, trying to look relaxed, even though he wasn't. "The kids at school teased him for a week afterward too."

Dev didn't respond. If anything, he looked even more unhappy, which put Val more on edge.

This was all spinning out of control too fast. He wished they could go back to that afternoon in the park, when things had been fun and light and full of sweet connection. After Vicki had died, he'd felt like a piece of him had been buried with her. A piece he'd feared would never feel happiness again. Then Dev had returned to town and his joy had returned tenfold, only he was supposed to keep that secret because it wasn't allowed. Val squeezed his eyes shut and inhaled deeply. God, why did he have to make things so complicated? Why did he have to fall in love with Dev when he shouldn't?

Because I'm an idiot.

Dev stood and raked his hands through his hair. "This is exactly what I feared would happen."

Val opened his eyes, preparing himself for battle. He wasn't ready to lose Dev yet, and he'd fight to keep this thing going between them for as long as he could, even if it meant denying his own heart. "He's seven, Dev. He'll be fine. I'll talk to him." He leaned forward, resting his forearms on his knees, his hands dangling between them. "Don't freak out, okay? He's good. We're all good."

"Are we?" Dev shook his head, throwing his hands up, his tone exasperated. "Because I don't feel good, Val. Not about any of this…" He huffed out a frustrated breath. "I don't know what we're doing here anymore."

Val knew he was on fragile ground here, and rather than chance a full meltdown of things, he tried to lower the temperature of the situation by avoiding the subject entirely. He grabbed the remote and clicked on the TV, scrolling through the on-screen guide to find something good to watch, and patted the seat beside him. "How about you sit down and we decompress a bit, watch a show?" He glanced up and met Dev's gaze. "This doesn't have to be any more than we let it be."

Dev's dark eyes held Val's for a few more tense seconds before he finally settled back on the sofa and stared at the TV screen, where a weekly medical drama that was so far from real life that it was laughable played out. Val hoped maybe the soap opera of the love lives of the characters might help divert attention away from their own mess, allowing some of the tension in the air to dissipate.

It didn't seem to work though, because next thing he knew, Dev was on his feet again. "I should go."

"Go?" Val followed him to the foyer. "I thought you were staying tonight."

Dev tugged on his coat before facing Val again. "I think it's best if we all get a little space right now." Val opened his mouth to argue, but Dev held up a hand, cutting him off. "I know you said Cam telling people he loves them is normal, but I said from the start of this I don't want him hurt when this is over because he's too attached to me. I know too well what it's like to be abandoned by someone you love."

Heart aching, Val stepped closer and slid his arms inside Dev's coat, his hands at Dev's waist. "I don't want my son hurt either. But I also don't want to lose what we have. Please stay."

Dev grabbed Val's wrists, his heat encompassing them as he whispered, "I can't."

"Sure you can." Val broke free of his grasp and ran his palms up Dev's sweater-covered chest to twine them behind his neck, toying with the hair at his nape. "Just take off your coat and we'll go to bed."

"Val," Dev said, his voice lowering to a growl as Val leaned in to nuzzle his neck.

"It will be fine. I promise." Val leaned back to look Dev in the eye. "Trust me."

A muscle ticked near Dev's tense jaw and Val flicked his tongue over it, causing Dev to fist the back of Val's shirt, pulling him even closer, if that were possible. "You know I can't."

"Yes, you can," Val said, before pulling him into a heated kiss that soon turned into a wildfire.

They somehow managed to make the trip to Val's bedroom blindly amidst a flurry of kisses and swallowed groans. Dev's coat ended up on the floor as soon as the bedroom door was locked behind them, cocooning them in shadowed intimacy. Val tugged Dev's sweater off over his head, then removed his own shirt, leaving them both naked from the waist up. He couldn't seem to be able to stop touching Dev, stroking him. "God, I swear you're like a drug to me. I can't get enough of you."

Dev flattened Val against the wall, skin to skin, grinding against him while he kissed and nipped the side of Val's neck. "I need you so badly."

"Yes," Val gasped, holding him closer, tracing his fingers lower over the planes of Dev's taut stomach, then around to cup his tight butt through his jeans, savoring every contour, the hidden strength, the solidity of him being there, right where he belonged. "I'm here. Whatever you want. I'll always be here for you, Dev. Promise."

"Stop it. Stop saying that. It isn't true. We're not doing that." Dev ground his hard length against Val's until they both moaned low into each other's mouths. "We agreed. Just sex. That's it."

At that moment, Val wanted him so badly, he would've agreed with anything Dev said just to keep him there, touching him like that. "Whatever you need."

"No." Dev pulled back, his expression angry, their jagged breaths mingling, the air charged. "Tell me what this is. Say it, so I know we're both on the same page."

Mind swirling with adrenaline and desire, Val panted, "Just sex. Just for fun."

Then they were kissing, their mutual need igniting into a wildfire fueled by past regrets and present desires. Dev slid his fingers slid through Val's hair, banishing any lingering space between them. When they finally parted, they each stripped away their remaining clothes then stretched out on the bed, bodies entwined, hearts beating in sync. Val took both their hard lengths in hand, stroking, caressing, driving them both nearer to the edge of oblivion. Dev thrust against him, harder, faster, seeking his release, his mouth hot on Val's ear. And when pleasure overtook them both, they held each other close, all the fears and uncertainties vanishing beneath a rush of endorphins.

As they lay together in the afterglow, exhaustion threatened to pull Val under into slumber, but he fought against it, snuggling into Dev's side, knowing what he'd promised. Knowing he'd already broken their agreement by falling so far and so deep for Dev that he'd never find his way out. This had gone beyond sex for him after their first night together, but he'd denied it. To Dev and to himself because he didn't want to lose Dev again. He didn't want to lie to Dev, but telling him the truth at that point might drive him away forever.

CHAPTER EIGHT

Dev woke up predawn the next morning and carefully got out of bed to avoid waking Val, who was still snoozing away beside him. The room was cast in shadows, except for a small Lego figurine on the nightstand highlighted by a shaft of light from a streetlight outside. He picked it up and brushed his thumb against the tiny plastic contours, each bump a reminder of Cam's earnest proclamation the night before.

Goodnight, Dr. Dev. I love you...

Chest constricted, Dev put the figurine back fast, as if it had burned him. God, what the hell was wrong with him? He never should have started this thing with Val in the first place. It made him want things that weren't possible, things he didn't think he was capable of giving, like his heart. Why did he think he could handle this?

What a mess.

With a sigh, he stood to collect his clothes off the bedroom floor, his mind churning through images from the day before, stopping repeatedly on images of Val and Cam together. He'd walked into their lives knowing he wasn't what they needed, but it had been too tempting to resist. And Cam was the one who'd be hurt the most if he stayed, if he kept pretending. It was bad enough he cared so much now.

And, regardless of what Val had said about Cam's teacher, those words weren't meaningless to Dev. He took another deep breath, lungs aching, like there wasn't enough oxygen in the room, in the world, for him. He needed to get out of here, figure all this out, decide how to handle this thing between them going forward.

He tugged on his jeans and shirt, feeling broken and bitter, berating himself for his own foolishness.

Val deserved better. Cam deserved better.

And since Dev had started this whole disaster, it was his responsibility to fix it now. By giving them all a chance to cool down and get some distance from things, to look at the situation logically.

He snorted softly as he searched for his missing sock. Logically? While Val was the epitome of calm rationality in the ER, outside of work his strong suit was his emotions, which only terrified Dev more.

Because Val knew him so well, and if he sensed that Dev might have crossed the line of their agreement, and let his own emotions get involved, then…

No. Distance was the best answer now.

A break. They all had busy schedules. They probably wouldn't even notice he was gone. They'd be fine without Dev. And it wasn't forever, just until things were back under control again.

He shoved his feet into his sneakers then picked up his coat, walking to the window again to peer through the curtains at the approaching sunrise, the dark night giving way to brilliant purples and oranges and pinks. It felt like an omen, a sign that Dev was making the right choice here for all of them. To avoid the risk of getting hurt even more. Dev didn't think he could bear that. He cared more for Val and Cam then he had for anyone in a long, long time—including Tom—but it was best to go for now, before Cam got even more attached to him. Let them all adjust to Dev not being around. They'd been good before him. They'd be good after him too.

But his heart ached like someone had gouged it out with a dull spoon. Part of him wanted nothing more than to crawl back into bed with Val and hold onto him for dear life. Which was exactly why he had to leave. He needed to rebuild his walls, to protect everyone, himself included.

"Hey…" A groggy Val rolled over then, sheets rustling, looking rumpled and ridiculously handsome, squinting at Dev. "It's still early. Come back to bed for a little longer."

Every cell in his body yearned to do just that, to climb back into Val's arms, sink into the imaginary comfort of the fantasy they'd built. But he had to stay firm, so he forced himself to shake his head. "Sorry. I can't. Need to go. Early shift this morning." Thankfully, his voice sounded steadier than his resolve. "Go back to sleep."

Val's sleepy blue gaze narrowed. "What's wrong?"

"Nothing's wrong." Dev backed toward the door, hating that he was lying to Val but not able to tell him the truth either. God, he'd let himself become such a hypocrite. Another strike against him. He wanted to go slink under a rock somewhere and hide. "I'm just thinking about my schedule and all the prep I have to do ahead of time."

He could just tell Val that his feelings had changed, that he was scared and shaken and unsure what to do now—but that was a conversation he wasn't prepared to have that early in the morning, so best to leave it for later. Right now, he just had to get the hell out of there before Val picked up on anything else in his behavior.

But Val let it go for once, flopping back onto the mattress and yawning. "Fine. Lunch later?"

"Uh, I don't know." Dev had his hand on the bedroom door handle now, the metal cool beneath his palm, eager for escape. "Text me later and we'll figure it out."

Or not.

He fled then, like a coward, grabbing his coat and rushing out of the house and into his car, driving back to his mother's house to shower and change for work. By the time he made it to the medical center, it was nearly time for his shift to start. He felt tired and achy and like he'd been run over by a train. Repeatedly. He slumped to his office and booted up his computer, then sat down at his desk to go over his case files for the day, hoping a cup of coffee would help. And he'd been right about one thing at least. His schedule was nuts for that day and for the foreseeable future.

Work had always been a balm for him though, so he was grateful for it now. Clicking through his patient files, he made notes and lost himself in the details, the heat blasting from the vent overhead the only sound filling the otherwise silent office. Matt Warden and his mother were due in for another follow-up today, sans Val this time, and from the latest blood work results, the teen was continuing to improve. Some good news at last.

The rest of that morning rushed by. The afternoon too. And despite what he'd said earlier that day, no text ever came through from Val, which was a relief. In fact, Dev had almost thought he'd dodged a bullet there, until Val arrived in person, just after practice hours. The rest of the staff had gone for the day, so it was just Dev there in his office.

"Hey," he said from the doorway. "Sorry I forgot to text. Time got away from me. Have time for a break now?"

"Actually, no." Dev hedged, his heart tripping just at the sight of Val. Knowing he was in big trouble here, he focused on rifling through his drawers to find the notepad he was missing. "I'm buried under documentation that has to be done before I leave tonight. Maybe another time?"

"How about dinner later then?" Val straightened, looking bummed. "I'm making spaghetti. Vicki's recipe. Your favorite. I'll save you some and you can heat it up when you get there."

Dev found the notepad, throat tight. He reminded himself of his decision to give them all space, and showing up at Val's house again tonight went against that entirely. Deep down, he knew the separation was for everyone's good, even though it felt like the exact opposite. "Sorry, but I can't. Late meeting, then I promised my mom I'd help with some projects around the house."

Val frowned as he walked into the office and leaned

on the edge of Dev's desk. "Are you sure there's nothing wrong?"

"Positive." Dev avoided his gaze by staring intently at his laptop screen. He really didn't want to do this right now. "See you later."

"Yeah. I hope so," Val said, straightening and backing toward to the door. "You're sure you're okay?"

"Yep," Dev managed to squeak out. "I'm great."

"See you later then."

He waited until he heard the elevator ding and the doors close again, before he slumped in his chair and covered his face. He was already second-guessing his decision, which didn't make it any easier, but he was determined to see it through, to protect them all the only way he knew how—by making himself scarce.

Soon, one day turned into a week, then two, and the less Dev spoke to or saw Val and Cam, the more he expected his craving to see them would ease, but it didn't. Because each time he went down to the ER for a consult, he found himself peeking around every corner, hoping to see Val. Not that he was ready to have that talk with him yet, about the status of things between them. Several times he'd picked up his phone, intending to just get it over and done with, but at the last second, he'd lose his courage and find another excuse to put it off for just one more day, and somehow, he'd almost convinced himself they could continue like this indefinitely.

But, of course, they couldn't. Deep down he knew that. And so, when he finally ran into Val late one night at the hospital, after a long, grueling shift during which Dev had lost two patients despite his best efforts, it almost felt like fate. It happened outside the staff break room on the first floor. Val's weary expression spoke of frustration and sleepless nights and Dev's first thought was to turn around and go back the way he'd come. But he couldn't, because Val had already seen him, and besides, Dev was too exhausted to avoid this anymore. The time had come to have it out, once and for all.

"Dev." The uncharacteristic harshness in Val's tone said he was clearly done with this nonsense. "Why are you avoiding us?"

Us. Not *me*. Because Cam was part of this too. Dev hid his wince as his stomach plunged to his toes, but he was too far into this mess to back out now. "I'm not avoiding you. I told you my schedule's crazy."

"Mine too, but I still find time for important things." Val followed him into the empty break room and shut the door behind them, the vending machines humming as they faced off. "Look, it's one thing if you don't want to sleep with me anymore. I'm an adult. I can take it. But Cam is just a kid. He cares about you. He thought you were his friend, and then you just disappeared on him like he didn't matter to you at all. I thought you of all people would know what that's like."

Ouch. A direct hit there to the soft underbelly of my decisions.

Time to explain himself, to make Val understand that this was what was best for all of them.

Even if it didn't feel like it now.

"I do know what it's like to be so attached to someone or something, only to have it taken away. That's why I needed to slow things down, to give us all some space to cool off and think rationally about all this, so no one gets hurts. Especially Cam."

"He's seven, Dev," Val said, giving him a flat stare. "He can't even spell *rationally*, let alone understand it. How could you just dump him like that? I thought we had an agreement."

"We did," Dev said, scowling. "And I didn't dump him. I was going to see him again at some point, once I had things back under control." Defensiveness prickled inside him, making him feel like a naughty schoolboy getting scolded by the headmaster. He didn't like it one bit. He was trying to do them all a favor here. Why couldn't Val understand that? "Trust me. It's for the best."

Val's derisive snort had Dev's hackles rising. "Trust you? That's rich. Why should I, when you don't give me the same courtesy? I'm sick of this, Dev. Of feeling like I have to walk on eggshells around you so you don't get upset or spooked or whatever and take off again." He turned away, his tanned cheeks red and his blue eyes flashing with anger. "And you still left. I did everything you asked of me and you still walked away like we meant nothing to you."

"That's not…" Dev ground his teeth, stopping himself because he couldn't find the right words to say what he meant, because he was afraid anything he said would only push them farther apart. He'd already botched this conversation so far and only wanted to get out now before he caused more harm. "Look. You're right." He huffed out a breath and shook his head. "It's not you. It's me. I can't do this. I thought I could, but I can't. You did everything I asked, but I'm just not ready yet. Even for a meaningless fling."

Even as those last words emerged, Dev regretted them. Because they weren't even close to true.

He was leaving because he cared too much and it scared the hell out of him. Because somehow, regardless of all his efforts, what he and Val had shared over the past few weeks had become the most meaningful relationship of his life, and if it blew up in his face or was ripped away or crumbled before his eyes, like love usually did for him, he wasn't sure he could survive it.

"Meaningless fling?" Val blanched, his usual warm laugh icy cold now. "Right. Sure. Okay. My bad. We agreed to that, I suppose. But Cam didn't. You swore you wouldn't hurt him, Dev." He stepped closer, furious hurt pulsing off him in waves. "Did you know he still asks about you every day? Asks when you're coming over again, or if we can go see Elaine." A muscle ticked near Val's hard jaw. "After everything he's been through, the last thing my son needs is someone else leaving him and that's exactly what you did. I don't care if you break my heart, but how dare you hurt my son? I don't want you near him ever again."

I don't care if you break my heart...

Confirmation of his deepest concerns—that they'd already grown more attached to each other than he'd wanted—only made Dev feel worse as guilt and regret twisted deeper in his gut, nearly dropping him to his knees. He'd only wanted to protect them all, so he'd done what he'd thought was best, but in the end, he hadn't protected anyone at all. He'd only made the pain worse.

And now it was too late. "I didn't mean for any of this to happen, I swear. I thought it would be better this way. I thought Cam would forget about me and move on. You said yourself he needed to learn boundaries."

"Not this way!" Val's voice grew sharper and louder. "Jesus, Dev. And FYI, this is about as far from healthy boundaries as you can get. Healthy boundaries would be getting to know someone before giving them your heart. Healthy boundaries would be talking about things, not just running away and avoiding the situation. Those are the kinds of boundaries I want my son to learn. Not to be an emotionless, careless bastard who's scared to feel anything for fear it will break him."

Val stalked across the room then, scrubbing his hands over his face, while Dev stood rooted to the spot, unable to move, because Val was right. That was who'd he'd become. A walking, talking self-fulfilling prophecy. He'd expected this whole situation to fall apart at some point and boom, it had happened. He'd known better and he'd done it anyway. Val glanced at him then, the hurt in his eyes slicing into Dev's soul deeper than any scalpel. One long beat stretched into two, then three, until Dev finally found his voice again. "You're right. You and Cam deserved better. You always did. This is all my fault and you're both better off without me. I'm sorry. For everything."

Shame scalding him from the inside out, Dev walked out then, the white walls seeming to close in on him as his clamoring pulse drowned out every other noise. It was done. Over. He was safe and secure again. Alone.

Just like he'd wanted. Even if it felt like Dev's heart would never recover.

He didn't need a heart.

Hearts only hurt you when they broke.

You're right. You and Cam deserved better. You always did...

As Val finished up his paperwork before leaving the ER for the night, Dev's words were running through his head on an endless loop. He liked being right as much as the next person, but this time it only made him feel worse. Because Dev wasn't the only one to blame here. After all, he'd crossed the line from fling to wanting forever a long time ago in their relationship—even though he'd sworn not to—and now he was so far gone he'd need a map to find his way back to normal. And for the first time in his life, Val had hidden his feelings away just to have more time with the man he loved. He'd betrayed them both by lying about it and it felt awful.

His whole life, people had told Val he cared too much, too soon, and eventually it would get him into trouble. In for a penny, in for a pound, as Vicki used to say. He'd never listened, never heeded the warnings, but he should have. Especially because there was more to worry about now than just himself. There was Cam too. God, he felt like the worst parent ever. How could he have been so stupid, so reckless? How did you explain to a kid that an adult he cared about didn't want to see him anymore because he was too damaged by the past? All those books he read to Cam every night covered a lot of emotional territory, but Val couldn't remember one that addressed this topic.

As he finished his last chart and headed for the staff locker room to get his coat, the lights of the hospital corridor blurred past him, his heavy steps carrying the weight of his bad decisions and his regrets.

How could he have thought going into this thing with Dev would be a win-win situation? It was so obvious now that it would never have worked, not when Dev had always had one foot out the door from the start, and Val had used their agreement as an excuse to hide the fact that he'd fallen hard and fast for his former best friend. Which made him just as much of a liar as Tom had been.

He drove home, parked in his driveway and cut the engine, resting his forehead against the steering wheel.

What the hell is wrong with me?

To Val, love was not something scary or something to be hidden away, but in Dev's experience, it only brought hurt and humiliation. And regardless of his motives for not telling Dev how he really felt, Val felt as much at fault for how things had ended up between them as Dev.

With a sigh, he got out of the SUV and walked up to the front door. He should have stayed true to himself and led with his heart first, even if it would have ended their affair before it had started. At least then, he wouldn't have betrayed Dev and himself by lying. All he wanted now was a hot shower and a long sleep, but he couldn't because Cam needed him too. He had to find a way to explain the truth to him, why Dev hadn't been around as much lately and wouldn't be around at all in the future.

His mind was still churning over that as he stepped in the foyer to find Nancy waiting for him. She had her coat on and slung her purse over her shoulder already, obviously in a hurry to leave. "Sorry, but I need to get home. Cam's in bed. His cold's back."

Val's heart sank further, if that were possible. The day just got better and better. "Did you give him anything for it?"

"Some children's Tylenol," Nancy said as she rushed out the door. "He's almost due for another dose."

"Thanks," he called from behind her. "Drive safely."

Once Val had locked up again for the night, he went down the hall to Cam's room. He placed a gentle hand on his son's forehead, and found it too warm.

This many infections in a row could indicate a potential problem with Cam's immune system. He frowned, wondering if he was just being a paranoid parent again, or if his medical instinct to be concerned was correct. Dev had checked him out after the last illness and found nothing wrong; he'd never ordered additional testing. Val took a deep breath and contemplated his options. Cam seemed to be doing okay now, sleeping peacefully, so the cold meds Nancy had given him seemed to be helping. She'd said he was nearly due for another dose, so that could account for the return of his fever. Without any signs of acute danger, Val decided to wait and see. Let his son sleep and reassess him in the morning. But just as Val reached the door again, a small voice behind him called out.

"Uncle Val?" Cam stirred, rolling over, his hair matted against the side of his head and his eyes sleepy.

"Hey, buddy." Val returned to the bed and sat on the edge. "Nancy said your cold's back."

"Yeah." Cam tried to sit up, but Val kept him down with a hand on his chest. "I feel yucky."

"I'm sorry, bud. But you need to rest so you'll get better." Val reached for the digital thermometer on the nightstand and held it to his son's forehead to confirm his temperature. One hundred and one. So not too worrisome.

"Is Dr. Dev here too?" Cam sniffled, looking hopeful.

Chest tight, Val brushed the hair back from the boy's flushed cheeks. He really didn't want to do this when Cam was sick, so he tried to buy himself more time to figure out what to say. "Sorry, bud. It's just you and me again tonight. How about I read you another story after you take your medicine, eh?"

"Okay," Cam replied, looking disappointed. Val knew the feeling.

Val went to grab the Tylenol from the kitchen, feeling like the weight of the world was on his shoulders. He'd weathered storms before—both in the ER and in life—but the forecast now promised turbulence ahead.

"Here you go, buddy." Val measured out a dose of the cherry-flavored syrup at Cam's bedside. "This should make you feel better."

Cam swallowed the spoonful, nose scrunched, then managed a weak smile. "Ready for my pirates."

"Pirates it is." Val grabbed the dog-eared book then settled in beside his son on the bed. "Where did we leave off?"

* * *

Hours later, Val awoke with crick in his neck from falling asleep against Cam's headboard. Early morning light streamed in through the window as he winced then straightened, glancing down at Cam, who still slept soundly, nestled beneath his covers and surrounded by pillows. The plush dinosaur toy clutched under his arm rose and fell with each congested breath, the rattling noise far too loud in the quiet room. A glance at his smartwatch said it was a little after 6:00 a.m.

Carefully, Val eased out of bed and set the book aside before crouching by the bed to gently smooth the ruffled hair away from his son's face. "Hey, buddy. How are you feeling today?"

Cam opened his eyes slowly. "A little better. Is Dr. Dev here now?"

"No. I'm afraid not." Val's throat constricted, knowing the sooner he got this over with, the better it would be for them both. Ready or not, the time had come. "Listen, Cam. Dr. Dev won't be hanging around with us anymore. I'm sorry."

"Oh." The boy looked so forlorn that Val nearly started crying himself. "Doesn't he like us anymore?"

"No, Cam. No," Val said fiercely. "He loves you."

It's me he doesn't want...

The knots in Val's stomach tightened as he took a seat on the edge of the mattress next to his son. "This is a problem between Dev and me, okay? Sometimes people just don't fit into the space we want them to. Like your Lego. You find a certain piece you think will be a perfect fit, but then you try it, and it doesn't quite work.

There's nothing wrong with the pieces themselves, they just belong somewhere else. Does that make sense?"

Cam went quiet for a moment, then whispered, "Is that why Mommy left? We didn't fit her anymore?"

"Oh, buddy." Heart completely shattered now, Val held his son tight, wishing he could shield him from all the pain in the world. "Your mom never wanted to leave you, Cam. You were her perfect fit. She left because of the sickness, not you. Never you. But you know what? I think we're a perfect fit too, you and me. And no matter what happens, I'm not going anywhere. You're stuck with me, bud."

Eventually, Cam pulled back to look up at him. "Like Lego?"

"Exactly like Lego," Val said, flashing a tremulous grin.

Cam sighed. "I'll miss Dr. Dev, but as long as we're together, I'm good, Uncle Val."

"Same, buddy. Same." Val hugged his son again, holding on because that's what family did—even when the rest of the world seemed to let go.

"Will you miss Dr. Dev?" Cam asked then, driving the knife deeper into Val's chest.

He swallowed hard, glad his son couldn't see his face right then as his voice thickened. "Yes, I will."

He stayed there, holding Cam until the boy fell back to sleep, then carefully tucked him in before leaving the bedroom to make some calls. First to the ER to tell them he wouldn't be in for his shift that day, then to Nancy to give her the day off and finally to Cam's school to let them know he was home sick again. Then he refilled the humidifier in Cam's room and set it a tad higher, thinking the gentle mist would help the boy breathe easier.

Once that was done, he took a shower and changed, then went to the kitchen to make a pot of much-needed coffee. While it was brewing, he contacted the pharmacy and scheduled a delivery of more cold medicine for Cam. He fixed himself a mug of liquid energy, then settled in the living room to figure out what their future would look like without Dev. Val still had his work and Alex, Cam had school and his activities. And speaking of Alex, he could really use a listening ear to help him work through all this. They hadn't talked since the pizza night—before everything with Dev happened—because of their crazy schedules, and he had a lot to fill his friend in on. The call rang twice before picking up.

"Hey, it's me," Val said, hearing the slight echo in the background. "Is this a bad time?"

"Good a time as any. I'm on the road, driving, as usual, between stops, so I've got a little time. You're on hands-free Bluetooth, if it sounds a little funny. What's going on?"

"I screwed up." The words tumbled out of Val in a rush of relief. It felt good to say them at last.

Alex chuckled. "I'll alert the media."

Val exhaled and scrubbed a hand over his face. "Remember Dev? I talked to you about him at pizza night?"

"The guy who texted he'd go with you to the Timberwolves game?" Alex asked. "Yeah, I remember. You guys used to be old friends, right?"

"Well, we became a lot more than that over the next few weeks," Val said, covering his face. "We agreed up front to keep things light and uncomplicated, because he has serious trust and abandonment issues. And I said I would, but I couldn't."

"Uh-oh," Alex said, as the muted sounds of traffic filtered through in the background of the call. "Why did you agree to that, Val? You know you're basically a walking ball of emotions. Even I could see that was a bad idea a mile away, and I'm basically the poster boy for missing signs and signals."

"I know." Val groaned, sitting forward. "I was just so glad to have him around again. And I guess I was just so desperate to spend more time with him that I was willing to agree to anything." He shook his head at his own wishful thinking. "Anyway, we'd been together a few weeks, hanging out together. Cam too. Then Dev got spooked one night when Cam told him he loved him and that was basically it. He ghosted us."

"Ouch," Alex hissed. "That's harsh. What about Cam? Is he okay?"

"He's sick again, but yeah. I mean, he's sad and misses Dev, but I think he'll be okay. I want to punch Dev for hurting him though. He promised he wouldn't and then he did." Val scratched the stubble on his jaw he hadn't bothered shaving. "Of course, it was my fault too, for not being honest with Dev about how I felt for fear I'd scare him away."

Alex huffed out a breath over the line. "Wow, what a mess."

"Tell me about it," Val said, shaking his head. "Sorry to dump it all on you. I guess I just needed someone to listen and bounce ideas off of, because somehow, I have to figure this out. We still have to work together at the hospital occasionally and I don't want things to be awkward for patients. That doesn't make for good care."

After cursing under his breath, Alex said, "Hang on a sec." Several seconds passed before he returned to the line. "Sorry, had to get through some road construction. Right. How do you feel about him now? Do you still love him?"

Val gritted his teeth. Leave it to Alex to cut right to the chase. But as mad as he was at them both for this fiasco, his feelings hadn't changed where Dev was concerned. "Yeah, I do." He flopped back in his chair and pinched the bridge of his nose, eyes closed. "But I have no clue where to go from here with him."

"It's a conundrum for sure." A low whistle came from Alex's end of the call. "Well, probably the simplest solution is to talk to him about it all, like adults."

"Yeah, that's what I thought too, but it feels too soon. We just had our blowout argument last night. I can't imagine he's feeling any better about all this than I am. And I don't want him anywhere near Cam again until we work this out." He sighed and stared out the window beside him, feeling awful. "God, I'm like the worst parent ever. I finally had to tell him that Dev wouldn't be coming around anymore because he kept asking. And then he asked if it was his fault. I never want him to think that again. I told him it was like Lego. Sometimes they just don't fit like you want them to. Then he asked if Vicki left because he didn't fit her. I felt like I'd been sucker punched right in the feels. I told him that his mom loved him, and they were a perfect fit, but you never know how kids will take things…"

"Dude. First of all," Alex said over the ticktick of his turn signal, "I have never met a person more suited for fatherhood than you, Val. Vicki used to say the same thing. You're smart, caring, kind, empathetic, funny. Cam couldn't ask for a better parent than you. And second, sometimes you have to make hard decisions and do things even when the timing isn't the greatest. That's life. I'm sure it wasn't easy to tell Cam that, but you did it. Wait a little while if you think you need to, then talk to this Dev guy and be honest with him. I mean, what's the worst that could happen? He can't leave you again, right?"

"No, I guess not." Val slumped farther down in his seat, sadness moving like sludge through his body. "I just feel horrible about everything. We were friends long before we slept together. I should never have lied to him, Alex. Especially after what happened with his ex-husband. And he lost his dad too, when he was about Cam's age. Just walked out on him and his mom. So Dev comes by his trust issues honestly. And then I go and basically lie right to his face again just to keep sleeping with him." He covered his eyes. "I called him an emotionless, careless bastard."

"Well, it sounds like maybe he might have deserved it." Alex took a deep breath and the sound of his engine cutting off sounded over the phone. "I just pulled into the lot for my next appointment, so I have to go, but listen, whatever you said or did, it takes two people to screw up a relationship. Him walking out on you and Cam without a word like that sounds like he's to blame in all this too, yeah? I think it all comes down to that conversation you need to have with him."

Val nodded and took a deep breath. "You're right. I need to talk to Dev. Thanks for confirming it."

"Sure thing." Alex's smile was evident in his voice. "Let me know how it goes."

"Will do." Val grinned. "Now go sell some drugs."

After the call ended, Val sat with his coffee and stared out the window beside him, needing to think about what he'd say to Dev once he finally set up a time to talk.

CHAPTER NINE

IN THE FOUR DAYS since his fight with Val, Dev had taken to running at dawn, the crisp Minneapolis air biting at his cheeks as he wove through the still-sleeping neighborhood where he'd grown up. In these solitary moments, with his breath clouding the air and the rhythmic thud of his sneakers against the pavement, he found a fleeting peace—a respite from the mess he'd created.

Today, he'd inadvertently left his phone back at the house instead of tucking it in the pocket of his running jacket like usual, but it was probably for the best. Saved him from checking it a billion times to see if there was a call or text from Val. Which was beyond pathetic. Because why would he contact Dev? Their argument in the break room had been a definitive ending.

An emotionless, careless bastard...

That's what Val had called him, and as much as it pained him to admit, it was probably true.

Stuffing down his feelings and getting on with life was how Dev dealt with things. It was how he'd survived after his father had left and again when Tom had betrayed him, but now it seemed he was doing it all the time. And when he'd spent those few blissful weeks with

Val and Cam and the walls inside had started to crack and crumble, that's when he'd panicked.

God, I really am a bastard.

Loneliness continued to dog his heels all the way home, through his shower and getting dressed, to the kitchen where he found his mother waiting for him at the table. He got his coffee, intending to sit in the living room to check his emails, but she caught his arm as he passed by.

"Wait, honey. Come sit with me for a second. Tell me what's wrong."

He couldn't look at her as he took a seat across from her, staring at the quilt draped over the back of the sofa just past her shoulder instead, his eyes tracing the patchwork of cloth as she waited.

Eventually, her motherly concern won him over, and Dev huffed out a breath, the tension inside him deflating as his stoic facade vanished, replaced by abject sadness. He ended up pouring out the whole story to her: his reunion with Val, their friendship crossing the line into something more, his decision to walk away and why. When he finished, he felt hollowed out, empty, for the first time in months.

"Oh, sweetie." She took his hand. "You really screwed up."

He snorted, and finally hazarded a glance at his mom, feelings raw. "I know. And the worst part is, I thought I was helping. It seems like I've spent every day of my life since Dad left us waiting for the other shoe to drop. Fearing everything good would disappear without warning." He gave a sad little shrug. "For a long time growing up, I wondered if him abandoning us was my fault somehow. Like if I'd just been a better kid, a more perfect son, he would have stayed. I wondered the same thing after Tom and I split up too. Thinking if I'd just done better, been better, he wouldn't have strayed." Dev shook his head, staring down at the black coffee in his cup. "Burying my emotions became easier for me. It felt safer not feeling anything, pushing it all down and locking it away. I felt more in control. But when Val reappeared in my life, it was like that control went out the window. Suddenly, I was feeling everything again and it was overwhelming and confusing. Terrifying, if I'm truthful. And the more time I spent with him and Cam together, the more it felt right. Which only made all those doubts and fears and anxieties I'd pushed aside return twice as strong later. And once I realized what had happened to me, that all my barriers were gone, my sense of impending doom grew to the point where I felt like the best decision I could make to keep us all safe was to remove myself from the situation entirely. Because even though I'd vowed not to, I love Val. Cam too." He hung his head and squeezed his eyes shut, ashamed. "So I left. To protect all of us from future heartache. I told myself it was for their own good. But in reality, I was just running away from the best thing that had ever happened to me. How messed up is that?"

"Honey." His mother took his hand. "Listen to me, please. Your father leaving never had anything to do with you. He had one foot out the door long before you were born. And I'm sorry you lived all these years thinking differently. I wish you'd told me you felt that way."

Dev managed a nod, eyes stinging as he focused on the tabletop, not trusting his voice.

"And as to you and Val, it does sound like you've gotten yourself into a pickle there, that's for sure. Trust is a tricky thing. Once you lose it, it's hard to get back. You have to earn it. And while I know you're scared by what you feel for him and his son—" her thumb brushed against his knuckles as she talked, a comforting rhythm that lulled him into relaxing for the first time in days "—that doesn't mean it isn't real or right. And it doesn't mean that you should give up either. Talk to Val. Tell him how you feel. Val isn't Tom. He isn't your father either. And he's been through his own pain these last few years. I think both of you need each other more than ever. You're good together. You understand each other. And that little boy loves you both so much. Show them that you can and will be there for them going forward. Show them the courage I know you have inside you. Real courage this time, the kind that comes from your heart and soul and isn't afraid to feel and love because, in the end, that's the only truth there is."

Dev looked into his mother's eyes at last, two wells of wisdom and understanding that seemed to see right into his soul. She knew everything there was to know about him, had guided him through scraped knees and broken hearts, through academic pressures and professional challenges. She knew his best and his worst, and she still loved and supported him, just like Val had always done. His heart swelled in his chest until it felt like it would burst. "I want to make a family with them."

"That's wonderful, honey." She smiled. "All the more

reason to talk to Val as soon as possible. Tell him what you just told me. No risk, no reward. Love—the real kind—isn't easy, but it's so worth it."

Dev nodded, then asked, "Did you hate Dad for leaving us?"

She shrugged. "Maybe a little, at first. But after a while, I realized it was for the best. Hard as it was raising you on my own, I think we were better off just the two of us, eh?"

He chuckled. "Agreed."

"Good." She grinned. "Now, go win back the man you love and his kid."

The warmth of his mother's unwavering faith in him seemed to shift something inside Dev. Her words didn't erase his insecurities, but they did remind him he wasn't alone. And maybe, just maybe, that was enough for him to mend fences and start moving forward again.

"Okay..." His voice caught slightly, and he cleared his throat. "I worried after Tom that I'd never heal, never find someone again, but I did. Right here where I started. Funny how that happens, huh?"

"Yes." His mom smiled as Dev continued processing everything that had happened to him since returning to his hometown. If anything, Val and Cam had taught him how to embrace life fully again. He yearned to be back at their sides and show them both they could depend on him, that he'd be there from this day forward, to beg for forgiveness and another chance to show them exactly how steadfast he could be.

"But honestly," his mother continued. "I was surprised you two didn't end up together all those years ago. Never seen two people so compatible with each other before. Then that idiot Tom swept you off your feet. All I can say is I'm glad you're back, honey, and I'm glad you've found your true home at last." She squeezed his hand once more then let him go. "Now, go and prove to Val and Cam why they can't live without you. And before you go driving yourself nuts, remember they don't need perfection. They just need you, Dev. All of you, even the imperfect parts that are still healing."

Dev nodded, knowing it was true. The possibility of loss and disappointment and hurt would always be there, lurking at the edges of life, but so was the possibility of something real and lasting and true. Love wasn't guaranteed or was forever, but perhaps the risk made it even sweeter.

As he grabbed his coat, he felt a new determination. The path forward wouldn't be easy, but he was no longer willing to allow the specter of past pain to dictate his future steps. He opened the front door, then paused. "Wish me luck, Mom."

"You don't need luck, honey," she called as he stepped outside into the brisk late autumn day. "You got this!"

The air hinted at the coming winter, but inside, Dev burned with the warmth of renewed purpose. With each step toward his car, his apprehension lifted a bit more. His mother was right. Val and Cam deserved all the parts of him—the good, the bad and the in-between—and everything he had to give. Before, he would've done everything in his power to hide the sides of himself he felt were broken, unworthy, unlovable. He would've kept his emotions under wraps and tried to logic his way out of it. But logic was what had gotten him into this mess. Now it was time to listen to his heart.

By the time he reached the medical center, he was brimming with determination to find Val and talk to him. Opportunity soon presented itself when he was paged down to the ER for a consult. There was no requesting physician listed in the text, so it was possible it wasn't Val, but still, it would put them in the same department and Dev could seek him out from there. He rode the elevator down to the first floor, squaring his shoulders as he stepped off and headed toward the busy nurses' station, determined to get it all out in the open with Val. "Dr. Harrison. I was paged for a consult."

"That was me." That familiar voice sent his pulse racing like a thoroughbred. Val. "It's my patient."

Dev turned slowly, feeling like every eye in the department was watching him, apprehension prickling his cheeks as nervous heat climbed from beneath the collar of his dress shirt. Thankfully, Val acted normally, handing Dev a tablet with the chart pulled up on it as they walked toward the trauma bays. He gave the rundown. "Twelve-year-old female patient with abnormal levels of serum tumor markers and liver function in the serology. Ultrasound imaging revealed a large mass in the left lobe of the liver. No lesions elsewhere."

"Symptoms?" Dev asked, his voice gruffer than usual as he studied the lab results. They would talk. He'd find the time, but first they had a patient to treat, and they both had to focus on that.

"None. But from what I read, that's not unusual in some cases." Val opened a curtain to reveal a girl named

Maria with large brown eyes peering out from a too-pale face beneath a dark mop of hair. "This is Dr. Harrison, pediatric oncologist. I've called him in for a consult."

Dev proceeded to introduce himself to the patient and her parents, then performed his own exam, palpating the patient's abdomen, aware of Val on the other side of the bed, watching him. He asked Maria, "Does this hurt when I press here?" Then to her parents when Maria winced and nodded, he asked, "How is her appetite?"

"Fine, I think," the mother said. "What's wrong with her?"

"That's what we're hoping to discover," Dev said, removing his gloves and tossing them in a nearby biohazard bin before washing his hands. "The ultrasound showed a mass on her liver, so I'd like to get a biopsy of that. The diagnosis will depend on those findings."

After getting their consent for the procedure and explaining it all to both parents and his new patient, Dev followed Val out of the exam room, speaking low to avoid being overheard. "Based on my exam, I'd guess we're dealing with a rhabdomyosarcoma, but I'll still need that biopsy to confirm."

Val grimaced as they arrived back at the nurses' station. "The prognosis isn't great for that type."

"No, but there are new treatments available and several clinical trials for new drugs she might qualify for. We'll see once we know exactly what we're dealing with."

They both stood there then, staring at each other. Dev suddenly tongue-tied now that the moment had arrived, his adrenaline skyrocketing. He could do this. He would do this. He swallowed hard, then said, "Val, I…" at the same time Val said, "Dev, I…"

"Dr. Laurent?" one of the nurses called from across the corridor. "You're needed in trauma bay two, stat!"

Val gave Dev an apologetic look as he backed away. "Sorry, I have to go. We'll talk later. Let me know when those labs come in."

Dev watched him walk away, feeling disappointed. Mainly in himself for not going for it when he'd had a chance. As he headed back upstairs, he thought Val had looked tired, his blue eyes shadowed, and wondered if he'd had trouble sleeping too. Dev had woken up last night, reaching for a warm body beside him that wasn't there.

We'll talk later, Val had said.

For Dev, later couldn't come soon enough.

Once the lab results were back, Dev headed back down to the ER to discuss treatment plans with Val instead of calling, hoping that after they met with the patient, they might have a chance to talk privately. Maria's diagnosis was as he'd expected. Rhabdomyosarcoma, a type of cancer that starts in the growth cells of soft tissue, like muscles and tendons, but can spread quickly to other parts of the body, which is most likely how it had ended up on Maria's liver.

He and Val stood shoulder to shoulder now in front of an ER computer screen, staring at the images.

"So, what's the treatment plan?" Val asked, arms crossed.

"We'll need to be aggressive, since it's already metastasized," Dev said. "Surgery to remove as much of the liver mass as possible. Then, once she's recovered from that procedure, chemotherapy and radiation for at least the next fifteen months. Agreed?"

"You're the expert," Val said, giving Dev some side-eye. "Listen, about that talk, I—"

"Code blue! Code blue! Trauma bay two! All available ER personnel required!" blared over the PA system and people began racing to the scene. Val swore under his breath, looking frustrated. "Sorry. You'll have to talk to Maria and her family yourself, I guess. Text me later about that talk."

Then he hurried off to his next emergency.

Gah!

Dev was starting to think there was some cosmic conspiracy to prevent him from telling Val that he loved him. He vowed next time they saw each other, he'd come right out with it, no matter what else was happening.

When he'd finished saving the code blue gunshot victim, who had gone into cardiac arrest, Val came out of the trauma bay hoping to find Dev waiting for him, but of course he wasn't. The man was busy too with his own patients to see, so it was silly to expect Dev to be standing around, waiting to talk to him.

He went back to the nurses' station to see if there was anyone waiting to be seen. Keeping busy would help make the last hour of his shift go faster. Before he grabbed a new chart, he pulled out his phone to send Dev a quick text to ask him if he was available later that night to talk and to text him a time. But before he sent it, his phone vibrated with an incoming call. His stomach bottomed out when Nancy's face appeared. It had to be serious enough for Nancy to call during his shift. He stepped off to the side of the corridor for privacy then answered. "What's wrong?"

"His fever came back a few hours ago. One hundred and one. So I gave him the cold meds, like you said, but then he started vomiting. I got him cleaned up from that but now I can't wake him up!" Nancy said, her tone panicked. "I called 911. They're here now and we're heading to the medical center."

Val's world slowed to a halt, his insides going into a full parental fear meltdown. Yes, he was a doctor himself. No, it didn't matter when it was your own child. He felt frantic and desperate to help his son in any way he could as quickly as possible.

The next twenty minutes were agony as he monitored the call-board and waited for Cam's arrival. According to the reports Nancy was giving as she rode alongside the paramedics in the ambulance, Cam's fever had now spiked to one hundred and four, and his breathing was shallow and strained, only interrupted by occasional wet, rough coughs. Cam had also moaned like he was in pain when the paramedics stabilized his neck on the gurney, and in one exam he displayed photosensitivity. Val's years of medical training pointed to a diagnosis that terrified him.

Meningitis.

He checked the hospital records for any reports of recent local outbreaks of bacterial meningitis, but couldn't find any. It didn't mean it wasn't the culprit though. The potentially lethal infection, which caused swelling of the brain and spinal cord, could also be caused by certain viruses and some fungi too. And the sooner Cam received treatment, the better. It could make the difference between a favorable outcome and...

No. He would not go there. Could not go there.

Cam would get through this. Had to get through this.

Val glanced up at the clock on the wall above him and wondered what the hell was taking them so long as he paced the floor of the ER in front of the ambulance bay, each minute elongating until his nerves were stretched taut.

Finally, after what felt like a small eternity, the ambulance finally arrived, and though he was forbidden to treat his own family members, Val still raced out to meet them as a concerned father. Poor Cam looked so small and helpless strapped to the gurney the paramedics rushed through the automatic doors, the boy's complexion gray except for the bright pink flush across his cheeks. An oxygen mask covered his nose and mouth, and he was unresponsive, though the paramedics assured him Cam had a steady, strong pulse.

Nancy was a wreck too, crying and shaking. She kept apologizing to Val like it was her fault, but he assured her it wasn't. She went to sit in the waiting room to wait for news, saying her husband was going to join her, so she wouldn't be alone while Val stayed with his son.

"Cam, buddy?" Val held his hand as he hurried alongside the gurney toward one of the special isolation trauma bays in the ER. They were taking special precautions to prevent spread of any infection until they had a confirmed diagnosis. Cam's eyes remained stubbornly closed, despite Val trying to rouse him. "I'm right here, Cam. You're going to be okay. Just stay with me, buddy. We'll make it through this."

Once they reached the assigned room, staff in special personal protective equipment rushed Cam inside then closed the door on Val, leaving him outside to peer in through the glass window as his whole life fought to survive on that gurney.

He'd promised himself, promised Vicki, that he'd always protect Cam. He could not fail now.

That evening, Dev returned to the ER to make sure he'd tied up all the loose ends for Maria's case before he left for the night. After their second foiled attempt to talk, Dev had sent Val a text asking if he had time for a drink after work. That was over three hours ago, and he still hadn't gotten a response. Not that that meant anything. Given how busy Val had been earlier, he could still be tied up with patients. He missed talking to Val, not just about work but about anything. And he longed to spend time with Cam again too, talking about his models or his latest soccer game. Anything, really...

He rode the elevator down to the first floor, resisting the urge to rub the sore spot over his heart. It had been there since seeing Val earlier, and was purely from loneliness and yearning.

He'd been so determined to keep to himself, keep his heart safe after the brutal betrayal by Tom. And yet, Val and Cam had both gotten around his barriers with their joy and laughter and sweet smiles. With their sunshine and hope. And now Dev couldn't live without it—without them—again.

By the time he arrived on the first floor, Dev had checked his phone again. Still nothing.

The elevator dinged and the door whooshed open to another brightly lit hall, and Dev stepped off thinking maybe after he was done with Maria's file, he'd just try to find Val again in person.

CHAPTER TEN

VAL SAT OUT in the hallway, anxiously awaiting any news about Cam and checking his smartwatch constantly. Three hours had passed and still no news, other than Cam was stable and still unconscious. Several of his ER colleagues had passed by on their way to other patients, all of them giving him sympathetic glances and encouraging pats on the shoulder. And while Val appreciated their concern, none of it made him feel any better.

Each time the door to Cam's room opened, Val's heart jumped and he stood, hoping for a new update, some good news. But as yet another specialist went into Cam's room, Val sank back into his seat, despondent. This must be how his ER patients felt when they brought in their loved ones for emergencies. Being on the other side of things from his usual perspective as the physician in charge was not fun. He wanted to charge in there and demand answers, but knew they needed to concentrate on his son right now, so he stayed put. Nancy and her husband had come back a couple of times to check on him and on Cam, but Val hadn't had much to tell them, and they'd both looked dead on their feet, so he'd told them to go on home with a promise he'd let them know as soon as he found out anything new.

He wished Dev was there to lend advice, or just be a warm presence for support. He finally got a chance to check his phone and saw a text from Dev asking if he wanted to get a drink. But they hadn't had their talk yet, and Val was exhausted, so adding alcohol to that mix probably wasn't a great idea at that point. Besides, he planned to stick close to his son's bedside until he was well again, so…

"Please," he prayed to whoever might be listening, including Vicki. "Let him be okay."

But Val knew Cam was in the best hands now. He worked with these people every day, and there was no medical team he trusted more to care for his son at this critical time. That was something at least.

He dragged a hand through his hair for the umpteenth time, then stood again, too restless to just sit there anymore, so he paced the hall for a bit before wandering down to the public waiting room out front. He stood at the windows, staring out at the glittering city lights of Minneapolis and beyond, seeking some solace or distraction from the nightmare his present reality had become.

As his initial burst of adrenaline from the ambulance's arrival earlier ebbed away, it left soul-draining exhaustion in its wake. Maybe Dev was still here. He could go up to his office and check, but didn't want to leave the ER in case something changed with Cam. So, finally, he sat down again, resting his head back against the chair and closing his eyes, memories of their day at the park filling his head. Cam's laughter as he'd played basketball with Dev or threw the Frisbee. Cam and Dev building Lego sets together, constructing new worlds from colorful bricks. The three of them eating ice cream, watching movies, doing everyday normal things that families did all the time. But every happy recollection now felt like a shard of glass, beautiful but painful, a sharp reminder of what he was fighting to get back…

"Come on, Cam," he whispered. "Beat this like I know you can."

When Val opened his eyes again, the clock on the wall in front of him ticked with maddening slowness, each second a drop of water in an empty bucket. He leaned forward, elbows on knees, head cradled in hands, willing things to move faster, for the team to find a diagnosis so they could begin treatment. What was taking so long? Had Cam gotten worse? Had he died in there and no one told him?

Then, as if summoned by him, the automatic doors leading into the ER finally opened and out walked one of the specialists—Fred, who'd been working on his son. He took a seat beside Val to explain the situation. "We're doing everything we can to narrow it down precisely so we can treat him the most effectively, but it's leaning toward viral meningitis. We'll need the lumbar puncture to confirm and type it, and I put a stat rush on the labs. But he's stable and holding his own, though he hasn't regained consciousness yet."

Val dug the heels of his hands into his scratchy eyes. Viral meningitis was the most common type in children, and the least lethal. It was easier to treat too and less contagious. With his recent spate of colds and sinus infections, Cam would've been more susceptible to it also. All the pieces fell into place. "Can I see him?"

Fred stood and clapped a hand on his shoulder. "You can. I'll let you know as soon as we get the results back."

"Thanks, Fred." Val stood to follow him back into the ER, Vicki's last words echoing in his mind.

Take care of Cam for me.

Her final plea, his final promise.

I'm trying, sis. I'm trying.

Dev froze in his tracks halfway to the nurses' station because of what he saw on the patient board—Cam's name and words *suspected viral meningitis*.

What the—

Heart lodged in his throat, he grabbed a tablet and typed in Cam's name to pull up the file. It looked like they'd already run a litany of tests, including a lumbar puncture to precisely type the virus involved, but they'd already started him on IV antiviral meds and steroids to help reduce the inflammation in Cam's body.

Oh, boy.

Val must be sick with worry. Dev checked the file again and saw that they were going to move him up to the PICU once a bed opened up, but until then he was still here in the ER, in a special isolation room. Dev hurried toward it, Cam's last words to him chasing at his heels.

Good night, Dr. Dev... I love you...

He stopped outside the door and looked through the glass to see Val at his son's bedside, hair disheveled, his blue eyes dulled by fatigue and worry as he held the hand of an unconscious Cam, who looked far too small in that great big hospital bed.

Then Val looked over, as if sensing him there, and Dev

went inside, words bubbling up inside him and clamoring to get out.

I'm sorry. I'm here for you. I love you, Val. I love you too, Cam.

He placed a hand on Val's shoulder and Val reached up to cover it with his own, a small sign of solidarity that helped ease the tension a bit. "I just found out, or I would've been down here sooner. Has there been any change in his condition? I looked up his file."

"No. Not yet." Val watched his son as he spoke. "He hasn't woken up since they brought him in."

"I'm sorry." Dev cursed quietly under his breath. He hated feeling helpless, but knew they were doing everything they could at present.

"I can't lose him," Val said raggedly, tears running down his cheeks.

Dev pulled Val up then and into his arms, offering whatever comfort he could. "It's okay. I'm here. Cam's going to be okay. They're giving him the best care possible."

"I know," Val mumbled, eventually gathering himself and pulling away. "I'm sorry to fall apart on you. I just hate the fact that I didn't see this coming sooner."

"How could you?" Dev said, pulling up a chair beside him. "You know as well as I do that the symptoms often start out mild and can turn severe without warning. Like you said before, those classrooms are petri dishes of infection. No telling where he might have picked it up. And most times, it never even manifests to this degree. There's no way you could have predicted this. Don't blame yourself."

Finally, Val nodded. "Thanks for saying that. And thanks for being here with us now."

Dev took Val's hand and shifted to look him in the eye. "I'll always be here for you and Cam, Val. If you'll forgive me. I was such an idiot before and I'm sorry. About everything."

Before he could say more, a nurse stuck his head in to say, "Val, a bed opened in the PICU, so they'll be moving him upstairs now. We're all optimistic that he'll make a full recovery."

"Thanks," Val said. "Me too."

The nurse left as orderlies came in to start moving Cam up to the PICU. Val walked out into the hall and gestured for Dev to follow. Once they'd found a relatively private alcove, he turned to Dev and said, "Thank you for being here and for the apology. And I want you to know I'm sorry too."

"About what?" Dev said, frowning.

"I broke our agreement."

Dev blinked at him. "How?"

Val sighed and shook his head. "We'd agreed to keep things uncomplicated, light. I tried, Dev. I really did, but I couldn't do it. I know you're scared to love, but I can't help myself where you're concerned. I fell in love with you, and I was afraid to tell you because I wanted more time with you. So, I lied. And I'm so sorry."

It took a minute for Dev to process what he had said, and once he did, he couldn't help the relieved laugh that came out of him. They'd been dancing around the truth when it was right there in front of them all the time, if only they'd been brave enough to see it and say it.

Val's brows knitted together. "This is funny to you?"

"What? No." Dev sobered, though he couldn't stop his smile. "It's just that I love you too, Val, but I was too terrified to tell you. Hell, I was too terrified even to admit it to myself for too long. That's why I left. I thought distance would make it go away on its own, but it didn't."

"Love isn't a disease, Dev." Val gave him a look. "It's okay to have feelings. They're normal."

"I know." He stared down at his hands in his lap. "But after what I'd been through, they also felt toxic. I didn't want to get hurt again, so it seemed better to not have them."

"And how did that work out for you?" Val raised a brow at him, his tone dripping with snark.

Yeah, he deserved that, Dev supposed, after walking away from the best thing that had ever happened to him. Not once, but twice. But now that they were putting it all out there, he needed to say his piece to be able to move forward. "I want to apologize to you properly. All of this was my fault. At the time, leaving seemed like the best way to protect all of us from being hurt, but I only made things worse. That's not an excuse for my behavior, but I wanted you to understand my thinking. My leaving had nothing to do with you or Cam. I love you both more than I can say, and I'm never going to leave again, unless you ask me to. Promise."

Val leaned over to rest his head on Dev's shoulder as Dev took a deep breath then continued.

"I've been trying to hide my feelings since my dad left, thinking that was how I could keep myself from ever getting hurt like that again. I know how ridiculous that sounds, but I was five and that's how kids think. Anyway, that's when I decided that locking my emotions away was the key to safety, and the easiest way to do that was to be alone. Keep everything under wraps, lock it down so I wouldn't be hurt again when things ended or people left, because in my experience, they always did. I had my mom, and then I had you, and I thought that was all I needed. Then Tom blew into my life like a hurricane and knocked me off my feet. For the first time in what felt like forever, I thought maybe, finally, I could try again. But I was wrong, and things fell apart once more, and to me, that just proved my point. Don't let anything show. Don't let people in. Otherwise, you'll get hurt. After we separated, the pain was too real, too raw, dividing up our lives like the weekly recycling. I shut down all my emotions again. Then I came back here and saw you on my first day, reminding me of what I'd left behind—true friendship and belonging and real love and caring—and I reinforced my walls and made them even higher and sturdier. But even then, somehow, you and Cam got around them before I even knew what was happening. And once I did realize how far gone I was, I panicked and ran away. Like an idiot..." He cleared the lump from his throat. "But I'm done running. I love you, Val. I think I always did. Even back in medical school. Which means I broke our agreement way before you, so you had nothing to lie about because our agreement was already void. I love Cam too. And I know what I did hurt you both, and I can't guarantee I won't screw up again at some point because, well, I'm a broken toy. A real mess. That's the truth. And you of all people should know that.

I carry a lot of baggage, and I'm not always the easiest person to deal with. I can be stubborn and opinionated and a real pain in the ass. But if you're willing to give it a go, so am I. You've seen me at my worst and at my best, and you're still here. That means so much to me. More than I can say. I love you, Valentine Laurent, and I want to be yours forever, if you'll have me."

Val didn't respond, and as a beat passed, then two, Dev's heart sank. That's when the nervous babbling started.

"I totally understand if you're done, Val. And I'll respect your wishes if you never want to see me again. I failed you when you needed me most. But I'd like to make amends, if you'll let me. Prove to you that you can trust me with your heart. I want to move forward, Val, and I hope we can do that together."

Finally, Val lifted his head, took Dev's face in his hands, and kissed Dev soundly on the lips. When they finally pulled apart, his blue eyes were bright as stars. "Of course I forgive you, you infuriating man. I've loved you from the first moment I saw you sitting alone in the corner of that classroom at the beginning of medical school. I thought you were the sexiest nerd on campus. And I love you even more now."

They hugged then, Dev not sure how he'd gotten so lucky, but so grateful anyway. "I meant what I said too. I plan to spend every day from now on proving to you and Cam that I'll be there for you both." He leaned his forehead against Val's. "For as long as you'll have me."

"Forever," Val murmured against his neck, holding

Dev like he'd never let him go again. "That's how long I want you with us."

After following the medical entourage up to Cam's new room, they took up their posts beside his bed, and Dev couldn't help glancing over periodically to confirm that Val was still there, not quite believing it yet. He'd done it. He'd been brave, he'd followed his heart and emotions, and it had worked out. Imagine that. Once they'd both settled in at Cam's bedside, they napped in rotation in case someone came in with an update. When it was Dev's turn after midnight, it felt like he'd just closed his eyes, but when he opened them again, early morning sunlight was streaming in through the window behind Val, highlighting his tawny hair and giving him an almost ethereal glow. Even rumpled and sleep-deprived, he was still the handsomest man Dev had ever seen. His palms itched to touch Val, hold him, but that could come later.

First, they had to get Cam well again.

Then Val looked over at him and Dev's heart thumped hard, whatever remnants left of his inner walls vanishing completely, allowing Val to see him—all of him—even though it terrified Dev. Then Val smiled, and Dev knew it would be all right. Whatever challenges the future threw their way, they'd handle it. Together.

Val finally broke the connection by turning his attention to Cam and taking the boy's limp hand as a nurse came in to check on the IVs. Hopefully, they'd see some sign of improvement in him soon.

Around noon, Val watched as the nurse fiddled with Cam's IVs and Dev got up to stretch his legs. Various medical staff had come in like clockwork about every twenty minutes to reassess his son's condition, but so far, all Val had received from them were platitudes and pitying looks. He and Vicki had gotten enough of those as growing up poor kids with deadbeat parents. Then, after his sister's funeral, he'd gotten more of the same. At least then, he'd been so wrapped up in helping Cam adjust to his new life that Val hadn't had time to notice. Now though, it felt suffocating. The only thing that made this weight bearable was Dev. Knowing that they were okay, that they were in love and would have a future together gave him a bright spot to focus on amongst the darkness. He needed that more than he could say.

The nurse left, and Dev waved him over to the computer in the corner of the room where he'd brought up Cam's file. "Val, come look at this."

Val walked around his son's bed to see the screen, taking strength from the other man's warmth. "What?"

"From the counts, it looks like the drugs are starting to work," Dev said, pointing to the most recent set of blood work drawn shortly after Cam had arrived in the PICU.

"Let's hope that continues," Val said, forcing himself to stay grounded. While his son's condition hadn't gotten any worse since he'd been in the hospital, it hadn't gotten noticeably better either. But Val was counting his blessings where he could. And having Dev's support in his hour of need helped.

He sat again and took his son's hand, warming Cam's small, chilled fingers with his own larger ones. "Come on, buddy. You can do this. Come back to us."

Val then proceeded to tell Cam what was happening, even though the boy gave no sign of hearing him. There'd been many studies that said unconscious patients could still hear and understand voices around them, and it made Val feel better to pretend things were normal anyway, even if they weren't. That's when he felt Cam squeeze his fingers ever so slightly. His heart stumbled and his eyes widened. His son was still there, still fighting. "That's it, Cam. Come back to me, buddy. Can you open your eyes? Please."

Dev rushed to the other side of the bed. "What happened?"

"He squeezed my hand," Val said, throat constricting and eyes stinging. "I think he's coming around."

"Yes!" Dev took Cam's other hand. "Hey, Cam. It's Dr. Dev. I'm here with you and your dad. I've missed you so much, and I'm so sorry I haven't been there these last few weeks. But I'm back and I'm not leaving again, I promise."

It took a few seconds, but soon Cam's fingers tightened around Dev's hand too. "I felt it!"

Val couldn't hide his grin as fresh tears fell down his cheeks. "He's going to be okay."

"Yes, he's going to be okay," Dev repeated, flashing Val a watery smile in return. "He's waking up."

Sure enough, Cam's eyelids fluttered before slowly opening enough to reveal the clear blue irises Val had longed to see again, his son's expression a mix of confusion and weariness. "Wh-what's h-happening?" Cam croaked out. "Wh-where am I?"

Val kissed Cam's hand, his tone laced with relief and joy. "Hey there, buddy."

Dev grinned down at Cam from the other side of the bed. "Welcome back."

"Uncle Val? Wh-why are you c-crying?" Cam's gaze darted between them. "Dr. Dev?"

"You've been really sick," Val said, his words rough with emotion as he kissed his son's forehead. "You scared me."

"S-sorry," Cam said, a hint of his usual mischievousness returning.

"It's okay, buddy." Val ruffled Cam's tawny hair affectionately. "Just know we both love you so much."

"How are you feeling now, Cam?" Dev asked.

"Better." Cam's voice grew stronger the longer he talked until the stutter disappeared. Another good sign. "Does this mean you'll come over to see me again, Dr. Dev?"

"I absolutely will," Dev said. "In fact, I'll be there so much, you might get tired of seeing me."

Cam's smile widened. "Yay!"

"Okay," Val said, glancing at the monitors. "We'll let you get some more rest."

"And we'll be here when you wake up again," Dev reassured him.

"Promise?" Cam asked, his eyelids drooping as his limited energy waned once more.

"Promise," both men affirmed in unison.

Once Cam drifted off, they remained at the bedside, Val feeling like he was home, even in this stressful environment, because the people he loved were there. Eventually, when he was sure Cam was doing better, he reluctantly agreed to leave so he could shower and change and maybe take a power nap. Or a thousand.

Dev said he'd drive, since Val felt ready to drop and didn't trust himself behind the wheel.

As they waited for an elevator, Dev brushed a stray lock of unruly hair from Val's forehead. "Thank you for giving me another chance. And thank you for letting me be part of your family."

The elevator dinged and both men walked into the empty car. Once the doors closed, Val wrapped his arms around Dev, pulling him close. "Thank you for wanting to be a part of it."

Once they were outside in the physician's parking lot, Val winced. "Man, I need a shower."

"Yes, you do," Dev teased gently, a hint of much-needed humor creeping into his tone.

Val winked at him over the hood of the gray sedan. "I also need to eat, so maybe you could fix us some food while I take care of business. I'm starving."

As Val climbed into the passenger seat and Dev got behind the wheel, it felt like a huge weight had finally lifted. The days ahead were looking brighter with each passing second.

CHAPTER ELEVEN

Three weeks later...

DEV ADJUSTED HIS GLASSES and smiled.

I can't believe I'm back here again.

"Look at it! Isn't it cool?" Cam's eyes were as wide as saucers, his finger tracing the picture of the spacecraft on the box for his new NASA Artemis Space Launch System Lego set with reverence. "We can build it together, Dev!"

Val beamed at them from the open kitchen, his expression a mix of pride and deep affection.

"Yes, we can," Dev agreed, taking a seat on the floor and ruffling Cam's hair. "We'll make it the best spaceship ever."

They opened the box and spread out the colorful Lego blocks across the living room floor, creating a galaxy of tiny plastic components that awaited their transformation. The afternoon light filtered through the window, casting a warm glow over the scene. Cam sat cross-legged with an instruction booklet in his lap, scanning the pages with eager anticipation.

"How about we start with the base?" Dev asked, picking up a gray piece and examining it closely before picking up a second piece that looked like it might fit and trying them together.

Cam shook his head, grabbing a different piece, snapping them together perfectly. "It goes like this."

Together, they assembled the launchpad, clicking each intricate piece into place with satisfying snaps. The activity was meditative, and Dev soon lost himself in it, his analytical brain overjoyed.

"Dev?" Cam's voice pulled him from his thoughts, quieter now, contemplative. The boy looked up at him, his hair falling into his eyes. "Are you going to stay forever this time?"

Dev's heart swelled with sweetness. Since Cam had been discharged from the hospital three days after he'd entered it, Dev had all but moved into their house, only going back to his mom's a couple of times a week to check on her. Eventually, they planned to sell both houses and buy a bigger one with a guest suite that would accommodate all four of them—Cam, Val, Dev and his mom. "I will, if that's okay with you."

"It's great!" Cam said, working a little slower now as he attached a cylindrical piece to the base before looking up again. "Are you going to be my second dad?"

Dev's steady hands faltered slightly as he tried adding another section to the structure. He and Val had discussed marriage—if they wanted to get married or not. And while they weren't rushing into anything, it was a possibility at some point. For now, they were just savoring every day together. "Would you like me to be your second dad?"

"I would!" Cam said, a grin lighting up his face. It was

the kind of smile that could turn a room from ordinary to extraordinary, and reminded Dev again of why he'd chosen pediatrics in the first place: to protect those smiles, to fight for them when the darkness threatened to swallow them whole. Cam was doing well, post-meningitis. In fact, Cam had been lucky, with no lasting issues from the disease. "You give me bigger ice-cream scoops than Uncle Val."

"Ask a silly question," Val chimed in from the kitchen.

"I know," Dev laughed. The kid deserved the biggest scoops he could handle. "Serves me right."

They fell into an easy silence then, Dev and Cam building, while Val made lasagna for dinner using his sister's recipe.

"There's an air and space museum in Ohio. Maybe next summer, we can take a trip there to see the planes and rockets," Dev said, thinking aloud as he connected another section of scaffolding to the model. "If you'd like that."

"Yes! I'd love that!" Cam's blue eyes lit up as he called to Val, "Did you hear, Uncle Val? We're going to the space museum next year! Maybe I can learn more about the stars before then. Like those big balls of gas burning billions of miles away from the book you read to me in the hospital!"

Val chuckled as he shoved the lasagna in the oven, then joined them in the living room and sank into a seat on the sofa. "Sounds like a plan, buddy."

As they continued assembling the Lego set, Cam added, "I love you, Dev."

Dev glanced at Val, his heart nearly bursting. "I love you too, Cam."

From the sofa, Val smiled, knowing what they'd been through to get there, and looking as grateful as Dev felt to have it at last—to have Cam home and healthy, and the new family they'd formed. An affirmation of their strength, the unity they'd forged through hardship, their unspoken commitment to the future.

"Let's get this rocket finished," Dev said, his voice cracking before he cleared his throat. "Our astronaut needs to get to space."

"Mission control is ready for launch!" Cam declared as he snapped the last brick into place with a gratifying click. "The rocket's ready for liftoff!"

The pride in Val's gaze mirrored his son's as he checked out their handiwork. "Wow, buddy. That is one impressive piece of engineering."

"It's not just a model, you know," Dev chimed in, leaning back on his palms. "It's a symbol of what humans can achieve when they come together, work together."

"Like us?" Cam asked, his gaze flitting between the two men.

"Exactly like us," Dev confirmed, emotion swelling inside him and stealing his voice.

"Then we should capture this achievement," Val suggested, grabbing his phone off the side table. "Let's take a picture. A family photo with our Artemis."

Cam's face lit up brighter than any launchpad flare. "Can we put it next to the one with Mom and me after my first build?"

"Of course," Val replied as Dev moved into position

behind the model, along with Cam. "I think that's the perfect place to hang it."

"All right, space explorers," Val announced, holding the phone at arm's length as he crowded in behind Dev and Cam to take the selfie. "Squeeze in close."

They huddled around the spacecraft, shoulder to shoulder, and Dev realized this picture would be more than just an image: it would be a keepsake of this very instant when everything seemed possible.

"Smile," Val said. "Everyone say 'Artemis!'"

Afterward, Val showed them the photo, his blue gaze locked on Dev's. "Perfect."

Dev nodded, knowing it was true.

* * * * *

*If you enjoyed this story,
check out these other great reads from
Traci Douglass*

Family of Three Under the Tree
Her Forbidden Firefighter
An ER Nurse to Redeem Him
Home Alone with the Children's Doctor

All available now!

MILLS & BOON®

Coming next month

A DADDY FOR HER BABIES
Becky Wicks

'Twins,' Theo announces, before Dr Priya can.

She nods and lets him wheel the monitor closer so I can see better.

Twins.

The word echoes through the room, doubling itself in my mind. Twins? I turn to Theo, who's still grinning in a way that makes him look ten years younger and twenty times more handsome. Here they are, right here. Two little beings, my babies, dancing in their own private universe.

'Twins are a huge part of my family. They have been for generations, but somehow I never really thought...' My voice trails off. I'm lost in a swell of emotions now, just looking at the screen. I am completely mesmerized by what I'm seeing and soon I'm hearing it, too—two tiny hearts beating in sync.

'They're cooking along nicely, Carter,' Theo says proudly.

'Would you like to know the genders?' Dr Sharma asks. My palm is warm and clammy now from my nerves, glued to Theo's. He's still mouthing the word *twins* to himself, and there's a look of disbelief and wonderment on his face that I've never actually seen before. Am I ready? I think I am. I tell her yes. I think I'm feeding off Theo's excitement.

Dr Sharma begins with another swirl of the cool wand over my abdomen. 'You're having a boy and a girl.'

'One of each, no...' Theo lets out a laugh, just as I do.

A boy and a girl. This is crazy. More tears gather in the corners of my eyes. 'Just like Rose dreamed,' I remember suddenly. Weirdly, Rose said she had a dream the other night, in which I announced this exact thing. I wish she were here now. She'd be wrapped around their little fingers already, too.

'Congratulations, Carter,' Theo whispers. I know I'm emotional, but his words tingle my ear and send a flush of adrenaline to my nerves. I can't help missing my sister, but I'm so relieved that someone's here to witness this. That *Theo* is here to witness this.

'Congratulations, *both* of you,' Dr Priya says, making me a printout so I can show Rose. She's going to be so thrilled. Just wait till she... Wait... *What did she say?*

'Oh, no,' I insert as it hits me what this lady just alluded to. 'Theo's not... I mean, we're not...'

'They're going to be so loved, right, wifey?' Theo finishes for me. He's still marveling at the screen. He really does look fiercely determined now and I let the comment go.

They will definitely be loved. But my friend and colleague has just been mistaken for the father of these babies, and more concerning, for a hot fleeting second there I caught myself wishing he really *were*.

Continue reading

A DADDY FOR HER BABIES
Becky Wicks

Available next month
millsandboon.co.uk

Copyright © 2025 Becky Wicks

COMING SOON!

We really hope you enjoyed reading this book.
If you're looking for more romance
be sure to head to the shops when
new books are available on

Thursday 22nd May

To see which titles are coming soon, please visit
millsandboon.co.uk/nextmonth

MILLS & BOON

FOUR BRAND NEW BOOKS FROM
MILLS & BOON MODERN

The same great stories you love, a stylish new look!

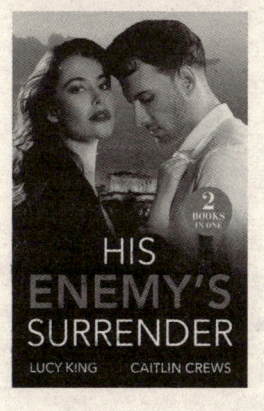

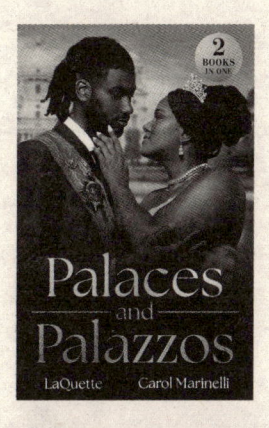

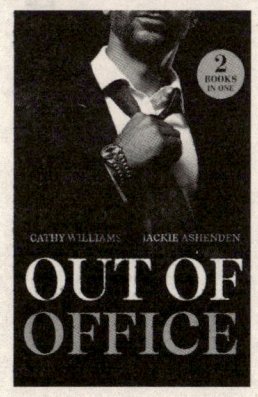

A Consequence Claimed
LOUISE FULLER — CLARE CONNELLY

Palaces and Palazzos
LaQuette — Carol Marinelli

His Enemy's Surrender
LUCY KING — CAITLIN CREWS

Out of Office
CATHY WILLIAMS — JACKIE ASHENDEN

OUT NOW

Eight Modern stories published every month, find them all at:

millsandboon.co.uk

afterglow BOOKS

Afterglow Books is a trend-led, trope-filled list of books with diverse, authentic and relatable characters, a wide array of voices and representations, plus real world trials and tribulations. Featuring all the tropes you could possibly want (think small-town settings, fake relationships, grumpy vs sunshine, enemies to lovers) and all with a generous dose of spice in every story.

♪ @millsandboonuk
◎ @millsandboonuk
afterglowbooks.co.uk

#AfterglowBooks

For all the latest book news, exclusive content and giveaways scan the QR code below to sign up to the Afterglow newsletter:

SCAN ME

afterglow BOOKS

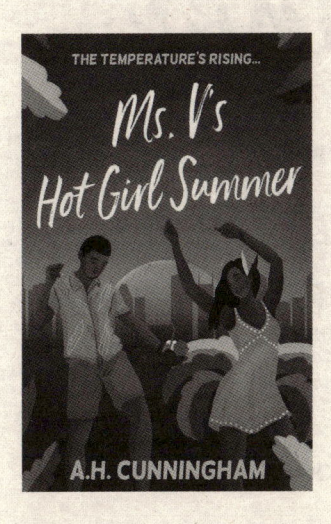

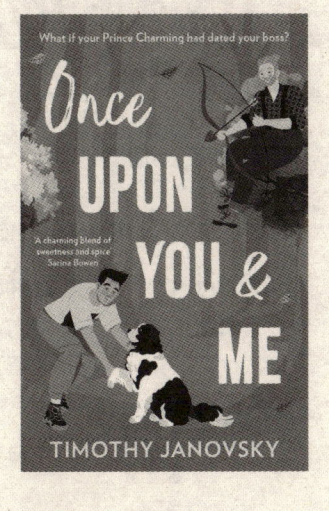

Ms. V's Hot Girl Summer
A.H. Cunningham

Once Upon You & Me
Timothy Janovsky

- ✈ International
- ☯ Opposites attract
- 🌶 Spicy

- 💻 Workplace romance
- 🚫 Forbidden love
- 🌶 Spicy

OUT NOW

Two stories published every month. Discover more at:
Afterglowbooks.co.uk

LET'S TALK
Romance

For exclusive extracts, competitions and special offers, find us online:

- **f** MillsandBoon
- **X** @MillsandBoon
- **◉** @MillsandBoonUK
- **♪** @MillsandBoonUK

Get in touch on 01413 063 232

For all the latest titles coming soon, visit
millsandboon.co.uk/nextmonth

OUT NOW!

Opposites Attract: Medics in Love

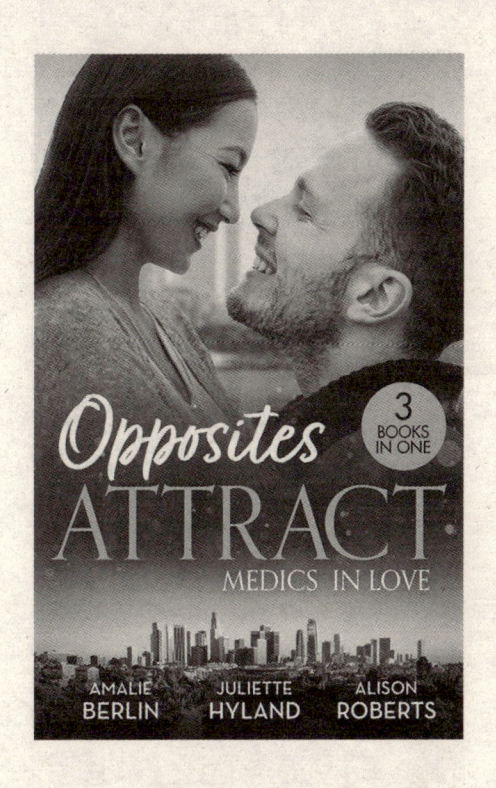

3 BOOKS IN ONE

AMALIE BERLIN
JULIETTE HYLAND
ALISON ROBERTS

Available at
millsandboon.co.uk

MILLS & BOON

OUT NOW!

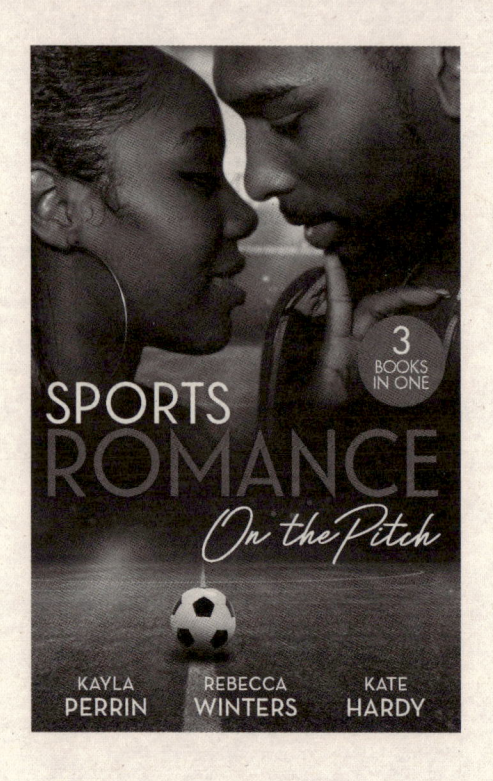

SPORTS ROMANCE
On the Pitch

3 BOOKS IN ONE

KAYLA PERRIN
REBECCA WINTERS
KATE HARDY

Available at
millsandboon.co.uk

MILLS & BOON

OUT NOW!

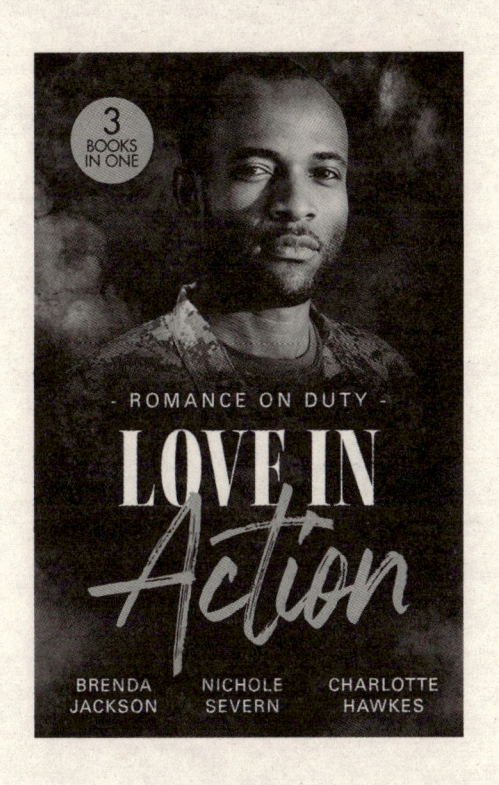

ROMANCE ON DUTY
LOVE IN Action

3 BOOKS IN ONE

BRENDA JACKSON **NICHOLE SEVERN** **CHARLOTTE HAWKES**

Available at
millsandboon.co.uk

MILLS & BOON

OUT NOW!

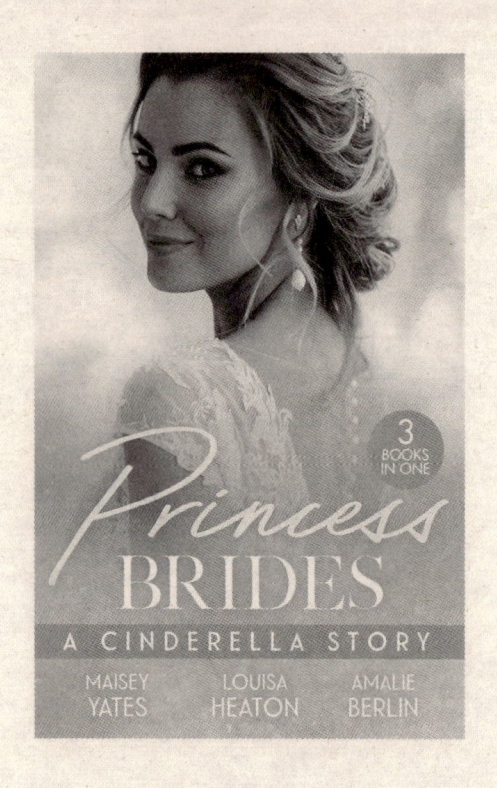

Princess BRIDES: A CINDERELLA STORY

MAISEY YATES · LOUISA HEATON · AMALIE BERLIN

3 BOOKS IN ONE

Available at
millsandboon.co.uk

MILLS & BOON